One Wilde Ride
Book Two

An Exceptional Boy

LM Foster

ISBN-10: 0692388915
ISBN-13: 978-0692388914

Cover
The Desperate Man, circa 1843
By French painter Gustave Courbet (1819–1877)
Self-Portrait - Oil on canvas
Private Collection
Design by
Ravenna Young
www.ravennayoung.blogspot.ca

9th Street Press
www.9thstreetpress.com

In cases of defense 'tis best to weigh
The enemy more mighty than he seems
                                        - William Shakespeare,
                                          Henry V

ONE

Not long after Adrian bumped his head at the tender age of three, Daina began to notice that her son could anticipate things. He would be in his highchair, busily smearing Spaghetti-O's on his face, then he would suddenly stop, pause, and look at the door. Adrian would say, "'Malky wants in, Mommy," and a second afterward, Daina would hear the old cat's scrabbling claws demanding entrance.

Or, instead of mentioning the old mama cat, Adrian would say, "AnTeen's here," or "Auntie Bellona's here," or "Daddy's home!" A heartbeat later, the person actually arrived. It wasn't as if it happened all the time: perhaps once or twice when he was three, and twice or thrice when he was four. Daina was intrigued, but not overly. She thought that perhaps her son just had an above-average sense of hearing. Maybe he heard footsteps before anyone else, like they say animals can sense an earthquake seconds before it occurs. Maybe he was just more observant than she was.

A little before Adrian's fifth birthday, Daina was carrying groceries into the house from the car; the front door was open. Adrian helped – Daina always gave him a sack to carry. Nothing pleased her boy more than to assist his mommy.

But as they approached the open front door, the preschooler paused, said, "Loud noise, Mommy." He had enough time to set his bag on the ground and cover his ears before the front door inexplicably swung shut.

Emotions staggered through Daina's mind like drunks at closing time, bumping into each other and rebounding. She was amazed, appalled, afraid – she was pleased, she was proud. Her aunts called Adrian *Capo,* the Boss. They said that they could ken that he would grow up to be something, that he would be *something else,* even if he might not live very long. Was this what they meant? Could it be possible that her darling little boy had some kind of telekinetic power?

"Did you close the door, son?"

"No, Mommy." Adrian blinked at the impossibility. "I'm over here. The wind closed the door."

Another possibility occurred to Daina. Not telekinesis. Instead – "But you knew? You *saw?"* Adrian didn't understand, so Daina began again. "Before the door slammed, you said, 'Loud noise, Mommy.'"

Adrian giggled. "It was loud."

"How did you know that the door was gonna slam, Adrian?"

He tilted his head, gestured at the door. He paused, inarticulate. He was not even five years old, after all. He shrugged, shook his head, unsure.

Daina spoke no more of it, changed the subject. "Do you want one of Aunt Bellona's chocolate chip cookies?" Adrian nodded, smiled. "Help me put the groceries away first."

TWO

Adrian sat on the bench on his aunts' deck, sliding his Slinky from the table onto the bench. Occasionally he would pause and take a bite from his cookie, then resume playing with the fascinating spring. His aunts and his mother stood a little distance away, watching him.

Daina had told them about Adrian and the slamming door. "He *knew* it was going to happen!" she whispered, still a little awestruck.

They watched Adrian being a little boy. Finished with his cookie, he clambered on top of the table. Standing, he held the Slinky above his head, over the side of the table. When it stretched to its full length, he released it. The Slinky seemed to hang in the air, to levitate for a split second: the bottom of it didn't fall to the ground before the top part dropped to meet it. The action of the toy was remarkable, and Adrian giggled.

Daina gasped. "Oh, my God! Did you see that? It was . . . It was . . . *magic!* " she whispered.

Penny was unconvinced. "What did I tell you about climbing on the table, Capo?" She approached and whisked him off of it, set him down on the bench. "We sit *on* benches, and *at* tables. We don't climb *upon* them."

"Yes, ma'am," Adrian said obediently. Penny picked up the Slinky. "It sticks in the air, Auntie Penny," he told her.

Daina and Bellona crossed the deck. "Do you *make* it stick in the air, Adrian?" his mother asked softly.

"No, Mommy. I just drop it."

Penny held the spring above her head and allowed it to uncoil to its full length. *"Abracadabra, iftaḥ yā simsim, sim sala bim!"* she intoned, and dropped the Slinky. Again, it seemed to hang in the air for a split-second before falling to the deck with a *zing!* sound. She recovered it again. "You try it, Daina. It's not magic. If it was magic, maybe I could explain it to you." She grinned. "But it's physics. Some property of the spring makes it seem to *stick in the air,* just like my clever boy said. It happens every time. Don't I remember you playing with a Slinky when you were little?"

"I don't remember it ever doing that," Daina said.

"Maybe it *is* magic," the almost five-year-old opined.

"Come, my boy," Bellona said. "I'll teach you some real magic." Adrian hopped down happily from the bench and took her hand. Bellona winked at them over her shoulder.

Penny smirked at her niece. Daina said, "Well. Maybe he can't levitate a Slinky. But he knew the door was going to slam. Sometimes he knows when someone's at the door, before they knock. Sometimes he tells me Ian's home, *before* Ian's actually home. Maybe he *sees,* Aunt Penny! Like you do!"

"Maybe," she concurred, still skeptical. "He's just a baby, Daina."

"Isn't there some way we could . . . test him?"

Penny threw back her head and laughed. "A witch's test! You've already had him in the lake. Does he sink or float? Have you searched him for a Devil's Mark? I've bathed him – I've never seen one, but perhaps it's hidden beneath that hell-black hair? Should we shave his head to be sure? We could make a witch cake and use it to reveal him – Bellona has an old recipe."

"A witch cake?"

"Yes. We could feed it to Grimalkin or Holt. Aren't they the boy's familiars? The ingredients are supposed to imbue the creatures with the gift of speech, in order that they may betray their master to the world. Adrian Wilde – Five-Year-Old Warlock!"

Daina frowned at her aunt's teasing. "You said he was exceptional."

"And indeed he is."

"So there has to be some way to test him."

Bellona and Adrian reappeared. She was carrying a bottle of Coke, with the cap still on it; Adrian clutched a plastic drinking straw in his chubby hand.

"Bellona, was it not once proclaimed that a witch, being damned, could not speak from the Holy Book aloud?"

"Our father, who art in heaven –"

"Not you, dear. Adrian, could you recite the Lord's Prayer for your mommy?"

Adrian blinked, confused. Not being religious, Daina had not taught the invocation to her son.

"Obviously, he is a witch," Penny concluded and smiled at Daina.

"Obviously," Bellona agreed with her own smile. "It's in his blood." She set the Coke bottle on the table, and lifted Adrian up so that he was standing on the bench. "Show your mommy magic."

Adrian rubbed the straw vigorously between his hands, then set it gingerly on top of the capped bottle. That he could get it to balance

4

with his baby's fingers was an achievement in and of itself. But he accomplished it. "What do I say, Auntie Bell?"

"Abracadabra."

"Abra . . . dabra," Adrian recited. He splayed one hand out above the straw, moved it in a circle. The straw followed his palm. He moved it in the other direction; the straw followed. He grinned at Daina. "It's magic, Mommy."

"Indeed," Penny said, her skeptical smirk returning. "He'd have a promising career in vaudeville, Bell, if vaudeville wasn't dead. Not so much witch as mountebank."

"It's not really magic," Adrian confessed. "Auntie showed me. It works 'cause I rubbed the straw first. 'Cause of stajic . . ." He looked at Bellona for the correct words.

"Static electricity," she reminded him.

"That's called a magic *trick*, Capo," Penny told him. "But still, you shouldn't reveal the secrets of how your tricks work." She ruffled his hair, then winked at her sister. "That's the first thing your Auntie Bell should've taught you."

"Look what else I found, in the drawer with the straws," Bellona said. It was a tiny deck of Old Maid cards, just the right size for a child's small hands.

"Ah," Daina said. "Those were mine. What did you call it, Penny? When I was little?"

"Vieux Garçon. The Bachelor."

"Not exactly the *Tarot de Marseille*," Bellona said, "but there's plenty of time to teach him cartomancy."

Penny smiled at Daina. *"Reading the future in the cards."*

"Here, Adrian, come sit on Auntie's lap," Bellona said. Adrian complied. She took the cards out of the box and took his hands in hers, showed him how to fan out the deck. "Time to learn a little prestidigitation."

"Presti-?"

"Prestidigitation," Daina supplied. "It means being clever with your hands, son."

"Okay. The first thing you say, Capo, to your mark –" Bellona winked at her niece, "– is, 'Pick a card, any card . . .'"

THREE

On the way back down to the house later, Daina said to her son, "You knew the door was going to slam before it happened, didn't you, Adrian?"

The boy looked up at her, and just like Nadine always did, Daina saw his father in Adrian's dark blue eyes, and thought, *Wait 'til Ian hears about* this.

Her husband had always listened calmly to her stories about Penny and Bellona's supernatural abilities. He claimed not to have an opinion either way, but Daina believed that Ian leaned more toward belief than he was willing to admit. He was imaginative; he loved verse and fairy tales. Daina was sure that such enjoyments allowed him to easily make the leap in his mind: magic and curses were real, the future could be foretold. This impression was strengthened for Daina, because whenever she would mention that her aunts considered themselves to be witches, imbued with clairvoyance, Ian never failed to reply, "Well, they *did* predict that we would find each other . . ."

Now the little boy with his father's eyes looked at his mother in confusion. Adrian had forgotten about the slamming door.

"The loud noise. When we got back from the store," his mother prompted. "Think about it for a minute." Daina stopped walking and crouched down beside him. "How did you know it was going to happen? Did you *see it?*"

Adrian concentrated for a moment. Then he shrugged, and again, Daina saw Ian in the gesture. "I guess so, Mommy."

"The next time? When you *see* something before it actually happens? Can you tell me?" Daina abruptly hugged him to her. "But don't tell anyone else."

She had suddenly pictured her *exceptional* boy in the dock, on trial for witchcraft. She imagined him derided as a freak of nature, a demon – *no one really wants someone around that can see the future, because the future's not always bright,* she thought. *His own future's in doubt.*

Sometimes, Daina's imagination could be as fanciful as her husband's; but when these flights seized her, it was seldom to show her anything joyful.

"Okay, Mommy," Adrian said and hugged her back. "I'll tell you."

FOUR

But Adrian's mother was not on hand the next time Adrian had a flash of precognition.

Ian and his boy had taken *One Wilde Ride* out on Lake Elsinore with Rob. Daina didn't accompany them; it was something that they enjoyed together, her men, and she didn't feel it necessary to tag along. Adrian was not yet old enough to ski – Ian figured maybe ten or eleven might be a good time to start him – but he was certainly old enough to act as lookout. "Daddy's down," he would tell his cousin, or "Uncle Rob fell," he would tell his dad, and the driver would circle back and return the rope to the skier.

These days, Rob and Ian spent more time tied up on the beach than they had in college. They looked forward to the day when they could once again ski from sun up until sun down, but Adrian was too young for all that yet, so they landed frequently to allow him to play in the sand or in the water.

Ian and Rob were sitting in camp chairs at the lake's edge, drinking beers. It was mid-July, 1975; Adrian had just passed his fifth birthday. He was plopped down in the lake in front of his relatives, studiously scooping up sand and water in a light-blue plastic pail and just as studiously dumping it back out. He didn't pause, nor look up, but said to his father, "Who's my new cousin, Daddy?"

Rob, oblivious, said, "That's right! I was just thinking about that – I keep forgetting to tell you. Marta's pregnant again. Baby's due around Christmas."

The former debutante and Will had encountered a similar situation to Ian and Daina's, a few years before: Marta found herself pregnant, and she and Will had thereby found it necessary to get married, the latest five year plan be damned. Marta was of Will's class, and marrying her hadn't even caused a blip in the ambitious Doctor Wilde's climb toward success.

On October 1, 1972, Robert William Wilde had entered the world. They called him Bobby, to differentiate between his uncle and himself. At the time, Ian had remarked that Rob already had two children named after him – Adrian's middle name was Robert – without ever having to produce one of his own.

"So . . . Yeah," Rob considered Adrian, who was listening, but not raptly. "You *are* going to have a new little cousin, Champ. A little brother or sister for Bobby." He looked at Ian; Ian shrugged.

"Sometimes he knows stuff ahead of time. Daina thinks he's psychic." Ian tapped the side of his head. "Maybe he just read your mind."

"Maybe." Rob concentrated. "What am I thinking right now, Adrian?"

Adrian looked up at his cousin, the man he loved almost as much as his dad, his *Uncle Rob*. He smiled. "That's easy. You wanna go skiing some more."

"Actually, I was thinking that you need to go fetch me another beer." Rob grinned at Ian. "But that'll do, too."

Adrian stood up and tossed his pail into the boat. *"Now is it time to ski: come, shall we about it?"*

His father and cousin smiled proudly at him.

FIVE

When he got home, Ian told his wife that Marta was expecting again, but neglected to mention the timing of his son's inquisitive question about his new cousin. *Yeah,* Ian admitted to himself, *it's true – sometimes Adrian seems to know stuff ahead of time.* Like the time Ian had knocked a can of soda off the coffee table with his elbow – it wasn't open – and Adrian had already had his hands out to catch it.

Adrian didn't see what was going to occur very often; his father was convinced of that. He was usually just as surprised by presents and unexpected visitors as was anyone else. Things got knocked over and he didn't automatically catch them; situations proceeded that he would have been better off to avoid had he know their outcomes, like the time he reached out to pet the old man's Doberman in front of the supermarket, and the cur had growled and lunged at him, giving him quite a fright. "Bad doggie," he had commented to his dad, after he'd stopped crying.

But sometimes, Adrian did anticipate things. Ian had noticed him look at the phone a heartbeat before it rang, had heard him say, "Rob's down," a millisecond before Rob fell. But Ian was hesitant to discuss these things with Daina. Maybe their son did have a little preternatural talent; maybe all little kids had it, and it had only been noticed in Adrian because of his mother's witchy upbringing. Maybe it would fade as he got older.

But Ian didn't mention his observations to Daina, because he didn't want her to think that there was anything unusual about their boy. He knew that such thoughts always led her back to her aunts' prophecy about Adrian's short lifespan.

SIX

Nadine enrolled in photography classes at UCR. Time passed; she saw her twenty-sixth birthday and her twenty-seventh. She spent an occasional evening at the same dark bar at which Ian had once been employed, and if the desire struck her and he had his own place, she sometimes went home with a college boy that reminded her of him. Nadine always picked ones that were in their early or mid-twenties; the same age Ian had been when they'd first met. This discrepancy in age wasn't really noticeable at first, but as the years passed, it seemed as if Nadine couldn't escape an attraction to younger men that reminded her of Ian at the same age.

Nadine became as Daina had been in college. It was simply a physical need that demanded to be serviced. She saw no future with any of these young men, and seldom went back for a second or third date. Nadine felt that her future had been amputated, stolen from her. The future that she had been fated to have, lived across the street with an aging whore and her little blue-eyed, growing-bigger-every-day chimpanzee.

When the term ended in June in the bicentennial year of 1976, Nadine announced with some pride that she had secured a job at National Geographic Magazine. It was a prestigious position for someone so young, but Nadine was an excellent photographer. She told the family across the street that she was sorry, but she was going to miss Adrian's sixth birthday party; she was leaving the country on assignment.

Adrian tried manfully not to cry when he heard the news. He was very fond of his AnTeen: she gave him candy whenever he asked for it, let him stay up past his bedtime when she watched him. She encouraged him in the simple magic tricks that his Aunt Bellona had taught him; AnTeen always had a moment *to pick a card, any card.*

Adrian solemnly told Nadine that he would miss her. He'd never had the occasion to miss anything yet in his life, except for old Grimalkin. A few weeks before, a thin, yellow-eyed, black mama cat had appeared on the deck, carrying one fluffy black kitten in her mouth. Aunt Penny had gently told Adrian that 'Malky had moved on; but this mama and her baby were hungry. They needed his love now.

Adrian dutifully took a bowlful of food out to the skittish new arrivals. Showing a patience beyond his years, Adrian eventually gained their trust. Soon Mama was rubbing on his legs and he was holding the kitten in his lap. But Adrian was sad about the loss of his old familiar.

Not long after, old Princess Plush was gone, too; Adrian didn't notice – the Siamese had never let him anywhere near her – but Penny mourned for a moment. Only Holt the tom remained to receive the mama and her kitten. Once again, there were three.

As they had when Penny told him that 'Malky was gone, now the tears ran silently down Adrian's face as he gave his AnTeen a hug goodbye.

SEVEN

When Nadine next returned to Riverside, it was August of 1982. She had been *a child of the world* in the intervening years – she'd lived here and there, in Europe, the States, and even Australia for a little while, taking pictures. She'd *had many lovers, as she chose,* just as Penny and Bellona had foretold when she was just a blushing schoolgirl.

But Nadine's relationships were always empty. The men she selected were always younger; they always reminded her in some way of Ian as he'd been when she'd first met him. They didn't necessarily look like him – there were only so many men in the world that actually *resembled* Ian – but there was always some attribute to them that personified him to Nadine. This one had squinty eyes; that one had a similar smile; another one had dark, shaggy hair; this one, the same muscular build; that one spoke in verse like Ian did.

It was effortless for Nadine to imagine that each was Ian, her soulmate, based on just one little characteristic, and it always satisfied her at first. But after a while, the fact that they were *not* Ian inevitably came home to her. And when it did, Nadine would abruptly, unceremoniously drop them like Third Period French, and move on. Sometimes to a different town, sometimes to a different country.

But after six years of rambling, Nadine was once again ready to come home for a recharge. Surely, she thought in the back of her mind, Ian and Daina's marriage must've grown stale by now. Perhaps now, true fate could be allowed to flourish.

Again her arrival was unheralded. Nadine simply showed up one Saturday afternoon on the doorstep of the man she loved, and rang the bell. Ian exclaimed, "Well, I'll be *god* damned!" and hugged her.

It seemed like a lifetime had passed since Nadine had last seen him; it seemed like she had waited a lifetime for this moment, to be in Ian's arms again. The desire for this tiny event had drawn her across oceans, across continents, like the ancient force that made salmon return to the place of their birth. It wasn't the idea of home and familiar surroundings, or her so-called friend, that called to her. It wasn't the joy of seeing her mom and dad that brought Nadine back. It was Ian and the anticipation of holding him against her for this too-brief hug.

Nadine had enjoyed all the infinite variety of smells and tastes and sights of the big, wide world; but she knew she'd never settle anywhere abroad. She might enjoy a few days' or a week's or a month's or a year's stay in one foreign locale, but she always felt a tug to move on after a while, to see the next ocean, to surmount the next hill, to taste the next cuisine. And just as this invisible pull had dragged her all over the world, it always brought her back, eventually, to Ian. Wherever her next journey led, however long it would last, Nadine knew that it would conclude with her returning to him. That return was the part to which she always looked forward most of all. Ian was her soulmate.

As always, when he hugged her, Nadine experienced the years of longing, all at once; distilled, like an inundation, a drowning. *Oh, God, Ian! I love you so much! What did I ever do to deserve losing you?* But Nadine knew she was innocent of blame for the cruel theft that she had suffered. It wasn't any kind of karmic retribution for unknown sins committed in a former life that had deprived her of her destiny, but the scheming of others. Nadine had been betrayed by those closest to her, those with whom she'd felt a magical kinship. She considered herself their victim, and she awaited the day – she often imagined the look of astonishment on their faces – when she would rise and smite them for their crime.

Ian released her and said, "Daina took a batch of candles to Mohini's. She'll be back in a little while. She'll be so glad to see you!"

The gods smiled on Nadine then: Ian hugged her again. It *had* been six years. Again she was enveloped in his scent, felt his chest against hers, his strong arms around her. After all this time, she was again in Ian's embrace – the place she was meant to be!

Resolve flooded through her then, complete, encompassing, like the rush of a powerful narcotic. *It isn't too late! The whore isn't here! I'll just tell him right now, what I should've told him that first night in 1969! Before the decade turned! The decade has turned again – I won't wait another second! Boldness be my friend! I'll tell him of our destiny, and at last he'll see, at last he'll –*

Nadine reluctantly backed out of his Ian's friendly hug – it was *so* difficult to do so, but if she spoke now, she could then return to his arms, she could remain in his embrace forever! She looked up at his smiling face, breathlessly said his name. "I –"

An ear-splitting whine of feedback rendered further words impossible. Nadine blinked, believing for a second that the sound had come from within her own mind. But Ian was shaking his head, rolling his eyes. He smiled indulgently. "Come see Adrian, Nadine. He thinks he's a rock star these days."

Ian stepped through the still-open front door and headed in the direction of the garage. Again Nadine blinked, in irritation this time. Again she had been cut off, right at the very second when all could've been redeemed! Again, her rightful fate had been blocked by one of Daina's kin! That detestable little *brat!*

Nadine followed Ian out to the garage. All manner of musical accoutrements were there, beside Ian's covered boat: amps and cables and pedals; guitar stands, a microphone. All that was missing was a drum kit. Ian was talking to two boys, each holding a guitar. One was a redhead with freckles, sporting a fairly good imitation of a Flock of Seagulls haircut. The other had black hair, parted in the middle, shaggy, falling off his brow and nearly to his shoulders.

Not shaggy, Nadine corrected herself. *"Feathered" is the modern term.* This had to be Adrian, but at first glance, Daina's son was unrecognizable to her. When last she'd seen him, he'd been not quite six years old, still a summertime away from starting first grade.

The boy's face lit up when he saw Nadine, and if she'd had any doubt that this tall, skinny, gangly kid was Daina's boy, it fled. Because he still had, and would always have, his father's dark-blue eyes.

"AnTeen!" he exclaimed. He set down his guitar on a stand and leapt over the snake pit of pedals and wires on the floor. Nadine was reminded of how his father had once upon a time vaulted over the bar at a little college tavern, before Adrian had ever even been dreamt of. Nadine reluctantly opened her arms and Adrian hugged her enthusiastically but clumsily, almost knocking her down.

He kissed her on the cheek; Adrian was not a shy pre-teen who still thought girls were yucky, it would seem. Or maybe he was – regardless, this was his AnTeen and he loved her. What little he remembered of her. "How have you been? *Where* have you been? I've missed you so much!" He hugged her exuberantly again.

"I've been all over, Adrian," she said, still amazed at the changes six years had wrought upon a six-year-old boy. He was still just a gawky kid, but he wasn't an ugly duckling anymore. He was already almost as tall as Ian, still had his mother's black hair and bow mouth, his father's guileless blue eyes, although Adrian wasn't squinty. With the long hair, he was as pretty as a girl.

But as soon as those hormones kick in, Nadine thought wryly, *Daina's little brat's gonna be a lady-killer. Just like his father was. And he won't even need a mahogany boat, because he plays the guitar.*

"Do you remember my cousin Will, Nadine?" Ian asked, out of nowhere.

"Not very well," she replied with a grin. Why not enjoy herself while the whore was away? If she smiled at Ian, he would smile back, and Nadine had waited six years to see his smile again. "I don't think I said more than three hundred words to Will in all the time I knew him. Although I seem to recall he bore an uncanny resemblance to someone I dated."

Ian ignored that remark; he told Nadine, "This is Will's son, Bobby."

Yeah, Nadine thought. *The past is an ancient can of worms best left unopened in front of the youngsters. I once dated this kid's Uncle Rob, his dad once dated Adrian's mom; Adrian's dad once dated his mom. All that was better left unremembered at this time. It would confuse them. Disgust them.*

The redheaded boy with the ridiculous hairdo politely shook Nadine's hand and said it was nice to meet her.

Nadine marveled: hadn't she read in some sociobiology text somewhere that children usually resembled their fathers? Yet it seemed to run counter to nature with the Wilde genes. As Adrian did, Bobby favored his mother in hair color: he had Marta's dark auburn hair and her freckles. One could only identify the boys' fathers by their eyes. Adrian's were the same incredible shade of dark blue as Ian's and Nadine could clearly see Will in Bobby's light green ones.

Adrian hopped back over the wires. He stood beside the mike and again picked up his guitar. It was black, crisscrossed by yellow lines of varying thicknesses. Nadine was inexplicably put in mind of the horrible knit dress his mother had worn on the night Ian had asked her to marry him. *You were already on the way then, boy,* she thought.

The pattern on Adrian's guitar looked like some kind of nightmare negative of that prim, ugly dress; it had been a similar shade of yellow, crisscrossed by thin black lines. If Nadine had been at all hip, she would've known that it was Adrian's pride and joy, a replica of Eddie Van Halen's guitar.

15

"What would you like to hear, AnTeen? We don't have a drummer, but Bobby and I have quite a repertoire. Request something."

Like his father had done earlier, Nadine rolled her eyes indulgently. She'd heard that squeal of feedback; she wasn't really in the mood for a twelve-year-old boy's rendition of what was passing for music these days.

Adrian caught her skeptical look. "We're what you call classically trained guitarists, AnTeen." He winked at his cousin.

Ian nodded, smiled in pride. "This guy at work has been teaching them since they were little. Says they're prodigies."

He says that right after he cashes your check, Nadine said to herself.

"No requests?" Nadine thought that Adrian's smile was a little crafty when he said to his cousin, "How about a little *Jesse's Girl?*""

Adrian started playing his ugly guitar, then leaned into the mike and whispered in his little-boy's voice. Nadine missed most of the intro, but caught, *Jessie's got himself a girl and I want to make her mine,* and then listened to the rest of the song. *And she's watching him with those eyes, and she's lovin' him with that body, I just know it . . .*

"*I wish that I had Jessie's girl,*" Adrian sang, then stopped abruptly. He grinned at Nadine, waited for her to compliment his musical skills.

"You wish that *you were* Jessie's girl," Bobby murmured to his cousin with a smirk.

Nadine was secretly in love with Ian. It was a secret that she'd kept from every living soul for more than a decade, and therefore, she was practiced at controlling her expression. She gazed blankly at Adrian. "I've been out of the country, honey," she said condescendingly. "I haven't heard that one."

It was true. Nadine hadn't before heard Rick Springfield's ode to misplaced affection, but now that Adrian had sung it to her, the lyrics wounded, reminded her of her own situation. A picture of Ian, wrapped up in Daina's green sheet, flashed, unwelcome, into her mind. *And he's holding her in his arms, late, late at night . . .* Why did Daina's brat choose that particular tune? *So wise so young, they say, do never live long . . .*

"Maybe something a little older, son," Ian suggested. "Something your mom would like."

16

Nadine thought that if Adrian played *Killing Me Softly (With His Song)* she would indeed kill him, on the spot, and it wouldn't be softly. And the redheaded bass player, too.

Undaunted by Nadine's lack of praise, Adrian said, "You like oldies, do ya, AnTeen? How 'bout one from before little Bobby was born? It's his favorite." He grinned. "Play it, Cuz."

The bassline was unmistakable, and Nadine recognized Three Dog Night's *Mama Told Me Not to Come* immediately. She had to admit that Will's kid played a mean bass for a ten-year-old. The boys were talented, even though it was humorous to hear a twelve-year-old sing, *This is the craziest party there could* evah *be.*

Again they stopped abruptly, in the middle of the song, right after, *That ain't the way to have fun, son.*

Nadine felt a tap on her shoulder. She turned, and then Daina was hugging her, exclaiming over her, telling her how much she'd been missed, just like her skinny boy had done.

"Adrian's quite the musician," Nadine commented, just for something to say, after the *How have you beens?* and the *So glad that you're backs!* had petered out.

At the sound of his name Adrian smiled at his AnTeen, then at his mother, and Nadine was amazed at how his smile was the same as it had been when he was five years old. *Still a mama's boy,* she thought with contempt.

"He even writes his own songs," Daina said with the same parental pride that Ian had earlier expressed.

Oh, sweet Jesus! Please don't force me to endure any of those! Nadine paused in talking to herself for a heartbeat, then thought, *Of course, he's confident enough to write his own lyrics, even at twelve years old. His grandfather is a scholar and his father can quote the classics as easily as breathing.*

But had he been my son, as he was meant to be – he would've been a poet, not a musician. He wouldn't be spending his time in this hot garage, squeezing feedback and common rhymes out of that hideous black and yellow instrument.

Nadine was spared any of Adrian's compositions for the moment. He said, "We learned *California Dreamin',* Mom." The *just for you* was left unsaid, but it hung there in Nadine's mind. The boy began the tune from his mother's past, and he sang it directly to her.

Adrian might like to play music for himself, but Nadine could see that his greatest thrill was to play for Daina. She knew that Daina had never understood poetry, but she had always been able to remember the lyrics to the latest transitory rock tune, and her boy was more than delighted to sing them all to her.

Ian put his arm around his wife and they listened to their boy and his cousin. Daina leaned into him, and Ian smiled at her. She looked at her son; Adrian smiled at her, too. Even Bobby smiled at her. This love for Daina, silently expressed in the smiles of her menfolk, became like a tangible miasma to Nadine; it seemed to condense in the air and choke her. And Daina basked in their love, *secure from worldly chances and mishaps. Here lurks no treason, here no envy swells, here grow no damned grudges; here are no storms, no noise* . . .

Nadine had to escape all this affection for the whore who had ruined her life. All this love – it should have been Nadine's – only through perfidious thievery was it Daina's. She had stolen Ian, and had through him produced a child that clearly worshipped her. An underhanded theft, and Nadine was left with nothing. No blue-eyed water-skier, no gangly boy. No one loved Nadine. And it was all Daina's fault.

The song ended, and before Adrian could begin to further serenade his mother, Nadine offered her stock excuse, the one that had allowed her to get away from them before: "I have to go visit with my mom and dad. It's great to see all of you again. And nice to meet you, Bobby."

Nadine turned and strode out of the garage, down the short concrete driveway. Sanctuary, puny as it was, was just across the street. Sam and Irene's house offered escape from Daina's happiness, from the homey contentment that she possessed, all as a result of what she had stolen from Nadine.

"Come to dinner, AnTeen!" Adrian called after her. "We're having spaghetti!"

EIGHT

But Nadine was able to avoid dinner with the happy family, by using her parents' desire to spend time with her as an excuse. She was astounded at the changes in them: retired now, they had become a little old man and woman. It was appalling; it underlined for Nadine how much time had passed, and yet still her life was empty. College, youth, were long gone. It was easy to avoid these truths when she was in the field; her days were filled with the task at hand.

But once she was home, all the girlhood memories assailed Nadine. Her room was as she'd left it when she'd run off to join the circus, er, the Peace Corps, with Chuck. The pictures she'd taken while searching for that one and only were still thumbtacked to the wall. They were yellowing now, turning in at the edges. There was Rob and Will, sporting crew cuts, as well as all the other men from her past, all the other men that had meant nothing to her. Nadine had folders more, accordion files stuffed with newer pictures, newer men. None of them had meant anything to her, either.

If all of these pictures were burned, and the negatives, too, Nadine would not mourn. They represented only ships that passed in the night, momentary needs that had been quenched. The only picture that Nadine valued was the little black and white one that she'd taken of Ian at the river. She always had that one in her camera bag. The original print had become creased and torn during her travels, and she had long ago discarded it. But she kept the negative in a tiny plastic sleeve, sealed against the ravages of the world. She frequently made a new print for herself.

Nadine had planned on staying with her parents for a while, but after a very short time she again longed to flee. Everything was the same, yet it was different. Her dad still read the paper, but he also watched a lot of television, because there wasn't much else for him to do. Her mom still cooked and cleaned and read the latest treatises on the empowerment of women, but Irene was far too old to ever escape now.

Nadine wondered if her mother was happy, if she had ever achieved one single part of the feminism that she'd always read about. Nadine had achieved it. She was a freelance photographer – a field still dominated by men – her career was her life. She had refused the narrow bonds of marriage and children. She was nearly thirty-four; Irene didn't ask if there would soon be prospects for a son-in-law or grandchildren anymore.

Irene had accepted that such simple joys were not to be hers. Her daughter was a world-traveler, and she would just have to content herself with Nadine's stories of far-away places and the triumphs of her craft. She was glad that Nadine had never allowed herself to be tied down, if that's how she'd wanted it.

Irene loved Sam and their daughter, and couldn't say that she had any regrets. But there had been a few achingly wistful times in her life when she had wondered what other, more fulfilling experiences she might have encompassed had she selected another path. Perhaps a solitary one, as Nadine had chosen. But it was not something that had often been offered to women of her generation.

Sometimes Irene thought she caught a haunted look in her daughter's eye, despite all her intriguing stories of exotic ports and foreign boyfriends, none of whom lasted for very long. Nadine wondered if her mother was happy; Irene wondered the same thing about Nadine.

Sam was just glad to see his baby whenever she came home. He congratulated himself. While she'd never quite grown out of the hippiness that she'd adopted in high school – this world-traveling shtick was proof of that – neither had she become a murderer or a druggie or an unwed mother. He had raised a successful adult.

Penny and Bellona seemed exactly the same to Nadine, just a little bit more wizened and gray. They were cheerful and polite, asked Nadine thoughtful questions about her travels, asked if she still practiced the old arts. Nadine proudly told them that she would always be a witch foremost. She still read the Tarot; still lit a candle and said a few words on the Sabbats. But she was a *solitaire,* as she'd always been. She shared her knowledge with no one.

"As you share your life with no one," Penny observed, eternally straight to the heart of the matter. "When are you going to settle down, 'Deen? Stay home?"

"We miss you," Bellona said and patted her hand.

"Reply hazy, try again," Nadine replied evenly, thinking, *Do you think that I've forgotten that it's because of you that I'm all alone? That I always feel the need to escape because of you? That I'd have the slut down the hill's life if you all wouldn't have conspired to steal it from me?*

Nadine shook her head and said, "It's not in the cards at the moment."

Penny wasn't averse to bringing up the past. "What did I tell you about reading your own cards, 'Deen? Your interpretation is skewed, by hope as well as resignation. You should have one of us read it for you."

"Concentrate and ask again," Nadine replied and forced herself to smile. "It can be your gift to me, before I leave the next time." *Only I wouldn't hold your breath waiting for me to make the request,* Nadine thought.

Daina was aging mellowly, as well she should. She had no responsibilities other than to love her husband and son. To amuse herself, she told Nadine, she still made candles for Mohini's. Nadine found Daina to be insufferably happy with her narrow lot.

She also discovered that Daina and Ian still couldn't keep their hands off of each other, even after all these years. *You'd think that they would've developed some decorum with a child in the house; but, no.* They still held hands, still walked around with their arms linked around each other's waists; they still took every opportunity to kiss. Daina still sat in his lap. It seemed to Nadine that they were rubbing her nose in their harmonic togetherness, pointing up the fact that Rob was long gone, and Chuck, and Charlie, and a legion more that they didn't even know about.

Ian looked the same to Nadine: perennially healthy, virile, sexy – always was Ian the epitome of manhood to her. He still waterskied whenever he could, although not-quite-famed-yet orthopedist Doctor Robert Wilde was not as available as he had once been in the carefree old days to accompany his cousin.

Adrian and Will's son Bobby were there to take up the slack, Ian said, but it was not as much of a passion with these cousins as it had been with the earlier generation. Adrian and Bobby would just as soon spend their weekends in the garage playing their guitars. They enjoyed dragging *One Wilde Ride* to Elsinore to ski – "Don't get me wrong," Ian said – but it was a secondary pleasure, a diversion from their music.

Adrian treated Nadine as if she was some kind of inexplicable curiosity. Nadine couldn't say that Adrian had a boyish crush on her; that wouldn't have been accurate. But still he was fascinated with her, and never missed an opportunity to talk to her. If they saw that she was at home, he and Bobby would stop *band practice* – how could they think of themselves as a band without a drummer? They would just drop in uninvited then, and Adrian would beg to hear more stories of the road. He said that he'd like to travel someday, to see the world as she had done, and Nadine relished the thought: *You're not fated to ever get out of Riverside, boy. You're gonna die.*

Adrian would give her his undivided attention, hang on her every word, almost as if he was studying her. It was a little unnerving, especially when he would tilt his head and stare inquiringly at her, and Nadine would get the unsettling impression that he wasn't listening to what she was saying so much at that moment; instead, it was as if he was listening to what she was *thinking.*

The odd phenomenon would only last for a split-second, but sometimes he would subsequently surprise Nadine by guessing what she was going to say next. When she mentioned doing some nature photography in Nagano, Japan, Adrian interrupted with, "Oh, yeah! Where the monkeys are. In the springs!"

How a twelve-year-old boy could know about the hot-tubbing Asian macaques was beyond Nadine; but she had had a picture of them in her head at that moment, and it was as if Adrian had read her mind.

Penny and Bellona had always claimed that he was *exceptional.* Maybe he *could* see a few seconds into the future, but if Daina's doomed son was psychic, Nadine believed that it came to him only in flashes. If he really had any kind of seer's gift, she figured that he'd be able to sense how much she disliked him, and wouldn't be dropping in and bothering her all the time. If he was anything more than momentarily clairvoyant, then Adrian would be able to see that his AnTeen wished nothing more than for Penny and Bellona's awful prediction to come true, and the sooner the better.

But he was only twelve, still years away from his majority, and his cousin was only ten. Nadine was thankful, actually, that Adrian almost always hauled Bobby along with him when he insisted on visiting. Bobby would get bored quickly; he wanted to go practice his bass. He didn't want to listen to boring stories about foreign lands that he had no desire to see. If Adrian possessed some of his father's imagination, Bobby had inherited *his* father's wholesale. Will had never been one for adventure stories, real or fanciful.

November 12th, 1982, marked Nadine's thirty-fourth birthday. She had cake and ice cream with her parents, as if she was still a child, then climbed the path to Penny and Bellona's for a party more befitting her years. Seated beside their amps in the middle of the deck, the pre-teen guitar players stayed up past their bedtime and serenaded the grown-ups. But mostly they were ignored, left to their own devices, as Ian and Nadine and Daina and her aunts sat around and reminisced about college, about skiing the river and lake, about the good old days.

Nadine hated to reminisce about the good old days. There had been nothing good about them, not one single thing, except for the brief period when Nadine had believed that Ian would be hers. And since that dream had been viciously shattered by these very women with whom she was forced into camaraderie at the moment, neither the conversation nor the company amused her. Her life was half over, and she had nothing to show for it because of *them.*

Nadine drank too much. It dulled the pain, helped her to keep a carefree smile on her lips, helped to submerge the eternal rage she felt for these people.

During a lull in the conversation, Adrian, always eager for attention, played the opening chords to *At Last.* Nadine looked over her shoulder at him and he grinned at her, played the intro again. *Of course he would know that ancient tune,* she thought. *It's no doubt part of the family history. Mr. and Mrs. Wilde's first dance.*

But Nadine was in her cups, and she pushed the thoughts of *Mr. and Mrs. Wilde* from her mind. She looked back at Ian, and now she saw only him. She smiled. "Remember that Hallowe'en, Ian? When we danced to this? Long before yon guitar player was even born?"

Hell, the evil imp said in Nadine's mind, *yon guitar player might've been conceived the very next day. Ha!*

But Nadine ignored its voice. She continued to smile at Ian. "Come on! Dance with me! For old times' sake!" Nadine extended her hand across the table.

Ian looked blankly at her. "Married men don't dance with beautiful young ladies," he said after a moment, ever the poet.

"Ah, *the heyday in the blood is tame, it's humble, and waits upon the judgment,*" Nadine said with a drunken giggle. It couldn't be further from the truth: the prospect of dancing with Ian, swaying to the old classic with his body pressed to her, suddenly electrified Nadine, fired her imagination. The prospect reminded her of one of those moments from the good old days that had actually been *good:* that long ago Hallowe'en when they had danced together, when she still had a chance.

Ian glanced at Daina, and she saw reflected in his eyes all the reluctance that had been there so long ago. He didn't want to dance with Nadine now, any more than he'd wanted to dance with her then. That was the night they'd first met; that was the night that they'd fallen in love at first sight, like in a storybook, a fairytale. That was the night when Daina's life had truly begun.

23

Now she smirked at her husband. The drunken birthday girl was obviously game. Daina recalled that Nadine had liked Ian once upon a time; perhaps the liquor and the stroll down Memory Lane, and the strains of *At Last* had reminded her of those long ago emotions.

"Go ahead, Ian. Dance with Nadine. For old times' sake." *Give the beautiful young lady a thrill,* she added wordlessly.

I'll give you *a thrill,* his expression replied.

You always do.

Their son might have sparks of precognition, but Daina and Ian had been telepathic since the moment they'd met. A smile, a raised eyebrow – they could speak volumes to each other without a single word. Now Daina winked at him, nodded at her friend.

Ian stood, masking his reluctance, as he had on that long ago Hallowe'en. In his mind, Daina was still the irresistible black-haired beauty that he'd met that night; their passion had never waned. The thought of any other woman, previously known or otherwise, had never crossed his mind in all the intervening years. He loved Daina to *the depth and breadth and height his soul could reach,* and he was confident that she felt the same way. He didn't want to dance with Nadine.

Nadine grabbed his hand and drew him to one side of the deck, away from his wife and her aunts, away from the *band.* Unabashedly, she wrapped her arms around Ian's neck, molded her body against his. It was *their song,* after all. Ian glanced over Nadine's shoulder at his wife in mock horror; Daina grinned at him.

Adrian sang the old favorite well. *He heard it in the womb!* the imp cackled in Nadine's mind. She ignored the derisive voice, put her head on Ian's shoulder, rocked gently against her soulmate. As always, his smell was intoxicating.

"You know, Ian," she breathed against his chest, "I've missed you."

"I've missed you, too, 'Deen," he replied immediately, neutrally.

Drink and Ian's maddening scent made Nadine bold, reckless. "I've always wished that we could've gotten to know each other better," she said, and gave him a little squeeze.

"Well, we're not dead yet."

Nadine looked up into Ian's eyes at this response. It could've been a flirt, a suggestion, and coming from anyone else, it might've been. But Ian's dark eyes were guileless as always, innocent. He'd always looked at her in this way: pleasantly, amicably, without a trace of longing, not a scintilla of lust. He could be looking at

Bellona. His next words underlined it for Nadine: "We'll always be friends."

Friends! Ha-ha-ho-ho-hee-hee! Nadine's eyes watered at the imp's vicious, crowing laughter. Again she ignored it.

"Always," she told Ian.

She hugged him tighter to her, and a wave of hatred for Daina and her aunts passed through Nadine again. They had hoodwinked Ian, bewitched him, made him blind to the truth. But what he'd said was true: *we're not dead yet . . .*

Still, as Adrian finished the song, Nadine suddenly felt silly, self-conscious, sober. Life was long, and the time might still come – hell, she didn't have one foot in the grave, after all, and neither did Ian – but the time was not now. He had not yet kenned the conspiracy, had not seen through to the deceit of his whore-wife and her conniving kin. Ian had been trapped, corralled, a lamb to the slaughter. But he didn't know it. Not yet. Someday, it would happen . . . But not now.

Nadine felt the need to run again, to go somewhere where the dream of Ian was so much more palatable than this reality. She had to escape the inescapable: Ian still believed himself to be in love with his wife.

On the last chord, Nadine released Ian immediately and stalked back to the table, her fake smile pasted on. She picked up her drink and downed it.

Ian, left standing alone, turned to Adrian. "You really need to learn some new material, son. Something from this decade."

"It's the classics that endure, Dad," Adrian disagreed.

Bobby grinned and played the bassline from *Rock This Town.*

Ian grinned back at him. "You're good, boy."

"Come over here, gentlemen," Penny requested. "'Deen has an announcement."

The boys set down their guitars and they and Ian crossed the deck. Ian sat in a chair; Daina, seated on the bench, stretched her legs out and put her feet in his lap. Adrian sat beside her on the bench and Daina put her arm around his shoulder and gave him a little squeeze. She smiled at Bobby. "You guys get better every day. Carnegie Hall awaits."

"The Hollywood Bowl, Mom."

Ian smiled at his wife and son, his cousin. Nadine observed all this and thought, *the time has come,* just as she had the first time that she'd escaped from their homespun bliss, when Adrian was only a baby.

"I just wanted to thank you all for the lovely party," she said, "and tell you that I'll be leaving again. Tomorrow." Up until that moment, Nadine hadn't firmed up her plans yet, but this evening had resolved her. She had to get away again.

"Where to this time?" Daina asked. "Rome? Paris?"

"I have a friend that's invited me to New York," Nadine said mysteriously. Anthony, with whom she'd spent a week the previous summer in Albuquerque. He had dark blue eyes, and a quick smile, just like Ian. He was twenty-six.

"Bite the Big Apple. Don't mind the maggots," Adrian said. His cousin grinned at him.

"Really, Adrian," Ian chided. "From this decade."

"The Stones, Dad. *Classic.*"

Nadine felt the urge to clear her throat, in order to return their attention to her. She wasn't even gone yet, and they were already ignoring her. When his son had no more immortal words, Ian looked at the birthday girl and said, "We'll miss you, 'Deen. As always."

No *Please don't go,* or even a request to know when she might be returning. Nadine had only stayed a little more than ninety days. *Small time, but in that small . . .* she'd been able to discern no cracks in Daina's marriage into which she might've poured discord. All was serene, solid, *sovereign* between her one-time best friend and her purloined soulmate.

Nadine was amazed as always at how completely these witches had ensorcelled Ian. He would awaken someday, though. Nadine was sure of it. But not tonight. Perhaps when his boy died. Nadine hoped to be on hand when that tragedy struck; the imp still whispered that perhaps she could even have a hand in it. Nadine would be back.

NINE

Life in New York City was a whirlwind. Anthony was in the fashion industry, and used his connections to get Nadine enough photo shoots that they lived quite well.

Nadine loved the change of the seasons, reveled in the cold, snowy winters. It allowed her to wear all sorts of stylish clothing: colorful hats and gloves and long wool coats, things never really necessary in her native clime. And the ice and wind reflected the coldness in her soul.

She liked young, blue-eyed Anthony, and enjoyed her days and nights with him. But Nadine knew that someday the heat of Southern California would call her home; the idea of holding Ian in her arms again (even if it was only for a moment) would draw her back across the continent.

But it hadn't happened yet, and time crept in its petty pace from day to day, until six years had again passed. Nadine was happy. Anthony was a lot of fun: he was a mere thirty-two to her more world-weary almost-forty, and she enjoyed his exuberance and lust for life.

On Wednesday, the 29th of June, 1988, Nadine had an odd, disturbing dream. All was darkness, then a door banged open, shattering the quiet. Then another lurid noise, and a man wearing a ski mask was silhouetted in the burst of light from a long gun as he fired it. Nadine snapped awake: the telephone was ringing.

Irene told Nadine tearfully that her father had suffered a heart attack. Sam was hospitalized; the situation was touch and go. Could Nadine return to Riverside as soon as possible?

She made it back home just as the sun was setting on Friday. The cab dropped her off at the head of the cul-de-sac, because the little street where she had grown up was choked with parked cars. It was the first of July; Nadine realized with a start that Monday was Independence Day. It would mark Adrian Wilde's eighteenth birthday. They must be throwing a party for him.

Parties could be hazardous events, Nadine thought with a grin, *especially for young men.* She wondered if Daina's anxiety level was off the charts at the moment. Perhaps not – the anniversary of her son's birth was still three days away – he hadn't come into his majority just yet. But it was close enough, and Nadine longed to see the whore a nervous wreck.

Maybe here was fate at work again. Nadine had been content in New York; she had forgotten all about Adrian's impending doom. Sam had never had any heart trouble in the past. Yet he'd had a life-threatening episode on the eve of the time when Adrian's life was also due to be threatened, perhaps even ended. Fate had called Nadine back home in order that she might bear witness to the monkey's comeuppance and his mother's sure-to-be unendurable sorrow.

Sam was home from the hospital; Nadine had talked to her mother while en route from the East Coast, and Irene had told her that he was weak and shaky, but the danger was past. The danger to Daina's *exceptional* son was just beginning, however, so Nadine decided to drop in on the party and see what was shakin'.

The house was dark, so Nadine climbed the path to Penny and Bellona's place. The clearing was ablaze with light, even though the sun had just set. Twenty or thirty young people milled around in groups of twos and threes. Nadine saw not a soul she recognized.

She found a teenaged girl sitting in a folding chair, blocking the egress to the deck upstairs.

"Hi," the girl said simply.

"Hi," Nadine returned. She was probably eighteen, with enormous blue eyes. She reminded Nadine a little bit of Daina at the same age, although when Daina was eighteen she had worn her black hair simply. This girl's was teased and fluffed around her face like a cloud. *It's the style these days,* Nadine thought, and again her advancing age was brought home to her. The new generation – young people, though approaching their majority, and therefore not so young – were alien to her. There was no commonality. The future now belonged to them.

And Daina had always been a conservative dresser. This young girl was wearing a short black skirt and a bulky, loud, ridiculous, multi-colored jacket; too much make-up; garish, plastic hooped earrings. And while Daina had never been poetic, she was not unintelligent. This girl gazed up at Nadine with the serenity and blankness of a cow. Surely, she reminded Nadine a little of her enemy, but it was a dumber, trampy-er looking Daina that sat before her.

"Can I go upstairs?" Nadine asked.

"Oh, yeah, sure!" The girl hopped up, moved the chair out of the way. "I was just keeping all the people back."

"Back from what?"

"We can't have everybody going up there."

Nadine wasn't getting it. "Why not? What's up there?"

"The band."

"Band?"

"Yeah. Urban Equinox. Adrian's band. He asked me not to let more than ten or fifteen people up there." When the girl spoke Adrian's name, Nadine sensed adoration, unrequited. It was familiar territory to Nadine and she was attuned to it.

Nadine said, "I'm Adrian's . . ." What was she to the despised brat? *His nemesis,* the imp in her mind whispered. "I'm Adrian's aunt."

"Like Miss Penny and Miss Bellona?" the girl said eagerly. "Are you their sister?" She looked at Nadine again, realized that she was not anywhere nearly as old as the beldames. "Their daughter?"

"I'm a friend of Adrian's mom," Nadine clarified. "I'm not really blood to him." *Because his father was stolen from me.* "My name's Nadine. No *Miss* required." Nadine extended her hand.

The girl shook it. "I'm Randi. Nice to meet you."

Nadine nodded, said it was nice to meet her, too. "I've been gone a long time, Randi. Adrian was just a little kid the last time I saw him. Are you his girlfriend?"

Randi looked at the ground, laughed nervously, self-consciously. "No. Adrian doesn't have a girlfriend. He's too busy with . . . his music." She looked up to see if Nadine was buying it.

Nadine pretended to, but she thought the sentence would've been different if this girl was honest with herself. *Adrian is too busy with all the girls to settle for just one.* Just like his father had been at one time. Until all the meddling witches had intervened, lassoed him, and tied him to a whore.

"I'm sure you'll get your turn," Nadine said conspiratorially.

Randi grinned, glanced up the steps. "One can only hope," she said, mostly to herself. Then, thinking that she had perhaps said too much to this stranger, *Adrian's aunt,* she added, "My boyfriend's name is Gil. He's around here somewhere." A pause. "I'm sure you'd like to see Adrian now."

Again, that wistfulness when she said his name. Randi was young, but she was obviously a grown woman, not a blushing schoolgirl. Nadine couldn't imagine why she was so impressed with Adrian. He'd been a skinny, graceless boy, all knees and elbows, the last time Nadine had seen him. Sure, he could play the guitar then, and he'd no doubt only gotten better at that . . . On the other hand, it *had* been six years. Nadine remembered how pretty he'd been on the cusp of puberty.

"He's upstairs with the rest of the band."

"Thanks, Randi. I'm sure I'll be seeing you later."

Nadine paused at the top of the stairs: three kids were grouped around the table, watching a fourth deal Three-card Monte. The dealer was wearing a white fedora with a black band; he had his head down, looking at the cards, so Nadine couldn't see his face. She recognized Bobby, even though the Flock of Seagulls haircut was long departed. His unmistakable, dark red hair – so like his mother's – was now swept back off of his brow. Beside him sat a young girl, blonde, her hair teased fiercely, like Randi's. On the other side of the Monte dealer, in the other chair, was a little kid, also with red hair. He wore it spiked like a punk.

Bobby saw Nadine and smiled; he nudged the dealer. The dealer looked at him; Nadine beheld Adrian's profile. Bobby nodded in Nadine's direction.

She steeled herself for a joyously chirped, *"AnTeen!"* She expected Adrian to leap up from his chair and hug her exuberantly as he had always done before.

But those days were gone. Although he still sported precisely the same long, feathered haircut he'd worn when he was twelve, Adrian was not a child anymore. He was too cool for school, above the childish joys of family reunions. One side of his mouth curved up in a little smirk.

No, Adrian Wilde was no longer a boy. Nadine saw it all in just one glance. Adrian was grown, twice the adult the little tramp at the foot of the stairs was, even though she was of an age with him. Nadine saw Ian's confidence reflected in his son's eyes, sans all the fake innocence that Ian had always affected.

"AnTeen," he said. Gone, too, was the little boy's piping tone. Adrian's voice was deep, silky, inviting; again, just like Ian's. His blue eyes glowed with interest when he looked at her. Adrian was sexy, *knowing.*

Jesus, Nadine thought, *he's only eighteen, and he's as fine as his father was at twenty-four!*

Adrian's grin grew inquisitive, and again Nadine got the unsettling impression that he could read her mind. He winked, nodded at the three cards. "Can you follow the queen?"

Nadine approached until she was standing across the table from him. "This game's fixed, Adrian." She glanced at his cousin. "Are you the shill, Bobby? Or is it this young lady?"

"I knew it!" the little redheaded kid exclaimed. "Give me my money back, Adrian, you son of a bitch!"

Adrian grinned and handed him the ten that was lying on the table. "Always be suspicious of a man dealing three cards, Nick," he said. He smiled at Nadine. "Let me introduce you to the band, AnTeen. You remember Bobby?"

Nadine nodded, and Bobby said it was nice to see her again. Nadine noted that the two years that separated Bobby from his cousin were like a gulf, a mountain range; the difference between day and night. Adrian's attitude made him seem twenty-five; Bobby was undeniably sixteen. "I heard about your dad. How's he doing?"

That's why Adrian wasn't surprised to see me, Nadine thought with a weird kind of relief. *He didn't* see *that I was coming; he'd been told to expect me. Mom must've told them that I was on my way.*

"He's doing better," Nadine lied. Dad would be all right; she'd see him soon enough. She was glad that she'd stopped by here first. The change in Adrian was unbelievable.

"This is Trace the Face," Adrian said and winked at the blonde. "She's Bobby's girlfriend. Our drummer. Tracy, this is my AnTeen."

The mangling of her name, which Adrian had stubbornly refused to give up from the time he'd first been introduced to her when he was three years old, was as dark and sweet as honey when Adrian said it now. She thought she might shiver if he called her *darlin'*, like Charlie used to. *Hot damn! How Daina's little brat has grown! Too bad he's not supposed to live too much longer.*

"It's Nadine," she corrected. Tracy nodded.

"This is Nicky, Bobby's little brother." Adrian clapped him heavily on the shoulder. "He's not much of a card player, but he's death on the guitar." The kid's smile bloomed under his cousin's praise. "Nick, this is . . . *Nadine.*"

It was even worse when he said her name properly, because Adrian sounded so much like his dad, and there was an extra little slyness to his tone, something Ian had never expressed.

Nick said hi.

Adrian gathered up the cards, stood up. He was just as tall, just as broad-shouldered and well-built as his father, a little more slender. Nadine watched him put the three cards with the rest of the deck and stick the deck in his back pocket. She wondered how many girls would be vying to *pick a card, any card* later in the evening. She imagined that Randi would be first in line.

Adrian nodded over Nadine's shoulder; she turned to see Randi herself standing expectantly at the top of the stairs. "It's time to start this dog and pony show, my friends." Adrian paused, then added, *"Music has charms to soothe a savage breast."*

Nadine was surprised to hear William Congreve come out of the pup's mouth; but then she reckoned that she shouldn't be surprised: he was Ian's son, after all. She replied with another of the poet's famous lines, *"Heaven has no rage like love to hatred turned, nor hell a fury like a woman scorned."*

Now Adrian feigned innocence, and Nadine saw his father in him. "I have no idea what you're talking about, AnTeen." He nodded again, and Randi skipped over, as if she'd been waiting for his permission.

Randi beamed up at Adrian – Nadine now understood the motivation for her crush: Adrian Wilde was *fine* – and he smiled fondly at her, plopped his fedora upon her head.

"They're waiting," Randi said.

Just like you are, Nadine thought. *It becomes a drag, honey, let me clue you.*

Adrian glanced across the deck. Partially obstructed by their instruments and amps, Nadine noticed three rows of folding chairs, about fifteen in all. "Only let about twenty people up here, Randi," Adrian instructed. "My aunts'll kill me if I collapse their deck."

Randi nodded, departed. A moment later, a stream of kids appeared at the top of the stairs. As if bored, Nick pointed at the chairs.

"Come on, AnTeen. Sit in the front row." Adrian took her hand; his grip was warm and firm. He led her across the deck to a chair, deposited her into it. "It's great to see you."

Adrian leaned over and kissed her on the cheek. Nadine smiled at him, thinking again, *Damn, you're cute, boy. Too bad you're gonna die.* She didn't think it was too bad at all. Adrian joined his bandmates. Still amazed by how splendidly Daina's doomed little boy had grown, Nadine watched them tune-up.

After a moment, a young man sat in the chair to her right. He smiled, stuck out his hand. "Hi, I'm Gil Hogan. Randi told me you're somehow related to . . . ?" He gestured vaguely in the direction of the band, then returned his hand. Nadine shook it.

"Not really," she said. "I'm an old friend of the family."

Gil's hand lingered in hers while she told him her name, and Nadine marveled. *Riverside has sprouted some attractive young men while I've been away!*

Gil was blonde, with striking, piercing green eyes. He was not natively cute like Adrian was or even like Ian, in his heyday; they were attractive, no matter their expression. Gil was rather plain, except for his smile, and a little game twinkle in his eye. There was a wolfish, expectant aspect to his gaze, something just the tiniest bit undomesticated to his smile. He looked at Nadine appraisingly, as if she was Randi's age, and Nadine discovered that she liked that. He was older than the kids she had encountered so far this evening: Nadine reckoned him to be about twenty-five or perhaps twenty-six. She thought Randi was a tad bit young for him, but not really. Age had always been just a number to Nadine.

Gil chatted her up. He told her that he worked in construction. Nadine told him that she had most recently been a fashion photographer in New York City, and before that, she'd been a world traveler. Gil seemed to be impressed, or it could've been that he was all ears because he was interested in Nadine. Even if she was almost old enough to be his mother.

To keep the conversation going, Nadine said, "I'm afraid I don't know too much about modern music, however," indicating the band.

"They're just a cover band," Gil said with a scornful smirk. "Mostly oldies, anyway. Their own stuff isn't very good. But if they play something you don't recognize, just ask me." He smiled at Nadine again, winked.

Are you feeling froggy, sonny? By all means, jump, therefore.

Nadine thought about the spare bedroom, scant yards away, where she'd once done nothing with Ian on that long ago Hallowe'en. Buildings remained, mostly unaffected, as the years sped by. Only the people in them changed. Nadine reflected that Gil had probably gone trick-or-treating on that Hallowe'en in 1969; he hadn't been old enough yet to cross the street by himself.

Nadine grinned inwardly, and the imp in her mind giggled. It was not like she was hard up: Anthony had given her quite the romantic send-off two days before. Nadine had no excuse whatsoever to be thinking impure thoughts about a twenty-five-year-old *boy*. But Gil was charming in his lupine way, and for the first time since *before* that long ago Hallowe'en, Nadine found herself attracted to someone who in no way reminded her of Ian, even if he

33

was way too young for her. It was an age Nadine had always liked on a man.

Randi came up and said, "I see you've met!" She sat on Gil's knee, and smiled at Nadine, all friendliness. She had not an inkling that her boyfriend was talking up an older woman, not a clue that the older woman was responding, considering. Nadine noticed that the girl was still wearing Adrian's hat; after a moment, Randi's attention was drawn to its owner.

Gil went to say something to his girlfriend, noticed her absorption. Nadine saw a flash of anger; it transformed Gil's features. He was neither charming nor attractive when he was angry. He was dangerous. Nadine thought that she would not want to see his anger prolonged, nor turned upon her.

"If you're gonna stare at him, don't do it sitting in my lap."

Randi grinned guiltily, arose and sat in the chair beside him. Gil's smile returned, and he recommenced flirting with Nadine. Randi didn't notice because she was in her own world, the world of watching Adrian.

"What's New York City like?" Gil asked.

"The same as here, only different," Nadine told him with a laugh. She didn't want to talk about New York; it would only underline their differences, the universe of years and miles and experiences that separated them. Gil had never been out of Riverside.

Nadine said, "Who are all these people?"

"Adrian's fans," Randi said absently.

The crowd had swelled. All the seats were filled, and probably ten more people stood around. Randi had proved an ineffectual bouncer; although perhaps Nadine was being unkind. There were more people in the clearing below that weren't trying to come up. Perhaps she had been instrumental in keeping them down there. Daina thought she heard the old deck creak. There was no sign of Penny or Bellona or Adrian's parents.

At last Adrian approached the mike. "I'd like to thank you all for coming to my party."

"Happy birthday, Adrian!" Randi called enthusiastically. Nadine watched Gil frown. More voices echoed her sentiment and Adrian again said thanks.

"What should we begin with?" he asked the crowd, and a few suggestions were voiced. Nadine recognized none of the titles, wondered if Adrian's own compositions were being requested.

Adrian paused for another moment, turned to look at his band. The drummer counted off, then Bobby started playing; young Nick did an impressive riff. Then they stopped.

Nadine didn't recognize it. She looked at Gil and he smiled. "That was part of *Back in Black,*" he told her.

"Too metal," Adrian said into the mike. The crowd laughed.

The drummer began again, as did Bobby, and Nadine recognized the intro to *Pretty Woman.* When they got to the part where Adrian would start singing, they stopped again. He said, "Too old." Once more, the crowd laughed.

Immediately, Bobby swung into the bassline from *Money.* Adrian let him continue for a moment; when the band stopped again, he said, "Still too old. You know what my dad always says, Cuz. *Something from this decade.*"

When the drummer busted out enthusiastically, Nadine didn't recognize the beat. Adrian smiled, took the mike off the stand. The little guitar player began.

"Addicted to Love!" Randi applauded, squealed, whooped. The crowed echoed her.

Adrian was mesmerizing; for a moment, he sang directly to Nadine. *The lights are on, but you're not home. Your mind is not your own.* She wondered if this was his own composition – she looked at Gil for confirmation. He shook his head, yelled in her ear over the music. "Robert Palmer. He's English."

"You can't be saved, oblivion is all you crave."

"Do you crave oblivion, Nadine?" Gil whispered in her ear.

Adrian sang, *"If there's some left for you, you don't mind if you do."*

Nadine looked pointedly at Randi. Gil glanced over at his girlfriend, enrapt with the singer, then he whispered in Nadine's ear again. "Oh, there's definitely some left for you." He patted her on the knee.

Nadine smirked at him. This boy was definitely flirting with her, and fearlessly.

Nadine found the song entertaining. The crowd applauded when it ended, and Adrian put the mike back in its stand. He picked up his guitar and immediately played the immortal opening riff to *(I Can't Get No) Satisfaction.* To Nadine's surprise, Nick had his own mike, and he sang this time, in a high girlish voice, though tunefully. The drummer also added her voice. Gil squeezed Nadine's knee this time, then again glanced over at Randi. She still was hypnotized by Adrian, but Gil wasn't angry now. He winked at Nadine.

The Stones' anthem concluded and the crowd on the deck cheered, echoed by the people in the clearing below. Nadine still had not glimpsed any of the adults responsible for the grounds – like a cliché, she wondered if Ian and Daina and her aunts even knew this party was taking place. Nadine didn't see any alcohol however. She was sure it was here – some of these kids, like Gil, were of age – but others seemed barely in their teens. No booze was in plain sight, so it led Nadine to believe that Adrian's parents were lurking around somewhere.

When the cheering died down, Adrian thanked his friends, his *fans*, then looked behind him at his band and said, "What next?"

The drummer began, and Bobby played the bassline to *Disco Inferno,* then stopped.

"Disco's dead, Cuz," Adrian said, and again the crowd laughed. In response, Nick and Bobby busted into *Play That Funky Music,* and then stopped again.

"Dead, Nick. Before you were born."

Nadine counted in her head: if Adrian was eighteen and Bobby was sixteen, then his little brother was only thirteen years old. Nadine recalled hearing the announcement of his birth; she had been in Austria at the time. But she had never seen the youngest Wilde heir before tonight.

Bobby quickly played the bass riff to *Iron Man,* in answer to Adrian's denigration of disco. The crowd laughed and applauded, and Nadine realized that Urban Equinox was more of an act than a band, with all of its members getting a turn to sing, and all these between song, scripted hijinks. Adrian and Bobby had been playing together for a long time, and little Nick had probably been with them since he could hold a guitar by himself. They were simpatico, like some ancient, touring band, and just playing a run-of-the-mill set probably bored them.

Now Randi took her cue. She stood up and yelled, "Play *I Ran,* Bobby!"

Bobby grinned at her, and the band swung into the song. Adrian stepped away from his mike and Bobby approached it. Nadine reckoned this was one of Bobby's favorites; she remembered his Flock of Seagulls haircut from when he was ten.

Had that really been six years ago? It seemed like it had only been yesterday; at the same time, it seemed like a lifetime had passed Nadine by since then.

Next Urban Equinox played some of their own songs. Contrary to Gil's estimation, they were pretty good. The crowd sang along; it seemed that this modern vaudeville act had a substantial following. Nadine, of course, knew none of the words, so she took the opportunity to study her companions. Randi still watched Adrian, fascinated. Nadine saw Gil frown at her enthralled attention; she saw a flash of jealousy mar his face, and it was even uglier to behold than his anger. He followed Randi's gaze and glared for a second at Adrian. Then he seemed to shrug mentally: Adrian was only a musician after all, and young women liked musicians.

Gil once again smiled at Nadine. Nadine smiled back at him, letting him know that she was unimpressed with musicians. She was impressed with *him.*

Nadine liked Gil. He was intent, sexy in a daring, sly way, and it didn't to seem to matter to him at all that she was pushing forty. The last man far too young for her had been some time ago, if one didn't count Anthony, who was still eight years her junior . . .

Nadine thought that it could be their little secret. It wasn't like she planned to take Gil away from young, black-haired Randi. At least not for more than twenty minutes or so.

The band's song ended, then Nick broke out with a rock and roll version of *Happy Birthday;* the crowd picked up the tune. At last the adults made the scene. Ian pushed a cart out of the house; upon it was a huge cake, ablaze with candles. Behind him followed the birthday boy's aunts and his mother. Nadine noted that Lily was also present; like a hound dog catching a scent, she suddenly glanced around and zeroed directly in on Nadine. She smiled and Nadine smiled back.

Lily had always been kind to her, and despite her being in league with these other traitorous witches, Nadine had always liked her, respected her obvious powers. Nadine noted that Lily had been to the altar of Maybelline, had recently paid homage to the Goddess of Hair Coloring: she didn't appear to be too much older than Nadine herself. It was amazing what a little cosmetics could achieve. Nadine also thought that the darkness and the warm glow from the birthday cake helped soften her age somewhat.

37

"I have to go and greet the happy family," Nadine said to Gil. "But I'm sure I'll see you later." Nadine stretched the *you* to include Randi, who nodded.

Gil said, "I'm looking forward to it," and Nadine didn't fail to catch the promise in his words, even if Randi seemed oblivious to them.

As Adrian blew out the candles – *I hope you're wishing for a long life, boy,* Nadine thought and smiled nastily to herself – she stepped up behind Daina and tapped *her* on the shoulder this time. Daina turned, hugged her tightly, exclaimed in surprise over her old friend's return, as she always did. Nadine noted with pleasure that Daina had lost a little weight. She hoped that the thought of the witches' prophecy concerning her pretty boy ate at her, kept her up at night.

Penny and Bellona also supplied welcoming hugs. Lily, more circumspect, took Nadine's hands and squeezed them, said it was fabulous to see her again, told her she looked great.

Nadine's long-anticipated reunion with her soulmate was truncated, however. Ian said, "Hey, 'Deen! Great to have you home again!" But he gave her only a far-too-quick, perfunctory hug. He was listening to something his son was saying, and whatever it was, it was more important than a proper greeting for his long-gone, *we'll always be* friend.

Nadine was disappointed, and since she could not possibly care less about whatever Adrian was saying, she looked around. Immediately, she found what she sought: Gil was standing a little ways away, motionless in the swirling crowd, watching her. She smiled at him. He returned her smile, winked. *Yes,* Nadine thought, *this definitely needs to go somewhere.*

"How long are you staying this time, AnTeen?" Adrian asked.

Nadine held Gil's gaze for another heartbeat, then turned to reply. "I just might stay permanently this time, Adrian. I don't know how much care Dad's gonna need, and . . . I think maybe I'm tired of roaming. Home is where the heart is, after all."

Home is where the attractive young men are, at the moment – the intriguing ones, as well as the ones decreed to perish. Nadine discovered truth in her own words: she discovered that she did want to stay home. She wanted to get to know Gil a whole lot better; she wanted to witness Adrian's fate, Daina's pain. Again Nadine thought that Daina's son's undoing might also undo her marriage . . . And then Ian would be hers at last.

TEN

The party continued. Nadine knew that she should be going home, but she lingered. The idea of seeing her parents, still older now – her dad sick – depressed her. Here was light, life; Gil. She saw him go inside, so she followed him. She watched him enter the bathroom, and positioned herself in the shadow of the doorway to Daina's old room. He would have to pass her on his way out.

She whistled softly to him when he emerged. Ian would've looked at her innocently, pretended that he couldn't read the invitation in her eyes. But not young Gil. It wasn't necessary for Nadine to crook her finger or even nod; she stepped backward into the dark room and Gil followed her, then closed the door softly behind them and silently turned the lock.

Immediately, he threw Nadine against the door; *somebody probably heard that,* she thought, though maybe not. The footsteps and conversation of the party echoed through the house, and Urban Equinox was tuning up for a second set.

Gil kissed her hungrily, and she kissed him back. It was exciting, but not overly so: Nadine was an old campaigner in the war of the sexes. She was still more amused than turned on at the moment.

"But what about Randi?" she asked when he broke the kiss.

"She's off chasing Wilde," Gil replied and bit her on the neck.

"You're not worried about that?"

"There's not much I can do about it. It's a free country. She can look at whoever she wants; she knows better than to do anything more than look. Wilde's not interested in Randi. He knows better, too."

This statement surprised Nadine. "She certainly seems to like him."

Nadine expected another flash of anger from the young, green-eyed blonde; she'd laid out his girlfriend's obvious lust for another man rather starkly to him.

But Gil just smiled and repeated, "He knows better. He knows I'd kill him if he touches her."

There's a lot of dog in a man, Nadine thought. Again she marveled that the oppressive patriarchy that her aunts had always railed against was still firmly entrenched, even now, in the Year of Our Lord 1988. Here was Gil, ready, willing, able, *eager* to cheat on his woman. But if Randi dared to trespass against him, Gil would hurt her. And her partner, too. Nadine shrugged mentally; none of that concerned her in the least.

"Tough guy, are you?" she asked him with a grin.

"I think you're down to find out," Gil replied. He whirled her around and rather forcefully threw her onto the bed; there was an audible creak. He paused to grin at her; but as he went to climb into the bed, there was a noise at the door. It wasn't really a knock, more of a shuffling sound, as if one of the party-goers had brushed up against it. But it was enough to divert Gil's attention, to put them both in mind of the vulnerability of the situation, remind them how likely they were to be found out.

Nadine sat up, then stood up, embraced him again. "Isn't there somewhere else we can go?" she whispered in his ear before biting it. "Your place, maybe?"

"I live with Randi. She'd miss me if I just took off. How about your place?"

Nadine shook her head. "I'm staying across the street with my parents."

"Really?" he asked, amazed that someone her age was still living at home.

Nadine caught the unspoken *still*. "I just moved back here," she said, a little defensively. "I just arrived tonight."

Gil kissed her quickly again. "How 'bout the woods?"

Again, Nadine shook her head. She wasn't as wound up as her young swain; she had no desire to roll around in the pine needles and dirt. Gil was hooked now; there was plenty of time to reel him in at some more propitious time, at her leisure, when there was privacy. Let him think about it for a while; anticipate. "There's too many people around. Someone'll catch us."

Now, there was a definite knock on the door, followed by Daina's voice. "'Deen? Are you in there? Are you all right?"

"Yes, Daina!" Nadine replied. She quickly adjusted her clothing, smoothed her hair. She put a finger to her lips, positioned Gil behind the door, then opened it. She smiled at Daina. "It's been a long day," she said with a sigh. "I'm exhausted. I just needed a moment to myself." Nadine stepped out into the hall and pulled the door closed behind her. "I feel much better now."

40

ELEVEN

Things at home were worse than Nadine ever could've imagined.

Her father seemed the very eye of age: he was frail, shrunken. His big easy chair seemed to swallow him, and although he wasn't using it, she noticed to her alarm that there was an oxygen tank standing like a grim sentinel beside it. Sam smiled weakly at his daughter, and Nadine got the impression that she might crush him if she hugged him with too much exuberance.

Stoically, dry-eyed, Irene had taken Nadine aside and given her the devastating news. Sam's heart attack had been mild, not really life-threatening at all. But while he was in the hospital, the doctors had run other tests, and they found that Sam had lung cancer. One optimistic doctor had given him three years, maybe four. Another, perhaps more realistic, had said that Sam had no more than another year left in this vale of tears.

Here was another prediction of an ending, as true and inescapable as anything Penny and Bellona had ever foreseen.

At this news, Nadine had wanted to run again, to flee. Her father was already a shadow of the man that had raised her. She didn't want to witness his further wasting away unto death. But because Sam *had* raised her, Nadine owed him her presence, now that the finale was on the horizon. She couldn't board a plane and escape this time, back to New York, or across the ocean. She had to stay home now, to see this through to its sad, inevitable conclusion.

Irene had another bombshell for her only child. "I'm thinking of selling the house, 'Deen. There are some apartments downtown, close to the hospital. The upkeep here, the yard work . . . With your dad's condition . . . It's too much for us. It's been that way for a while, really. Adrian's been cutting the grass for us.

"The money'll help pay for his treatments. I thought that you could stay there with us. Help me take care of him . . ."

"Sure, Mom." Nadine hugged the sorrowful old lady that used to be her vibrant, forward-thinking mother. Irene was still looking toward the future: her plan was unemotional, logical. What was a house, when the money it would bring might help to prolong her husband's life? After Sam was gone, the memories here would be too much for Irene, anyway. Better to get rid of the house now, while those memories were still of happier times.

Nadine was appalled. She had not lived under the same roof as her parents for more than a short time, upon each return, since she'd been in her twenties. She was almost forty now; she had her own habits, her own peccadillos. She couldn't return to her youth. Perhaps she could rent her own apartment in the same building with them.

It was all too much to digest at one time. Nadine couldn't flee across the world this time, but she still had to get away from her elderly mother and her dying father for a minute. So first thing in the morning, she returned to the place that had given her solace as a child, as a teenager and young adult, though never again afterwards. But she had no place left to go. She went to Penny and Bellona's.

Nadine was surprised to find Randi upon the deck with them. She was picking up plastic cups and throwing them into a trash bag when Nadine surmounted the steps.

Randi smiled in her open, friendly, Bambi-like manner, said hi. Then, "I have to go find a broom." She disappeared into the house as if she lived there.

Nadine looked at the old witches for explanation.

"The new generation of the craft," Bellona supplied. "She reminds me of Daina a little bit."

"Daina's smarter than her," Nadine observed, *sotto voce.*

"But Randi's far more eager to learn," Penny countered. "Like you were. And Adrian is –"

"Adrian knows the old ways?" Nadine asked in amazement.

"It's in his blood," Bellona said.

"He's as knowledgeable as his mother and about as interested," Penny replied with a sigh. "He's always been more attuned to magic *tricks* than magic." Penny looked significantly at her sister and Bellona grinned. "But he knows his spells and his stories. He says his prayers on the Sabbat."

"It's in his blood," Bellona repeated.

Randi reappeared and began sweeping on the other side of the deck, out of earshot.

"Was Randi interested in witchcraft before she met Adrian?" Nadine thought that no matter the subject – be it the ancient arts, musical oldies, *hang-gliding* – if Adrian was into it, then Randi would attempt to follow.

Bellona nodded. "That's how we came to know her. She's one of Lily's apprentices. Adrian was dropping off an order of candles, earlier this summer. Randi was there in Mohini's, and –"

"It was love at first sight," Nadine said.

42

"History repeats itself," Penny said archly and grinned – *dared to grin,* Nadine thought. "As in other epochs, it's a one-sided affection. Adrian is young, carefree – he has little time and no inclination to saddle himself with one girl, when there are so many."

He has little time, period, if your prediction is to be realized, Nadine thought.

"The world's his oyster," Bellona added.

At the word *oyster,* Nadine couldn't keep herself from grinning. She said, *"'It seems a shame,' the Walrus said, 'to play them such a trick, after we've brought them out so far, and made them trot so quick!'"*

But Penny and Bellona didn't smile back. In fact, Bellona looked a trifle shocked. Their prophecies were gospel: Adrian was going to die, just like the oysters, and they didn't appreciate Nadine's making light of it.

Nadine didn't care. She allowed her grin to flourish, but changed the subject slightly. "Do they practice together? Adrian and Randi?" She wondered what Gil thought about *that.*

Penny shook her head. "Adrian is *solitaire,* as you've always been. It's second nature to him – not religion but reality. Randi, on the other hand, prefers a more celebrant role. She likes to lead the ritual."

"And so young." Nadine looked over at the black-haired girl with renewed interest. She was sweeping, and dancing around happily at the same time. Nadine thought that Gil had no doubt exorcised his unspent lust for a little strange on familiar territory; she wondered if Randi had the imagination to close her eyes and pretend that Gil was Adrian.

"It's just with us, so far," Bellona said. "We don't want her getting mixed up with all those silly Wiccans that patronize Mohini's. It's bad enough that she works there, and has to listen to their claptrap."

"Their money's green," Penny observed. "And Lily has her on a true path."

Randi finished sweeping and approached. "Is there anything else I can do for you ladies?" she asked brightly, and Nadine saw the same reverence in Randi's eyes for the older witches that Nadine herself had once encompassed.

Nadine imagined that, despite Gil, the old crones would probably like to pair Randi with Adrian, *with their blood,* to continue the black-haired, blue-eyed dynasty of sorcery. Except there wasn't going to be enough time for that, now was there?

TWELVE

Adrian Wilde was stoned.

He was floating on his back in his cousin's pool, considering the shapes in the clouds. Bobby was poolside, flung across a lounge chair, with this month's copy of *Guitar Player* over his face. Eddie Van Halen was on the cover. Neither Eddie nor Bobby were considering much at the moment.

Nick wasn't around. Nadine had been a little off in her calculations of ages at Adrian's party the week before; Nick wouldn't be thirteen until the day after Christmas. He didn't smoke pot.

He just acquired it for his brother and his cousin when they had a yen to expand their horizons for the afternoon.

Earlier that summer, Adrian and Bobby had been sitting in Bobby's room, trying to write a song. A baggie was on the desk – it was on the desk because it was empty. Nick came upstairs and stood in the doorway. "How's it coming?"

"We lack inspiration," his brother said mysteriously, and winked at Adrian.

Nick disappeared for a minute, then returned and tossed a full baggie of weed onto the desk beside the empty one. "And don't leave the goddamn empties laying around, Bobby. You're gonna get us all busted."

Adrian and Bobby stared at Nick, agape, speechless.

"Shut your mouths, you're attracting flies," the kid said with a grin. "You act like I can't tell when you people are stoned, like I *don't know*. Christ, if you giggled like that all the time, I'd have to find another band."

Bobby was nonplussed. "How long have you been –"

"I don't smoke it. I leave that to you assholes."

"You kiss your mother with that mouth, Nicky?" Adrian asked. "When did you become a pint-sized pusher-man?"

"I know a couple people. Up the street. Down the block. Sometimes a guy needs to make a buck. For guitar strings."

"Christ, son!" Adrian exclaimed. "When I was your age –"

"Times have changed, Grandpa. *Perhaps you'd understand it better, standin' in my shoes. It's the ultimate enticement, it's the smuggler's blues.*"

Adrian grinned, but brotherly concern overwhelmed Bobby. "You can't be selling weed, Nick. You're only twelve years old. If you get caught . . . Promise me you won't do this anymore."

"Unless it's for us," Adrian suggested. He opened up the baggie and smelled the contents.

Adrian handed Bobby the bag for inspection; he approved. After a moment, he reluctantly nodded. "But only for us."

"Deal," Nicky said. "I have a little bit of a credibility problem anyway, what with being only twelve years old." He looked at his cousin. "I don't see you reaching for your wallet, Adrian."

"I thought the first time was always free."

"This ain't your first time, my brutha."

Since then, Nick had kept his promise and acquired an occasional bag of cheer only for his bandmates. When Adrian asked him why he wasn't curious to sample some himself, Nick said, "I understand it stunts your growth." He tapped the side of his head. "And I like to stay sharp. Besides, somebody's gotta look after you guys."

THIRTEEN

Adrian dove down and put his fingers through the grate in the bottom of the pool; he held on as long as he could before letting go, allowing his body to float upwards at its own pace. He liked to be in the water; Adrian could swim before he could walk, because Ian had made sure of it. And it was nice to be mellow, while he was in the water, every now and again. It allowed him to think. It allowed him to differentiate between what was real to the world at large and what was real only to him.

Adrian resisted the specific labels that his mother tried to buckle onto him. He preferred his aunts' more generic *exceptional.* Adrian didn't consider himself a psychic or a clairvoyant; he didn't believe he possessed a gift of precognition or ESP. Those terms were all too narrow.

Adrian, being a musician, had come to think of it in terms of sounds and echoes. It you snap your fingers in an empty room, you'll hear the sound twice. Adrian believed some mechanism unrevealed allowed him to see an echo of time, every now and again. It was never more than a flash, a moment, like a stutter, like a frame slipped in a movie and doubled.

He would see something happen, then it would actually happen, with barely a heartbeat's pause in between. He might have time to blink or dodge or hold his hand out to catch something knocked over; but that was it. He couldn't use the phenomenon to pick the winner of a horserace ahead of time, and he couldn't summon the power at will. It was just something that happened sometimes.

Corollary to this talent, however, was Adrian's ability to hear a flash of thought before someone said it, or more importantly, before they *didn't* say it. He considered this gift far more useful, because it was under his control. Sometimes he just had to look at a person and he could actually hear their precise thoughts, as if they were speaking to him. Other times, he was just able to get a vague vibe – nothing more concrete than a nebulous mood.

It wasn't like Adrian could sustain this peek into people's thoughts; it wasn't like the whole splashing, swirling stream of others' consciousness was open to him. He didn't have access to the entire text of their inner monologues; just a few words, or perhaps a declarative sentence. No paragraphs.

Adrian couldn't do it with everyone. He couldn't read his aunts or his dad at all, while from his mom he got only emotions: love, confidence, occasionally fear. When he was a little kid, Adrian just had to look at his mother to gauge what was happening in situations that he couldn't understand yet. If his mother was calm or happy, so was he. If she was afraid, he would stand behind her and cling to her legs, worriedly peep around her. But Daina wasn't afraid very often; whatever scared her always passed quickly, and she would pick Adrian up and hug him, and then he would feel that love and confidence again. All would be right with the world.

Uncle Rob fairly broadcast his thoughts, usually the ones about the attractiveness of the women passers-by. Adrian had heard *Hod day-um, what an ass!* at least ten or twelve years before he could even begin to comprehend Rob's appreciation. Sometimes Adrian could hear Bobby's mom or dad if he really concentrated, but seldom were they thinking anything that either concerned or interested him.

FOURTEEN

Daina and Marta had wisely decided that their sons should get to know each other early. They considered it a pity that their fathers didn't particularly get along. It was Rob, childless, who was Ian's best friend, not Will. But since they were solitary children (at least until Nick showed up), Daina and Marta wanted to give their boys the opportunity to each have a brother.

Marta loved her brother – *even though he's quite the asshole,* Adrian had often thought – and Daina was an only child. She'd had a best friend once, someone who'd been like a sister to her . . . But their friendship hadn't endured. Nadine had left town at the first opportunity and had only visited sporadically over the intervening years. Daina believed that perhaps 'Deen had found it so easy to just leave their friendship behind because they hadn't been raised together.

She wanted Adrian to have the kind of life-long companionship that she'd once believed that she was going to enjoy with Nadine. Daina volunteered to watch Bobby for Marta most days, so he and Adrian could play together. This arrangement freed Marta to pursue her doctor's wife's activities, and whatever other activities she wanted to pursue, and it was surely better than paying some stranger to care for her boy.

Then Nick came along, and Marta really valued Daina's assistance. She didn't think she could've handled a newborn and a three-year-old at the same time. Marta cared for the baby on her own – she loved babies – but she continued to drop Bobby off at his cousin's.

Bobby and Adrian owed it to their mothers' foresight that they were raised like brothers, but it was their temperaments that made them best friends. Adrian and Bobby were simpatico; they finished each other's sentences, like twins, like Will and Rob did. All his life, Bobby had known that Adrian could read his mind – sometimes he thought he knew it more than Adrian knew it. Sometimes he'd only have to glance at his cousin, and Adrian would speak aloud Bobby's very thoughts.

Adrian had started guitar lessons when he was six. The boy needed a hobby besides legerdemain with a deck of cards, cat's cradles and walking quarters across his knuckles. He needed something more than reading the Tarot and studying grimoires with his aunts with which to occupy his time. Ian was friends with the music teacher at work, so learning an instrument was chosen as an after-school activity for Adrian over some organized sport. Ian wasn't going to stand around on a hot soccer field wasting daylight of a weekend, watching his boy chase a ball, when both of them could be on the water somewhere.

"It's best to start them off playing early," Ian's colleague at the middle school had told him. "It's not like it's rocket science," the teacher, Mr. Johnson, said with a grin. "But it's something he'll enjoy all his life."

So Adrian started learning the guitar when he was six, then he and Bobby started going to Mr. Johnson's house together when Bobby turned six. And Bobby was nine and Ian was eleven when Nick got started.

Daina, who drove them to their lessons each week, thought that of the three of them, Mr. Johnson enjoyed tutoring Nick the most. The youngest Wilde was truly a prodigy, he told Daina on more than one occasion. It all seemed to come naturally to him, and he practiced his lessons with all the single-mindedness that a little boy could muster. Nick was a stubborn child; if he transgressed in any way at home, if he neglected to take the trash out or if he received a bad grade in school, the only punishment that affected him was a grounding from his guitar.

Nick wanted to be like his big brother and his cousin, but he wasn't worshipful about it. He learned the next piece in order to impress them, but he never let them know it. By the time he was ten, his proficiency equaled, if not surpassed, Adrian and Bobby's.

Adrian was a little more than two years older than Bobby; but he was five and a half years older than Nick. It was too great of an age gap for little boys to bridge; they shouldn't have been friends, even if they were cousins. Nick looked up to Adrian, as much as he did to his brother, the bass-player; but from about the time he was ten years old, from the time he started to get really good at the guitar, Nick had simply *fascinated* Adrian.

A ten-year-old boy doesn't have the same interests as one who is fifteen and a half. It wasn't the years so much as it was the time in their lives that separated them – even today, a week after Adrian turned eighteen, Nick was still only on the very brink of puberty. Adrian had already been kissed, and more than once, by the time of Nicky's tenth birthday, but still Nick kenned the motivations and desires of the older boys without having yet felt them himself. It was his unusual perception that made his cousin so fascinating to Adrian.

50

Nick was an old soul, or so he was proclaimed by Penny and Bellona. Once they said that, Adrian was put in mind of Claudia, the character from *Interview with the Vampire*. He was not much of a reader – Adrian took after his mother in that regard – but he'd seen the novel lying on a table at his aunt's house, and, his curiosity piqued by the title, he'd picked it up and had skimmed it.

Claudia was an ageless vampire, a grown woman trapped forever in a little girl's body. That was how Nick seemed to Adrian: as if he had already known dark desires and hidden secrets, even though, outwardly, he was just a little boy. Perhaps he was just unusually observant of the adults and wanna-be adults that surrounded him. Adrian never ceased to be amazed at some of the things that Nick said.

By the time he was ten, Nick was a member of the band. Bobby and Adrian gave him a hard time, because he was just a little kid, but they weren't cruel. They respected his amazing talent, and the fact that he was never a whiner; never, ever, a snitch. The worst behavior Nick demonstrated would be to wear out his welcome when his brother or his cousin brought over a young lady to hear them play. Practice over, Bobby and Adrian would expect the little kid to make himself scarce.

But Nick liked to hang around and observe, and Adrian was always surprised by his cousin's astute, accurate, often penetrating commentary about things that he just wasn't supposed to know anything about yet. And Christ, the mouth he had on him.

While Adrian could sometimes guess what Bobby was going to say or do next out of familiarity, and while he could also sporadically *hear* it – Adrian and his younger cousin were telepathic. It was a two-way street between them, as it never was with anyone else: Adrian heard Nick's thoughts in his mind because Nick put them there. To answer his cousin, all Adrian had to do was think what should be said in reply.

The band had tried out drummers, kids they knew from school, but none of them had meshed with the Wilde boys. Just about the time they would get one broken in, he would lose interest, or he would make fun of Nick's youth a little too much. Adrian would point out that his young cousin had forgotten more about music than the new drummer was ever going to know; since it was the truth, that would be one more drummer down the road.

When Bobby was fourteen and Adrian sixteen and Nick not quite eleven yet, they still all took lessons from Mr. Johnson. His set up

51

was simple. He would tutor the musician on his screened-in back porch, adjacent to which was a concrete patio. Pupils arriving early could wait there, as long as they remained quiet, and didn't make a mess. And there was no cussing, no smoking. Despite his rock and roll chops, Mr. Johnson was a Christian man.

The student receiving a lesson at the moment was aware that he had an audience nearby. They wanted to be rock stars, didn't they? And rock stars' talent was *subject to the breath of every fool.* So, Mr. Johnson figured – since kids were brutally honest – his students would grow thick skins and learn to disregard the scorn of their peers, if they knew there was someone outside listening to them.

The guitar players of Urban Equinox didn't all take their lessons on the same day, but when Adrian turned sixteen, he became the chauffeur; and since there was no use practicing without Nick, Bobby went along and waited on the porch with his cousin while his brother had his lesson.

The Wilde clan arrived early on this particular day. Someone was drumming inside: Mr. Johnson taught damn near all instruments. The boys knew the drill. They went around and sat on the porch and waited for Nick's turn at the master's knee. They listened with a critical ear to the drummer; he wasn't half bad. They were thereby quite surprised when Mr. Johnson brought a young girl out and introduced her to them.

Adrian and Bobby and Mr. Johnson chatted with the girl for several minutes; they talked about Van Halen's new album, the first with Sammy Hagar. Adrian didn't care about who was singing, one way or another; as long as Eddie was still there, he was happy.

Nick had his own opinions of Adrian's idol, mostly summed up by the word *overrated,* but he kept them to himself at the moment. He was silent, observing the interactions between his relatives and the girl, teenagers whose emotions, motivations and agendas were yet worlds removed from his own. Nick was eleven; he just wanted to play the guitar.

At last it was time for Nick to go inside for his lesson. *There's our new drummer, Cuz.*

Adrian heard Nick's voice clearly in his head, so he turned to look at the guitar prodigy. *You think so?*

Nick rolled his eyes. *And Christ on a crutch, isn't it about time? Tell Bobby – but let him talk to her. She already digs him.*

Adrian nodded and Nick went in. He watched Bobby talk to the drummer; her name was Tracy. He saw that Nicky was right, even though he was not even eleven, and couldn't really have any concept about what it meant to *dig* somebody yet. Hell, Bobby and the girl were only fourteen, themselves. From his vast mountain of experience – at sixteen, Adrian had kissed probably four girls – he figured Bobby hadn't even kissed anyone himself. But it wouldn't be long now: here was obviously love at first sight.

After that first meeting at Mr. Johnson's house, Bobby and Tracy became inseparable. Urban Equinox was now complete, a four-person combo. They finally had a drummer. They were a real band.

And Adrian thought that they owed it all to one hyper-observant little boy, wise beyond his years about the workings of attraction and chemistry.

FIFTEEN

As far as attraction and chemistry was concerned, Adrian was philosophical. He watched Tracy and Bobby's love grow; after about a year of hand-holding and making out, he listened to Bobby talk about how they had decided that they were finally going to *do it,* the very next moment that the opportunity presented itself. Bobby spoke of romance, candlelight, promises. Adrian considered that to be cute and sweet – a vow to seal the physical manifestation of their teenage passion for each other.

The Monday after the momentous event had taken place, Bobby left Tracy and his brother out in the garage, and sought out his cousin for a word. No mind-reading was necessary this time. Adrian took one look at his cousin's astonished expression and believed that there would never be another girl for Bobby – or at least he believed that Bobby believed it.

"Hot damn, Cuz!" Adrian said, and slapped the bassist on the back. "Ain't love grand?"

The witchcraft in his blood had lead Adrian to the door of manhood some months before. His parents told him that he could throw himself a party to celebrate his seventeenth birthday on the 3rd of July. The 4th was to be reserved for family this year – they planned to gather on Penny and Bellona's deck to barbeque, for cake and ice cream, and to watch the fireworks.

At about six o'clock on the 3rd, Ian and Daina retired up the hill to Adrian's aunts' house. They reminded their son that they didn't want to see any evidence of teenage drunkenness, and that he needed to run all his guests out by midnight.

Adrian had invited his school chums, the ones he could scare up – school had been out for a few weeks and some of them were out of town. Chiefly, he had invited one AnneMarie Chalmers. She had graduated in June; she was a grade ahead of Adrian. They had shared a study hall together the last semester and had waltzed around the idea of going out on a date a couple of times, but nothing had ever come of it.

They'd hit it off in study hall, even though they never did find time for that night on the town. Adrian thought she was lovely, and AnneMarie had enjoyed his admiration. She'd confessed to Adrian that her father was a cop, that he was strict and watchful. Even though his daughter was of age, Detective Chalmers still ruled her life with an iron first; she still had to be in the house by eleven on weekends, and nine-thirty during the week. AnneMarie told Adrian that she couldn't wait until she got to go away to school in the fall, so she could at last escape her dad's tyranny.

But she'd escaped it tonight, on this Friday, the 3rd of July, 1987, just to wish Adrian Wilde a happy birthday. She'd found him adorable in study hall, and had wished she'd been able to sneak out and see him before now. Like many daughters of dictatorial daddies, all of the detective's oppressive rules for AnneMarie had come to naught. Since she'd turned sixteen, every chance she got, she'd sneaked out to engage in activities with boys that would've made her father have a coronary. But AnneMarie was careful and clever, and dear old Dad didn't have a clue that his daughter wasn't even remotely the blushing virgin that he believed her to be.

But there had never been the opportunity to give fine Adrian Wilde a try. Until now.

Adrian was sitting at his kitchen table with his cousin and his cousin's girlfriend and some little kid, playing poker, when AnneMarie threaded her way through the not unimpressive throng of partiers to find him. She paused in the kitchen doorway and thought to herself, *Man, you're cute, Adrian! I wonder if you'd like to go back to your room with me for a minute, so I can give you a special birthday surprise?*

The birthday boy paused in mid-shuffle and looked up at her, nonplussed. "Yes," he said. "Yes, I most certainly would."

AnneMarie's eyes widened in shocked surprise. Adrian Wilde had just read her mind. He stood up and set the deck of cards on the table in front of him. "That is . . . if you're serious."

AnneMarie nodded slowly, his incredulity superseded by anticipation. She smiled.

Adrian returned her smile, and said to the kid sitting next to him, "Deal me out, Nick." Not taking his eyes off of AnneMarie, he added, "In fact, you can play my money." He slid a pile of chips in front of the kid. "This might take a minute."

Adrian stepped away from the table, took AnneMarie's hand, and without a backward glance at his bandmates, led her to his room.

Bobby looked over his shoulder at the empty doorway for a heartbeat, shrugged, then looked back to the card game. Nick shook his head, smirked, and dealt.

"Who was that?" Tracy asked.

"That's Adrian's first piece of –" Bobby looked sharply at his little brother, and Nick stopped, grinned, made a *What? Am I wrong?*

face. He said, "That's Adrian's new girlfriend." He looked at his watch. "For at least the next couple of minutes, anyway."

Tracy blinked at Nick, appalled as always by his filthy little mind. *Christ only knows what he says about me,* she thought. She looked at Bobby. He shrugged again and asked what the ante was.

SIXTEEN

AnneMarie gave Adrian more than a few minutes for his birthday. She gave him time enough to figure out how the whole process worked: the things he'd more or less guessed and a few things he hadn't even imagined. And she gave him plenty of opportunities to hone his skills over the rest of the summer.

It wasn't that AnneMarie loved Adrian; she wasn't in the market for love at the moment. She was going away to school in the fall, and her father would've frowned, still, upon the concept of her having a boyfriend, anyway. AnneMarie just thought that Adrian was cute, and a lot of fun; a summertime fling to enjoy before college life began. She wouldn't have time for some kid still in high school then, and long distance romances seemed like they'd be a drag.

It was Adrian that was to be instrumental in disabusing Detective Chalmers of his woefully inaccurate opinions of his daughter's innocence, however.

As Ian had once observed, Adrian wasn't wholly precognitive. Events occurred that the guitar player would've been better to avoid, had he been able to *see* them ahead of time. And the first afternoon he spent alone with AnneMarie in her ruffled pink and white bedroom was one of those times. They had always enjoyed their assignations at his house, previously. It was also the last afternoon he spent with her.

The cop stopped by home early, unexpectedly. He had a touch of indigestion and thought that a little Pepto would be just the ticket to alleviate it. He was surprised, disconcerted, to see a strange car parked in the driveway. Suspicious, he stealthy crept into the house, knocked on his baby's door, immediately opened it.

Detective Chalmers didn't catch them *in flagrante delicto,* but it was close enough. AnneMarie was still in bed, the sheet gathered demurely up to her chin. She was talking to Adrian, who was standing in front of her dresser, shirtless, looking at himself in the mirror and running his fingers through his long hair.

As Mark Twain said, *Let us draw the curtain of charity over the rest of the scene.* Suffice it to say that Adrian exercised the better part of valor, dodging quickly around AnneMarie's red-faced father before he even had a chance to work up a head of steam and start screaming. In a moment he was in the driveway, in his car; then he was in the wind. *He who fights and runs away, lives to fight another day,* Adrian thought, feeling a little guilty for leaving AnneMarie to her father's fury.

It wasn't like they were embroiled in some monumental love affair; for both of them, it was just a fun way to spend the afternoon. It wasn't like Adrian would have allowed himself to be compelled, and he surely wouldn't have volunteered, to stick around and make an honest woman out of AnneMarie in some manner. And neither would she have wanted him to do so. She was leaving for college in a few weeks.

They spoke on the phone a couple of times before she left, but Adrian never saw her again. Her father had her under what could only be termed *house arrest.* It was as good a way as any to end it. Adrian never did get his shirt back.

After dodging a bullet – perhaps literally – on that day in late August, 1987, Adrian had reflected on the idea of love. What he and AnneMarie had shared – that was sex, and Adrian had certainly enjoyed it. It was great and all, but not something that he would devote the better part of his waking thought to achieve. Adrian would never become what Nick indecorously called a *pussy-hound,* a term that had not inaccurately been applied, once upon a time, to all three of the earlier generation of Wilde cousins.

Adrian would become picky. Just as he had with AnneMarie, he found that he had a knack for gauging a young woman's willingness, so it wasn't like he had to waste time guessing which ones were down. His mother and his aunts would've call it *precognition,* or *extra sensory perception. Seeing.* His dad and his cousins had a more matter-of-fact name for it: they believed that young Adrian simply *had a way with the ladies.* They didn't know that he could more or less read their minds, at least on this particular subject.

But Adrian soon discovered that the young women that he met had no originality to them. The girls would be alternately coy or flirty if they found themselves attracted to good-looking, blue-eyed, black-haired, guitar-playing Adrian Wilde. Or they would try to play aloof and disinterested. It all bored Adrian; it was so common, always the same shtick. He knew what they wanted. Try as they might, they couldn't hide it from him: he could read their minds. He knew that it would take only a wink or a smile, a few words or a song, and they would be his.

Ian had always been amazed, fascinated – perhaps even a bit grateful – with how effortless it was to get girls. His astonishment and gratitude at young women's willingness had certainly never stopped him from taking advantage of it, however. His son had no feelings of amazement, and certainly no gratitude. Adrian came to expect it that girls were game, and game for him especially.

But he didn't love any of them, and he was careful to pick ones that didn't – not at first blush, anyway – think that they were in love with him.

Cupid's arrow had yet to strike Adrian; he was precisely as his father had been at the same age. At eighteen, Adrian had never been in love, even though his looks and his talent and his confident, easy-going personality had offered him more than his share of opportunities to find it. But while Ian had once been unsure that love even existed as the poets spoke of it (until it happened to him), Adrian knew that love was real, that it was the happy congruence that could exist between two people. Adrian believed that love made the world go 'round. He saw young love every day between his cousin and his drummer. *A little ditty, 'bout Jack and Diane.*

But more importantly, Adrian had grown up watching the love that existed between his parents.

For their fifth wedding anniversary, Rob had thrown a surprise celebration for Daina and Ian at the country club to which all the Doctors Wilde belonged. Perhaps Rob had been feeling nostalgic or even wistful. His relationship with Andrea hadn't lasted past his residency; no doubt because Rob would not be compelled to pop the question. He hired a photographer and a cameraman to film his cousin's anniversary shindig for posterity, maybe because he knew he'd never be hiring the like for his own wedding. Rob wasn't the marrying kind.

Another ten years would pass before Adrian's parents had the old celluloid converted to VHS. He would be fifteen before he ever saw the video that, to him, epitomized his parents' affection for each other.

There was a part where Ian and Daina danced to The Platters' immortal *Only You.* By the following week, Adrian played it for them on the guitar, and even did a fair impression of the vocals, just so they could dance to it again.

Adrian enjoyed the video; past a few fading photographs, it wasn't often in life that a kid got to see his parents when they were young. But here were Ian and Daina in living color – the cameraman was talented, or perhaps the lighting was just good – he'd caught the fire in Daina's eyes as she danced with her husband; the tender smile on Ian's face as he softly sang, *When you hold my hand, I understand the magic that you do. You're my dream come true, my one and only you,* to his beloved.

It was obvious to whoever watched, but especially to their son: for Ian and Daina, when they were in each other's arms, there were no other people on the planet.

Adrian believed in love, because it had happened to his father. There would never be another woman for Ian, and this came though as he danced with Daina. It had come through for Adrian every day of his life. And Daina's love for Ian was the same. It was undeniable, eternal.

When he watched the video of his parents' anniversary dance for the first time, fifteen-year-old Adrian was surprised to see his not-quite-five-year-old self run out onto the dance floor at the end of the number. He hugged his parents around the legs – the cameraman caught this moment of familial cuteness brilliantly – the crowd laughed. But what teenaged Adrian didn't fail to notice was that his parents held each other's gaze for just one more heartbeat; they simply ignored their only child for *just another moment.*

Then Ian picked Adrian up and the crowd applauded.

What he'd known all his life was distilled for Adrian in that moment: his parents loved him – they loved him more than anything else in the world – except that they loved each other more than they loved him. Ian and Daina's love had existed before Adrian had arrived, and their love for him would always be secondary.

Adrian felt no jealousy or resentment about this, or at least not any that he could recognize within himself. His parents' love for each other compelled Adrian to want to find that special woman, precisely as his father had done. He longed to have some girl look at him the way his mom looked at his dad; but more importantly, he longed to look at some girl the way his dad looked at his mom. Girls looked at Adrian with love all the time, but he had yet to return it.

This acknowledgement that true love existed also made Adrian cautious. His parents had found each other. They were in love. Bobby and Tracy were in love. But Adrian also saw, all around him, couples that slogged through life, chained to each other, not in love at all. Couples that, even though they had forsaken all others, were not even in the same ballpark of contentment as his mom and dad.

For example, there were Bobby's progenitors, parents of two. Adrian sensed that Marta and Will were resigned, maybe even satisfied; but Adrian didn't get what he would call a happy vibe from them. There were vague resentments, suspicions; perceived slights and inequalities, desires to win and punish that he never detected in his parents.

Adrian's Uncle Rob had gone the opposite route. Claiming that he'd just never found the right one, Rob had never had to forsake anything. He still lived the exciting, varied life of a bachelor. Rob seldom lacked a date – he was a doctor, after all – but Adrian sometimes recognized a deep loneliness in Rob, despite the revolving door on his bedroom.

A week after his eighteenth birthday, Adrian had no prospects for true love at the moment, nor even the prospect of a fun afternoon with someone like AnneMarie. This lack of diversion, coupled with the fact that Bobby and Nick were going to Europe on Monday with their parents, combined to make Adrian feel annoyed, disappointed, restless; his buzz was wearing off far too quickly. His cousins would be gone for the rest of the summer, until school started, and Adrian was at a loss as to what he was going to do to amuse himself while they were away.

Adrian had graduated from high school the month before, but all year, he had balked at filling out college applications. He didn't know where he wanted to go to school, didn't know what he wanted to study, didn't know what he wanted *to be*. He finally told his parents that he'd like to take a year off to consider these things. His dad had asked him to think a little more about it, but his mother had said it was okay. He felt a small, inexplicable sadness pass in her when she said, "There'll be plenty of time for you to go to school. You have your whole life ahead of you."

Adrian could've chosen to go with his cousins to Europe, of course, but a) he didn't want to spend any more time with Doctor and Mrs. William Wilde than was absolutely necessary – they were just too uptight for Adrian, compared to his own parents – too likely to splash acidic sarcasm across the conversation at any moment, completely unbidden, uncalled for; and b) it wouldn't be fair to just leave Tracy behind.

Adrian knew that she'd love to accompany Bobby and see the *auld sod* – but Bobby's mother refused to acknowledge that her sixteen-year-old first born, swanlike, was already paired for life. It couldn't be true – her son had not chosen some poor girl *that played the drums*, of all god awful things.

And Marta certainly wouldn't pander to the ridiculous notion that Tracy might be her daughter-in-law someday by taking the girl with them on vacation now. She hoped that a change of scenery would also change Bobby's mind; or maybe if her son was gone, the little blonde might imprint on some other bass player. Adrian knew better. As the saying went, absence would only make their hearts grow founder.

Tracy wasn't too upset about the invite to Europe that hadn't come – she cared for Bobby's parents even less than Adrian did. It wasn't like it was forever, and she was going to be a camp counselor at a girls' camp in the mountains until school started; she was leaving the day before Bobby and Nick went to the airport.

Only Adrian was left at odds and ends for the entire summer.

SEVENTEEN

When Adrian got home from enjoying his cousins' exquisite pool, he was surprised to see a *For Sale* sign stuck into the yard of AnTeen's house. He'd heard that her dad had cancer, that he might not live for too much longer. Adrian was saddened by that, but only peripherally; though he had lived across the street from Mr. and Mrs. Germaine for his entire life, he didn't really know them. And he'd never lost anyone in his life, past a few pet cats. Their disappearances had affected Adrian; he could not imagine what it would be like to contemplate the loss of a parent.

Adrian paused on his front porch for a moment; he considered that actually, he really didn't know his AnTeen very well, either. Throughout his life, she had made only infrequent visits, and then stayed only briefly. And it wasn't as if she'd ever brought Adrian gifts from her travels, trifles for him to remember her by while she was gone. She hadn't made over him effusively on her returns, had neither hugged him nor kissed him nor told him that he had been missed. Most children would've forgotten such an emotionless, absentee family friend.

But as he was with Nick, Adrian had always been fascinated with his AnTeen. As a child, he had sensed a power within her; he had always pictured a deep, dark well – he thought that if something was dropped into it, it would be a long time indeed before a splash was heard. He could only catch a random thought from her – about a place she'd lived, perhaps – but never anything about people or emotions.

But that wasn't exactly correct, either.

Adrian hated the New Age claptrap about auras and how the enlightened could read them. It was second nature to him that everyone, every living thing, possessed a field of energy: that was the very definition of being alive. But whether such a thing could be *read,* interpreted . . . He was not so sure about how that was accomplished. Adrian could sometimes see things before they happened, and he could sometimes read a person's thoughts; he had always kenned a darkness, a malevolence in Nadine. If she had an aura, that was it.

It had never frightened him; he didn't feel evil, like spiking, deadly bolts of lightning within her, at the ready, to be unleashed for instant devastation. Her wickedness was more like the hum of a transformer. Adrian knew that the current was there, potent; it was just controlled. It was an intrinsic part of his AnTeen, this darkness. All his life Adrian had felt it, and wondered at its cause, its source. He wondered at its outlet, its destination; its object.

Nadine had always seemed austere to him, cold. He wondered why she even bothered to visit, as he could tell that she cared for none of them. Except for his dad. That was something that Adrian had also always sensed, but he could never quite put his finger on. AnTeen and . . . Something about his dad.

When she had arrived last week, when he'd looked up to see her standing there, Adrian had felt that malice again, coupled with an anticipation, an expectation. The emotion had been so strong that it had turned Adrian watchful immediately; he hadn't leapt up and hugged her as he had always done when he was little. AnTeen didn't miss it, and Adrian perceived her coldness for him fully at that moment: he had always been the one doing all the happy greetings. She had simply stood still for them.

Adrian wondered: *what is she waiting for?* He sensed a womanliness about her – something that he had been too young to see before – something he was not used to reading in women her age. It was a primitive, animal quality, akin to the eagerness he could unfailingly sense in girls his own age. But it wasn't directed at him, and it was colored, overshadowed, tinged with that darkness, that anticipation. His AnTeen *wanted* something. And whatever it was, it wasn't very nice.

She'd said, *Heaven has no rage like love to hatred turned, nor hell a fury like a woman scorned,* apropos of nothing, and again Adrian had felt a wave of wickedness roll off of her. Was that why she was so cold? Had someone scorned her? Was the darkness that Adrian had sensed in her for his entire life the outgrowth of hatred? Of rage? But whom did she hate? Who had scorned her?

EIGHTEEN

Adrian considered the *For Sale* sign down the street for another moment, then went into the house. Daina was sitting on the couch watching television. Adrian kissed her cheek, then sat in a chair across from her. *Who's the object of AnTeen's hatred?* he thought. *What is she waiting for? Something about Dad.*

"You've known AnTeen all your life, Mom?"

Daina glanced at her son and realized that he was concentrating, waiting patiently for an answer to his question. Her response was important to him at the moment; she had Adrian's undivided attention.

To capture Adrian's attention was sometimes a daunting experience. It seemed like he was always doing something with his hands; shuffling a deck of cards, tuning his guitar; reading the liner notes to an old record, squinting at the small print on a CD. So a person invariably had to *call* him; sometimes he wouldn't look up, and if that person really thought they needed him to look at them, they'd have to call him again.

Thus summoned, Adrian would stop what he was doing and turn the full scrutiny of his probing blue eyes upon the caller. This was sometimes more than the caller had bargained for: Adrian's full, expectant attention. His expression would ask, *What do you want?* Sometimes Adrian would actually say this out loud. If the person was male, the effect was either one of challenge – *Why are you bothering me about this?* – or it was one of camaraderie and friendliness: *No way, man, really?*

If the person that had called Adrian was female, no matter what her age, the girl realized that she suddenly had the interest of a very special individual. *You've got my attention – now what are you gonna do with it?*

It was a most extraordinary expression to all who encountered it. Daina thought that she could remember each and every time that she had commanded her son's full attention. It unsettled a person, made them feel like the mongoose might, when he caught the eye of the cobra, or like an ant who had captured the fancy of an evil little boy with a magnifying glass on a sunny day.

Daina clicked off the television. "Her family moved in across the street when we were nine." Her light blue eyes reflected the curiosity in her son's dark blue ones. This was all old news. "We were practically inseparable, until . . ."

Daina saw Adrian's eyes widen, almost imperceptibly: *Until what, Mom?*

"Until she joined the Peace Corps. I don't think you were even walking yet." Daina waited, wondering what was on Adrian's mind.

"So you guys went to high school together, and college? Did you ever date the same guys?"

What does he want to know? Daina thought. There had never been any kind of in-depth discussion of the couplings and un-couplings, the realignments in relationships that had eventually resulted in her marriage to Ian, or Will and Marta's union. There had never been any discussion at all, in fact. It was none of Adrian's or Bobby and Nick's business, really, who had dated whom in college. *What is he suddenly so curious about?*

"No," Daina said. "We never dated the same guys."

Adrian didn't know about his parents' and his cousins' parents' partner-switching, nor did he know that his AnTeen had once gone out with his Uncle Rob. It had all been before he was born, had only lasted a very short time. There was no way that such short-lived occurrences had ever been mentioned to Adrian.

"So, AnTeen never went out with Dad? Like before you guys met, or –"

"No, Adrian. Nadine never went out with your father. They went waterskiing a couple of times, but she was seeing . . . someone else then, and so was your dad." *And so was I. These were all people you know, although you couldn't possibly know, and besides . . .*

"Whatever gave you that idea? That your dad dated Nadine?"

Adrian shrugged, noncommittal, but didn't take his eyes from his mom's. "I just get a vibe from her sometimes. Like she couldn't care less about the rest of us . . ."

Now Daina's eyes widened a little bit – Adrian was stating aloud what she had felt all along – Nadine's once unbreakable family fealty for herself, for her aunts, even for her son, had long ago dried up and blew away. Could it have been the result of some feelings she'd once harbored for Ian – was that what Adrian saw?

"But I always get something else . . . I don't know how to describe it. I couldn't call it a crush – she's too old for that, isn't she? Not even affection so much as . . ." Adrian shrugged again. "I can't quite describe it. Something about Dad. So I thought maybe, once upon a time, maybe they dated or something."

"Once upon a time, she might've had a crush on your father."

Where does he come up with this stuff? Vibes, substance he gets *from people. He is* exceptional, *just like they always said. Could Nadine really still have a crush on Ian, after all these years?* It was ridiculous. Daina shook her head. "But if she did, she never told anyone about it. She'd known him for a while, through . . . Rob and Will. Like I say, they used to go skiing. She invited him to a Hallowe'en party we threw, and that was the night we met."

"And it was love at first sight." Adrian smiled.

He had heard the expurgated, PG-version of his parents' first meeting, about the gladiator outfit and the Queen of Diamonds costume. He knew that their courtship had been brief, that they'd married less than three months later. He knew that he had come along two weeks earlier than had been predicted, but even his slated due date was too quick for the customary time limits between nuptials and the birth of heirs. That he had been conceived out of wedlock was not a family secret, not to Adrian or anyone else.

Ian came in the house then, and as always, Daina arose from the couch to embrace him. "Your son was just asking me if you and Nadine ever had a love affair. He gets a *vibe* about you from her."

"I never got a vibe from her," Ian replied with a shrug.

Although that wasn't completely accurate, was it? Ian *had* sensed that perhaps Nadine liked him on that long ago Hallowe'en. She'd invited him to her party, then abandoned him to Penny and Bellona's wiles. They'd spoken of two girls, a rich one and a poor one, and – he'd never really given it a great deal of thought until just this moment – they'd spoken of two girls, either of which would love him *with her entire being.*

Ian had thought that they'd been trying to fix him up with Nadine. He'd thought that she might've liked him, then, to set up the whole future-telling business, so he'd thought it only nice to dance with her. He'd sensed that she liked him a little bit whilst they danced – she'd been drunk and had let it show – but . . . Lots of girls liked him when he danced with them, especially if they were drunk.

And once he'd beheld Daina, the idea that the other girl – Nadine – also would've loved him *with her entire being* had fled Ian's mind.

Now he said to his son, "Who knows? Maybe she did have a little warm for me back then. But if she did –"

"She should've spoken up," Daina said and hugged him.

"They do not love that do not show their love," Ian said. But still he was curious; he'd never considered that Nadine might've had a real crush on him – but now that he'd remembered the witches' exact

words, and his son was asking if he'd ever had a *love affair* with her – "What kind of vibes, son? Surely, after all these years, 'Deen couldn't possibly think that I would ever –"

"Smoke and mirrors, Dad." Adrian shrugged. "I just get a mood; like I told Mom, I wouldn't call it *affection,* per se . . ." He shrugged again. "But she thinks something. And it's about you."

"Whatever it is, it's years too late," Daina reiterated.

"Indeed," Ian agreed and they hugged again, and had a little chortle over the possibility of Nadine's long ago feelings, unspoken, misplaced then, and certainly misplaced now.

Adrian thought that if they sensed the blackness within Nadine the way he did, perhaps they wouldn't be laughing.

But still it fascinated him, this deviltry that he sensed in her, whether or not it sprung from ancient feelings unfilled, from before he was born. He also remembered the expectation, the anticipation that he had read – Adrian reasoned that Nadine was single – maybe she was just on the make. She was the same age as his mother, and his mother certainly wasn't dead yet; he could tell by the way she looked at his dad. Maybe AnTeen had decided to settle down after all these years of roaming, and she was just looking for a boyfriend. Maybe it didn't have anything to do with his dad at all.

NINETEEN

Nadine discovered that her mother hadn't just been *thinking* about selling the house. She had called about Dad's heart attack on Wednesday, the 29th of June – here it was only July 9th, and already the agent had caused a sign to be planted in the yard. Nadine thought that her mother must've called the agent the very day of her father's diagnosis, or her parents had already decided to sell out and move to smaller accommodations before Sam fell ill. Either way, Nadine hadn't bothered to unpack. It fact, she went to the grocery store up the road and acquired a few boxes. With those and a roll of trash bags, she began cleaning out the memories from her old room.

The Southern California housing market was good in 1988; the Germaine hacienda was well-kept and reasonably priced. Within two weeks, the *For Sale* sign was updated with a *Sold* banner. Without a hitch, escrow closed on the 26th of August. Nadine discovered that their house had been purchased by the real estate office that had listed it. They intended to list it again, believed that they could sell it for a profit. Regardless, it wasn't her home any longer.

As she had said she was going to do, Irene had already rented an apartment in a building not far from Community Hospital in downtown Riverside. Nadine was fortunate to secure an efficiency in the same building.

That weekend, Ian and Adrian helped them pack up and move out. Rob was on duty, and since the other able-bodied Wildes were on sabbatical in Europe, Adrian even scared up Gil to lend a hand.

Daina didn't make an appearance to help with the moving chores. *She figures that this is men's work,* Nadine thought. *She's lent me her men – why should she have to help, too?*

Her enemy's absence was more than okay with Nadine. Not only did she get to watch Ian work – he was still undeniably attractive to her, still virile and sexy at forty-two – she also got to observe his boy and Gil. Adrian was not hard to look at and Gil never missed an opportunity to smile or wink at her, or whisper a filthy suggestion in her ear, or give her a little pat on the bottom when no one was looking.

On a Hallowe'en night almost nineteen years before, Daina and Ian had shared a telepathic congruence: each knew that at the very next available moment, there would be consummation of their love at first sight. So it was with Nadine and Gil, although it was certainly not anything as lofty as love that they planned to complete. She let him know, with winks and nods, with a whispered word, that as soon as she was settled into her tiny pad, he was welcome – nay, he was *expected* – to drop by and help her break the place in.

Nadine was chipper as she packed up her parents' house. The desire she felt for Ian, always present, eternally denied, was still there, but it was dimmed to a tolerable level by her anticipation of entertaining young Gil. Sam was having a good day; he seemed almost his old self, at least in the morning, before he began to tire. He and Irene remained at their new apartment, putting things in their places as they were delivered; Nadine stayed at the house and gave directions as to what should be taken downtown and what should be taken to storage.

At one point, she and Gil enjoyed a quick make-out session in the closet of her childhood bedroom while Adrian and Ian tied down a load of furniture on the truck. As with their earlier interlude, Gil became far more wound up by the encounter than Nadine did. Nadine kept one ear cocked for discovery, and was amused more than moved by her young friend's passion.

"Just have a little patience," she told him, when they heard the truck's horn honk, signaling that the load was secured and ready to go. "You'll live longer."

By sundown on Sunday, the house was cleared out and cleaned up. Nadine, emotionless, took one last tour through its walls. The place meant nothing to her; it had just been the site where she had slept as a child, where she had accomplished the necessary interactions with her parents. Nadine had always considered the decked house in the woods across the street to be her real home. And for a while, the house at the bottom of the hill was a happy home, too . . . But all that had ended with her adopted family's betrayal, their theft.

Without ceremony, Nadine locked up and dropped the keys into the little door-box that the realtor had left for her, and walked out of the yard without a backward glance. There was not one single thing left to bring her back to this neighborhood, except for the chance for an occasional visit with Ian. And his detested family.

Nadine gratefully thanked her never achieved soulmate and his son for all their help, and bid them goodbye. She hopped into the car and headed downtown, tired but excited. A new life awaited. She'd already secured herself a little nine-to-five at Ritz Camera, selling lenses and film and offering advice to Riverside shutterbugs. It wasn't the fashion district in New York City, nor was it National

Geographic, but neither was Nadine twenty-eight any more. It would pay the rent and keep the lights on, and it was within walking distance of her new apartment.

So she was again gainfully employed, and a new adventure was about to commence, a local one this time. Nadine thought of her imminent comingling with Gil as that adventure, although she didn't consider that he would soon be her new man, that they would embark on some sort of May-December romance. Nadine found that she relished the concept of a tiny little place, all to herself. She wasn't in the market for a boyfriend – she realized with a start that neither her parents nor her treacherous *family* across the street had ever met any of her beaux except for Chuck.

Nadine could never parade a boyfriend in front of Ian, anyway. And even if she could see her way clear to doing that, it wouldn't be Gil. Gil was a cheating son of a bitch, for one thing, and besides that, he was entirely too young for her.

It wasn't that Nadine was ashamed of considering a fling with a taken, younger man. Shame was not an emotion she encompassed. If Randi couldn't keep her green-eyed, blonde boyfriend to heel, that was certainly not Nadine's problem. She liked the idea of a little intrigue, a little secrecy. The thought of a clandestine affair with an already partnered-up young man warmed her icy soul.

Another reason that Nadine wished to keep any interaction they might have on the down low, another reason that she liked Gil just where he was: the idea that Gil was involved with lil' Randi, and Randi was so obviously besotted with Adrian, and Adrian was supposed to die . . .

From observing their interactions today, Nadine was sure that Adrian had no fear of Gil, regardless of what Gil believed. Adrian was fond of Randi, and Randi wanted him to be fonder still. Gil was volatile – who knew what permanent, irrevocable actions might occur from such a mixture?

But in the meantime . . . Nadine barely had time to dig a sheet out of a cardboard box, throw it on the bed, and take a quick shower before Gil was knocking on her door. Wordlessly, she let him in, and wordlessly, they commenced, free from all the restraints inherent when the possibility of getting caught had been hovering nearby. Words were unnecessary, regardless. A physical culmination was all either sought.

What would they have talked about, anyway? Nadine was a world traveler, seventeen years his senior: she'd discovered to her chagrin that Gil was only twenty-three. Nadine had experiences, plans and agendas that Gil couldn't even guess about. He didn't care about them anyway. Here was a good-looking older woman who was hot to trot; Gil didn't think that Nadine was going to ask much more from him than he was more than willing to give her.

TWENTY

On Thanksgiving Day, 1988, Adrian noticed a red roadster parked in the driveway to his AnTeen's old house. He also noticed that the *For Sale* sign had been removed from the yard. Adrian didn't know much about cars, but like any other young man his age, he remembered the red 1933 Ford coupe from those ZZ Top videos; after Eddie Van Halen, Billy Gibbons was his favorite guitarist.

But Adrian didn't have a lot of time to speculate on the automobiles owned by his new neighbors. He had to shuttle his mom's green bean casserole up to his aunts' house – not being much of a cook, it was Daina's only contribution and she had worked hard on it – as well as help set the table, help with all the other arrangements.

Nadine hadn't had Thanksgiving dinner often with her parents, although she was dining with them this year. She had sent her regrets to Daina, but Dad was sick, and Mom wanted to cook this year, seeing how it might be his last . . .

Bobby and Nick were the same – from little on, they had enjoyed the feast with their cousin and his parents, at his aunts' weird little house in the woods, leaving Marta and Will to their own devices, usually socializing with powerful, childless couples.

It was a hectic scene this year, a houseful of people: Penny and Bellona, Ian and Daina, Bobby and Nick, Adrian. Now that he was driving, Bobby was able to pick up Tracy, and Uncle Rob showed up with a stunning young nurse from the hospital. Nick opened his mouth to comment, but then closed it again at a stern look from his brother and his cousin. No need to start off a wholesome family get-together with one of Nicky's blue remarks.

Adrian didn't have time to think about the red car again until later in the evening when he and his parents returned home. The roadster was gone and a large U-Haul truck was parked in its place.

Adrian was out in the garage by mid-morning the next day, waiting for his band to show up, practicing Eddie's riffs to *Finish What Ya Started*. Nick already had Sammy's rhythm parts nailed, and had threatened to start learning something new, something fresh, like *Cult of Personality,* and "Fuck that fat, overrated, outdated Eddie Van Halen."

Adrian could read music – he hadn't had guitar lessons for twelve years for nothing – but he played by ear. And Adrian liked

Eddie, and he liked the song, so he practiced the opening riff over and over again, until he felt that it started to sound right.

After repeating the intro for about an hour, Adrian heard a voice from the end of the driveway. "What the fuck *is that,* kid? And why do you keep playing it? Exclusively? Over and over?" Adrian looked up. A stout, mustachioed man in his late twenties was leaning against the corner of the fence.

"That's Van Halen, sir," he replied and played the breakdown from *Finish What Ya Started.*

"Don't you know anything else?"

"I dunno." Adrian nodded and shook his head at the same time. "I just picked up this here gee-tar a little while ago." He nodded behind him at the garage full of equipment: amps and mikes and stands and pedals and wires; Tracy's drum kit. "Request something."

The man thought for a moment. "How about *Smoke on the Water?"*

Adrian grinned. "A little before my time, but . . ." He played the intro to the Deep Purple song flawlessly. It was one of his favorites. Adrian looked at the man, saw that he was impressed, but not quite amazed yet. "Anything else?"

Before the man could open his mouth to make another request, Adrian played the opening to *Johnny B. Goode.* Now the man had taken a few steps into the driveway. Adrian began *Purple Haze,* and the man smiled and walked the rest of the way up to the garage.

When Adrian stopped, the man extended his hand. "I guess you can play something else. Hi. I'm Allan Coleman. I just bought the house across the street." Adrian put his guitar pick in his mouth, shook the guy's hand, introduced himself. Allan said, "I always wanted to learn how to play the guitar. But my fingers are too fat." He held up pudgy, work-calloused hands. "What else do you know?"

"Request something."

"Surprise me."

Adrian began *Stairway to Heaven.* "Not much of a surprise. Request something," he said again.

"Okay. How 'bout, *Paranoid?"*

Adrian grinned. "Another oldie." He played it, then began *Ain't Talking 'Bout Love.* Allan looked blankly at him. "Not a big Van Halen fan, are you?" Allan shook his head. "We'll have to work on that." Adrian grinned and played the intro to *Layla.*

"That's awesome, Adrian," the older man said.

"Thanks." Adrian played *Walk This Way,* and again Allan smiled, shook his head. Adrian had achieved amazement, and what he'd always loved most: an audience.

Adrian played *Aqualung;* Allan applauded. He played *Sunshine of Your Love,* then *The Boys Are Back in Town;* Allan cheered. Adrian grinned and looked up to see Nick, carrying his guitar case, standing in the mouth of the garage.

Adrian just looked at him questioningly. It wasn't necessary to actually say, "Where's Bobby and Tracy?"

"Tomorrow, my brother and only friend," Nick said. "Something about Christmas shopping." He looked askance at Allan and Adrian heard his cousin's voice in his head: *Who's this asshole?*

"This is our new neighbor, Allan. He just bought AnTeen's old house. Allan, this is my cousin, Nick."

Nick set his guitar case down and shook Allan's hand. "I bet you wish you were as good as Adrian, huh, sonny?"

Nick rolled his eyes. "I sure do, Grandpa." He picked up his guitar case and went over to his amp.

They entertained Allan for the entire afternoon, mostly just playing parts of songs, another thing Adrian enjoyed. Allan would shout a suggestion – *Sweet Home Alabama!* – and if Adrian couldn't play it immediately – *Rock You Like A Hurricane!* – then Nick invariably could. But Allan liked oldies, and while Nick could play anything after he'd heard it only twice, Adrian was more familiar with the ancient tunes. Allan came away from the afternoon believing Adrian to be the superior talent, even though Adrian himself didn't believe that to be true. Besides, Allan didn't care for the kid's attitude.

"I've gotta be heading back home," he said at last. "My wife's pregnant, and she'll be wondering where the hell I've been."

"Come back any time," Nick said, the picture of insincerity. Adrian looked over his shoulder at his cousin, and Nick made his signature *What?* face.

"Was that your roadster I saw parked in the driveway yesterday?" Adrian set his guitar on its stand and walked down the driveway with Allan.

"Nah," Allan said. "I just painted it for the guy. That's what I do. I just took the shop up the street."

Adrian was familiar with the place. It had been boarded up for as long as he could remember.

Allan caught his dubious expression. "I know. It's gonna take some work. But it was cheap. Stop by tomorrow and check it out."

"I'll do that." Nick played the intro to *Cult of Personality,* and Adrian looked over his shoulder at his cousin again. Nick was ignoring him. "Definitely," Adrian said to Allan. "After band practice."

"I'll see you then." Allan shook his hand. "You're really great on the guitar, Adrian."

"Thanks. I've had a lot of practice."

"Is that all you do?" Allan asked curiously. "A good looking kid like you? Play guitar in the garage with little kids?" Allan grinned to let Adrian know he was kidding him.

"We've got a CD of our own stuff," Adrian replied. He tried not to sound defensive, but didn't entirely succeed. "Our music teacher helped us record it. We play parties." He realized he didn't have to defend Urban Equinox to this complete stranger. "If it's not past Nick's bedtime."

"I can't wait to hear the rest of the band," Allan said. "But come see me tomorrow. I might have a job for you."

"Okay. After practice."

TWENTY-ONE

Eileen Coleman was happy. Her mother couldn't understand why: Eileen was more than three years shy of her twentieth-first birthday – the baby would be here, up and walking, in its terrible twos, before its mother could legally have a drink – and she was married to a fat deadbeat. But Eileen didn't look at it that way. She had a good job, typing and filing and making copies for a large title company. And already, at eighteen, her life was complete. She was married, she'd just bought a house; she was going to have a baby.

And Allan wasn't a deadbeat. He was an entrepreneur, a businessman; he was his own boss. It was true that he'd had to leave the last shop he'd rented under rather acrimonious circumstances: the rent was in arrears at the time that he'd packed up all his roll-aways and paint guns and compressors and moved them out of the place in the middle of the night. And it was true that the rent was also late on the apartment they'd shared downtown when he'd packed all their furniture into the U-Haul, in front of his tools.

But he'd made a killing, he'd told Eileen, painting that roadster – it was the last project completed at the old shop – he'd made enough money for the down payment on the house *and* a couple of months' rent in advance for the new shop.

So many things had happened in Eileen's life in such a short period of time. In April of 1988, she'd turned eighteen; she'd graduated from high school in June; the next month she'd been hired at the title company, right off the street. In August, she'd met Allan. In October, they'd wed, and by Thanksgiving, she was pregnant.

The way Allan and Eileen met had always seemed like a remarkable twist of fate to Eileen, all coincidences and happenstances, all I-would've-missed-him-had-I-stopped-by-a-minute-later. It was a Saturday afternoon. She had just started her job at the title company. The office manager had taken Eileen under her wing, and had told Eileen that she had some textbooks for learning the title game.

The textbooks were boring, and Eileen didn't have a lot of ambition. So after a short while, she decided that she was thirsty, and walked across the vacant lot in front of the office manager's house to a little hole-in-the-wall liquor store.

On her way out of the store, she noticed an auto repair shop across the street; as she watched, a gleaming black 1963 Cadillac DeVille convertible hove into the parking lot, and a chubby blonde guy with a mustache hauled himself out of it and went into the shop. The guy wasn't much, but the car was splendid. Eileen liked cars. So she crossed the street to look at it.

Eileen walked around the Caddy, peered in at its blindingly white interior. She was careful not to touch any part of it – she'd been to enough car shows to know that people that owned cars like this loved you to look, but they frowned if you decided to touch. After a few minutes, the blonde guy came back out and smiled curiously at her.

"Do you like it?" he asked, even though it was obvious from this little chickie's round eyes and big grin that she did. He was not unaware of the effect of a good-looking car on a good-looking woman, especially a young one.

"It's beautiful," she said breathlessly, confirming his guess.

"It's for sale."

Eileen looked up from the car in shock. "I'm sure it's out of my price range."

"I'm sure it is," he said with a chuckle.

Eileen noticed that he wasn't bad looking, even if he was a little on the stout side. He had light blue eyes, straight, bright, towhead blonde hair, nearly to his shoulders, and a cute little mustache. He was older than her; she would soon find out that he was a whopping ten years older than her. But it was okay with Eileen. No eighteen-year-old kid had a car like this.

"Hop in, I'll take you for a ride."

Eileen hesitated, a lifetime of admonitions against accepting rides from strangers leaping to her mind. She didn't know this guy. Even if he did have an awesome car, that didn't mean he wasn't a bad person.

The blonde guy read the reluctance in Eileen's eyes, so he introduced himself. "I'm Allan," he said. "This is my shop." He gestured behind him at the two bays and the little office. Two guys about Eileen's age had come out and were standing in front of one of the bays, smoking cigarettes and watching the conversation.

"I'm not going to bite you," he said blithely, "unless you ask me to." He winked quickly at her. "I've just got time for a little spin, anyway. This guy's bringing an IROC in for an estimate in a half hour. Hop in. I'll bring you right back."

Eileen's trepidation evaporated. He was a businessman, nice enough to take a minute out of his busy day to take a young girl for a ride around the block in his beautiful car. *He probably does it all the time,* she thought. *That's why he has a car like this. What could it hurt? It's a convertible. If he tries to grab me, I'll just jump out. I'm a big girl.* The danger rationalized away, Eileen opened the door and got into the immaculate Caddy.

Allan roared the car out onto the street. He grinned at Eileen's smile of appreciation at the old Caddy's power, and to make conversation, she introduced herself. They chatted; Eileen told him that she liked old cars, and Allan said, "What a coincidence! I paint old cars!" He was a perfect gentleman, although Eileen couldn't help but notice that he leered at her a little bit. That was okay; it wasn't the first time that a fat guy had leered at her.

Allan didn't drive very far, so she didn't have time to worry again that he was a stranger, that he might hurt her. And then he brought her right back, just like he'd promised. He put the Caddy in park, and patted her on the knee. "Come back later. I'll show you that Z." Allan's hand lingered on her knee, but then he removed it before Eileen had a chance to become uncomfortable.

"I'll do that," she said, and smiled at him. "Thanks for the ride. It's a beautiful car." She got out of the Caddy and asked Allan how long his shop was open.

He glanced over at the two guys, still lounging around in front of the garage. Eileen noticed that they were grinning at him. He looked back at Eileen and winked again. "As long as it takes."

"I'm over at my boss's house," Eileen gestured across the vacant lot. "I'll come back in a little while."

"I'll look forward to it." Allan hauled himself out of the Caddy. "See you then."

Eileen started to walk away, then turned back and looked at Allan again when she heard him say, "Did you guys take the trim off of that Ford yet? What am I paying you for?"

"You haven't paid us yet," one of them said.

"Buy your own beer then, sonny," Allan said and clapped him on the shoulder. "In a couple of years." The three of them went into the garage and Eileen went back to her boss's house.

But once there, Eileen discovered that she couldn't concentrate. The text she was skimming was fairly meaningless to her, and trying to get through it was as boring as watching paint dry. Paint. Allan painted cars. Eileen liked cars, and she'd surely liked Allan's car. Now that she thought about it, she decided that she liked Allan, too.

Sure, he was a little old for her, but the two guys that she'd dated when she was a senior in high school had both been older than her.

One of them had even been married, Eileen remembered with a little giggle. It wasn't anything serious – she hadn't aimed to take him away from his wife – and it had only lasted for a few months. But he was very attentive and respectful, almost grateful that she'd consented to go out with him. He always had plenty of money and took her to nice restaurants, unlike guys her own age, who always seemed to be reaching between the couch cushions for one more quarter so they could treat her to McDonald's. That was a drag. Eileen liked older men.

Eileen thanked her boss for the tips, said she'd see her at work on Monday and crossed the vacant lot to Allan's shop.

The bays were deserted, so she knocked on the door to the office. One of the kids she had seen earlier peeped through the blinds at her. He said something to the others in the office, then unlocked the door and let her in.

The office was hazy, redolent with marijuana smoke. "You just missed the afternoon's entertainment," said Allan, who was seated behind the empty, scarred wooden desk. "This is Tony," he said and indicated the younger of the two kids. Tony looked to be about sixteen. He grinned shyly at Eileen. "And this is Peter." The other kid also smiled shyly. She recognized Peter from high school – he was a year behind her.

Tony peered through the blinds again. "Herbie's here."

"Let's do this thing," Allan said and rose from the chair.

Herbie was a thin, dark-haired, bearded fellow, probably in his late-thirties. He was smoking a cigarette, lounging against the fender of a brand-new, banana-yellow IROC Z: it didn't even have license plates.

Herbie and Allan smiled at each other. "You remember Tony and Peter? They're gonna help me . . . paint your car."

"Sure," Herbie said, and nodded at the two boys. "But who's this?" Herbie nodded over his shoulder at Eileen, who was walking around the Chevy, admiring it.

"That's my new friend, Eileen," Allan said and winked at the older man. "She likes cars."

"Does she now?" Herbie said. He pushed off the fender and stood next to Allan, the better to admire Eileen. "A little young, isn't she?"

"How old are you, Eileen?" Allan asked her.

"I'm eighteen," she said, coming back around the car.

"Old enough," Allan said to Herbie, *sotto voce.*

"It's brand new," Eileen said, gesturing at the car.

"Yep. I just . . . picked it up from the dealer." Herbie grinned at Allan, and he grinned back. "Last night, as a matter of fact."

"Why are you having it painted?" Eileen asked, confused. "Couldn't you have picked out the color that you wanted beforehand?"

Herbie exchanged another glance with Allan. "Well, honey, this is all they had in stock. But I hate yellow, so Allan's gonna paint it . . .?"

"Black."

"Right. That's a good color. Allan's gonna paint it black for me."

"It seems like a lot of trouble . . ."

"No trouble at all," Allan said. He elbowed Herbie and they grinned at each other again. Herbie handed him the keys. "It'll be ready in a few days."

"Okay," Herbie said, then smiled at Eileen, told her it was so nice meeting her, said he hoped to see her again when he picked up the Chevy. Then he shook hands with Allan and loped off down the street.

"Can we take this one for a ride, too?" Eileen asked.

"No," Allan said quickly. He smile faltered for a moment, then returned. "No, this one needs to go into the garage. Immediately." He tossed the keys to Peter. "And shut the bay." Peter and Tony got into the car, and Peter did as he was told with the now-yellow, soon-to-be-black car.

Allan smiled at Eileen. "It doesn't pay to keep Herbie waiting. We need to start on his car right away." He moved closer to her, put his arm around her shoulders. She allowed it. Sure, he was a little on the chubby side, but his blue eyes twinkled; he was cute in a teddy-bear kind of way. "But I don't have to start on it this instant. They have to take the emblems and the trim off, tape it. Come back inside with me. We'll talk."

Eileen complied. She sat across the desk from Allan and watched him roll a joint. She demurred when he offered it to her. She was not averse to getting high every now and again, but she'd just met this guy. He was older than her, and she wasn't of a mind to be getting stoned with strangers right off the bat.

Allan asked her what kind of cars she liked; a lot of 1960s era Fords were mentioned. Allan took a large, battered photo album out of the bottom drawer of the desk and invited her to come around to his side and look at the pictures. There were plenty of old Fords for her to marvel at: Mustangs and Torinos, Rancheros and even a 1968 Mercury Cougar with sequential tail lights, painted a deep midnight blue. There were several Thunderbirds, coupes and convertibles. They were all beautiful.

"You painted all these?"

"Every one," he said. "But I like Corvettes best." Allan flipped further through the album. There were Corvettes of ever year and model, candy-apple reds and pearl whites, blacks, blues, greens.

"Friends don't let friends drive Chevys," Eileen quipped, and went back to the Fords.

Allan put the roach in an ashtray and pulled Eileen down onto his lap. "What kind of car do you drive?" he asked, and fondly brushed the hair out of her eyes.

"I have a Volkswagen bug," she said. "Stock. It's not much, but it gets me around." Eileen liked sitting in his lap; she liked him. She liked cars, and it was obvious from the pictures that he was an artist. A professional. Not someone who just changed his own oil in the back yard – that was about all she was able to do.

"So . . . You don't have a boyfriend, Eileen?" he asked brightly. The pot didn't seem to have much of an effect on him.

"How do you know?" she returned as brightly.

"Well, I wouldn't think you'd be sitting in my lap if you had a boyfriend, a nice girl like you."

"And you'd be right," she said. He was fun; he was moving a little quickly, but on the other hand, he wasn't a high school kid.

"What else do you do, since you don't have a boyfriend? With someone like me?"

"I guess you'll just have to find out." Eileen waited. She thought that she would like him to kiss her, and after a heartbeat, he did. His mustache tickled. Allan started to kiss her a little bit harder, and Eileen just had time to think that he had a lot of confidence for a chubby guy, when there was a knock on the office door.

Allan smiled at her. "Go away," he said. "I'm busy."

Eileen heard Peter's muffled voice through the glass; she marveled at how well trained he was. The door wasn't locked, but apparently, if Allan said he was busy, his employee knew better than to barge right on in. She was impressed.

But the moment was lost, and Allan knew it. "Let me see what he wants," he said, indicating for her to get up.

"I have to go, anyway," she said. Eileen was young, but she already knew the value of always leaving 'em wanting a little more. "My mom's expecting me for supper."

"But you just got here!" Allan seemed disappointed, but not overly so. If this young chickie aimed to tease him, he wasn't going to beg her. He told Peter to come in.

He peeped around the door. "Do you want us to take the tail lights out?"

"No. Just tape 'em."

"Okay." Peter looked curiously at Eileen, standing beside Allan, then closed the door.

"Come back tomorrow," Allan said, looking up at her. "Maybe we can discuss this you not having a boyfriend thing a little bit more."

"Okay." Emboldened, Eileen bent over and kissed him quickly. "What time?"

"Anytime. We'll be here all night, and all day tomorrow, too."

TWENTY-TWO

Their courtship, Allan's wooing of teenaged Eileen, proceeded quickly. Allan had known his share of women – he'd even been married once, for a year and a half, when he was twenty-two. But at twenty-eight, he'd never known anyone as fresh and cute as this one. A lot of girls who liked cars had been willing to give the fat painter a little action, but he'd always felt it had been out of some feeling of obligation. That was all right with Allan – he would take it any way he could get it – but none of them had lasted very long. Not even his marriage.

But Eileen genuinely liked him, and after a few days, he started to like her, past just angling to get in her pants. She joked with the boys, but didn't look twice at them, and she listened raptly to all his stories about all the cars he'd worked on, the days and nights he'd spent as a kid at the old Cali drag strips, now all closed and forgotten.

Eileen liked Allan because of his car stories, his expertise. But she also liked him because she was on the brink of adulthood. High school was past, and she had to get dressed up every day to go to work. Her mother was a widow – Dad had passed suddenly when Eileen was twelve – and she had never been any kind of a rebellious teenager. But now a new sort of rebellion called to her.

By the time she had known Allan for two weeks, Eileen had already spent the night with him at his tiny, shabby apartment, not far from his shop. Her mother recognized that she was an adult, but was surprised and a little disconcerted at the much older, working man, that her daughter brought home for dinner not long after. Eileen said he owned his own business, that he painted cars. But Allan came off as shifty to Mrs. Artus, slovenly, fat. He might be a businessman, as her daughter insisted, but she'd have wagered that he wasn't a very successful one.

But Allan had everything that Eileen wanted. He was free from parental constraints. Hell, he was a grown man, with his own business. Although it turned out that the Caddy wasn't his – it was just another one that he had painted – she still got to be around all the other vintage rides that he got in. She didn't see too many more brand new IROCs.

Allan had his own place, even though it was tiny and desperately in need of a woman's touch. So Eileen had no trouble moving in with him when he asked her, about the middle of September. She was tired of arguing with her mother about him anyway, and now she could be free, too.

But Allan was anxious to placate Mrs. Artus. He discovered that he was in love with her pretty, cheerful little girl, and decided that he wanted to hang onto her. After a lifetime of living more or less on the fringes, after one failed marriage, Allan decided that maybe it was time for him to settle down. He took the money that he was supposed to use to pay October's rent on the shop – courtesy of the job he did for Herbie – and bought her a ring.

Eileen hesitated for a moment. Freedom was one thing, but marriage was something else entirely. She told Allan to give her a day to think about it. But she didn't think too much. His place was small, but now it would be her place, too – she had a good job – maybe they could get a bigger place. She said yes. They were married at the County Recorder's Office on October 25th, 1988. Mrs. Artus cried.

On November 9th, Eileen found out that she was pregnant. The baby was due in late July or early August. Again her mother cried. Allan got that roadster in to restore the next day. The guy had long admired Allan's work, he'd told him, so he paid up front. With this windfall, unbeknownst to his bride, Allan bought the little house across the street from Adrian. A few days before Thanksgiving, escrow closed and Allan surprised Eileen with it. They moved in on Thanksgiving Day.

Eileen's pregnancy was a difficult one. She was plagued with morning sickness, at all hours of the day. She still gamely drove her little Volkswagen downtown to work every day, but spent a lot of time in the bathroom once she got there. The office manager liked her, and understood her troubles, or else Eileen might've been let go. She worried about that, and she also worried about the situation she'd so hastily gotten herself into – married and pregnant and not even nineteen. For the first five months, Eileen was despondent. If it rained, she cried. If it didn't rain, she still cried. She went to work, and sometimes cried there.

Eileen's mother and her doctor assured her that this sadness was hormonal. It was all part of the pregnancy process, and by her sixth month, the depression Eileen had been feeling lifted. She was still tired all the time, however, and rarely left the house except to go to work. She didn't feel up to the housework, and Allan dutifully scared up a neighbor girl to help out.

Randi wasn't really a neighbor, but she hung out a lot at the house on top of the hill across the street. Or at least that's what Allan told Eileen – she hadn't been outside much since they'd moved in, and had yet to meet the neighbors.

Eileen liked Randi – they were both eighteen – and she was glad for the black-haired girl's help. Randi stopped by and did the dusting and the laundry on the weekends. Allan was always at the shop, working. Peter and Tony had quit – something about Allan not paying them – and he had hired some new kid to help out, the neighbor from across the street. But Eileen hadn't met him yet, and it seemed that Allan was always working any more. There were a lot of bills connected with a house, as well as food and buying stuff for the baby's room. Eileen was lonely, feeling tired and fat and out of sorts, so she was glad for Randi's company.

They didn't talk a lot; Randi was shy and seemed a little awed at Eileen, a girl the same age as she was, but already with a fancy job and a house and a husband and a baby on the way. Eileen had not grown up rich by any means, but she had been rather sheltered. She thought about that sometimes, how she had always been a good little girl, how she had never even stayed out overnight before she had met Allan. She considered how innocent and unworldly she had been, once upon a time. She thought this at the same time that she was thinking *Marry in haste, repent in leisure.* Have a baby right away, and – *Oh, God, what have I done?* And the tears would threaten again.

Randi, on the other hand, was a high school drop-out. She'd left home at sixteen to move in with her boyfriend, and had worked at convenience stores and fast-food places ever since, to help support them when he was between construction jobs. They had a little apartment in Rubidoux. Randi worked during the week at Mohini's House of Magic, downtown, presently, and while the pay wasn't much, she told Eileen that she enjoyed it very much. That was how she'd met the sisters that lived across the street; they were friends with the owner. That was how she'd met Adrian, the kid that was working for Allan. It had been Adrian that had suggested her to help with the housework.

Randi was closed-mouthed about all these people, and she didn't say much about her boyfriend, either. Eileen had only met him once, when he'd dropped Randi off on a Saturday. He was another blondie, younger, trimmer, and a shade better-looking that Allan. He was friendly, and he'd smiled appreciatively at Eileen, even though she was fat and tired and pregnant. Eileen had always liked blondes; a friend in high school had once remarked that Eileen was the only girl she'd ever known who would look twice at an ugly blonde. Mrs. Artus thought she had married one.

But Randi didn't talk much about her own blonde. They'd been together for a couple years, and sure, they planned to get married someday. "I don't know if I'm ready for kids yet, though," Randi said, looking a little fearfully at Eileen's big belly. She said that Gil was good to her, and that she loved him, but Eileen got the impression that the honeymoon was long over, that maybe Randi was bored with being married without actually being married. But Eileen wasn't really sure. Randi didn't talk much.

Unless it was about Adrian.

Allan had mentioned him a couple of times, said he'd bring him over for dinner sometime, after Eileen was feeling better, when she felt up to entertaining.

"Maybe after the baby comes," Eileen had said and considered taking a nap.

"I'll cook dinner!" Randi had volunteered with an unaccustomed enthusiasm. "If you invite Adrian!"

Allan wasn't much on dinner parties, and the event had never come to pass. But he had mentioned his helper on another occasion as he left the house, and Randi had again enthusiastically chirped, "Tell Adrian I said hi!" Allan had said he would, then left.

Randi sighed, and Eileen, eager for a little conversation, sensed she had a subject that she could get her own helper to talk about. "Tell me about Adrian," she began.

Randi looked nervous for a minute. "Ah, Gil doesn't like Adrian," she said, non-sequitur.

"But you do."

Now Randi grinned. "Yes, I do. Very much. Adrian Robert Wilde . . ." She smiled dreamily for a second, then sighed once more. "But he's not interested in me. There's Gil – and Adrian plays guitar. He's in a band. He doesn't have time for a girlfriend."

Eileen had heard music from across the street. From her tired and worn-out pinnacle of pregnant, working adulthood, she had wished that they would tone it down, or maybe turn it off altogether, so she could get some rest. But Randi had no such problem. She was young and liked loud music. Eileen was the same age as she was, the same age as the guitar player himself, she would learn – but she didn't feel very young at the moment.

"What's he look like?" Eileen pressed.

"Oh," Randi said softly. "He's *so cute!* So . . . *sexy,*" she whispered. "He's tall. He's got the bluest eyes. He's got straight, black, shoulder-length hair –"

"I thought you liked blondes," Eileen said, looking for common ground between them. "Like I do." She smiled. "Like Allan and Gil. And Don Johnson."

Randi shrugged. "I used to. Gil is . . . But . . . Ah, Adrian! Adrian's *incredible.*"

TWENTY-THREE

Randi had just finished her junior year in high school when she'd met Gil. She had turned sixteen in May; she had a driver's license, but there was no money for a car for Randi. Her older sister had one – but she needed it to get to her job at Wal-Mart, and besides, her sister was a bitch, and she wasn't about to allow Randi to use her car. So Randi walked down Avalon to her job at the Tastee-Freez on Mission, then back to the little house where she lived with her mom and her bitchy older sister and her two little brothers.

Randi was on her way home from work, in fact, on that day in July of 1986, walking through the gravel on the side of the road, when Gil pulled over in front of her in his dusty red Ford Ranger. He got out of the truck, asked her if she needed a ride.

He was a wearing a green tank-top and jeans; he was muscular, good-looking, blonde, older than her. But guys stopped and asked her if she needed a ride all the time. Randi knew better. She said, "No, thank you," and walked past him. Gil shrugged, got back in the truck, and drove away.

This went on for three days. Randi began to wonder if maybe he was watching her, waiting for her get off of work. On the third day, he said, "Why won't you let me give you a ride home? I'm not a murderer."

Randi's eyes widened in surprise, with a touch of fear thrown in. She hadn't thought he was a murderer – just another guy trying to pick her up – but now *that* possibility was in her mind. But he was cute, and chances were he wasn't a murderer. Chances were that he was just another guy trying to pick her up. Her fear faded, replaced by defiance. "How do I know that?"

Gil reached into the truck and shut it off, then walked around and let the tailgate down. He sat on it, and said, "Come here and talk to me. I can't abduct you sitting on the tailgate. You can run if you get scared."

That seemed reasonable enough to Randi. How else was she going to meet anybody? It seemed like she worked all the time, and she was always dead tired when she got home. She hadn't gone out with her girlfriends since school had ended. It had been an awful summer so far.

So she walked up to the back of the truck, but not too close, and waited. The blondie asked her name, and told her that his name was Gil. Randi was still a little bit afraid – he was cute, but he had a kind of mean look to him. She found that attractive – he reminded her of a blonder Paige Fletcher, the guy from *The Hitchhiker*. But Randi wouldn't have picked Paige up, 'cause he looked like a bad-ass, and she wasn't so sure she was going to let Gil pick *her* up – not yet, anyway – 'cause he looked a little dangerous, too.

But he was friendly, and he had a charming smile, and the most beautiful, dark green eyes she had even seen. They put her in mind of an enchanted forest, where elves and fairies might live. After a while, Randi sat next to him on the tailgate. He didn't try to grab her, to *abduct* her. He didn't try to touch her at all. He said that he had a little apartment over on Rubidoux Boulevard, and that he'd seen her walking home from work for about a month or so.

"So you *have* been watching me," she said, her fear returning.

"You're beautiful," he said seriously. He gestured at the cars going by. "I'm sure all these guys are watching you. You shouldn't be walking out here all by yourself."

He thought she was beautiful. Randi smiled and her fear fled entirely. "Are you gonna protect me?"

"If you'll let me," he said, still serious. It was quite an offer, not one that she'd heard before. "Let me give you a ride home."

"I don't want to go home yet," she said.

"Let's take a ride then. Where would you like to go?"

And just like that, Randi relented. She had Gil take her up to the top of Mt. Rubidoux, where they could see the whole town laid out before them. It was a beautiful view, and Randi didn't get up there much because she didn't have a car. Gil smoked a joint with her, which relaxed her completely. He was cute, and he thought she was beautiful. He was gentlemanly; he didn't try to touch her, which surprised her a little bit. They talked for a while longer, then he drove her back to her house and asked for her phone number. He didn't even try to kiss her good-bye. He promised that he would be there to pick her up from work the next day.

"I'm off tomorrow," she told him.

"Then we should go to the movies."

"All right."

They caught *Top Gun* at the Rubidoux Drive-In, right around the corner from Randi's house. Gil wasn't as much of a gentleman now, but it wasn't like he forced her to do anything she didn't want to do. After the movie was over, she consented to go back to his apartment, so he could show her a little more of what he'd shown her at the drive-in, but in privacy.

90

Randi liked his place, and not unlike Eileen, she enjoyed being away from her mom and her little brothers and big sister. So, just like Eileen, Randi didn't think twice about packing her meager belongs and moving in with Gil when he suggested it about two weeks later. Hell, she spent practically every moment she wasn't working with him, anyhow. Why not move in with him?

Randi's mom objected a bit more strenuously than Mrs. Artus had about her daughter leaving home – Randi was still in high school, after all, still a minor. But unlike Mrs. Artus, Mrs. Green liked her daughter's choice in boyfriends – she found Gil to be polite, attentive; charming, even – she felt that he had her little girl's best interests at heart. He had a good job, always had plenty of money; he brought the family groceries a few times. As long as Randi went back to school in the fall, she was glad to be able to give her oldest boy his own room at last.

But Randi hadn't gone back to school. She felt that she was a grown woman now, with her own little apartment, and her own little job, and her big, strong, hardworking boyfriend.

"You really should go back though," Gil had advised. "You are eighteen, after all." He grinned.

"I'm sixteen," she said.

"Let me see your driver's license."

Randi was skeptical, a little fearful. "What do you want with it?"

"Just give it to me. You're not driving anywhere, now are you?"

Reluctantly, she gave it to him.

A week later – Randi didn't have a car, wasn't old enough to buy beer, so she hadn't missed her ID – Gil handed her driver's license back to her. "Now you're eighteen," he said, and kissed her.

Sure enough, her ID now said that her birthdate was May 14, 1968, instead of 1970. She turned the little laminated card over in her hands, titled it up to the light. It seemed legitimate to Randi, but on the other hand, she had zero experience at spotting fake IDs. It wasn't necessary to card anyone at the Tastee-Freez.

A test came a few weeks later, when Gil decided to take Randi to Vegas for the weekend. It was more for the change of scenery than for the gambling – even with a fake ID that said she was eighteen, Randi was still too young to be on the casino floor. But Gil thought it would be fun to get out of Dodge for a couple days, so they packed a few bags and hopped on the freeway.

It was just about dusk when Gil came out of the office of the little motel on the outskirts of Sin City to find a police cruiser, lights turning, blocking in his red Ranger. Randi was sitting in the passenger seat, looking terrified, looking not a second older than her sixteen and a half years. The cop was leaning in her window, speaking to her.

Gil approached, and the cop looked up. Gil, careful to put both hands on the roof of the truck where the cop could see them, said the customary cliché: "What seems to be the problem, Officer?"

"You go stand in front of the truck," the cop replied. Gil complied. The cop said to Randi, "How old are you, honey?"

"She's eighteen," Gil replied. "Her mother knows where she is." That wasn't entirely true. Her mother knew she was with Gil, but she didn't know that Randi was in Nevada. And Randi wasn't eighteen, despite what her ID said.

"Was I talking to you?" the cop said. Gil shut up.

Randi was terrified. She imagined spending the night in some lock-up – it might be even longer, if they decided to keep her until her mother could be made to come fetch her. God only knew what the penalty for giving a fake ID to a cop was. She repeated Gil's words. "I'm eighteen. My mother knows where I am. He's my boyfriend."

The cop smiled kindly at her. "Are you familiar with the Mann Act, honey? He's not allowed to take you out of California, if you're underage, even if he is your boyfriend." Randi realized the cop thought he had himself some kind of transporting minors across state lines bust on his hands, some kind of saving the innocent thing; maybe he thought he'd get his picture in the paper. She wasn't innocent, and Gil wasn't taking her across state lines against her will; but she was underage, and now she was scared to death that this cop was going to discover it.

The cop frowned at Gil. "How old are you?"

"I'm twenty-one." Which was true. *Gil* didn't have a fake ID. "I've got my license in my pocket, if you want to see it." Gil knew better than to reach for it, however. He'd been hassled by the law before, and knew to keep his hands where the cop could see them at all times.

"I'll deal with you in a minute," the cop said gruffly, then smiled paternally at Randi again. "Can I see your ID, honey? I don't think you'd lie to me, but, well . . . I wouldn't be doing my job if I didn't make sure, would I? Then we can wrap this up, and you can go on your way."

Randi slowly reached into her purse for her wallet. She felt trapped; there was no way to get out of the truck, nowhere to run. She trusted Gil, but this was a cop, and she knew that he would know that her ID was fake. But what else could she do?

She handed it to him, and it seemed like he looked at it, peered at it, *studied* it, for a lifetime. He said, "What did you come to Vegas for, Randi? You know you're too young to gamble, right?"

"We're getting married," Gil said from the front of the car.

The cop looked at Randi for another heartbeat. "Well, you're old enough to do that." He handed the fake ID back to her. "Congratulations. You kids have a nice night."

Gil waited until the cop got back into his car and pulled out of the motel parking lot. Then he opened Randi's door. "Good job, baby. What did I tell you? You're eighteen!"

Tears welled up in Randi's blue eyes. She didn't look eighteen, she didn't feel eighteen. She was not eighteen! She had never been so scared in her life.

"Come on," Gil said gently and took her hand. He could tell that she was frightened, and thought that she looked even more beautiful when she was vulnerable like this, dependent on him to show her the way. "Everything's okay. No more cops, I promise. Let's go inside."

For the next two years, until she really was eighteen, like some kind of Post-Traumatic Stress Disorder, the same fear would rise up and almost choke Randi every time she saw a cop. Even after she reached her majority, the feeling didn't lessen, because Gil insisted on getting her another fake ID that said she was twenty-one, then, so they could go to the bar together. She trusted Gil, but . . . The whole ID thing made her absolutely petrified of the law.

But other than making her afraid of the cops, Gil was good to her. They'd never had a single argument, and even if he did stay out all night with his friends every now and then, Randi had always considered him to be a great boyfriend. He made good money most of the time – there were sometimes a few weeks or a month of no money, when he was between construction gigs, but that was why she had a job, wasn't it? She had her own car, something she wouldn't have if she was still living at home.

She had a car, and a little apartment; she had the witchcraft that she was learning at Lily's knee. And she had Gil to look after her. And she loved him, and she was sure that he loved her, because he told her all the time that he did. And she was confident that they would get married someday, and maybe have a baby like Eileen and

Allan. Yes, Randi was more than happy with Gil; he was wonderful, the best boyfriend in the world.

And she had always believed all of that implicitly, until she met Adrian Wilde.

TWENTY-FOUR

Now Eileen smiled conspiratorially at her. "Tell me more, Randi. I haven't seen anything incredible in a while." *Not since before I started on this irreversible phase of my life,* she thought.

Things really weren't that bad: Eileen wasn't unhappy, just tired, and a little scared. Allan always seemed to have trouble coming up with the house payment; it was ten days late last month. But she was sure everything would turn out all right. He worked all the time, so he would be bringing in more money soon, right? Everything would be better once the baby was born, and she got back to feeling like herself again. She felt like a slightly nauseated elephant these days; she only had two more weeks to go.

Listening to Randi talk about this guy she had a crush on would be just the ticket to take Eileen's mind off her troubles for a minute. "What's so incredible about him?"

Randi smiled. "What's *not* incredible about him? He plays the guitar. He sings. He's smart, funny. He has the most beautiful smile. He told me once that I could do better than Gil." She giggled.

"Sounds like he was flirting with you." Eileen couldn't help feeling a little superior, listening to Randi's schoolgirl appreciation. She felt so much more grown up than her helper; she had so many other things to worry about besides some guitar player's smile.

"No." Randi shook her head firmly, sadly. "Adrian doesn't flirt with me. Believe me, I would know it." Again she smiled. "I think about *that* all the time. What I would say if Adrian suddenly came on to me . . . What I wouldn't give . . . But he's just friendly. Like a brother. He doesn't have time for a girlfriend."

Eileen sighed. It seemed like she and Randi were not going to bond after all. Randi just wasn't much of a talker, or perhaps she lacked imagination. She obviously liked this kid, but apparently couldn't find the words to make Eileen understand why. From Randi's description, there didn't seem to be anything *incredible* at all about Adrian Wilde.

TWENTY-FIVE

It was fortunate that Randi was on hand, helping with chores, on the afternoon of Saturday, August 5, 1989, because it was on that day that Eileen's water broke. Randi gleefully skipped up to the shop and told Allan, "Honey, it's time!" She was happy for the parents-to-be, and she was also happy because she got to spend the rest of the afternoon with Adrian while Allan and Eileen went to the hospital to undertake the blessed event.

Adrian and Randi didn't spend the afternoon alone, as she would've liked. He called the rest of his band, and they came over and practiced – Adrian had neglected band practice somewhat lately, because he'd been working so much with Allan – but still Randi was delighted to just stand around and watch him.

From the moment that they had been introduced, Randi had gotten the impression that little Nick was sweet on her. And now, whenever it was his turn to sing, this impression was underlined because he would always sing directly to her, with an earnest, solemn expression on his face. Wasn't that cute? What was he, nine?

But sometimes Adrian would sing directly to her, also. *My, my, my, I'm once bitten, twice shy, baby,* and he would give her a little wink. There was nothing serious about Adrian singing to her – not like the kid – it didn't signify anything. Randi knew that Adrian wasn't flirting with her, no matter how much she wanted him to.

TWENTY-SIX

Eileen and Allan's daughter, christened Carmen Michele, was born at 10:52 that evening. Eileen's labor wasn't as difficult as her pregnancy had been, but it was lengthy and exhausting. After spending the requisite time with her new bundle of joy and her ecstatic husband, Eileen just wanted to sleep. When the nurse took Carmen back to the nursery, she was not at all upset that Allan clearly didn't want to hang around at the hospital. He wanted to go hand out cigars and congratulate himself. That was okay. She wasn't at all sad to see him go – she would see him and the baby again, soon enough. Now she just wanted to rest.

The new daddy threw an impromptu party went he got home. Allan had a lot of acquaintances, but these were not people he would want coming to his house, or even knowing where he lived, for that matter. He had few friends. He was a known burner of bridges; acrimony was the last word on most of anything he'd ever called a friendship. But Adrian was his friend, and he brought over his cousin Bobby to aid in the celebration. Tracy wasn't interested in watching three men get drunk, and it was one of those times when it was past Nick's bedtime.

They smoked a few bowls, and Allan had bought a case of Budweiser. In the nine months of their association, Allan had given Adrian a beer every now and then, but Adrian had never seen the painter have one himself.

"I've been known to lose my temper," was all Allan would say about the fact that he didn't drink.

But he wasn't angry on this night, and it didn't take long for him become what could only be described as a happy, sentimental, falling-down drunk. He asked Bobby repeatedly if he had any clue at all about how good his cousin was at playing the guitar. Bobby smiled good-naturedly and assured the new father that he knew all about Adrian's musical abilities.

"Why don't you have a girlfriend, Adrian?" Allan slurred. "Why, if I could play guitar like you, I'd have hot and cold running women. Women love guitar players. I'd have to install one of those swinging doors, like in an old-timey saloon. One would come in, another would go out . . ." Allan grinned drunkenly. He seemed to have forgotten his young bride for the moment, the birth of his child – the reason for all the hilarity.

Adrian reminded him, using his Uncle Rob's favorite line. "Unlike yourself, I just haven't found the right one yet."

"Not for lack of trying," Bobby said. "Every party we play, Adrian gets a different girl. There was even two, on one occasion, if memory serves."

"All you old married men, so smug," Adrian said, and slapped his cousin on the back. "Your search has ended. Us single guys, we gotta keep looking, keep plugging along." Adrian grinned craftily, winked at his cousin. Had Randi been present, she would've swooned at his killer smile. "And you make it sound like there were two girls, one right after the other, like Allan's swinging door, Bobby. There was a good five or six hours between them."

Allan looked at him expectantly. Adrian sighed, but continued to grin. "We played this party – or, we were supposed to play it. We were there at six o'clock, starting to set up. But this guy's dad showed up unexpectedly – some kind of domestic dispute began, and we thought it was best to put our equipment back in the truck. There was some girl there – Amy, Emmie . . .'"

"Emily," Bobby supplied.

"Really?" Adrian gave drunken Allan a look of wide-eyed surprise. "I would've sworn it was Amy." Allan grinned at Adrian's arrogance, shook his head.

"No, it was Emily," Bobby said. "Tracy knows her."

Adrian shrugged. "Anyway, she comes out of the house while we're putting our equipment back on the truck, and says we can come over to her place and play. The kid had already paid us –?"

Bobby shook his head. "I don't remember his name."

"Me, either. But he'd already paid us, and he'd said that his parents' fight would blow over in a little while, and then we could come back. Besides, Nick was having a snit."

Bobby rolled his eyes. "Wasn't he, though? He was so mad that we weren't going to play."

"So I told Amy –"

"Emily."

Adrian grinned. "Right. So I told Emily that we didn't want to set up some place else, that we were gonna just go back home and wait for this kid to call us back. She looked over her shoulder at the house – you could still hear Mom and Dad screaming – and said, 'This might take a while. Why don't you come over to my house by yourself then?'

"She was cute, so I thought, hell, why not? I gotta couple hours to kill, and what better way than that to kill 'em? I told Bobby that I'd see him no later than eight o'clock, back at my house.

"We got back to Amy, uh, Emily's house. Mom and Dad aren't home, but all of a sudden, she's not so . . . *friendly* any more. She wants to sit in the living room and watch a movie. I'm kind of on a time schedule here . . . So I made a little move, and she pushed me away. It occurs to me that she thinks she's so fine that I'm gonna beg her. She actually *wants* me to beg her."

"Don't they all?" Allan said.

"I dunno about all that. The closest I got to begging her was – I said, 'Well, I guess I'll just go then . . .'"

Emily was concerned about appearances; she had just met this good-looking guitar player. What kind of girl would she seem to be if she just went right on ahead and . . . But as he turned to leave, Adrian heard her thought: *He's so cute – what do I care what he thinks?*

"Needless to say, she changed her mind. I had to make it quick, but that was all right with her."

"Quick was better than nothing," Allan said in admiration.

"Well, it wasn't *that* quick. But I was on a time schedule, and she'd mentioned that her parents would be home soon –"

"And you didn't want to get caught again." Bobby slapped his cousin on the back. "You didn't see that one coming, did ya, Kreskin?" Bobby said to Allan, "Daddy was a cop."

"Oh, shit!" Allan declared.

Adrian shrugged again. "It was what it was. He didn't shoot me, so I thought it turned out okay."

"What about the second girl?" Allan wanted to know.

"Oh. Yeah." Adrian grinned sheepishly. "So, Emily didn't want to go back to the party."

"She was exhausted," Allan theorized.

"Maybe. She also had to wait for her parents. Or something. I dunno, maybe she *was* exhausted." He shrugged again. "Or maybe she didn't like it."

"That's not what I heard," Bobby said.

"Anyway, I met up with the band back at my house. Domestic tranquility had been restored at that kid's house, so we went back and played his party."

"And the second girl?"

99

"There's always a girl waiting for him after a gig," Bobby supplied. "If I didn't know better, I'd think that was the only reason he has a band."

"I'm a classically trained guitarist," Adrian protested. "It's all about the music."

"The groupies are just an added benefit," Allan opined.

"The groupies are a pain in the ass," Bobby said.

"Only if you're married, Cuz. Only if you're married." When Allan looked confused, Adrian explained. "Bobby's married to our drummer."

"Really? Aren't you a little young to be –"

"We're not really married," Bobby said.

"But they actually are," Adrian countered.

"'Till death do us part, Cuz," Bobby said. "I'm not ashamed of it. I'll never want anyone but her."

"That's the cutest thing I've heard all day," Allan said and sipped his beer.

"Nothing to be ashamed of, Bobby," Adrian said seriously. "I think it's wonderful. You guys love each other. That's how it is with my parents. That's how it should be."

"And I'll never have to worry about furious fathers and jealous boyfriends." Bobby grinned. "Speaking of groupies and jealous boyfriends, how's Randi, by the way?"

Now Adrian rolled his eyes.

"You're dumb, Adrian," Allan said. "What's wrong with Randi? She's got an ass that just does not quit."

"Can I get an amen?" Bobby said, and they clinked bottles.

"I've never heard her speak more than five words," Allan continued, "unless it's 'Tell Adrian I said hi!' I think she's afraid of me."

"You are pretty scary," Adrian admitted.

Allan grinned. "But what's wrong with her, boy? She's obviously down for anything you might have a mind to do."

Bobby burst into song. He was a little drunk himself. *"I think I love you, so what am I so afraid of?"*

"I'm afraid that I'm not sure of, a love there is no cure for." Adrian grinned. "Like a disease. There's no cure for Randi's love. I'll pass."

Allan shook his head. "You're a piece of work, you know that? Why would you turn that down?"

100

"Just last Thanksgiving, my Uncle Rob gave me some advice," Adrian said. "He's not married – he's a doctor, and this last year, he brought some hot nurse to dinner with him."

"Now there was an ass," Bobby said.

"Indeed," Adrian agreed. "I don't know if he was talking about her specifically or not, but he said to me, 'Some women are like gum, Adrian. They're sticky. Clingy. They get attached. You remember that time Nick got gum in his hair at the river?'"

Bobby rolled his eyes. "Christ, what a mess!"

"That's just what Rob said. 'It was a bitch to get out, remember? Eventually his mom just took a pair of scissors and cut it out. Ruined his 'do. Some women are like that, Adrian. My advice to you is to avoid them. It's impossible to get them out of your hair.' And since nobody knows more about women than my Uncle Rob –"

"If you don't believe him, just ask him," Bobby said.

"I figured he knew wherein he spoke. Randi's like that. Clingy. I don't feel anything for her, and if I –"

"You'd never get rid of her," Allan finished for him. He shook his head. "You're a saint, Adrian. It never enters your mind to just use up what the chickies are offering you."

"Oh, it enters my mind. I just don't want any clingy ones."

"You're a saint," Allan repeated. "That's what you are. No wonder I like you so much." Allan gave Adrian a drunken squeeze, and Adrian grinned in surprise. "You're a fucking saint."

"And you're a brand new daddy," Adrian replied and hugged Allan back. He winked at his cousin. "Ain't love grand?"

"I bet you'll have your little girl helping out at the shop before you know it. All you guys ever do is work." Bobby looked significantly at Adrian, letting a little of his resentment show – his cousin wasn't around as much as he used to be.

"That's not all we do," Adrian said. He made a gesture to indicate that there was also a lot of pot smoking and sitting around. "I don't think he'll be having his little girl hang around there any time soon. It's no place for a kid." A new thought struck Adrian. "Tell Bobby about the redhead, Allan."

"That was your deal, boy."

Adrian shook his head. "No, she offered to be grateful to *you.*"

"But you got into her car." Allan said to Bobby, "Your cousin's a natural. He's got *car thief* written all over him."

Bobby looked at Adrian in surprise. "Is that a fact?"

"Just a little prestidigitation, Cuz. Besides, *he* taught me how to do it."

"I *showed* him how to do it. I didn't *teach* him anything. I can't even do it." Allan grinned proudly at his protégé. "Your cousin can break into a car with a piece of string, Bobby. In under a minute."

Bobby blinked. "You don't say?" He grinned at what he thought was Allan's drunken exaggeration.

"He's got an old car door at the shop," Adrian explained. "He tells me that it's possible to unlock it by making a slip knot in a piece of string, then jamming it down into the door. Then you just scooch it down the sides of the window until the loop slides over the lock. Then you pull the knot closed around it, and pull the lock open."

Bobby was skeptical. Allan said, "I can't do it. I don't have the patience. But he can."

"I practiced," Adrian said. "That's all it takes."

"So, this redhead, probably about thirty-five, prances into the shop the other day, all dressed up in high heels and this tight blue dress," Allan said. "She just walks right in, stepping over hoses and tools.

"'Can one of you help me?' she asks. 'I'm up at the market. I've locked the keys in . . . It's my boyfriend's car and he'll just kill me if I have to call him about this. I'll do anything.'"

"And it was clear she meant *anything,*" Adrian said and wiggled his black eyebrows. "Allan doesn't answer her – he just goes out in front of the shop and looks up at the building. The woman follows him, and after a minute, she asks him what he's looking at. 'I'm looking for the sign that says *locksmith* on the front of my shop, lady. I paint cars. I don't break into them.'

"This, of course, is bullshit." Adrian winked at Allan.

"Don't be telling tales out of school, boy," Allan warned through his drunkenness, and Bobby looked curiously at him, then just as curiously at Adrian. What exactly was his cousin trying to tell him?

"'I'll pay you,' the redhead says. 'Or, maybe . . .' She winked at him."

"You're making this up," Bobby said.

"No," Allan said. "Apparently, whatever she was offering was worth it to make sure the ol' man didn't find out that she was locked out of his car. But I'm married. I don't want to get involved in some situation with some silly bitch that's dumb enough to –"

"So I said I'd do it," Adrian continued. "I told him it would be a chance to try out the string trick."

"Don't you have one of those metal things?" Bobby asked. "What do ya call 'em? To get the door open?"

"A slim jim. And I'll tell you the same thing I told her. Do you see a tag on my shirt that says *locksmith?* Slim jims are illegal." Allan considered for a moment, then added. "Well, they're not really illegal, but if you got one on you, all a cop has to do is prove intent . . ." Again Bobby blinked and Allan looked at Adrian as if he had said too much. "Yeah, I've got one."

"A few, actually."

"But I'm not gonna go busting them out for some strange chick that just wanders in off the street." Allan smiled fondly at Adrian. "But he volunteered, so I walked up to the market with him and his string and this woman. Not only had she locked the keys in the car, but it was running. How dumb can she be? I thought.

"Adrian whipped out his string, tied the knot. I didn't think he could do it. It was a brand new BMW – not just the door to some old Chevy. But he stuck the string down into the top of the door, worked it down onto the lock . . . Damned if he didn't pop that lock right open. It was amazing. He's a natural."

"And what does the redhead do?" Adrian said. "She goes, 'Oh! Thank you so much!' and hugs *him.* I just opened the car for her, saving her from God-only-knows-what, and she hugs *him!*"

"You were just a kid to her." Allan grinned. "She also shoved a fifty into my hand."

"I didn't know about that," Adrian said suspiciously.

"How do you think we ate lunch?" Allan asked. He looked at Bobby. "It was amazing."

"My cousin. The car thief." Bobby wondered how much of it was true, wondered why Adrian seemed so proud of this little fat drunk's praise.

"Shush," Adrian said, and winked at the bass player. "Don't be telling tales out of school."

What Bobby didn't know, and what neither Allan nor his cousin were going to tell him, was that Allan had a large selection of slim jims, and it wasn't because he was a locksmith. He was an automotive painter, true, a restorer of all those vintage rides that had so ensorcelled his young bride. He was a legitimate businessman, but just as Mrs. Artus had speculated, he wasn't very successful at it.

Adrian knew this already: Allan didn't charge enough for the cars he painted; he ran out of money halfway through the job and had to ask for more – very unprofessional – and then he took too long in the accomplishment of the task. He lipped off to the customers. No matter how many photo albums he had crammed full of pictures of the cars he had painted, in nine months' time, Adrian had not seen Allan draw in any repeat business. A few guys walked in off the street, but apparently any word of mouth about him was all bad.

So to augment his income, Allan had a whole 'nother automotive business. Sometimes, he would just change the numbers and paint ones that someone else had stolen – that had been the deal with Herbie.

Adrian had guffawed at that story. "Your wife wanted you to take her for a ride in a hot car?"

"She wasn't my wife yet," Allan replied. "And she doesn't know –"

"She doesn't know?" Adrian asked incredulously.

"No, she doesn't know." He looked sternly at Adrian. "Maybe I shouldn't be letting *you* know."

"Who am I gonna tell?" Adrian asked with a grin. Allan smiled.

They had finished painting some dude's Model A a week before – Allan had made about two hundred bucks on the deal, and Adrian had gotten twenty out of it. No work had come in since.

Adrian didn't hang around and help Allan because he was making money working for him. Adrian hung around and helped out because he liked to work with his hands. He liked to take things apart and put them back together, and he discovered that wet sanding was like being stoned in the water: it was mindless, therapeutic; it gave Adrian time to think about what was real and what was not.

And Adrian liked Allan. He enjoyed his car stories as much as Eileen did, although the stories the painter told to Adrian were often bluer or a little more violent than the ones he told to his wife. *If only half the shit he says is true,* Adrian thought, *then he is a genuine bad-ass.* Adrian also appreciated Allan's talent. The cars he painted – once he got around to actually finishing the jobs – were always beautiful.

But as far as making any money in his employ – Allan talked a lot about big paydays, but Adrian had not seen a single one.

But that was about to change.

It was going on ten o'clock on a Wednesday night. Allan was using his wife's VW – he had just taken Adrian to the empty parking lot of an office building and taught him how to drive a stick shift. Like anything else to do with manual dexterity, Adrian had caught

104

on quickly, and now it seemed that they were just driving around randomly.

"Where are we going?" Adrian asked.

"I'm looking for something," Allan replied. He smirked. "You'll be the first one to know when I find it." They drove down side streets, through parking garages, finally arriving at a dark corner of the parking lot of Riverside Plaza.

"And there it is." Allan pulled the Volkswagen into the parking space next to a red Acura Legend.

Allan and Adrian got out of the car, then Allan reached behind the seat and brought out a slide hammer and a long, thin strip of metal with a notched end. He tossed the VW's keys to Adrian over its roof.

"When you see me back out, follow me."

Adrian stood beside the VW and watched Allan slide the piece of medal between the weather stripping and the glass. Allan wiggled the tool around; Adrian noticed that he stuck his tongue out like a little kid working on a particularly challenging math problem. Then he stopped and grinned at Adrian; he pulled the lock up on the Acura's door.

With a speed surprising for a fat guy, Allan jumped into the car and shut the door. The slide hammer forcefully met the car's ignition switch. Allan turned it; the car started and he again grinned at Adrian through the window. He backed the Acura out of its parking space; Adrian hopped into the VW and followed him back to the shop.

Allan pulled the roll-up door down in front of the Acura and looked innocently at Adrian through the windshield of the VW. Adrian got out of the car and tossed him the keys. His feelings were mixed: there was a little guilt – had he been religious, a stentorian voice in his head would've pronounced, *Thou shalt not steal.* Adrian wasn't religious, but he knew that stealing was wrong; in this case it was a crime. A *big* crime.

"What do you get for that?"

"I'll tell you what she brung tomorrow," Allan replied. He studied Adrian for a moment. "Oh. You mean . . . Scared are ya, guitar player?"

"No. I'm not scared." Adrian hadn't stolen anything, now had he? "I'm just curious."

He also realized that he was excited, that he was enjoying the danger inherent in standing – red-handed, so to speak – on the other side of a roll-up door from a stolen car. Adrian reckoned that right about now, someone was standing in that empty parking space with a wondering look on his face.

"Well, they gotta catch me first."

Adrian was confident beyond his nineteen years: his family had money; he was a classically trained guitarist; he had a way with the ladies. Sometimes he could see things happen before they happened. But Adrian suddenly felt a new respect for the fat painter. He appreciated the older man's audacious disregard for the law, his fearlessness. He had just stolen an Acura out of the parking lot of the Riverside Plaza, like it was the thing to do.

Adrian had yet to meet Allan's wife, but from what he said about her, Adrian got the impression that Allan thought his wife loved him because she considered him a tough guy, a bad-ass, the type of person she'd never before known in her sheltered little life. But his wife didn't know he was a car thief.

Adrian had also admired Allan for being a bad-ass, but now that Adrian knew he was a criminal, too, he found a new respect for him. He was daring; he'd just taken what he wanted. Adrian realized that perhaps he'd led a sheltered life, too, and recently, he'd thoroughly enjoyed smoking pot and hanging around with tough guys that turned out to be criminals. There *was* more to life than just playing guitar.

"But if fate decrees it, and you did get caught . . ."

"It's sixteen months the first time, three to five the next time. You scared yet?"

Adrian shook his head.

"I'm not gonna get caught. This ain't my first rodeo." Allan leaned closer to Adrian and said seriously, "If you ever get caught, you just say, 'I didn't know it was stolen.' And that's all you say. What can they do? Just because you have it, doesn't mean you stole it, right?"

In the morning, the Acura was gone, and Allan stuffed five twenties into Adrian's shirt-pocket. "That's for you," he said. "The rest goes to keep the lights on for another month. Here and at the house."

Adrian reflected that it wasn't a lot of money for the risk involved, but on the other hand, he didn't know how much money Allan had received. It was a quick hundred bucks for him, and besides, Adrian hadn't stolen anything, now had he?

TWENTY-SEVEN

After the celebration on the night of Carmen's arrival, her father arose, bleary-eyed and hung over, to go to the hospital to fetch his newborn and her mother. Adrian had slept on the couch; Bobby had passed out on the floor, and now sat on the couch with his hands splayed out across his face, holding his head as if it might explode.

The house was in shambles. "This is another reason why I don't drink," Allan said, indicating the beer cans and empty pizza boxes strewn all over the living room. The curtains in front of the sliding glass door were askew. "What happened to the couch?"

The couch on which Bobby sat leaned forward and touched the floor along its front. "You threw Adrian onto it," he said.

"Actually, you picked me up and jumped on it with me," Adrian said. "We broke the front legs."

"Why did I do that?"

Adrian shrugged. "Celebratory joy, maybe?"

"Christ, what a mess. Do me a favor, would ya, Adrian? Get Randi over here to clean this place up a little? I should be back in an hour or so."

TWENTY-EIGHT

Randi was waiting at the house when the proud parents arrived home with the new baby. She had made the mess disappear; Eileen would later hear tales, but she didn't see any evidence that her husband had gone on a bender and practically wrecked the house. Randi even got Adrian and Bobby to scare up a couple of red bricks to put under the front corners of the couch. She had a similar set-up at her apartment: Gil could be an exuberant drunk on occasion, too.

Randi squealed and hugged Eileen in congratulations. She cooed over Carmen, but didn't ask to hold her. It was too soon for that. Randi hoped that she might be called upon to babysit when Eileen went back to work, but . . . This tiny creature hadn't even *been here* yesterday at this time. Randi vaguely remembered helping her mom when her brothers had been born, but she'd just been a little kid then. Babies were fragile; there'd be plenty of time for her to hold Carmen.

"Penny and Bellona asked if they could bring you a casserole. They figured that you wouldn't want to cook tonight."

"Who?"

"Adrian's aunts," Randi supplied. "I told them that the baby had arrived, and they immediately started bustling around in the kitchen and chittering like squirrels. They're great cooks."

Eileen collapsed on the couch and sighed. She wouldn't notice the busted legs until later. "I don't know, Randi, we just got home –"

"I think that sounds great," Allan said. He had gingerly removed the sleeping newborn from her car seat and was gazing tenderly at her. "A free meal's a free meal, and it's nice of them to offer. You're right – you just got home – why pass up a little help?"

Eileen nodded. She certainly wasn't in a mood to entertain the neighbors, but she wasn't in the mood to cook dinner, either.

"And besides. You'll get to meet Adrian." Randi grinned. "I'll go up and fetch them."

Allan and Eileen looked at Carmen in silence for a moment, then Allan kissed his wife. "I love you," he said. "She's so beautiful."

"I love you, too," Eileen replied. "And she is beautiful. She looks just like you. I don't see myself in her at all," Eileen added with a grin.

It was true. Carmen had the same nose, precisely the same eyebrows as her father. She was nearly bald, but the wisps of hair that she did have were blonde, like his. Carmen looked like him;

Allan didn't really know how to comment on how proud that made him feel.

A baby girl should look like her mother, he thought. But such was not the case in his new family, although the baby did have tan eyes, very close in hue to her mother's hazel ones. Carmen had not inherited Allan's blue-eyed genes.

There was a knock at the door, and Allan was saved from making further comparisons between his young bride and the child that, for all intents and purposes, looked like he *spit her out,* as his grandmother used to say of family resemblances. He opened it and admitted Randi and two little old ladies.

"Adrian'll be along in a minute," Randi assured them, then made introductions.

Allan felt a little out of place at the sudden hen party, so he accepted Penny and Bellona's congratulations, handed his daughter to her mother, and stepped out onto the porch to wait for Adrian.

Eileen had expected the ladies to be a little younger, but after a moment of conversation, she realized that they were not the as yet unmet Adrian's *mother's* sisters; they were the kid's *grandmother's* sisters. They were actually his *great-aunts.*

Bellona, the shorter one, asked if she could hold the baby, and Eileen dutifully gave Carmen to her. Her own mother had not been very grandmotherly – she had stopped in at the hospital, had peered in at Carmen through the nursery window. She was like Randi; she believed that a newborn baby was too delicate for everyone to be manhandling. "I'll pick her up when she can hold her head up," Mrs. Artus had told her daughter. "Until then, she's all yours."

But Bellona had no such reservations, and Eileen smiled at the old woman as she clucked and cooed, when she told Eileen that her baby was adorable.

The taller one also smiled and echoed her sister's appreciation. "We made you some lasagna," she said to Eileen.

"Thank you so much." Eileen arose from the couch and took a large, aluminum-foil-wrapped dish from Penny. "I love lasagna."

"It's an old family recipe, perfect for new mothers. It's not spicy or anything."

Eileen took the casserole out to the kitchen. She moved a few things around in the refrigerator, then slid the big dish onto the shelf. When she returned to the living room, Bellona was holding her daughter out to a tall, black-haired kid. He shook his head, smiled. He didn't want to hold the baby yet either.

Eileen stopped dead, gobsmacked. She closed her eyes; surely she was imagining this. But no, when she opened them again, he was still there. This stranger, standing beside Allan and Randi and the two little old ladies, was simply the best-looking, sexiest man Eileen had ever beheld. He was wearing a faded red tank top – it was August, it was very hot outside – *when did it get so hot in here?* The shirt showed off his flawless shoulders, his muscular arms. He was about six feet tall, taller than Allan, her husband, the father of her new baby. Allan suddenly looked like a stumpy, fat, blonde troll to Eileen, compared to this black-haired vision.

Eileen swallowed hard. *That's no way to be thinking about my husband,* she told herself, so she ceased thinking about him entirely and just stared at the gorgeous young man. *Who are you?*

Adrian looked over at her – he had the bluest eyes she'd ever seen. Eileen felt breathless, faint. *Oh, my God, he is incredible! Just like Randi said!*

Adrian heard Eileen's thoughts as clearly as if she had spoken them aloud. He blinked in surprise at their intensity, and glanced at Randi, then at Allan. But they were both making over the baby, along with his aunts, so he had no other choice but to look at Eileen again.

Adrian could read the new mother like a street sign; her attraction to him was undeniable, uncontrollable. It jolted him – it was the strongest that he had ever felt. She was undressing him with her eyes, but her expression wasn't sly or flirting; the things she was imagining filled her with wonder, with amazement. Adrian could *see* this sudden desire in his friend's wife: it crackled in her mind like the lightning bolts coming out of the high voltage tower in the old RKO Pictures logo.

"Are you all right?" Allan had at last looked in her direction.

Eileen tore her gaze away from Adrian and looked at her husband. She opened her mouth, discovered she was speechless, closed it again. Unable to stop herself, she looked at Adrian again.

Allan looked over his shoulder to see what had caught his wife's attention; Adrian blinked innocently at him. Allan looked back at Eileen, then again at Adrian. He told his wife, "This is Adrian."

The guitar player heard that one word, *incredible,* in his head again. Eileen hurried across the room, and Allan said, "Adrian, this is my wife, Eileen."

Adrian offered his hand, and Eileen took it in both of hers. He was sure she was going to tickle his palm with her finger, because he saw her think about it. But she restrained herself. *I'm a married woman, for God's sake! I just had a baby! I can't be making a pass at some random guy! But, oh, my God, he's so fine!*

Eileen didn't speak, nor did she release Adrian's hand. She just stared up at him, dumbstruck. He was absolutely incredible; never in Eileen's life had she been so instantaneously, utterly attracted to anyone. She hadn't even heard him speak yet, but still she longed to touch him, to run her fingers through his black hair. She wanted to kiss him, she wanted to . . . *Jesus, he's unbelievable!*

Before the moment could grow uncomfortable, before her husband could notice that she wasn't letting go of his hand, Adrian said, "Congratulations. Your baby is beautiful."

His voice was deep, full of life. *Full of promise,* Eileen thought. She wanted to hear him whisper her name, wanted to feel his breath, hot in her ear, on her neck . . .

Eileen seemed to come out of her trance at the mention of her newborn; she looked over at Carmen, still in Bellona's arms. Adrian used the opportunity to remove his hand from hers. She looked back at him and said, "Thank you."

Eileen suddenly felt like everyone was staring at her, so she held out her hands to retrieve her child. With Carmen in her arms, Eileen felt like she was again in control of herself. She would ponder the *incredibleness* of her husband's newest helper later. At length. Eileen kissed the baby on the forehead. "She looks just like her daddy," she said and smiled at Adrian.

Adrian looked at Allan; the painter narrowed his eyes and considered him with interest. *So he saw it, too,* Adrian thought. *Christ, who could miss it?*

Adrian grinned at Allan. "I think she's a lot prettier than he is." He held Allan's gaze – he knew better than to look at Eileen again – until Allan at last smiled.

"She's pretty like her mom," he said, and embraced mother and child.

There was a heartbeat of silence, during which Adrian noticed that now his aunts were also staring inquisitively at him. Then Penny said, "Well!" and looked at Eileen. "I'm sure you're exhausted, dear. We'll let you rest."

"If you need one little thing," Bellona said, "just send someone up to get us." She kissed Eileen on the cheek, gave her a little hug, said congratulations again.

111

"Thank you," Eileen said, as the sisters filed out the door, followed by Randi. "And thanks for the lasagna."

"Anytime, dear!"

Before Adrian had a chance to also follow, to escape, Eileen turned and said, "It was *so* nice to meet you, Adrian." *You incredible, blue-eyed masterpiece.* "Thanks for helping Allan."

"It's no trouble at all." Adrian clapped his friend on the back, so he wouldn't have to look at his wife anymore. "I'm guessing the shop's closed for the rest of the day?"

Allan still looked keenly at him. "Yeah. But I'll see you in the morning."

"Bright and early!" Adrian said, angling for the door. "It was nice meeting you, Eileen." He didn't wait for a reply, didn't wait to again hear her think about exactly how nice it had been to meet *him.* He slid out into the hot August air and loped quickly across the street to his house.

Allan watched him go, until Eileen sighed. He looked curiously at her, and again he asked, "Are you all right?"

"I'm fine," she said. Carmen opened her eyes and began to cry. "I'm just a little tired. I'm going to go lie down with your daughter for a while."

TWENTY-NINE

Eileen had six weeks of maternity leave, and anytime she was not actively engaged in the task at hand – feeding, bathing and playing with Carmen, or cooking dinner, or talking to her husband or her mother or Randi – she daydreamed about Adrian.

She had not thought it prudent to mention her abrupt, all-encompassing affection for her husband's employee to Randi, however. The black-haired girl had a crush on Adrian, too, and while neither of them was in a position to act upon their yearnings, Randi was surely in a better spot than Eileen. If Adrian gave her the word, all Randi would have to do was dump Gil. Eileen was married, had a baby; she considered herself on a higher level of maturity and responsibility than her part-time housekeeper. And since she was on a higher level, it just wouldn't do to wallow with Randi in a shared appreciation for Adrian Wilde.

But Eileen's appreciation was unqualified: she had never in her entire life been so wholly fascinated with anyone. She wanted to talk to him, listen to his voice; she wanted to get to know him. She wanted to kiss him; most of all, she wanted to . . . *Oh, my God, Adrian! What have you done to me?*

Eileen knew that she couldn't do anything but think about her all-encompassing desire for Adrian: she had a husband, a job, a house, a baby. She couldn't just throw all of that away for a dark-haired guitar player. Adrian wasn't interested in her – he hadn't even come back into the house since the day they'd met. Eileen glimpsed him at the gate sometimes, when he'd stop in the morning to walk up to the shop with Allan. But he hadn't come back inside, not even to say hi. Adrian wasn't interested in Eileen any more than he was interested in Randi.

And that's just as well, Eileen thought. Because if Adrian so much as hinted that he was interested . . . all the responsibility in the world, all the maturity – nay, *wild horses* – would not have stopped Eileen from answering his interest.

So Eileen didn't plot or scheme to actually possess Adrian. That would just be too ugly, too messy . . . unless he made some kind of move . . . But Adrian wasn't interested in her. He wouldn't even come back into the house.

But still, he was constantly in her mind. He was the first thing she thought about when she arose in the morning, the last thing when she drifted off to sleep. She thought about him when the baby woke her up in the middle of the night. All too rarely, she dreamt of him.

Allan sometimes stared at her, like he knew what she was thinking about, so Eileen made it a point to never mention her husband's helper. None of it was real. It was just a pleasant thing to think about. He was *incredible*.

THIRTY

Adrian managed to avoid running into Allan's wife for a month. But with two weeks still to go on her maternity leave, Eileen dropped in at the shop one day, out of the blue, transporting Carmen with her in a little carrier.

"I decided to take a walk up to the market," she said, by way of explanation.

It escaped neither Allan nor Adrian that Eileen had never come by the shop before. In his mind, Allan tried to explain it away – she had been pregnant before, then a brand-new mom. Now she was back to her old self, sleek and slim and ready to go back to work. Of course, she would want to see what her husband was doing, admire whatever old ride he was working on at the moment. Her visit didn't have anything to do with Adrian at all.

Adrian knew better. Even if he hadn't been able to read her mind, the reason was plain on her face: she wanted to *see* him, to stare at him. She wanted to think about all the things that she wanted to do to him, that she wanted him to do to her. Adrian thought she could not be more obvious if she dropped the baby carrier on the concrete floor and launched herself into his arms.

But Adrian couldn't read all that was in Eileen's mind. She was tired of waiting around for him to make visits to the house that he never made. So while she was at the grocery store the last time, she'd picked up one of those FunSaver disposable cameras. Eileen aimed to get a few pictures of *incredible* Adrian Wilde to aid in her daydreams about him.

And she wasn't above using Carmen as a prop in her scheme. She made small talk with her husband and his helper for a few minutes, until Adrian wandered outside and sat on one of the grimy white plastic chairs in front of the shop. When she saw that he was seated and couldn't escape, she said, "Here, Adrian, hold the baby," and plopped Carmen into his lap. "I want to get a couple of pictures of her." She pointed the camera at them. "Say, *cheese!*"

Eileen was able to take and wind off about three shots before her husband came outside and looked curiously at her. But she was ready for Allan and his suspicious looks. "Okay, now it's your turn!" she chirped, and indicated for the proud papa to sit and hold the baby. Allan complied without comment and Eileen took a few more pictures. "Just like Olan-Mills!" she said.

No one would ever know that this exercise in motherly photography didn't have anything to do with being motherly at all. Eileen already had hundreds of pictures of her daughter. Now she wanted a few of Adrian.

When her task was completed, there was an awkward silence: Allan watched his wife stare at the guitar player for what seemed like minutes, until at last she said, "Well, we'd better get on up to the market." Eileen retrieved Carmen from her father's arms and deposited her back into her carrier. She hugged and kissed her husband, but couldn't just leave without saying, "Goodbye, Adrian."

Adrian waved silently.

Allan watched his wife and baby toddle off up the street, then said, "Come into the office with me a minute, boy."

Adrian followed. Allan sat behind the scarred and chipped old desk. It was devoid of paperwork: Allan did all his business verbally, legitimate or otherwise, and took payment only in cash. There was a sign on the wall, though, which never failed to amuse Adrian:

Hourly Rates
$65.00 per hour
$75.00 per hour if you watch
$85.00 per hour if you ask questions
$100.00 per hour if you help
$125.00 per hour if you ask when it'll be done
$135.00 per hour if you complain about when it'll be done
$150.00 per hour if you worked on it first, then brought it
in for us to fix it

Allan gestured at the chair opposite; Adrian sat. Allan sighed and folded his hands on the desk in front of him. "I've got something to ask you," he said. "And I'm only gonna ask you once."

Adrian nodded. He knew what was coming. If there had been astronauts in orbit, he reckoned that they would know, too. His friend's wife's desire was just that unmistakable.

"I haven't failed to notice that Eileen has taken a shine to you."

You have no idea, Adrian thought, but kept his expression neutral. "Happens to me all the time," he said, smiling, thinking humor might be a good tack.

It wasn't. Allan didn't smile back. He stared at Adrian for a heartbeat, then looked down at the desk, wiped some of the dust off of it.

"She likes Don Johnson, too. But I'm not concerned that Don's gonna drive out here from Miami in his Ferrari and sweep her off her feet. So she can like Don all she wants." Allan shrugged, then looked back at Adrian again. "You, on the other hand . . . You're right here in River City. You're the same age as she is, and you live right across the fucking street." Allan glowered; Adrian remained expressionless.

Again Allan looked down at the desk. "Don't get me wrong. She can like whoever she wants." Now Allan looked up and skewered Adrian with his light blue eyes, full of threat. "It takes two. So, I'm asking you, guitar player – my young wife likes you – what do you plan to do about that?"

"I can't help it if your wife likes me, Allan," Adrian replied slowly. "Randi likes me, too, and I already got a similar speech from her boyfriend. I'm kinda getting tired of you people threatening me." Adrian dared to grin, then added quickly, "Although I'm about as afraid of Gil as I am of the wind blowing."

Despite the gravity of the situation, one corner of Allan's mouth twitched up in a grin; derision about fear of nothing, *of the wind blowing,* was one of his favorite expressions.

"Randi could be had for the asking . . . But, here's the deal. I don't want someone else's woman. Not her, and certainly not your wife. I don't care about her ol' man – he's an asshole.

"But you're my friend, Allan. I would never – you're married, you've got a little girl, for Christ's sake. Even if you weren't around, that's way more responsibility than I could handle. You've got my word, Allan. I am in no way, shape or form interested in your wife. Not now, not in any future I could imagine." Adrian grinned again. "No matter how much she likes me."

Allan considered him sternly for another moment, then smiled. "That's all I needed to hear. You're right – you can't help it if she likes you. I trust you." Allan paused. "But I had to say something . . . She doesn't hide it very well."

She doesn't hide it at all, Adrian thought. *She's not capable of hiding it. The things she thinks* . . . "No harm, no foul," he said, then reiterated, "You have my word."

"That's all I need," Allan repeated. "Let's go look at that Pontiac."

Adrian was true to his word – he wasn't interested in Eileen. She was cute enough, but she was bad-ass Allan's wife, the mother of his kid, and thereby, she wasn't that cute. Besides, she was ridiculous in her naked desire. After she went back to work, when she came into the shop, she stared at him, open-mouthed. If there was space to sit next to him, Eileen sat next to him, even though Adrian would immediately get up and sit someplace else. And then he would find some reason to make himself scarce at the soonest opportunity.

Sometimes, Allan would frown at her, but he usually just ignored it. What was he going to say? *Quit looking at this kid like you want to eat him?* It was a delicate situation for Adrian: he couldn't insult Eileen, or tell her to get lost, tell her to leave him alone. That would offend her husband.

So Adrian pretended to be afraid of her; he pretended to be afraid of Allan. When Eileen made goo-goo eyes at him, he would look fearfully at her husband, as if Allan might suddenly become aware of his wife's thoughts – *Christ,* the things she thought – and have a mind to kick Adrian's ass. It was not the case – Allan and Adrian had had their talk – Allan trusted his friend. But it was the only method Adrian could think of that might dissuade Eileen from gaping at him.

Adrian's policy of zero encouragement didn't work; Eileen continued to stare hungrily at him whenever their paths crossed. But Adrian was confident in Allan's trust, and he really wasn't afraid of either husband or wife. He didn't want Eileen, regardless of the situation – she was just too damned obvious.

Adrian thought that Eileen would be like one of those clingy women of which his uncle told tales. Gummy. Sticky. Way too attached. Even if there was no Allan; she was cute enough, but she liked him *too much,* and she didn't even know him. She was just like Randi.

Adrian wanted a girl with a little more mystery, maybe one that wasn't immediately so sure, maybe one he would have to use a little charm upon before she gave in. One who wasn't all decided simply because of his looks; one whose mind wasn't so easy for him to read.

And overwhelmingly, Adrian wanted to feel the same kind of grand devotion for a girl that he saw in his dad's eyes whenever he looked at Daina. The infatuated Randis and Eileens of the world were all right – if they were single. But Adrian didn't want to get too involved with any of them. It was okay that they loved him, but he made it a point not to encourage them.

Adrian thought he'd know the right girl when he met her. She would be the one that he couldn't live without.

THIRTY-ONE

On Tuesday night, June 26th, 1990, Allan and Adrian stole a 1969 Stingray that was left unfortunately unsupervised in the unpatrolled parking lot at General Hospital. Corvettes were too hard to move in one piece, Allan told Adrian, so by the following Sunday, the only components left were the chassis, the engine, and the drivetrain. Allan had secured buyers for every single other part of it.

A middle-aged man driving another Corvette came by the shop on the second of July to look at what was left. Allan was suspicious. It wasn't like he'd advertised *Hot 'Vette parts for sale* in the local *PennySaver.*

The Chevy owner told Allan that he'd just serendipitously *heard* that the chassis and engine were available. "A friend of Eddie's told me." The guy smiled expansively.

"I don't know any one named Eddie," Allan said.

"How about Benjamin?" The guy shoved an envelope crammed full of hundreds, fifties and twenties into Allan's grimy paws. It was more than sufficient, and Allan nodded. "I'll be back with a trailer in the morning," the guy said, and left.

All the dead presidents hadn't entirely alleviated Allan's suspicions, however. "I want you to take this money to your house," he told Adrian, as he watched the guy drive away. "All of it. Hide it. If this goes south . . ."

"What's wrong?"

"Maybe nothing. I just didn't care for that guy too much."

The following morning, Adrian and Allan were sitting in the tiny office when two deputy sheriffs kicked the door in, guns drawn, and ordered them to lie on the ground. They complied without argument. The cops handcuffed them and sat them back in their chairs.

"What seems to be the trouble, officer?" Allan said amiably.

"You're under arrest. Suspicion of grand theft auto. You have the right to –"

"No, no, Vickers." The detective waltzed in, grinning. "Please allow me. Adrian, my dear friend."

Adrian hung his head, and Allan looked at him in astonishment. The good-looking guitar player from down the street was apparently on a first name basis with the law. That wasn't good.

"You have the right to remain silent. Anything you say can and will be used against you in a court of law. You have the right to an attorney. If you cannot afford an attorney, one will be provided for you. Do you understand the rights I have just read to you? With these rights in mind, do you wish to speak to me?"

"No, sir, Detective Chalmers. Sir. Not at this time."

"Why am I not surprised? What about you?" Detective Chalmers looked at Allan, who shook his head. The cop looked back at Adrian. "You're going down, Lover Boy. You should'nt've tried to sell that 'Vette back to the guy you stole it from."

Adrian looked back at him impassively. It was an expression that he'd learned from his Aunt Penny. "How's AnneMarie?"

Chalmers backhanded Adrian, shocking bad-ass Allan into blinking stupidity. Adrian was on a first name basis with the law, but the law seemed to have a bone to pick with him. This must be the cop-daddy that had caught Adrian in the kip with his daughter. Oh, shit. This day was just getting worse and worse.

Adrian grinned, spit a mouthful of blood onto the concrete. *He's got some guts for a kid*, Allan thought with admiration. *He's not afraid.*

Like something out of a bad cop drama, the detective snarled, "Get 'em out of here," and the uniforms hustled Adrian and Allan into separate patrol cars, then the one carrying Allan sped off.

Chalmers had the other deputy roll down the window so he could speak to the remaining handcuffed captive. "You don't have to go to prison, Adrian. You're just a kid; this is the first time you've been in trouble."

"Been checking up on me, have you, Detective?" Again Adrian grinned. His teeth were pink with blood.

"Let me explain this to you, smart-ass," Chalmers replied. He gestured at the open garage. "I see that the VIN plate's gone. No doubt, your buddy's gonna say that he bought a rolling chassis and drivetrain to part out, so he hadn't been worried about the missing VIN plate. You better hope to Christ we don't find it lying around here somewhere. Without a VIN plate, you're thinking, there's no way to prove whose car that is.

"But you're wrong, Adrian. You must be new to the stolen car game, though I'll bet your buddy's not. The engine has its own ID and VIN, and it's stamped right on the block. He knows that – he just thought he'd get rid of it before anybody checked. But that car's owner kept very accurate records. You cut up one of his babies, you see. He's got the paperwork. That's his car. You're going to jail, boy." The detective smiled, shark-like. "Unless you make a deal. Unless you roll over on your buddy."

120

Adrian blinked in innocent surprise. "You're telling me that chassis's stolen?"

Chalmers nodded. "You know it is."

Adrian shook his head, said the only six words that he could be compelled to say, throughout the ordeal that was to come. "I didn't know it was stolen."

Adrian spent Wednesday, the 4th of July, 1990, his twentieth birthday, in jail.

His parents threw his bail, of course, but it was Ian alone that showed up when he got out. Adrian tried to read his dad, as always, and as always, he failed. He got only watchful solemnity, which was what anyone would get, just from the look on Ian's face.

"What's going on, son?"

"We didn't know it was stolen, Dad." That response had gotten him this far; Adrian didn't plan on deviating from it now. *The truth is what ya make it,* Adrian said to himself. "A good lawyer –"

"There'll be plenty of time for all that," Ian began as they drove home. "Rob already called his guy. I'm not worried about your day in court. Right now – you're mother's distraught, Adrian. You know how she gets."

Adrian nodded. He knew exactly how she got. Adrian owed most of his confidence to his mother; he had never been at a loss on how to behave in any situation, growing up – he couldn't read his mother's thoughts, but he could read her emotions. It was like having a translator for the adult world on hand at all times. Adrian would be calm in the face of strange situations, simply because his mother was calm.

The first day of school had been a breeze because Daina had smiled and greeted his teacher, so Adrian knew that the tall, scary-looking man with the hooked nose was all right, even if he did look a little menacing. Mom was okay with him, so he had to be okay – and he was. The same with his first guitar lesson – Mr. Johnson always came off as a little stern to his new pupils. But Daina liked him immediately, so Adrian knew he really wasn't the hard-ass he appeared to be; and he wasn't.

As a child, Adrian was never nervous in a new situation if his mom was with him, and this had blossomed into self-confidence, and more than a little daring as he'd gotten older, as recent events would attest.

Daina had even contributed to Adrian's confidence with the opposite sex.

Even though they didn't live in the district where he taught, it had been arranged for Adrian to attend Ian's middle school. Adrian was in the eighth grade, would turn fourteen in July, after the term ended. Ian had been picked to be one of the judges for the annual Science Fair, and his wife and son and Aunt Bellona had accompanied him for an evening at school.

Adrian didn't have an entry: he played guitar, and didn't have time to make a simple electric motor out of a Duracell and a magnet, had no interest in cobbling together a solar hot dog cooker. But it was pleasant to spend time with his mom and dad and his aunt, on his dad's home turf. Adrian was just starting to notice girls, and he enjoyed looking at his female peers, although none of them had really started looking back at him yet.

The woman at the superintendent's office had been shrewd in placing charming Mr. Wilde at the eighth grade level. At a time in their lives when the little boys Ian taught were just starting to consider the little girls – the little girls saw only little boys. They were looking curiously at older, teenaged boys and even grown men. But they were not yet mature enough to do anything more than look.

As the lady at the superintendent's office would have predicted, the little girls gathered eagerly around Mr. Wilde. He grinned at his wife over their heads.

"That's going to be you soon, Adrian," his mother told him.

Adrian smiled wryly. "I can only hope, Mom."

He looked over at his dad again, listening indulgently to the gaggle of 8th Grade girls that all thought he was dreamy. As a Science Fair Judge, they might've just been angling for his vote, but Adrian knew better. All of his female peers just *liked* his dad – he had overheard Ian tell Daina that he thought it was the only reason that the administration had placed him on the panel for the Science Fair: his presence inspired the little girls to try for the prize. There was the blue ribbon, of course; but what all the budding Marie Curies and Mary Leakeys really sought was praise from Mr. Wilde. Maybe even a smile.

"Your dad just has a way with the ladies, Adrian," Aunt Bellona said with a little twinkle in her eyes. "Young or old, his charm ensorcells them. He is quite unaware of it."

"Oh, he's aware of it," Daina countered.

She thought of the life she shared with Ian. Their love was equal, in her mind; she worshipped Ian as much as he worshipped her. But she knew that her sexy, blue-eyed husband didn't see it that way. Ian

122

was a slave to a yen for her that had never diminished, but he seemed unaware that Daina was slave to the same yen.

Daina had never looked at another man from the moment that she'd met Ian; she was in thrall to his body, his smile, the things he did behind closed doors. She had often reflected that had Ian been of a nefarious bent, all of her own morality would've gone out the window. She would've done anything he requested – rob a bank, steal a car – she was just that devoted to him.

But Ian had never seen their love that way. He had always believed that it was the opposite – *he* was the slave, he would do anything that *Daina* requested. He never realized that he had all the power; he thought it all resided with her. Theirs was the best possible relationship: an identical obsession. Daina often remembered her Aunt's words from childhood, when Daina hadn't even know what love meant: *Heed me: you will share a love, as Romeo and Juliet, as Anthony and Cleopatra, as Napoleon and Josephine.* Ian was Daina's other half. She would never love another.

But Daina always thought that Ian was a little free with his charms. It wasn't jealousy that she felt: Daina was secure in Ian's love for her alone. But she felt that he allowed all the women that were attracted to him to take advantage, to waste his time. All the little girls gathered around him now – he knew that they weren't interested in advice on their science fair exhibits, but still he listened attentively to each and every one. Daina thought she may have been unfair about the little girls – paying attention to them was his job, after all.

But Ian allowed adult women to take advantage of him, also: the twenty-something English teacher who always asked for his help with lesson plans; the middle-aged women at the grocery store who sometimes asked him to help them put their groceries in the car, like he was a bag-boy. Ian knew what they really wanted, and he and Daina both knew that he wasn't going to give it to them. So why did he bother catering to them?

Daina said this to her son. "Your dad wastes his time, being so nice to all the ladies." Adrian looked at her in surprise. He looked for jealousy in her statement, but found none.

Daina gestured at his dad. "This is what you are," she said simply. "You can let all the pretty girls waste your time, Adrian, just because they like you. Like your dad does." She smiled at the string of giggling teens that were following Ian as he went around to each exhibit, making notes on a clipboard. "Or this is what you could be."

Daina nodded at Mr. Johnson, who stood by the door, talking to the principal. He smiled and waved at Daina and she smiled and waved back.

Mr. Johnson was also an attractive man, though several years older than Ian. *Whether they're in their thirties or their forties, dreamy teachers are all the same to teenage girls,* Daina thought wryly. *Teacher, teacher, teach me love, I can't learn it fast enough.* And he was a musician, another aspect to fire the imaginations of women, young and old.

Daina was sure that many of his young charges started off the school year with a crush on Mr. Johnson, just like they did on Mr. Wilde, but she imagined that these girlish dreams didn't last very long.

Daina had observed women her own age, mothers of his pupils, try vainly to flirt with him when they picked up their children from lessons at his house. But Mr. Johnson was a Christian man, devoted to his wife and family. Daina wouldn't go so far as to say that he was cold, but he was certainly austere. He was friendly, but business-like. He didn't smile and converse and *indulge* the women that took a shine to him, the way her husband did.

Adrian waited for further clarification from his mother. He wasn't yet fourteen, after all, and wasn't entirely sure just what it was she was trying to impart to him. "Don't let girls waste your time, Adrian," she said at last. "The ones you like . . . Well, treat them well. But the ones that you don't have any . . ."

"Use for," Aunt Bellona threw in and giggled.

Daina smiled at her aunt, then at her son, who was still a few years away from having any *use* for women. "The ones that you're not . . . interested in . . . Don't let them waste your time. Don't fuel their hopes. Be polite, but be . . . a little more distant than your dad. Or else you'll never get rid of them."

"You're in control, Capo," Aunt Bellona added. "Always remember that. Be poised."

"Not so . . . *familiar,"* Daina said and smiled at her husband again, still trailed by his adoring students.

"Always realize your power, Adrian," Aunt Bellona said and winked at him. "Look at a situation from all angles. Use a little self-control, and you'll always be able to turn things to your advantage."

And Adrian had taken his mother and aunt's advice to heart. He never chased after girls he didn't really want, just because he knew he could catch them. He could read their thoughts, after all. He had liked AnneMarie, but in retrospect, he thought what he liked best about her was that he had sensed that she wasn't the type that thought she was in love with him.

Adrian sought what his parents had: a mutual attraction. The girls he chose, he liked them well enough, but he had never felt that all-consuming love and desire for a girl that he saw in his dad for his mom, so he was aloof to women, indifferent.

Like his father's once upon a time, feigned innocence, Adrian was not unaware that his standoffishness made him all the more attractive to them, however. He was by no means a choir boy – from the time he was seventeen, Adrian Wilde could more or less get any woman that he wanted – but he was picky. He was sure he didn't want any of the clingy ones, the ones that thought they had achieved love at first sight the moment they cast peepers on him – so he took his mother's advice and didn't lead them on; he didn't allow women he didn't want to waste his time.

Adrian had always gotten his best advice from his mother.

But the last couple of years, from about the time he started driving, Adrian sometimes sensed a groundless, inchoate fear in his mom, and that fear had made him afraid at first. If Mom was fearful, there was something dangerous around, even if Adrian couldn't see it.

He remembered the time he had tried to peel an orange with a butcher knife when he was about seven – another time when a little precognition, absent, would've served him well. *Just like when Allan suggested that we drive by that big ol' dark parking lot at the hospital,* Adrian thought. A little *cryptesthesia,* as his Aunt Penny often called it, a little paranormal perception, would've certainly been welcome. *Maybe then I would've seen what a dumb ass move this was going to turn out to be . . .*

He'd tried to peel that orange with the big knife – *another dumb ass move,* Adrian recalled. He'd cut three fingers, but not severely. It didn't hurt very much, but it bled, and Adrian was fascinated with his own injury for a moment. He was standing in the kitchen watching his fingers bleed when his mom came in.

"I cut myself, Mom," he said matter-of-factly, and held up his bloody hand.

"Oh, my, God! Adrian!"

Daina dashed across the kitchen and Adrian felt the fear roll off of her like a heavy, icy wave as she took his hand and quickly held it under the tap. The cold water bit, and suddenly being cut wasn't so interesting anymore. The bleeding didn't stop immediately, and as Daina alternately held a wash cloth to his fingers, then examined them, Adrian felt her worry, her fear, and reckoned all at once that he might just bleed to death. Mom was frightened, and if Mom was frightened, Adrian became frightened, too.

At last the cuts stopped oozing gore, and Daina put a little Band-Aid on each of them, and kissed his fingers. "All better," she said. "If you want something peeled, ask me or your dad. No more giant knives, okay?"

Adrian's distress lasted another heartbeat. "Okay." He hugged her, and felt that she was calm again, and his own fear faded.

Adrian hadn't been a clumsy child. The thing with the knife had been a one-off; it had just been too big for his usually dexterous hands. There had been the time he when was nine and he'd dumped his bicycle in the street: a moment's inattention, a little rock, and he had gone flying over the handlebars, and had scraped one arm from baby-finger to elbow. But Daina hadn't been around for that calamity; she'd been up at his aunts' house, and Ian had doctored him up. "Don't show your mom," he'd said. "She'll have a cow."

Adrian waterskied with his dad and his cousins, but his mother didn't come along very often. He didn't play sports; he played the guitar. So, growing up, Adrian didn't often have cause to be fearful because of his mother's unwarranted fears for his safety.

But once he turned sixteen, once he started driving – if he was five minutes late coming home, when he walked in the door, Adrian would again feel his mother's terror, followed by her relief when she saw that he was okay. Daina's anxiety was always palpable, almost like smoke in the room. Adrian loved his mother, so these episodes puzzled him more than annoyed him, and he always called immediately if he was going to be late so she wouldn't worry.

But Adrian could never understand *why* she was *so afraid* – he was a safe driver. He wasn't out drinking or getting into fights. Nick had come home from school just last week with a black eye and *his* mother hadn't freaked out. Adrian figured that Daina was just a protective parent; he knew that other than his dad, his mother loved nothing in the world more than her only child. So after a while, he came to ignore her sudden baseless, irrational fears.

Adrian hadn't been thinking about his mother's love or her worry when he and Allan had boosted that Chevy out of the hospital parking lot. He had the guts to do such a stupid thing, the confidence, the daring, because for most of his life his mother hadn't been afraid, and she'd passed her own fearlessness and confidence on to him.

But now he'd gone and gotten himself arrested, had spent the night and the better part of the next day in jail. It surely hadn't been a bed of roses, but no one had bothered him. It was uncomfortable, and demeaning, but Adrian hadn't been afraid. But he knew that Daina had been afraid *for* him.

Now, driving home with his dad, Adrian wasn't worried that his mother would be ashamed of him – he hadn't known the car was stolen, right? And he would never do anything like this again, because nobody was going to believe that the next time. It had been fun, an adventure. Adrian had to admit that maybe he had admired Allan's own brazen audacity a little too much to let himself get talked into such a thing.

A mutual appreciation had developed between Allan and Adrian over the months they'd spent together. Allan always took time off to listen to Adrian's band rehearse, and never failed to compliment him on his skill with his instrument. Adrian admired Allan for his artistry and guts. But this whole deal with the cut-up Corvette was *beyond the pale,* as his dad would've said. Adrian had allowed his admiration for a criminal to run away with him.

And just as his close personal friend Detective Chalmers had said, Adrian had never been in trouble before. He was sure Rob's no doubt high-priced lawyer would get him off with a slap on the wrist.

Daina wouldn't be ashamed of her boy – he had just taken a little misstep.

But, oh, Christ, how she must've worried! Adrian thought guiltily. Her baby boy in the slammer overnight, with junkies and gangsters and murderers! Lions and tigers and bears.

Adrian suddenly remembered the time, when he was twelve, when he'd discovered a lady's wallet, left behind in the cart at the store. It had just been him and his Aunt Penny.

There was no cash in it, just credit cards and a driver's license, an ATM card, the family's Kaiser Hospital cards. Penny said, "What shall we do with it, Capo?"

Adrian thought that had there been money in it, he would've kept that. Adrian was a good kid, but he had more than a touch of miscreancy in his soul. Even at twelve years old, he knew that there were realms outside of that which could be seen. He knew that they *could be* seen by those with the right kind of eyes, the right kind of perception – and he had always encompassed a touch of superiority, a scintilla of corruption because of this knowledge.

But, he'd considered at the time, maybe finders keepers, losers weepers wasn't the way to be thinking. He looked at his aunt – she was expressionless, impossible to read, as always. Adrian would have to come to his own decision.

"We should take it to her," he said at last.

Penny smiled then, a rarity which he always enjoyed. Adrian knew he had made the right choice.

When they knocked on the door, the woman's husband answered, and they saw the lady seated at the kitchen table. They could tell she'd been crying.

Penny let Adrian do the talking. "We found this at the market. Your address was on –"

"Oh, thank you so much!" the woman flew to the door, hugged Adrian, much to his discomfiture. He read suspicion from the man – he thought that maybe Adrian had stolen the wallet, and the old woman was making him return it. The lady said, "Let me run to the bank – give you a reward for being such an honest young man!"

"That's okay," Adrian said immediately, and he sensed that the woman's husband was reevaluating him. Maybe he wasn't a thief after all.

"Are you sure?" he asked.

"I'm sure," Adrian replied.

The woman hugged him again, said thanks again, then they went back into the house.

As Adrian and Penny walked to the car, she asked, "Why didn't you let her give you a reward, Capo?"

Adrian shrugged. He hadn't wanted to wait around while the woman went to the bank, and besides – "I didn't do anything to be rewarded for. It was just the right thing to do."

"Indeed." Penny offered him another smile – that was two in one day. Adrian knew she was proud of him. "We should always do right because it's right. Not because of hope for reward." She studied him for a moment. "And we shouldn't do wrong because it's wrong. Fear of punishment for doing wrong shouldn't be the reason for not doing it. If fear of the stick is the only basis for our morality, and for some reason the stick is removed – then we have anarchy."

Adrian had not considered the stick this time: he had done wrong, and he'd done it because he didn't fear punishment, not from the law or from his parents. He'd gotten caught, and that was enough of a lesson for him. Do wrong if you can get away with it, but don't be a dumb ass and do wrong for fun and then get caught.

Adrian didn't feel bad about his crime; he didn't really even feel bad about getting caught. It had learned him, put him back on the path on which he'd been raised. Adrian might be a little wicked, but he was no thief. This theft had been fun and exciting, but jail had not been. Like a contagion, Adrian had caught larceny from Allan. But the Gray-bar Hotel had cured him. Overnight, as a matter of fact.

He didn't feel bad about stealing the guy's car, even though he wouldn't do anything even remotely so stupid again. But Adrian felt bad about the terror he knew his mother had encompassed for his sake, what she must've gone through, just because he'd let his darker nature have a free reign. Just because he'd been slumming with a criminal, being a dumb ass.

Adrian felt horrible about his mother's worry, worse than he'd felt about anything in his life.

The house was dark when he and Ian arrived. "She's up with your aunts," his dad told him, and Adrian turned to go and find her, to tell her he was sorry, to show her that he was all right. He wanted to make her fear go away – he thought that he could feel it from down here.

Ian remained standing in the doorway. "You're not coming?" Adrian asked in surprise.

His father's dark blue eyes, so like his own, mirrored his surprise. "She wants to see *you,* right now, not me. Besides, I've seen her cry enough. I'll be along in a minute. And Adrian?"

"Yes?"

"Don't do anything like this to her again. You know how she worries about you."

"We didn't know it was stolen, Dad," Adrian began, but at the look his father gave him, he shut up.

It didn't matter what he had done, only that he had caused that fear in his mother. Ian's acknowledgment of this fact cut Adrian, wounded him. Ian could be mad, he could be ashamed – his son had *stolen a car,* for Christ's sake, for no other reason than it was fun, easy, and he could – but Ian didn't care about any of it.

Adrian realized in that moment that he couldn't remember a time in his life when his dad had so much as raised his voice to him. But he was disappointed now, not because of the hot car, but because Adrian had hurt his mother, the woman that Ian loved above all others.

"Never again, Dad," Adrian said. "I promise."

"Go on then." Ian remained expressionless. "I'll see you in a minute."

"I'm sorry, Dad." He'd never been so sorry for anything in his life.

"Go see your mom, son." Ian closed the door.

Adrian sprinted up the path, up the steps to the deck. It seemed like all the lights in the house were on, like beacons, welcoming him. His aunts and his mother were sitting around the little table in the corner, like he'd always seen them, his whole life. Adrian knew he'd made a mistake, been a little cavalier with right and wrong; but seeing his womenfolk made him know for sure that everything would be okay.

It didn't take mind reading for him to know that his mother would say, *"Oh, my, God! Adrian!"* It didn't take second sight for him to foretell that she would leap up and hug him. Adrian felt her fear when she spoke, her relief when she embraced him. It was like a sudden spring downpour, and again he felt guilty for making her afraid for him.

"I'm okay, Mom," he said, and hugged her tightly, kissed the top of her head. He was taller than her, and she felt small, almost frail in his arms. He wiped the tears from her eyes, felt his own well up at her pain. "I'm so sorry, Mom!" he said and hugged her again.

"We're just glad that you're all right, Adrian," Aunt Bellona said. She smiled at him, then her face went somber.

"We need to talk, Capo," Penny said with a stern frown. "Have a seat."

"I didn't know it was stolen, Aunt Penny," Adrian said, wondering how many more times he was going to have to repeat the words. *At least a few more,* he thought with resignation.

Penny curtly waved her hand. "Never mind about that. Sit."

Adrian did as he was told. Daina sat next to him in the other chair. She hadn't said a word other than, *Oh, my, God! Adrian!*

Penny ignored her sister and her niece; she stared directly at the wayward guitar player for a moment. Then she said quietly, "You're gonna die, boy."

Adrian opened his mouth to say, "What?" but at the gasp from his mother and his other aunt he closed it again.

Now Penny looked at them. "It's time he knew. Then maybe he'll guide himself accordingly. Maybe he'll be a little more careful with the time he has left, and stop doing stupid shit like stealing cars." The profanity stung Adrian like a slap: he'd never heard his erudite, poetic aunt utter a curse word; a rare curse, perhaps, but never a curse *word*.

"I didn't know it was stolen, Aunt Penny," Adrian repeated.

"So you've said. Tell it to the judge. I've got bigger fish to fry." Penny sighed, but neither her tone nor her expression softened. "When your mother was barely more than a child, we foresaw that she would someday bear a child of her own. A clever, exceptional boy, he would be the joy of her life, and so you have been, up until this little piece of senseless mischief."

Adrian considered daring to smile, thought better of it, and remained expressionless.

"We also saw that you wouldn't have a long life, Adrian. You've already reached eighteen, your first legal majority. You can now get married, sign a contract, go to war —"

"Go to jail," Bellona noted with a tiny grin, which came and went in a flash.

"But you can't yet buy a drink," Penny continued, ignoring her sister. "That is also considered *majority.*" She sighed again. "The auguries have always remained maddeningly vague. Only that word. *He will reach his majority.* You have passed one such milestone — but what does the word actually mean? Eighteen, twenty-one? When you get married? Buy a house?"

"When I inherit one?" Adrian said flippantly.

"Very doubtful," Bellona said darkly, and her words chilled Adrian. He felt his mother's fear again and squeezed her hand. "Far sooner than that," Bellona added. Then she suddenly, inexplicably brightened. "There is a way for you to live on, however, Capo, through an ancient means. All you need is a woman. We were thinking perhaps Eileen —"

"Eileen?" Adrian and Daina said in unison. Adrian added, "Allan's *wife?"*

"Ask again later," Penny said and glared at her sister. "Not Eileen, Bell. I've seen that her path and Adrian's path will soon diverge. For him to continue . . . It won't be through Eileen."

Adrian laughed. *"This dream is all amiss interpreted!"* It was something he'd heard his father say once. "You've got it all wrong, Aunt Bellona! Sure, Eileen likes me. That's undeniable." Adrian rolled his eyes. They had no doubt seen it on the day when they had all met. *"Inescapable.* But Allan already knows. I gave him my word. He's not going to kill me because his wife —"

"Forget about all that, Adrian." Penny shook her head firmly. "Your fate was foretold long before you were born. It has nothing to do with Allan and Eileen."

"But he needs to find some woman!" Bellona insisted. *"The Incantations of Thoth –"*

"Belay all that now." Again Penny shook her head. "You're not going to die today, boy. You don't need a woman yet. When the time comes . . . We'll find her for you."

THIRTY-TWO

Adrian held his mother's hand as they walked down the path to their house, just like he had done when he was a little boy. "Do you really believe I'm gonna die, Mom?" he asked quietly.

Daina looked up at him, her eyes brimming with tears. "I've lived with it since I was fourteen, Adrian. They told me I would meet the love of my life, our love would endure, but our son . . . There would be a *tragic blot*. When you were three, you fell down the deck stairs –"

"Really? I don't remember that."

"You weren't hurt. But I freaked out –"

Adrian smiled. "You tend to do that."

"I've lived with this my whole life, Adrian," she said, and her son stopped smiling. No wonder she was afraid for him all the time. "Penny said it then – the tragic blot was that you were going to die. Your dad said –"

"Dad knows about this?"

Daina nodded. "They said you would reach your majority. Your dad said not to worry about it 'til then, and I've tried. But you'll be twenty-one in a year." She sobbed and hugged him.

Adrian hugged her back. "You know this is ridiculous, Mom."

Daina sniffled and regained her composure. "That's called *denial,* son. Just like me, you've been cursed with them your whole life. You've seen their predictions –"

"Old cats disappearing. Freak rainstorms. I wouldn't exactly say they're Nostradamus."

"They're never wrong."

Adrian perceived that his mother was steadfast. She entirely believed that he might not have more than another year to live. He knew that he couldn't talk her out of it, so he thought it best to play up to her delusion. "Bellona said something about . . . I could . . . *go on?* Something about . . . a woman? *The Incantations of Thoth?"*

"I don't know, Adrian. They've never mentioned anything like that before. But you can be sure I'm gonna find out."

THIRTY-THREE

The charges against Allan and Adrian were knocked down from grand theft auto to receiving stolen goods. Adrian's conviction would be sealed and would fall off his record after ten years – *if I live that long,* he thought – because it was his first time in any trouble, and because he was not yet twenty-one, and because he had a very, very good lawyer. Allan was given three years' probation, didn't do any time. Even the whiff of involvement with anything hot, however, and they'd both be going back to jail.

Detective Chalmers reminded Adrian of this, after sentence had been pronounced. Again, Adrian felt as though he was in trapped in a cop show: his mom and dad had gone to get the car, and he was standing on the courthouse steps, waiting for them to come back and pick him up. Allan had disappeared like a summer mist, immediately after court.

AnneMarie's dad was no Sonny Crockett, but the same menace was in his voice, even if the linen suit was missing.

"You skated this time, Adrian."

"We didn't know it was stolen," Adrian repeated, grinning. "I told you that all along."

"Right. Here's what I'm gonna tell you. It's time you found a better class of friends. Get a real job. Go to school."

"Where's AnneMarie going to school these days?" Adrian smiled brightly.

He didn't believe that Detective Chalmers had suddenly morphed into the good cop. During the interrogation, he'd told Adrian, "Your buddy rolled over on you, my boy. Said it was all your idea."

"I didn't know it was stolen," Adrian replied.

He would find out that Chalmers had told Allan the same thing. "The kid said you made him do it."

"I didn't know it was stolen," Allan had also replied. "I bought it like you saw it from some guy. I think his name might've been Eddie. I didn't know it was stolen."

By sticking to the script, by having faith in each other, the Corvette thieves had indeed skated. There just hadn't been enough evidence to prove that it had been they, and not the mythical Eddie, who had actually taken the entire car, because the entire car was a whole lot more than what they'd been apprehended with.

Now Adrian smiled at the detective. "Is she still going to Arizona State? My cousin's got a little house in Parker. Maybe I could look her up some weekend."

Detective Chalmers shook his head. "Always the smart-ass, aren't you? I'm trying to give you a little bit of fatherly advice –"

"I've already got a father, Detective. And you're not even in the same league with him."

"Maybe not. I wouldn't've made it as a schoolteacher. But he didn't teach you not to steal cars, did he?"

"We didn't know it was –"

"Save it. Here's what I want you to know, Lover Boy. I'll be watching you. You and your buddy. And if you as much as *look* at another hot 'Vette –" Ian pulled up at the curb and honked. Chalmers winked at Adrian. "Keep looking over your shoulder, *son*. I'll be seeing you." Chalmers waved at Mr. and Mrs. Wilde, then walked away down the sidewalk.

Adrian didn't take the detective's advice and find a better class of friends. Adrian liked Allan, and against his parents' wishes, he continued to work for him, even though he got paid even less than he had not gotten paid before.

While Allan didn't steal any more cars, he had always run a word-of-mouth, cash-only business. Even his clientele that could be termed marginally honest tended to be almost as shady as he was. The presence of Detective Chalmers and his unmarked police car, parked across the street – he was there once or twice a week, at all hours – tended to give Allan's friends pause.

Custom slowed to a trickle. Then it dried up entirely. The money Adrian had hidden for Allan, what he'd received from the guy who turned out to be the owner of the Corvette they'd stolen, was long gone. Funds at the Coleman house became tight.

Like Adrian's lack of paydays, Randi also found that if she still wanted to help out around the Coleman house and babysit, she'd be doing it only for the occasional meal; there were no more envelopes of grimy twenties. Gil didn't like it, but Randi enjoyed watching Carmen, even if it was for free. She liked the idea that she was helping someone who desperately needed the help. The Colemans needed a babysitter, and right now, there was no way they could afford to pay one.

When Eileen was at work, Randi took Carmen over to Penny and Bellona's most days. She said happy spells over her, allowed her to use an oversized pentacle as a teether. The old ladies were delighted

135

to have a toddler in the house once again. Randi was also delighted, because by being frequently at his aunts' house, she got to see Adrian more often. She didn't miss the pay at all.

THIRTY-FOUR

By Hallowe'en, 1990, Allan's finances were in desperate straits. His house was about to go into foreclosure; if he didn't get some money coming in soon, he and his wife and fourteen-month-old child would be out on the street by Thanksgiving.

Adrian wasn't at the shop on that Wednesday afternoon. He and the rest of Urban Equinox were scheduled to perform at a party that evening; it was the first real gig they'd had in months. Allan could hear them from down the street, getting in one last rehearsal.

He made a decision, and walked across the street to where Detective Chalmers was sitting in his government-issue Ford.

THIRTY-FIVE

Adrian, Nick, and Bobby had just finished putting all their equipment in the *band truck*. It was an old Chevy pick-up that Rob had given to Bobby for his sixteenth birthday, just to tote their instruments around. Tracy was already in the cab, and Nick climbed in next to her. Bobby was just about to squeeze in on her other side, when Detective Chalmers pulled into the driveway.

"Oh, shit," Adrian said, and rolled his eyes at Bobby. "Go ahead, get in the truck. Lemme see what he wants."

Bobby hesitated; he knew the story. Deciding that he didn't want to talk to any cops if he could help it, he did as he was told.

"What can I do for you on this fine evening, Detective?" Adrian said amicably, as AnneMarie's daddy got out of the car.

"I need to have a word with you, Adrian, my fine ex-car thief," the cop returned, just as amicably. He even smiled, then glanced over his shoulder at the waiting truck. "It might take a minute, though."

"We're playing a party in half an hour."

"Better tell them to go on without you. You'll get there about the time they finish setting up. I won't keep you much longer than that." Again the detective smiled, shark-like, as on the day he'd arrested Adrian. "I promise. Trust me."

Adrian sighed, and went to tell Bobby to go on and set up at the party.

"What the *fuck*, Adrian?" Nick swore.

"I have not a clue. But he's says I'll make it, so go on. If I don't make it, you can sing lead. That should wow 'em. A little kid –"

"Fuck you, Adrian," Nick said. "At least I don't have cops showing up at my door."

"I'll see you soon."

Bobby reluctantly pulled away, leaving his cousin standing in the driveway with the cop.

"What do you want?" Adrian asked.

Chalmers reached through the window of his car, took a folded piece of paper off the dash, and handed it to Adrian.

When Adrian didn't immediately open it, Chalmers said, "That's a search warrant, Lover Boy."

Adrian unfolded the paper; sure enough, at the top of the page it said, *State of California, County of Riverside, Search Warrant and Affidavit.* Adrian read it out loud. "Peace Officer Clancy Chalmers swears under oath that the facts by him/her in the attached and incorporated affidavit are true and that based thereon, he/she has probable cause to believe and does believe that the articles, property, and persons described below are lawfully seizable pursuant to Penal Code –"

"That's enough." Chalmers snatched the warrant back, refolded it, and stuck it in his pocket.

Adrian grinned. "What are you looking for, *Clancy?*"

"Drugs, my boy."

Adrian's eyebrows went up. His grin widened. "What kind of drugs?"

Chalmers grinned also. "Any kind I can find."

"Well, I dunno about all that, Detective. You just go right ahead and search –"

"Do you really think you want that, Adrian? The boys will turn Mommy and Daddy's house upside down, if I tell 'em to. Just think of the mess!"

Adrian blinked, thought about his mother's fear again. But it didn't matter – Chalmers was gonna do whatever he was gonna do – Adrian was above begging him not to do it. Besides, he wasn't gonna find any drugs. There wasn't even a baggie of pot around. Adrian was dry. Nick had been unable to score a little cheer for his bandmates for several days.

"I don't want any of this, Detective. I don't even want my parents seeing you here." They were helping out at a Hallowe'en celebration at Ian's school.

"Relax, my boy. I don't think there are any drugs here. At least not any worth wrecking your house to find."

"Then why are you here?"

"Let me tell you about my day, Adrian."

"Let me guess. It started out at the doughnut shop –"

"I have a warrant, Adrian. You might want to shut the fuck up for a minute."

Adrian shut up. He reckoned that he really wasn't in the best position to continue being a smart-ass.

"I spent the morning at the office, went to lunch, came back and did some paperwork. Then, not too long ago, I decided to continue my surveillance of your buddy's chop shop."

"Your harassment of an honest businessman, you mean."

"Let me tell you how honest your "friend" is, my boy." Chalmers made quotation marks in the air. "I was sitting there, and he comes across the street and says to me, 'Why are you staking me out, Chalmers? You're not going to see anything illegal going on here.' He looked back across the street, then said, 'You're not gonna see *anything* going on here, thanks to your continued harassment. You're wasting the taxpayer's money.'

"Then he puts his pudgy arms on the window and leans closer to me. He says, 'If you really want to make a bust, you should make a little visit to Adrian's house. I understand he's got a couple of kilos of coke under his bed. You know how those rich kids are.' So here I am."

Adrian blinked, dumbfounded. Then he recalled his interrogation, how Chalmers had lied and told him that Allan had tried to pin the 'Vette heist on him, how he had lied to Allan the same way. This had to be some kind of similar iteration of police lies. Allan hadn't narced him off about non-existent cocaine, hadn't sicced the cops on him so that he could go out and steal another –

"You're making this up," Adrian said at last.

"You saw the warrant."

"Allan would never tell you that I had drugs." *But do I really know that?*

He knew that the painter was about to lose his house; there hadn't been a single significant payday since they'd gotten busted with that Corvette. There'd been one scuff and shoot job: some old woman had gotten lost on her way to the local Earl Scheib, and Allan had graciously painted her car for twice Earl's price. But that still wasn't very much, and there'd been nothing since. Allan was desperate for cash.

But surely he wouldn't sell Adrian down the river like this, as a diversion, so he could get out from under Chalmers's ceaseless surveillance for a few hours . . . That was just nuts.

"Why aren't you searching, then?" Adrian asked defiantly.

"Because I know there aren't any drugs here."

"Then why are you talking to me?"

"Look, Adrian," Chalmers said, and put his arm around the guitar player's shoulder. Adrian looked at his arm and Chalmers removed it. "I won't lie and say that I like you. You're a lippy smart-ass, and you're not nearly as cool as you think you are.

"But my daughter likes you – she said that if you said that you didn't know that 'Vette was stolen, then she believed you."

Good ol' AnneMarie, Adrian thought, then discovered that he had a little trouble remembering what she looked like. It had been a brief thing, and it had been a long time ago. Adrian had been with a lot of girls since his initial forays into adulthood with AnneMarie.

"But I don't believe you. You knew that car was hotter than a Mexican lunch – for all I know, it was you that drove it away from the hospital."

"I didn't know it was –"

Chalmers held up his hand. "Save it. Here's why I'm here. My daughter likes you, so I figure, beneath the entirely unwise bravado, you're probably a good kid. You've just fallen in with the wrong crowd." He nodded up the street. "You think the tough guy car thief is your friend. But I'm here to tell ya, there's no honor among thieves, Adrian."

Chalmers paused, then said, "So I told Coleman I'd come over here and check you out, since he told me you had a good chunk of Peru stashed under your bed. I told him I'd have to go get a warrant first, and drove off. He didn't even call to warn you I was coming, did he?"

"I dunno," Adrian said. "I've been in the garage all afternoon."

"Check your machine," Chalmers advised. "But I guarantee there won't be any messages. You're his pal, right? He just put the law on you – if he couldn't get you on the phone, he could've stopped by to let you know about the shitstorm that he'd just sent your way. He's just up the street." Chalmers grinned again. "But he was in too big a hurry – to go out and boost another car, I hope. I didn't go anywhere. I just went around the corner and called it in. Wherever he is, your little fat buddy's got a tail on him."

"But what about the warrant?"

"That was just to get your attention, son. It's for a different case. That's why I didn't let you read any more of it."

Adrian considered for a heartbeat. "I don't believe you."

Chalmers shrugged. "I didn't think you would. See what reward I get for doing a good deed?" He winked at Adrian. "But why would I waste my time telling you all this if it wasn't true? There's nothing in it for me."

"There's nothing in it for you, either way."

"Here's what's in it for me. I did a good deed – I showed you that your "friend" is just as crooked as you always knew he was, and that someone that crooked will sell your ass out just as easily as he'll take something that doesn't belong to him. And I'm showing him that I'm not as dumb as he thinks I am, and he's not nearly as smart as he thinks he is.

"All ya gotta do is ask him, Adrian. You'll be able to tell by the look on his face." Again the detective smiled. "I know you're not gonna thank me, so I'll just be on my way." Chalmers turned, and without a backward glance, he got in his car and left.

Adrian was furious. He stood in his driveway and tried to get a grip on his anger. No matter how much he tried to deny it, he knew that Chalmers had told him the truth. There was no reason for him to make up such an off the wall story.

It sounded like something that Allan would pull, anyway, if Adrian really thought about it. Allan knew there were no drugs at Adrian's house, so in the end, no harm would've come from it, and Allan figured he'd be able to light out and steal another car while Chalmers and a couple of cruisers were busy searching Adrian's house.

Allan didn't have to take whatever he stole back to the shop – he was about to lose the shop, anyway – the rent was behind there, too. Maybe he already had someone waiting to take delivery. He'd just go steal whatever they had ordered, while the cops were busy with Adrian, then collect his money.

Allan apparently didn't care that it would've been a major headache for Adrian if his parents had come home while the cops were ransacking their house, looking for non-existent drugs. All's fair in love and war and grand larceny, set your friend up – if only temporarily – remind his dad that he had already made one dumb-ass move, make his mom *worry* . . .

Adrian noticed that there was a light on at Allan's house. *All's fair in love and war.* He crossed the street and rang the bell.

Eileen opened the door and stared at him, nonplussed. Adrian never came to the house, especially not when her husband wasn't – "Allan's not here," she told him.

"I know," Adrian replied and smiled at her.

Eileen's heart skipped a beat. Adrian had smiled at her. She blinked and glanced over at Carmen, asleep in her playpen. It was the equivalent for Eileen of pinching herself to see if she was dreaming. She had imagined it like this, *so many times* . . . Adrian would just show up one day, when her husband wasn't home, when her baby was asleep, and then he would . . .

"Would you like to come in?"

"Yes. Yes, I would."

He walked into the living room, and Eileen shut the door. As an afterthought, she turned the deadbolt. Allan always had trouble with that lock, always had to jiggle his key in it, so they would hear him if he came home, if they were . . . She looked at Adrian. He was standing by the playpen. *He's making sure that Carmen's asleep! This can't be happening. I must be dreaming.*

Oh, my God, Adrian, I want you so bad!

Adrian turned at her thought and smiled at her again.

Eileen returned his smile. If she *was* dreaming, she was going to make the very most of it. She thought about him *all the time,* she thought about it happening *just like this,* and now he was *right here.*

"I don't get to see much of you, Adrian," Eileen said. *And I'd like to see* all *of you.* She took a few steps closer to him. "Why don't you ever come in the house?" She pouted. "Sometimes I think you don't like me."

Adrian observed that Eileen was actually quite pretty; she had lustrous brown hair, and big hazel eyes. He noticed that she looked tired, and thought that being married to someone who worked all the time but never brought home any money would make anyone look tired. Adrian noticed that she had quite a nice body, and contemplated for a moment what she might look like undressed. He closed the distance between them. It would be *so easy* to find out . . .

"I like you, Eileen. I like you just fine." He put his hand on her cheek, ran his thumb lightly across her lips. Eileen shuddered. Adrian made her wait for a heartbeat, then kissed her, ever so slowly.

Without hesitation, Eileen kissed him back passionately. She tangled her hands in his hair, molded her body against his.

Oh, yeah, Adrian thought, *this is going to be fun.*

Without breaking their kiss, Adrian picked her up; Eileen wrapped her arms around his neck. Adrian aimed to carry her into the bedroom – it wouldn't be right to just do Mommy on the floor in front of the playpen – Carmen might wake up at any moment. Adrian would just take Eileen to her bed – *Allan's bed* – and give her what she had so clearly wanted from the minute she'd laid eyes on him. *How 'bout them apples, Allan, you backstabbing son of a bitch?*

But before he could take more than two steps toward this destination, Adrian heard the unmistakable metallic rattle of the VW's exhaust in the driveway. Eileen heard it, too. She stopped kissing Adrian, stared wide-eyed at him. He set her down, and she said, "Wipe your mouth. I'll be right back. Don't tell him –"

"Why would I tell him?" Adrian grinned at her, and wiped his mouth on the back of his hand. He saw pink lipstick. "Am I good?"

"You're great!" Eileen hugged him quickly.

"I mean – the lipstick?"

"It's gone. I'll be right back. I'm gonna go get Carmen's Hallowe'en costume. Just . . . Just stand there." Eileen skipped across the room and turned the deadbolt, then fled into Carmen's room.

Adrian stepped back to the playpen, and noticing that the toddler was awake, he picked her up. Then her father opened the front door.

"What are you doing here, Adrian? I thought you'd be –"

"Handcuffed in the back of a patrol car?"

Adrian waited. If Chalmers had made the whole thing up, Allan would look confused, demand to know what the hell Adrian was talking about. But he didn't. He just looked sheepishly at the floor for a moment, then said, "Ah, I knew they wouldn't find anything. You're no cokehead. I just had to get him away from in front of the shop for a minute, so I could see a man about a horse. Herbie had an idea –"

So it was all true. "He had you tailed."

"I figured. I drove around for a while. Herbie wasn't there, anyway, so I came back home."

Adrian waited for the apology, waited for his *friend* to tell him that he was sorry for using him as a decoy, so he could go out and collude with another known felon about the possibility of committing another felony. But no apology came.

Adrian heard Eileen's voice in his head. *Oh, Christ, Adrian, I want you to kiss me again!* He looked up to see her staring at him from the hallway. She was holding a little pink bunny suit by its Peter Cottontail ears: Carmen's Hallowe'en costume.

Adrian returned her gaze mildly, innocuously, and thought, *You better keep all that to yourself, sister. I don't want to have to kill your husband over a kiss, but I'm just pissed off enough at what a traitor he's turned out to be, that I'm up for it.*

He said, "Well, you guys have fun trick or treating. I've got a show to do." He nodded at Eileen; she came into the living room and took Carmen from him. She made a point of not looking him in the eye.

"Hey," Allan said as Adrian opened the door. "No hard feelings, huh? I couldn't think of any other way to get that fucking cop off my back."

"Sure, Allan. All's fair in love and war." *You're fucking with the wrong guitar player, Fat Boy,* he thought. "No hard feelings."

144

Adrian was unmoved by Allan's puny remorse. There had been no apology. Adrian resisted the urge to make eye-contact with the painter's wife, but he could hear her thinking about him.

"See you in the morning?"

"Sure."

But Adrian woke up in Emily's bed the next morning; she had her own place now. She had come to the show at Tracy's invite, and from the first song, she had stood up front and watched the band in her aloof manner, all the while angling in her mind for Round Two with Adrian Wilde. He had been surprisingly easy to catch – she didn't know that her willingness was as plain as the handwriting on the wall to him.

Emily thought she was playing hard to get. As had been his father's MO in a different era, Adrian just let her think it was all her idea. Emily was a game-player, another kind of girl of which Adrian was not particularly fond. And she wanted him – not as much as Eileen did, but on the other hand, Adrian reflected that no one had *ever* wanted him as much as Eileen did.

Emily's desire and its fulfillment had taken Adrian's mind off his traitorous friend and his needy wife for the evening.

Adrian had a hangover, even though he was still nine months' away from being able to buy a drink. *Nine months left to live,* he thought wryly. *Why am I wasting my time with this chick? I should go to work . . .* But then he remembered Allan's betrayal, how close he had come to answering that betrayal, and in spades, with Allan's wife. *All's fair in love and war.*

Adrian covered his face with Emily's pillow. He didn't want to go home right away. He smelled coffee and bacon and decided that she wasn't so bad after all, if she could cook. He could see his way clear to at least spending the day with her, and maybe one more night, if she asked nicely.

THIRTY-SIX

When Adrian returned home the next afternoon – Emily had asked him to stay, in the *nicest possible way* – Ian told him that his cousin had called like twelve times. Something about the band.

Nick answered when Adrian phoned the Wilde manse. "Oh, my Christ, Adrian! If you'd stop trying to get your dick wet for five seconds and check in sometimes –"

"You kiss your mother with that mouth, Nicky? You kissed anybody with it yet?" Nick would be fifteen the day after Christmas.

"You forget, Cuz, I play guitar, too."

Adrian could hear the smugness in Nick's tone, but he wasn't buying it. "Do tell."

"Never mind about that now. While you were out on the boulevard, we lined up four more gigs. We got a little party on Saturday; then another one on the tenth, then one on the sixteenth, then some kind of big block party deal for the Saturday after Thanksgiving."

"Where?"

"All in that neighborhood where we just played. From kids at the party, and one guy's ol' man – that's the block party deal. So . . . Have you been to the clinic? Made sure you didn't catch anything? We've gotta rehearse. Bobby wants to cover *Too Many Puppies*. You know how much he likes Les Claypool." When Adrian didn't answer immediately, Nick said. "We'll be there in an hour. Take a shower, will ya?"

Adrian thought about calling and leaving a message for Allan, but he knew he wasn't home: it was a work day, after all. Randi was no doubt babysitting, and she'd pick up the phone when she heard his voice. He didn't want to talk to Randi, didn't want her hanging around all afternoon while they rehearsed. Nick had more than a little bit of a thing for Randi, and his timing was invariably off when she was around.

Besides, just leaving a message struck Adrian as rather a chickenshit move, anyway. He and Allan were still *friends,* were they not? He wouldn't want the painter to think that he harbored any *hard feelings* over the idea that his one-time partner in crime had sold him out to the cops, now would he? Plus, he had an hour to kill before his band arrived, so he loped up the street to the shop.

Allan grinned at him. "Don't tell me. Let me guess. You met a girl at the party."

Adrian also grinned, but kept Allan's betrayal at the front of his mind. This man was not really his friend. "One I already knew, actually."

Allan glanced around the empty shop, nodded across the street at the black and white sheriff's cruiser parked there. "Not like there's been any trade."

Adrian glanced at the cop car and thought that Detective Chalmers had apparently delegated the stake-out duties. He truly was wasting the tax-payers' money: Allan wouldn't steal anything with a cop parked across the street. If he couldn't catch him in another felonious act, Adrian reflected, running Allan out of his legitimate business would be sufficient for AnneMarie's dad.

"The band lined up a bunch of shows for the rest of the month, so we have to rehearse. You won't be seeing a lot of me 'til after Thanksgiving." *And probably not even then,* Adrian thought. Spending the night in jail had cured him of the thrill of stealing cars, and the knife Allan had planted firmly between his shoulders had cured him of trusting car thieves.

"I'll be gone by then, my friend." Allan said.

What an ironic choice of words, Adrian thought.

"It's time to cut my losses," the painter continued. "The realtor we bought the house from said they'd buy it back – at a loss, of course. But I'll get a little change out of it – and we're about to lose it, anyway. These bastards . . ." He gestured at the sheriff across the street. "Fuck 'em. I'm getting out of their jurisdiction. I've got a little shop lined up in Moreno Valley. Eileen and Carmen are gonna stay with Eileen's mom until I can get enough scratch together to get us an apartment."

"I'm sorry to hear that." Adrian wasn't sorry at all.

Allan shrugged. "Shit happens. I was looking for a shop when I found this one. We'll be okay. Come up and see me when you're done being Mick Jagger. The place is on Day Street, almost to Alesandro. You can't miss it."

"I'll be sure to do that." There was a moment's silence, and Adrian got the impression that Allan knew he wouldn't be joining him in further automotive hijinks, certainly not all the way out in Moreno Valley. "Good luck, Allan." Adrian turned to go.

"You, too, kid."

Adrian would not only never see Allan or his family again, they wouldn't even cross his mind. This felonious chapter of his life was concluded.

THIRTY-SEVEN

Sam Germaine was still hanging on by Thanksgiving, so Nadine helped Irene cook. There was a pall over the festivities, however, because all three of them knew that he wouldn't see the holiday again. *If Penny and Bellona's predictions are correct – and they always are – neither will Adrian,* Nadine said to herself, and the thought cheered her immensely. She ramped up the pleasant conversation; told little happy vignettes about her customers from the camera store. Her good spirits eventually infected her mom and dad, and the day passed as happily as could be expected with Death hovering so nearby.

Just as Allan had predicted, he and his family were moved out and a *For Sale* sign was once again in the yard when Adrian carried Daina's green bean casserole up the hill. Because he knew that Adrian was busy with his band, Allan hadn't asked his former partner in crime to help him pack up. Or maybe Allan had sensed that he and Adrian weren't really friends anymore.

Randi had spent a lot of time with Penny and Bellona while she watched Eileen's baby, so even though that was over now, Adrian's aunts had invited Randi to help prepare and enjoy the feast. The older witches were quite fond of the nascent one, and were delighted to have her on hand to help handle the houseful of people.

Randi brought Gil along. He didn't really want to attend, but there was no escape, no excuse not to be there with his woman. He didn't care for the men present, because he felt that none of them were even remotely like him: Ian's dad and his cousin spouted stupid quotations at each other, sometimes in verse. Gil considered that to be snooty, effeminate; he got the impression that they were looking down on him, this rich doctor and confident schoolteacher.

Bobby was a non-entity to Gil. The bass player didn't have much to say to Randi's boyfriend, and Gil thereby got the impression that the red-haired kid was afraid of him. That was fine with Gil.

His little brother Nick, on the other hand, was openly hostile, and it was effortless for Gil to grasp the reason. The little squirt had it bad for Randi, so he was unable and probably unwilling to mask his hatred and jealousy for her man. Gil found this amusing; had he been a little more charitable, he might've found it cute, even flattering, that the kid set so much store by his girlfriend. But Gil was unfamiliar with charity, so he took great relish in baiting Nick. He never passed up the chance to touch Randi, to embrace her or kiss her, when he saw that the little guitarist was watching. Nick wasn't even fifteen yet; he was a child to Randi. Gil knew there was nothing to worry about from that camp.

Adrian, on the other hand, was not a child, and as always, Randi's obvious affection for him galled Gil. He'd seen it from the first Urban Equinox show that he had attended, had deemed it necessary to warn Adrian the very day they'd met. Randi had already gone to two or three of the dinky little parties they played, and she had dragged Gil along this time.

"They're so *good!*" she had effused.

Gil thought Urban Equinox was fair for a cover band, though he found their between song banter annoying. He found their own compositions tiresome and trite, and by the conclusion of their set, he was bored, ready to leave. So it was with an added dismay that he watched as his girlfriend went up and practically launched herself into the singer's arms when they took a break.

Gil reckoned that the black-haired guitar player had hugged her back a might too familiarly, and when Randi wandered off to talk to someone else, Gil walked up and introduced himself to the singer. Friendly-like. Shook his hand and everything.

"I'm Randi's boyfriend," he said.

Adrian blinked; he thought that this blonde stranger was confessing some stripe of homosexuality to him, telling him that he was some dude's boyfriend. That had never happened to Adrian before, and he didn't know how to take it. But this guy was clearly waiting for some response, so Adrian just said, "Who?"

A thin wire of rage whipped through Gil. Randi obviously liked this asshole; she'd just given him a big, entirely-too-friendly *squeeze,* had she not? And he didn't even know who she was. *Christ, how I hate musicians,* Gil said to himself.

He looked around at the crowd until he found his girlfriend, talking to some blonde chick. As Gil watched, Randi turned and smiled at the guitar player, then whispered something in the girl's ear. The girl giggled and waved at Adrian. Adrian smiled and waved back.

"That's Randi," Gil said.

"Oh," Adrian said, relieved. *"That* Randi. From Mohini's." This guy wasn't going to make a pass at him after all. "Randi with an *i.*"

"Right," Gil said, momentarily confused. How many Randis did this guy know? Gil waited while a good-looking redhead came up, told Adrian, "Great show!" gave him a little pat on the arm, then

149

wandered off again. Adrian followed her departure with interest, then turned back to Gil again.

"Rock and roll sure impresses the ladies, huh?" Gil looked appreciatively after the redhead, then back at Adrian for confirmation.

Adrian read his hostility, remembered his words: *I'm Randi's boyfriend.* He shrugged. "The ladies are easily impressed."

"Impress them all you can," Gil advised. "But if you touch Randi again, I'll kill you."

Adrian's eyebrows went up in surprise. He'd thought earlier that Gil had been flirting with him, announcing that he was some dude's *boyfriend.* That had been a first for Adrian, and this – an out-an-out threat from some *chick's* boyfriend – this was a first, too.

He wasn't quite sure what reaction was expected, so he just gave an honest answer. "I'm not interested in your girlfriend, pal. But maybe you oughta say something to her."

"Oh, I will," Gil assured him. "But right now, I'm saying something to *you.*"

Nick and Bobby sauntered up; Bobby looked questioningly at his cousin. Adrian heard Nick's voice in his head: *Who's this asshole?*

"This is Randi's boyfriend. Gil."

"Is he now?" Nick looked the blonde tough guy up and down. Adrian heard his cousin's unspoken words once more: *I remain unimpressed.* Nick had imprinted on Randi from the first time she had showed up at one of their shows, several weeks earlier. *I think I can take him.*

You might have to. He's a jealous one.

Nick looked at Gil with renewed interest. "What can we do for you, Randi's boyfriend? You wanna make a request?"

Gil's gaze flickered over to the little kid: he wasn't worth the time it would take to put him on the ground. He looked back at Adrian. "I've already made my request. And I think your buddy's gonna honor it, kid. If he knows what's good for him."

"Oh, most definitely," Adrian replied. "I have been warned." He turned his back on Gil and grinned at his cousins. *"Now is it time to ski: come, shall we about it?"*

"Ski?" Nick asked, as they walked away from Gil, still glowering.

"It's something that Ian and Rob always say," Bobby told him. "He means, *let's go play another set.*"

"Then why doesn't he just say that, then? Ski." Nick revered Bobby and Adrian, but he drew the line at waterskiing with them. After one horribly unsuccessful attempt when he was about ten, when he felt like he had swallowed half of Lake Elsinore being dragged behind *One Wilde Ride,* while his Uncle Rob and Adrian's dad and his brother and his cousin laughed at him, Nick had refused any further inveiglements to go skiing.

Bobby looked over his shoulder, found that Gil was still staring at them. "What the fuck, Adrian?"

"That's a jealous boyfriend," Nick told him.

"Really? Whose?"

"Randi's." Nick couldn't suppress a little sigh. "And look how worried Adrian is about it."

"She's all yours, Nicky," Adrian said, and clapped him on the shoulder. "I'm sure you can take him. Whip his ass, sweep Randi off her feet . . ." He grinned at Bobby.

"Fuck you, Adrian," Nick said.

THIRTY-EIGHT

Now, forced to have Thanksgiving dinner with this smart-ass guitar player that he loathed, as well as his chickenshit bassist, and the little kid that had a crush on Randi, Gil wondered vaguely if maybe the front for Urban Equinox liked guys. Hell, if he was in Adrian's shoes, he would've snatched Randi up after their first gig. She didn't try to hide how much she wanted him, so . . . Why not? Gil would've bet that it didn't matter to Adrian if some chick had a boyfriend, so why hadn't he jumped at the opportunity? Randi probably didn't even tell him she had a boyfriend, until she'd dragged him along, so what was Wilde's problem? He had to be queer.

But Gil had seen Adrian with plenty of girls since. He might swing both ways – Gil knew musicians were notorious for that – but it was clear that Wilde wasn't exclusively into dudes. Gil decided that Adrian hadn't returned Randi's obvious interest because he was afraid of him. And well he should be.

Gil had expressed a few choice words to Randi, too, told her that he didn't appreciate her drooling over some no-talent musician. Randi had denied the attraction at first, but when Gil had insisted that it was as plain as the nose on her face, Randi said, "It doesn't mean anything, Gil. I just like . . . I just like how he sings. But I *love* you." Randi had then gone on to demonstrate just how much she loved him, and Gil had let her.

And Randi did love him, with all her heart. It was just her *mind* that kept returning to Adrian, to his voice, and his blue eyes, and his fabulous body . . . Surely, Randi loved Gil, especially since Adrian wouldn't give her the time of day. *He's too busy with his music for a girlfriend,* she always told herself. But if Adrian ever decided that he *was* interested . . . Well, that would just never happen. She loved Gil.

Gil had less than no use whatsoever for the male members of the Wilde clan, but the women were all right. He would surely give the curvy blonde drummer a twirl, if she would disengage herself from her bassist boyfriend's hand for half a second, so he could have a word with her. Wouldn't that be turnabout and fair play and all? Randi wanted to do the singer, so Gil would just run off for a few hours with the drummer . . . But that would get back to Randi, and besides the uppity blonde pretended that she didn't even know Gil was there.

The doctor had brought a hot young nurse (Gil didn't know that it was a different one from the year before), and he thought he caught her looking at him inquisitively a few times when the doctor was spouting verse with the schoolteacher. *You should try a guy a little closer to your own age, honey,* Gil thought. *I'm not a doctor and I don't know any poetry, but I do know how to . . .* He smiled at her. She smiled back, then turned to listen to her date. *Whatever,* Gil thought.

He flirted gently, harmlessly, with the two old ladies. The taller one wasn't having any, although he did coax a smile out of her once, and he got the other one to giggle a few times. Gil liked women, and even though these two were way past their expiration dates, he wasn't unamenable to giving them a little smile and a few kind words. It was practice for the more eligible ones.

Gil was most intrigued by the guitar player's mom, however. He knew that she had once been friends with Nadine – Adrian considered Nadine his aunt – but apparently, not so much anymore. He had never heard Nadine say a nice thing about Adrian's mom. Or Adrian either, for that matter. She referred to him as *that little brat* when she spoke of him. As in, *You're not going to let that little brat move in on your girlfriend, are you?*

Gil liked Nadine; he liked her quite a bit. He liked the fact that she was always down, whenever he could get away for a visit with her. He liked that she expressed no jealousy over his relationship with Randi – she understood that Randi was his future: they were planning on getting married someday, starting a family – Nadine knew that she was just a very enjoyable part of his present. She had never once expressed any kind of ridiculous thoughts, nothing along the lines of maybe he should leave Randi and take up with her full time.

Gil couldn't believe his luck in finding Nadine, actually. Their relationship was perfect: she was sexy, if a little long in the tooth, and she never asked for anything he didn't want to give, didn't pout or cry if he said he'd be there and then couldn't make it. Nadine had not a jealous bone in her body.

Sometimes, this lack of jealousy irked Gil a little bit, made him wonder if perhaps Nadine had someone else besides him. She assured him that she did not – "One tomcat is more than enough for me" – but maybe Gil might have liked it if she expressed just a *trace* of jealousy once in a while. It might've demonstrated that Nadine actually cared for him, if she talked a little shit on his gullible girlfriend, if she acted like perhaps she didn't like the younger woman to whom Gil always returned.

A little jealousy would've been better than what Nadine did say about Randi. She would start off by complimenting her, saying how lovely she was – that was all right with Gil – but then, Nadine would always end up by adding something about Adrian Wilde.

"I hope you're taking good care of your pretty little girlfriend," she'd say with a wicked grin. "When the cat's away . . . You know what they say about musicians. And Adrian . . . Well, we both know how much Randi likes Adrian, now don't we?"

Gil didn't like Nadine very much when she would talk about Randi and Adrian Wilde, but he had to admit that it was undeniably the truth. His girlfriend had a thing for this guy, just as surely as his snot-nosed little cousin had a thing for Randi.

As they sat down to dinner, Gil grasped Randi's hand and kissed it, all the while grinning at Nick. Nick frowned and looked away. *Life's tough, ain't it, my son?* Gil thought.

Gil reasoned that just like this kid was powerless to act on his yen for Randi – how pathetic and ludicrous would that be? He wasn't even old enough to drive! Gil pictured the kid's dad giving them a ride to the Junior Prom and almost laughed out loud.

Just like Nick couldn't do a damn thing about his itch for Randi, Gil was just as powerless to stop Randi from having a little warm for the black-haired guitar player.

Bitching about it wouldn't do any good, and bitching about it would make it seem like he perceived Randi's crush as a threat. It was all good: Adrian didn't want Randi because he was afraid of Gil; and he had more women than he could handle, anyway, from what Gil had heard. Good for him. As long as he stayed away from his girlfriend, then Gil wouldn't have to kill him.

Gil watched Randi watch Adrian, who ignored her other than when it was absolutely necessary to interact with her. Gil didn't worry about Randi making a move – she was basically shy, though she had her pride; she wasn't the type to just throw herself at random musicians.

So, all in all, the situation wasn't unbearable for Gil, and the dinner was excellent. He got to look at the hot nurse, and the blonde drummer, and he also got to look at Wilde's mom. She was still hot – she was the same age as Nadine, so he knew that she was undoubtedly still hot to trot, too. She only had eyes for the schoolteacher, however. Gil saw them share a smoky glance or two during the afternoon. She only gave Gil the occasional polite smile: she ignored him as thoroughly as her chickenshit son ignored Randi.

Your loss, Mrs. Wilde, Gil thought. *The things I could do for a woman your age . . .* Thinking of a woman her age put him in mind of Nadine once more. He thought that he might drop Randi off at home after dinner, tell her that he was going to pay a visit to his mother, what with the holiday and all . . . Randi knew he didn't talk to his mother, but, what with the holiday and all . . . she would believe him.

Yeah, life's good, Gil said to himself. *I'll just drop in and say hi to Nadine later this evening.* It would be a nice gesture, since it was Thanksgiving. Gil smiled to himself and asked Bellona to pass the mashed potatoes.

THIRTY-NINE

Christmas had always been one of Adrian's favorite holidays, for the simple reason that his aunts marked it quite a bit differently than anyone he'd ever known. Sure, it was the celebration of our Savior's birth, and the Wilde home always had a huge, good-smelling tree, and lights and tinsel and ornaments; a big ol' ham on Christmas Eve, Christmas cards and presents.

But December was also the time of the winter solstice and Saturnalia, when gift-giving was once upon a time augmented with drunken licentiousness in the streets of Rome. December 25th marked the Roman festival of *Dies Natalis Solis Invicti*, the birthday of *the unconquered sun.* The holly and the ivy were Dionysus and his maenads.

Sinterklaas would bring Adrian largesse if he was a good boy, but if he was not – Penny would grin at him, as if she suspected that he often was not – then he would be harassed by Sinterklaas's dark helper, Black Pete.

Yuletide meant that Adrian might behold Odin leading the Wild Hunt across the winter sky: ghostly huntsman on horseback, accompanied by their slat-ribbed hounds. The part of the legend that prophesied that he would meet his doom soon after seeing them was not related to Adrian – there had been quite enough prophecies of doom concerning the boy – so as a child, he often scanned cloudy December California skies, hoping for a glimpse of the god and his minions.

All the common trappings of Christmas had ancient origins, and Adrian's aunts had familiarized him with them from little on. Roman, Norse, Druid; all pagan, pre-Christian: he enjoyed these stories so much more than *'Twas the Night Before Christmas* and no room at the inn.

On his twentieth Christmas morning, Adrian sat on the couch, flanked by his aunts, while his dad sat in a nearby chair and his mom knelt beside the big Douglas Fir and handed out presents.

His father always gave a book to each of his aunts. They had thousands; the collections of two lifetime readers who had lived long lives indeed. So Ian strove not so much for content: how many *Collected Works of Shakespeare* did any pair of old witches need? Instead, he always found them either obscure titles, long out of print, or first editions of more familiar works. This year, he presented Penny with the initial publication run of Harper Lee's *To Kill A*

Mockingbird, and to Bellona he gave a copy of Hemingway's *For Whom the Bell Tolls,* printed in 1940.

Penny and Bellona always gifted their favorite English teacher in kind, and since they had quite a bit more money to spend, they wowed Ian with an outrageously expensive 1906 first edition of Upton Sinclair's classic, *The Jungle.*

That was all well and good for his aunts and his dad, but there were a couple of large boxes under the tree, and like a little kid, Adrian wondered if they were for him. But the large, fat one that could've almost been an amp turned out to be a handmade quilt from his aunts to his mom, and the tall, skinny one that might've hidden a guitar was in fact a strange painting by a local artist, from his mom and dad to his aunts.

Adrian's parents always exchanged their Christmas gifts in private – Daina had told him once that they simply wrote each other love letters. Upon hearing of this charming custom, Nick had made one of his blue remarks about precisely what it might be that Ian *gave* his wife for Christmas. Refusing to speculate about all that, Adrian had never mentioned it again.

His parents' love letters – or whatever – that was all well and good, too, except that Adrian had not received any Christmas presents yet, and while the two presents still left under the tree did have his name on them, they consisted only of an envelope and a box, small enough that he could hold it in the palm of his hand. Adrian discovered that he was a trifle disappointed.

Daina handed him the envelope. It said, *To Adrian, From Santa,* so he knew it was from his parents. He smiled. Some things never changed. All the Christmas presents he'd ever received from his parents had said, *To Adrian, From Santa.*

Good things could come in envelopes, Adrian reasoned – *like cash* – and he wasn't disappointed. Daina and Ian had given him a quite generous gift certificate to Guitar Center. It was a surprise and Adrian enthusiastically said his thanks, leapt up and hugged his parents.

That left only the small box. Adrian knew it was from his aunts, and he wondered what it might be. They never gave him either cash or gift certificates, considering both to be lazy and thoughtless, so what sort of thing, valuable to a young man, could be contained in such a little box?

Adrian blanched – it might be prophylactics. His aunts had taken it upon themselves to sit down and tell him about the birds and the bees when he was about thirteen, about a week before Dad had given him the same speech. The three of them might think such a gift would be humorous, as Adrian hadn't been spending a lot of nights at home during the past holiday season, seeing as how Urban Equinox had been playing a lot of parties, attended by a lot of eager fans. But Adrian didn't think that Penny and Bellona and his dad would collude to give him such a joke gift in front of his mother.

Even though the box was small, Adrian knew it would be something good; his aunts had always given him *the best* presents. One year it had been an expensive, metal-studded guitar strap. His old one broke when he played a New Year's Eve shindig a week later, and Adrian would've been lost without his aunts' thoughtful gift.

The Christmas after he'd turned sixteen, they'd given him a Triple A membership. It came in handy, because the car he bought the following month – he'd worked the holiday rush at K-Mart to earn the money for it – had turned out to be a dog, and he'd had to have it towed frequently, until his dad took pity on him and bought him a better one. If he'd still been driving that clunker when Detective Chalmers caught him with AnneMarie the following summer . . . He probably wouldn't have escaped, because it would've stalled in the driveway.

Adrian realized with a start that quite a few of his aunts' Christmas presents had seemed odd at Christmas, but they had never failed to come in handy not long after. Like the expensive ski parka and snow pants they had given a few years back. Adrian had said thanks, but later joked with his dad that his aunts had the wrong kind of skiing. Adrian had never even *seen* snow, except when it graced the mountains surrounding Riverside.

But damned if Doctor Wilde hadn't been feeling generous at the end of January and invited Adrian along on the family's annual trip to Aspen. Adrian hadn't taken to the slopes – Nick had laughed at his clumsiness, apt revenge for his own disastrous day waterskiing – but Nick quit laughing when Adrian found a snow bunny at the lodge to keep him warm for the weekend.

Now Adrian looked at the small box, and remembered that his aunts, and his mother, too, believed that he wasn't going to live more than another seven months or so. He pushed the thought away; it was Christmas, a happy, family time, and besides, the whole idea was just nuts. Sure, his aunts had often given him seemingly precognitive Christmas presents, but that didn't mean they were right this time.

He wondered if whatever was in the box had anything to do with their dire prediction.

There was only one way to find out. His mother held the box out to him, and Adrian took it, tore off the paper. Inside was a common Schlage key, attached to a festive red ribbon. Adrian held it up, looked at his aunts, grinned uncertainly. Thinking of his predicted doom, he said, "What is this? A good luck charm?"

Penny furrowed her brow, considered Adrian as if he'd suddenly become stupid. "That's a house key, dear."

"To whose house?"

"To *your* house, Capo!" Bellona leapt up and kissed him. "Merry Christmas!"

Adrian looked at his parents, but they were as stunned as he was. He said to his aunts, "You bought me . . . *a house?*"

"Your Aunt Nadine's old place," Penny said.

"You're a grown man now," Bellona said, with an impish twinkle in her blue eyes, and Daina was suddenly awash in déjà vu. "You need your privacy. You can't be cooped up with your parents anymore. You need a place of your own. But we didn't want you to move too far away."

Daina had a flash of what could've been precognition. She knew that Penny would next say, "You're going to need some furniture," and hand Adrian a roll of cash. She was almost right: Penny said the words, but instructed Adrian to look under the padding in the box. The money was right there.

"It's time," Bellona said, then repeated, "You're a grown man now."

Adrian felt his mother's fear bloom at the mention of how grown he was, and he gave her a reassuring hug. "Did you know about this? Dad?" Daina and Ian silently shook their heads.

"I don't know what to say. I don't deserve this." Adrian embraced his aunts, felt the energy of their love flow from them as he had for his entire life. He laughed shakily. "I kinda thought it might be a lump of coal. You know, after the thing with the 'Vette –"

"You didn't know it was stolen," Bellona said and winked at him.

"It's also a tremendous tax write-off for us," Penny suggested.

Adrian stopped objecting and gave his aunts another grateful hug. It was the best Christmas *ever.*

FORTY

"Now I can finally put the boat in the garage again," Ian said.

It was the day after Christmas, and he and Bobby and Nick were helping Adrian move across the street. The singer for Urban Equinox wanted to install their instruments in the living room – the set-up of amps and guitars and drums had grown so as to squeeze *One Wilde Ride* out into the driveway – but at a frown from his dad, Adrian changed his mind. "Don't make your first place into a frat house, son."

Adrian decided that the band's equipment and rehearsal area would be fine in his new garage.

Ian experienced his own species of déjà vu while helping Adrian clear out his room. He remembered the odd afternoon more than twenty years before, when out of the blue, Sam Germaine (poor Sam!) had stopped him in the driveway and asked him to help move Nadine's stuff out of the very same room. At the time, Ian had thought it peculiar that Nadine would suddenly want to once again live under parental scrutiny. He'd believed that she'd been happy living with him and Daina, so her abrupt, unexpected flight back across the street to her mom and dad's welcoming arms had surprised Ian.

As he helped Adrian carry his bed and dresser and desk across the street, Ian recalled that it had been on the very afternoon that Nadine moved out – back here, to her parents' house, now *Adrian's* house – that Daina had told him that she was pregnant. Daina's childhood bedroom had become Nadine's room had become Adrian's room. Now it would become a library, Ian's *study,* as he liked to call it; an office where he could grade papers and work up lesson plans.

Sam Germaine's house had been his for a long time, since Nadine was nine years old, Ian knew; then it had been bad-influence Allan's for just an eye blink of time, and now, thanks to the unbelievable generosity of his loving aunts, it was Adrian's house.

Ian reflected that past a fresh coat of paint or a new rug, a new roof or some structural improvements, maybe some updated wiring or plumbing – houses never changed. Only their inhabitants, like the forces of nature, grew, thrived, matured, faltered, died; the architecture remained unaffected. Each individual was *only a poor player that struts and frets his hour upon the stage and then is heard no more,* but the houses remained.

Macbeth's doleful observation put Ian in mind of Penny and Bellona's prediction regarding his son. Generally, Ian accepted their seemingly supernatural gifts, regardless of how their unrealistic claims clashed with his perception of the modern world. He had no other choice: had they not shown him the path to true love, the real meaning of life, something he had once not even believed was possible?

But Ian would not accept their augury in this case. No matter how precognitive they had proved themselves to be in the past, he stubbornly refused to believe them now. His intelligent, healthy, happy-go-lucky son was not going to inexplicably die, just because they said he would. Such an event would decimate Ian; it would kill Daina. It was impossible. It could not occur.

With little effort, Ian threw off the gloom of the old witches' long-standing, supposedly preternaturally-informed proclamation. Ian had always enjoyed stories of fantasy and magical realms, and if it was truly a world where Oedipus could seal his own fate by returning to Thebes, it was also a world where Quetzalcoatl had never returned, and the world had not yet ended, despite legions of prophets who believed that their information came from on high.

Neither the coasts of the United States, nor Japan, nor England had sunk into the sea as Edgar Cayce predicted; the waters of the Great Lakes had not emptied into the Gulf of Mexico. So Ian was not troubled with what two little old ladies residing in Riverside, California claimed that they had foreseen. Far greater seers than they had been wrong. His son would live a long and happy life.

Adrian took the master bedroom for himself, of course. It was reached by a short, T-shaped hall off the living room, and had a second door that opened into the kitchen.

"Perfect for midnight snacks," he told his dad with a grin. At the other end of the hall was the bedroom that had been Nadine's. "And this is gonna be Bobby's room."

Ian smiled, considered that history had a way of repeating itself. Penny and Bellona had gifted Daina with a house, and the first person she wanted there was her best friend. They had done the same for Adrian, and of course he would want Bobby to share it with him. Nadine and Daina's living arrangements hadn't lasted, nor, really, had their friendship. And Ian considered that maybe that had been his fault in some way. But Adrian and Bobby were blood, like brothers – Ian believed that a woman could never come between them.

161

"What the fuck, Adrian?" Nick said, and Ian winced at the profanity. "What about me?"

"About that, Cuz," Bobby said. He worried a loose thread in the carpet with the toe of his shoe. "It's my Dad . . ."

"Dad can't say anything about what you do anymore," Nick said. "You're eighteen. I should live so long."

"What did he say?" Adrian asked.

Bobby glanced up at his cousin, then at Ian, then down at the floor again in embarrassment.

Ian grinned at his son. *"Once more unto the breach, dear friends, once more.* Your dad has never had much nice to say *to* me, Bobby, nonetheless *about* me. I'm sure it's the same with Adrian. You're not going to hurt our feelings. What did he say?"

Bobby sighed. "He said he'd cut me off. 'You're not moving in with goddamned Cousin Ian's deadbeat son when you're only a freshman in college.'"

Bobby had enrolled in his parents' (and Adrian's parents') alma mater in September, but was still undecided on a major. That was still more than Adrian had ever accomplished. He'd never had any desire to go back to school, and his parents had never pushed it. Adrian now knew why: they thought he was going to die, so why bother with school? But that was just nuts. Perhaps he would join his cousin in the fall. It was high time he did something with his life.

"Then Mom chimed in," Bobby continued. "She said I just wanted to move out so I could . . ." Nick grinned, and Bobby shot him a warning frown. "So I could be with Tracy."

"Maybe it's just as well," Adrian said. "You couldn't leave Nick in that big ol' house all alone. He might have nightmares."

Nick opened his mouth to retort, but his brother cut him off. "I'll be here, Cuz," he promised. "Fuck my dad."

Ian grinned at *this* profanity, despite himself. Bobby had echoed his own sentiments. Just like he had never liked Ian's friendship with Rob, Will had never liked his son's brotherhood with Adrian. *But that's just too goddamned bad, now isn't it?*

"As soon as we get back from Europe this year, I'll be here," Bobby said. "Expect me on your door step sometime in August." He looked at his little brother. "And you can visit."

"Sounds like a plan," Adrian said.

162

FORTY-ONE

Like Nadine and Daina had done before any of them were even a twinkle in their fathers' eyes, Adrian and Bobby and Nick scoured used furniture stores, hit all the after-Christmas sales. They bought a couch and a coffee table, a couple of armchairs, a nice little dinette set. A television.

Adrian told his number one fan to spread the word: Urban Equinox would be seeing out 1990 with a bang on New Year's Eve at Adrian Wilde's very own new house. Randi squealed in glee and got on the telephone. The result of her enthusiasm was a big crowd, which spilled out of the house and filled the front yard when the band started tuning up in the garage.

Penny and Bellona stopped in to wish Adrian and his band happy new year before the party began. "Any requests?" Adrian asked, after giving them each a hug and a kiss. "I'm sure you'll be able to hear us up on the hill."

"I like everything you play," said Bellona, ever the music fan.

They departed, and then Ian and Daina walked into the garage. Nick blinked stupidly at them and tried to be slick about setting the beer he was drinking down on his amp. Nick usually liked to remain sharp; he did not defile the temple of his soul with intoxicants, mostly because he'd been around more than his share of drunks and stoners at the parties they'd played, and had been more or less disgusted by all of them.

But it was New Year's Eve, and he felt like cutting loose. Randi's asshole boyfriend had dropped her off earlier in the afternoon, and seeing Randi never failed to warm Nick's soul, as well as its temple. Sure, she only had eyes for Adrian, but Nick still liked having her there. Adrian didn't want her, so someday, Nick might get his chance . . .

Ian grinned at Nick's lack of craft in hiding his beer. "Don't worry. I won't tell Doctor Wilde." Nick smiled gratefully. *"To be bowed by grief is folly; naught is gained by melancholy; better than the pain of thinking, is to steep the sense in drinking."* Ian looked at his wife, who rolled her eyes. "On the other hand, *Drink not the third glass, which thou canst not tame, when once it is within thee."*

"Good advice for all of you," Daina said.

Adrian felt his mother's anxiety again, and squeezed her hand. "I'm not gonna get drunk, Mom."

He understood his mother's fear: 1990 was about to be history, and she believed that he was going to die in 1991, apparently after he reached his majority at twenty-one (since he'd made it this far). And Adrian loved his mom; but he was glad when she left and took her fear with her. It was New Year's Eve, for God's sake. It was time to have fun. He wasn't going to die tonight.

FORTY-TWO

Gil dropped Randi off in the afternoon, then left, because he wasn't in the mood to stick around and watch her fawn over Adrian Wilde until midnight. He'd gone to the bar and enjoyed a little solitary hilarity. Then he'd returned to Wilde's house to see the year out with his woman.

Now, at eleven o'clock, even though he was half in the bag, Gil was not having a good time. He didn't know anyone at the party, except for the members of Urban Equinox, and he didn't like any of them. But Randi would've pouted if he'd made her miss her favorite band's first gig at Adrian's new house. Gil would allow her to reward him for his munificence later. In fact he would insist upon it.

Gil had a few more drinks, and joined in a few conversations. Randi flitted around from group to group as though this was *her* party. That annoyed Gil, and he decided that midnight just couldn't come quickly enough, so he could blow this pop stand, and just go on home and celebrate the first hours of 1991 alone with Randi.

But the clock seemed to be stuck at five minutes 'til twelve for two hours, so Gil abandoned the crowd and went out to the kitchen. There were people in there, too, but no one talked to him. He called Nadine. "Guess where I am?"

Not here with me, Nadine thought, but that was just being petty. She had grown fond of Gil, liked it when he called her, when he visited her. But that didn't mean she wanted him with her all the time. So there was no reason to be petty.

"I have not the foggiest," she replied.

"I'm at your old house. Adrian's aunts bought it for him. *As a Christmas present.*"

"You don't say?" Nadine had read somewhere that Aztec youths slated for sacrifice were feted to a year of wine, women, and song before the obsidian knife was inexorably unsheathed. *And the old crones are only giving Adrian seven months . . .*

"Randi wanted to see his stupid band," Gil was saying. "So here I am."

"Keep an eye on your girl, honey," Nadine advised. "Especially when the clock strikes midnight."

Gil laughed. "What's she going to do, turn into a black cat?"

Gil was well aware of Randi's witchy studies; since her babysitting job had dried up, she worked full time at Mohini's now. She brought home books and charms and incense, and twirled around in their living room, gesturing at the walls with a dagger and saying prayers. Gil had made it clear to her that he would always remain a staunch unbeliever, so Randi didn't talk to him about it.

It turned out that Nadine knew Randi's boss at the occult bookstore, and Nadine seemed to know all about that ridiculous magical shit, too. She'd also tried to explain it to him once; but Gil could not possibly care less, and had changed the subject.

"No, I think Randi's a little inexperienced for shape-shifting," Nadine replied with a giggle. "But there's a black cat there already, isn't there? A black tomcat. Your host. Just as unlucky. Just as sneaky.

"I do believe there's a quaint tradition of kissing strangers on New Year's Eve, is there not? *Stanley, look to your wife."* Nadine giggled again. She consulted her television: on *Dick Clark's New Year's Rockin' Eve,* the ball was dropping all over again. "The countdown has commenced."

"How 'bout if I come by and see you later?" Gil asked.

"That would be great. Happy New Year, honey." Nadine hung up.

Gil couldn't wait to get away from these people and go see Nadine, but for right now, he wanted to find Randi. He'd kiss his girlfriend as the clock struck twelve and shout *Happy New Year!* Then he'd hustle her out of there, take her home and show her how happy he wanted her new year to be. Once she fell asleep, he'd leave her a note, telling her that he had to go help Tim from work – his car had broken down – and then he would go see Nadine.

But Randi wasn't looking for her boyfriend to kiss as the drunken guests raucously counted down. Gil paused in the kitchen doorway and watched as Randi zeroed in on Adrian across the room. He wasn't looking back at her: he was arm and arm with his bass player and that blonde chick that drummed for them. But just as Nadine had said, Wilde's inattention wasn't going to stop Randi. She was going to kiss him at the stroke of midnight, and the consequences be damned.

But just as the clock ran out, as everybody screamed and kissed whoever they were with, Nick stepped in front of Randi, effectively blocking her from getting to Adrian. Oblivious, Adrian hugged his cousin, kissed his drummer on the cheek.

"Happy New Year, Randi," Nick said softly.

Randi knew what he wanted; she knew Nick had an enormous crush on her. She was flattered – he was an awesome guitarist – and she always tried to be nice to him. But he was just too young, and she was with Gil; it would be unkind to encourage Nick. Giving him a kiss on New Year's would be encouraging him, so she turned and looked around for Gil to come to her rescue. To Randi's surprise, her boyfriend nodded good-naturedly, effectively giving her permission to give the kid a little thrill.

Fuck you, Randi, Gil thought. *You weren't looking for me ten seconds ago. You wanted to kiss* him, *thought you might just get away with it, too, all in the name of a little holiday cheer. But he didn't even notice you. He* never *notices you. But the little redheaded kid did, and now you're stuck sharing a little holiday cheer with someone who doesn't even shave yet. Happy fucking New Year, Randi!*

Gil thought that Timmy might call about that car trouble the moment he got home. He knew Nadine would want to kiss him, and anything else he had a mind to do. On New Year's Eve or any other time.

Randi looked back at eager, just-turned-fifteen Nick. She wished him Happy New Year, and moved to kiss him on the forehead.

But Nick backed up a half a step and said, "Hell, Randi, if you're gonna kiss me, kiss me. It's New Year's Eve. What are you afraid of?"

Randi looked at Gil again. He shrugged, so Randi allowed Nick to kiss her on the lips. The kid was bold, Gil observed to his surprise. He put his arms around Randi's neck and prolonged the kiss; Gil was just about to step up and say something when he released her.

"Thanks, Randi," Nick whispered to her. "My year can't get any better than this."

Randi was touched by his earnest affection; she smiled and patted him on the shoulder. Nick wanted to kiss her again, but he figured he'd just gotten away with more than he'd ever expected, what with her asshole boyfriend standing right there. So Nick turned and winked at Gil, then quickly blended into the crowd.

Gil was amazed at the guts shown by the youngest Wilde kid. His lover boy cousin didn't have the stones to kiss Randi at midnight, but this little kid . . . Gil could've been amused by it, but he chose not to be.

Now Randi came over to give him a belated New Year's kiss. She went to put her arms around his neck, but he shook his head. "How was that?" he nodded over her shoulder.

"Jesus, Gil. He's just a little kid."

Gil decided that a little jealousy might be just the ticket. "He didn't kiss you like a little kid."

"Oh, for Christ's sake, Gil!"

"Is there anybody else here you want to kiss?"

Gil's expression dared Randi to turn around and look at Wilde. He thought that if she did, he would just go on ahead and backhand her, right here in front of God and everyone. There wasn't a dude in attendance that had the guts to say anything to him about it, and maybe that would remind Randi why she was with him, and not any of these chickenshit Wilde boys or their friends.

But Randi didn't turn around.

"No? Are you sure?" Gil asked again. "Good. Let's go." He grabbed her by the hand and dragged her across the living room. Embarrassed, Randi didn't look at Nick, and she surely didn't see Adrian put a restraining hand on his cousin's shoulder as Gil pulled her through the door.

Gil wasn't going to hurt Randi. He wasn't really even angry with her for letting that little kid slobber on her. He was angry with her for wanting to kiss the other guitar player, for thinking that she could get away with it. Even when it was obvious that Wilde didn't want anything to do with her, she still wanted to do it. And Gil wasn't even that mad about that. Sometimes, Randi seemed like a child to Gil, with her stupid crushes on guys who didn't even know that she existed.

But if Randi thought he was jealous, angry at her for kissing Nick, then maybe she'd think twice about whom she'd really wanted to kiss. And if Randi thought Gil was pissed at her, then he wouldn't even have to bring out the lie about Tim and his car. He could use that one some other time. He would just drop her off at home, tell her he was gonna go have a nightcap, leave in a huff. He knew she hated using her fake ID; she wouldn't actually be twenty-one until May.

Randi wouldn't want to go to the bar with him, and Gil would be free to go wish a grown woman a Happy New Year. Nadine didn't have any ridiculous crushes. Nadine didn't want to kiss anyone but him.

168

FORTY-THREE

On Valentine's Day, 1991, Robert William Wilde, aged eighteen, got down on one knee and asked the love of his life to marry him. An exact date wasn't specified, but the engagement ring was impressive. Bobby's parents provided him with an insanely generous allowance, and he'd saved the better part of it for some time.

He didn't relate the momentous occasion to Will and Marta; his mother would've started to bitch again about his *ridiculous infatuation with that peasant girl,* and his dad probably would've threatened to cut him off again. Unlike his little brother, who had almost from birth been stubborn and unruly, Bobby had only recently discovered a rebellious streak. It had tapped him on the shoulder on Christmas Day, when his father had forbidden him from moving in with his cousin.

This unreasonable mandate was a sore spot to Will's firstborn; it still stung, and Bobby found that the best salve was to undertake other endeavors that might also piss his dad off, such as buying Tracy an engagement ring. Bobby made it a point to save most of his money these days; he aimed to move in with his cousin (Adrian had graciously said he could bring Tracy along with him) as soon as the summer was over, whether his dad cut him off or not. If it meant some kind of break with his parents, then so be it. He wasn't a little kid anymore. They could now attempt to boss Nick around, because Bobby was going to be gone. He'd even made a few perfunctory inquiries about getting a job.

Valentine's came and went and Adrian still didn't have a girlfriend. He'd hadn't met anyone lately that had captured his attention enough even for a night on the town, not to mention anything more intimate. Nick still carried a torch for Randi, an impossible five and a half years his senior, and ignored any hopeful high school freshmen that attempted to catch his eye.

Sam Germaine passed away in his sleep on Easter Sunday, March 31st, 1991. *I am the resurrection and the life,* Nadine thought, but didn't believe it.

There were scattered clouds, but not a breath of wind when Sam was interred at Evergreen Memorial Cemetery at one o'clock on April 4th. It was unseasonably warm, but Ian and Adrian appeared cool and sad and fine in their almost identical black suits, white shirts and black ties. Penny and Bellona and Daina were veiled, like the good witches that they considered themselves to be. Lily, also veiled, came to pay her respects. After the Christian ceremony concluded and all the mourners departed, Ian walked with Irene the few blocks from the cemetery to her apartment building.

The pagan prayer for Sam's soul commenced after they were gone. The witches raised their veils. Lily stood to the north, and carried a stone, representing the earth. Bellona was at the east, a feather in her hand, signifying air. Penny stood opposite her, to the west – the river on the other side of Mt. Rubidoux was the water. Daina stood to the south and lit a stick of incense for fire. Nadine and Adrian completed the circle.

Penny called upon the four elements, invoked the powers of the cardinal directions to bless them all. Then she intoned, "By the earth and wind and the fire and rain, his soul travels. We will remember him. Take his body back to the earth from whence it came. He is not afraid. We will remember him." She turned to Nadine. "Blood of his blood, bone of his bone, flesh of his flesh, within you he continues. He will live forever within our hearts. We are not afraid. We will remember him."

The six witches closed their eyes and observed a moment of silence. Nadine felt the power of the circle, but still she hated them all, except for Lily, and she wasn't entirely sure about her. She was *their* confederate, after all.

Nadine's father had gone to his rest without ever experiencing the joy of a son-in-law or a grandchild, because Nadine had wandered the globe, rootless, husbandless, childless. She had been deprived of the man that should have been her mate by these very women that now prayed for her father's soul. And the one that should've been her son . . . Adrian would pay the ultimate price for his family's betrayal, their theft.

Nadine had never doubted the inexorable path of fate. Her own happiness had been diverted by the machinations of these women, but the universal powers would see to her revenge. And when Adrian was dust, then his father would see what a mockery they had made of his life, what a fool they had made of him. And then, at long last, Ian would see Nadine . . . *The golden age is before us, not behind us.*

Urban Equinox played a party on May 18th, but Randi wasn't there. Nick became frantic; she never missed a show. That little stunt of Gil's – dragging her out of Adrian's New Year's Eve party after Nick kissed her – Gil's overreaction had led the guitarist to believe that her boyfriend was way too jealous, that he had an abusive streak.

This view of Gil as a tyrant meshed well in Nick's mind with his fantasy of stepping in one day, as soon as he was grown enough, and rescuing Randi from Gil and showing her a better life.

Now, when she didn't show up at the party, Nick talked himself into the idea that Gil had hurt her in some way. Adrian said that was just nuts, told him to mind his own business. He claimed to not know Randi's phone number. Nick thought his cousin didn't want him to call because he thought it would provoke Randi's asshole boyfriend. But Nick wasn't afraid of Gil any more than was Adrian, but not for the same reasons. Adrian simply dismissed Randi's ol' man and his baseless, macho jealousy; Nick was willing to brave anything if it meant saving Randi.

On Sunday, Nick inquired of Adrian's aunts. They didn't have a phone, even in the Year of Our Lord 1991, so they didn't have Randi's number, either. They suggested that Nick call Mohini's and ask after her there. Lily told Nick that Randi had called in sick to work the day before; something about a sore throat. Nick asked for her number so he could check up on his friend, and Lily gave it to him.

The machine picked up; Nick left a message: "Hi, Randi, I heard you were sick. I was just calling to see if you were feeling better, or if you needed anything." That was just being neighborly, showing concern. *If her boyfriend doesn't like it, he can kiss my ass,* Nick said to himself. But Randi didn't return his call, and nothing but the machine picked up when he called back.

Sore throat notwithstanding, since Randi never returned his calls, by Monday, Nick was convinced that Gil had murdered her and skipped town. So he cut school and took a bus to Rubidoux. Nick knew where Randi lived because Tracy had picked her up for one of their earliest shows, when her car had broken down. Nick had eagerly gone along for the ride. Her worthless boyfriend couldn't even keep a car running for her.

Nick was relieved to see no police tape around the door, so maybe Gil hadn't murdered Randi after all. But why wasn't she answering the phone? Maybe she was dead, inside, and no one had discovered her yet. Nick's hatred for Gil flared as he knocked on the door; he vowed that if that son of a bitch had hurt Randi in any way, he would hunt him to the ends of the earth.

An old woman, chubby and tired-looking, answered the door. Nick blinked in surprise, stammered, "Is . . . Is Randi here?"

"Randi's sick, sweetie," she answered with a smile. "She's got strep throat. The doctor says she's very contagious."

But Randi wasn't dead, and no mere germ was going to prevent Nick from seeing her. From comforting her. He heard her sweet voice. "Who is it, Mom?"

"It's me, Randi! Nick Wilde!'"

Randi's mother stepped aside so this visibly worried kid could come in and see her daughter. "Don't say I didn't warn you if you catch it."

Randi was lying on the couch, wrapped in an ugly black and yellow afghan. She looked pale and drawn, her face was puffy, but she was still beautiful to Nick. She introduced him to her mom, who asked if she needed anything else. Randi consulted the array of remedies on the coffee table: she had tissues and cough medicine, cough drops and Vitamin C tablets. A bottle of antibiotics, Nick noted.

"It looks like I'm set, Mom," Randi said. "Thanks for babying me."

"I'll bring you some chicken soup later." She told Nick that it was nice meeting him and left.

"Where's Gil?" Nick asked.

Gil had come home from work on Friday night to find his girlfriend hacking and coughing and sneezing. Her face was swollen, her eyes red and teary. She looked haggard, homely. He was shocked when she told him that she'd called in sick at work. Randi liked being at Mohini's almost as much as she liked going to an Urban Equinox show.

Like a good boyfriend, Gil took her to the doctor, but when the medico pronounced *strep throat,* that was the last straw for Gil. He didn't want to sleep next to a puffy, sniffly, uninviting girl anyway, and certainly not one that had also become a runny-nosed germ-factory. The moment they got back home, Gil was on the phone.

"Can I stay at your house for a few days? Randi's sick. She's contagious."

There was a pause; a heartbeat, then two. At last Nadine said, "Sure, honey."

"Thanks. I'll see you soon." Gil hung up the phone and told Randi, "Tim says I can stay at his house until you're not contagious anymore. I'm sorry, Randi. I can't afford to get sick right now." *Or any other time,* he thought. "If I call in, they'll replace me with someone else."

Gil had been working at the big Lusk Homes development in Menifee for about six months. He'd told her that his job was practically permanent – the homebuilding project was supposed to go on until 1995 – so she didn't know why he was scared of getting fired for calling in sick.

Then Randi realized that it was really her sore throat: Gil was scared to death of getting sick, but it wasn't because of his job. He'd told her about the horrors of the tonsillectomy he'd undergone when he was a little boy: he said he'd almost died. But if they'd taken out his tonsils then, they couldn't take them out again, so Randi couldn't understand why he was so frightened of catching a common cold every now and then. It happened to everybody.

She considered him silently for a moment, a trifle taken aback that he would abandon her. The thought crossed Randi's mind: *I bet Adrian wouldn't take off just because I'm sick.* But Adrian – fine, *awesome* Adrian – he wasn't Randi's boyfriend. Gil was her boyfriend, and what could she do about his irrational fear of a simple sore throat? The doctor *had* said that she was contagious.

So Randi just shrugged, and told him it was okay. "Leave me Tim's phone number, and I'll call you when I'm feeling better."

Randi thought that putting Gil up for a few days was the least Tim could do, anyway. She hadn't met Gil's co-worker yet, but the guy was always calling Gil for a ride across town, or to help him when his car broke down. She reflected that neither Tim nor Gil was much of a mechanic: sometimes when Tim's car would break down, Gil would be gone all night.

Gil scribbled the number down on the pad beside the phone, then went into their bedroom and threw a couple changes of clothes into a small duffel bag. Randi stood in the doorway and watched him.

"You'll be okay. If anyone tries to break in, shoot 'em." He nodded at the closet, from which he'd pulled the duffel bag. Standing against the back wall, mostly hidden by winter coats and clothes neither of them wore anymore, were two dusty shotguns and a slightly rusted rifle.

"I don't know how to use a gun, Gil. I'm not even sure *you* do."

"I went hunting with my dad when I was a kid," he said, and pulled the drawstring closed on the bag. It wasn't a pleasant memory, hunting with his dad. He didn't have too many pleasant memories of his dad at all, and he surely didn't want to talk about them now. Randi was producing pathogens as they spoke, polluting his air with them. And Nadine was waiting for him.

Gil smiled at his girlfriend. "Remember the last time I kissed you goodbye?"

"Yeah. It was this morning."

"Well, just remember that one, 'cause I'm not getting anywhere near you right now." Gil grinned. "I promise I'll make it up to you when you're better." He told her that he would call her later, told her that he loved her, and fled their apartment.

Nadine greeted Gil with open arms. "Turn your machine off. If Randi calls, you're Tim's wife."

Gil had called Randi three or four times in the three days since he'd been gone. Now Randi rolled her eyes and answered Nick's question. "He's petrified of sore throats. He told me that he almost died from a tonsillectomy when he was a kid, so he's afraid of catching any kind of a cold. The doctor said I've got strep throat, so Gil freaked out. He's staying at his friend's house until I'm not contagious anymore."

Nick was appalled. "He left you here all by yourself, when you're sick?"

Randi regarded him with a touch of embarrassment for Gil's lack of chivalry. "I'm a big girl, Nick."

"I'd never leave you alone when you're sick." Randi glanced away at this declaration of his fealty. "Is there anything I can get for you?"

Randi smiled kindly at him. He and his affection were sweet. "Another glass of orange juice would be nice."

Nick simmered in his hatred for Gil while he waited on Randi. He was pretty sure that you couldn't get strep throat if you'd had a tonsillectomy – he'd have to ask his dad – but even if you could, it was just a sore throat, for Christ's sake.

Gil was a coward to let Randi suffer alone. *Someday, she'll see what a bastard he is,* Nick thought. *And I'll be there waiting for her when she does.*

FORTY-FOUR

Nick took the bus to Randi's house after school on Tuesday. She was improving, but still had a touch of a cough. They watched TV for a while, then Nick went around the corner to the market and bought eggs and cheese, onions and poblanos, all the fixin's for his famous chili rellenos.

Technically, Randi wasn't Nick's first crush. That had been the Wilde's former housekeeper, the beautiful, doe-eyed Esmeralda. She had left their employ when she got married, about the time Nick was thirteen, but prior to that, from about the age of ten, he had haunted the kitchen before mealtimes, just to gaze at her sultry Latina beauty. Nick was fascinated with Esmeralda: her jet black hair, her dimpled smile, her accent. Like Randi, she was kind to the boy, and since he insisted on hanging around and getting underfoot, Esmeralda had taught him how to cook.

Nick's meal was scrumptious. It was just spicy enough, and Randi was convinced that the heat helped to heal her sore throat. He really was an adorable little kid, and the old chestnut played through Randi's mind: *he'll make someone a great boyfriend someday.*

But Nick wasn't going to find himself a girlfriend – someone his own age – if he was spending all his afternoons with her. Randi saw the love shining out from his pale green eyes each and every time he looked at her. She liked him very much – but not in the way that he wanted her to – and she was worried that he was becoming too attached. She didn't want to see him get his feelings hurt.

On Wednesday, Randi went back to work. She was still feeling a little weak, but the crisis was past, and she was sure that she was no longer contagious. When she arrived home at the close of the day, she called Gil's friend; neither he nor Tim were back from the jobsite yet, but Tim's wife assured her that she would give Gil the message the minute they walked in the door.

Randi primped and perfumed; she was looking forward to seeing her boyfriend. When he knocked on the door, she was a little bit surprised and thought that he must've left his key behind in his panic to flee from her sore throat.

Randi opened the door, saying, "I've missed you so much! Did you leave your –?"

But it wasn't Gil; it was Nick. Randi was disconcerted; if the kid had called, she would've told him that she was all better now, and that it was nice that he'd been so thoughtful . . . But she would've told him not to come over anymore. Gil was on his way home, and . . . But Nick hadn't called, so Randi was just going to have to tell him in person.

She frowned at his eager, love-struck smile, and let him in the apartment. "You can't come visit me anymore, Nick. I'm better now, and Gil . . . Gil's gonna be home any minute."

"So?" Again Nick's hatred flared. The fact that Randi had chosen an asshole for a boyfriend shouldn't mean that they couldn't be friends.

Randi unconsciously spoke to Nick's thought. "He's jealous, Nick. He wouldn't like it if he came home and you were here."

"I'm not afraid of Gil, Randi."

"Maybe you should be. He's . . . He's got guns."

"Here?"

Randi nodded and showed Nick the arsenal, standing against the back of the closet.

Nick had never seen a long gun before, nor even a pistol, for that matter. "Does he hunt?"

"I guess his dad did. He told me that his mother said she didn't want them in the house. He's got two little brothers. So they've been here for as long as I've known him."

"Are they loaded?"

Randi shrugged. "I don't know. He's never taken them out of the closet. Like I say, they were his dad's and his dad passed on when he was nineteen. I don't even know if he knows how to use them."

Randi slid the closet door closed and quickly exited the bedroom. What would Gil do if he came home and found her with Nick *in the bedroom?* She sat on the couch and Nick sat down next to her. That really wasn't good either.

Randi didn't think that Gil would shoot Nick. He wouldn't shoot anybody. But if he came home and Nick was there . . . It could get ugly. Nick was a nice kid. Randi thought that it was endearing that he had such a crush on her, but he was just a kid, and she wouldn't want to see him get hurt. Gil wouldn't shoot him – she hadn't ever seen him so much as even touch one of those guns – but he might smack Nick, just for hanging around.

"The point is, he *has* them. And he's jealous," Randi repeated.

She remembered New Year's Eve, how Gil had dragged her out of Adrian's party for allowing Nick to give her a little holiday kiss. She remembered how he'd left her all alone in the wee hours of the first day of the new year and gone to the bar. Randi didn't want to put up with Gil's groundless jealousy again, just because this *boy* had a crush on her. Randi was looking forward to her boyfriend's return, and she certainly didn't want to fight with him, so she had to get rid of this kid.

"I'm feeling better now, Nick. I went to work today. You don't have to come here anymore."

Nick remembered New Year's Eve too, but he wasn't afraid. He only felt an overwhelming hatred for Gil and the frustration of being only fifteen and in love with someone who saw him as a child. Nick wasn't a child; sometimes he thought that he'd never been one. But his quick, exceptional, *adult* mind was trapped in an only half-grown body at the moment, but someday . . . Someday, he just might kick Gil's ass for the fun of it, whether or not it meant that Randi would see how much he loved her. But she probably would, and then she would be his . . .

But that day was still a long way off. "I understand, Randi. I'm glad you're feeling better."

"Thanks for coming to visit me." Randi arose and opened the front door. She thought about giving Nick a hug and maybe a little kiss on the cheek – he was so nice – but then she decided that such a gesture would only encourage him. "I'll see you soon," she said. "At your next show."

Nick nodded and walked out the door. He was despondent as he shambled to the bus stop, gripped by the agony of unrequited love. He sat on the bench and sighed. *What does she see in that creep?* But Nick knew what it was: Gil was twenty-five, had a car and a job. He didn't have to take the bus to see the woman he loved.

Nick doubted that Gil truly loved Randi, anyway. Surely not the way that he loved her. If he did, he wouldn't have left her to fend for herself when she was sick.

Nick longed to be older; it seemed to him as if he'd longed to be older for his entire life. Penny and Bellona had said that he was an old soul; he had grasped peoples' adult desires and motivations from a far too early age, even if he hadn't initially felt them in himself, as he did now. He wished that he could think up some way to demonstrate his love for Randi, some kind of mature gesture, something more than just babysitting her when she was sick. Something more than just cooking dinner for her.

Nick sighed again and looked at his watch. The bus wouldn't be along for twenty more minutes, and the weather was hot. It was May 22nd – he knew because there were two little windows on his watch that told him the date – and Nick reflected that summer was already, undeniably, here.

Nick looked at his watch again and brightened. If today was the 22nd, then Randi's birthday was on Saturday, the 25th. He only remembered because he'd asked her sign, the very night they'd met.

She'd looked so pretty then, standing up front while they played. Nick had always noticed the attractiveness of his band's fans – he was an old soul, after all, and had possessed a man's discerning eye and mind long before the rest of him caught up – he'd considered their charms in the same way Adrian did, without ever possessing the desire to act on this consideration. Until he saw Randi.

She'd been talking to Adrian after their set, and Nick had just rolled on up and said hi, and asked her sign. Nick had observed girls always asking Adrian what sign he was, so he knew that it was something that they liked to talk about.

Randi told him, "I'm a Gemini. My birthday's the 25th of May."

Nick had gone to the library and looked up Geminis, read that they were supposed to be clever but soft-spoken, spontaneous but sometimes inconsistent. That certainly seemed to describe Randi.

Nick smiled to himself. He would bet that Randi didn't even remember telling him her birthdate. He knew exactly the grown-up gesture that would please her.

FORTY-FIVE

The minute Nick walked into the house, he got Adrian on the horn. "How many favors do you owe me, Cuz?"

Adrian grinned. "I can't think of a single one, my brutha."

"How about the time I told that cross-eyed chick that you were going with Tracy, so she'd quit following you around at the party?"

"She wasn't cross-eyed, Nick. She was just –"

"Annoying? How about the time I confided to Emily that you'd been going to the doctor a lot – something about a rash of an unfortunately intimate nature – so she would stop coming to *every single one* of our shows, and thereby putting a crimp in your style? How about the time –"

"All right. Maybe I do owe you a few." Adrian had to admit that Nick was right. He was quite the little wingman, at least as far as getting rid of bothersome girls was concerned. It was something that as-good-as-married-since-he-was-fourteen Bobby had never been.

"You can make it all up to me at once, Adrian. Here's what you're gonna do. You're gonna get your aunts to call Randi at about four o'clock on Saturday and tell them that she has to get over to their place immediately. In the meantime, we're gonna plan a surprise birthday party for her."

Adrian sighed. "I dunno, Nick." He didn't really want to throw a party for Randi, because it would mean that he'd have to put up with her ol' man glowering at him for the entire time. Randi was cute, and she was sweet, and Adrian appreciated that she liked him, but Gil was a drag.

"I could call Emily and let her know the good news, that the doctor has given you a clean bill of health. Your rash is all cleared up, and you're just dying to see her."

Adrian smiled again. It was a weak threat. He thought Emily was okay, just a little clingy, and Nick knew it. But his cousin had never asked for a favor before, and Adrian knew how much the kid liked Randi, so, "I guess, if it's important to you."

"Thanks, Cuz. I'll get Tracy to invite some of her and Randi's friends. But not Emily."

FORTY-SIX

Penny and Bellona thought a surprise birthday party for Randi was a delightful idea.

"It's not every day that a young woman turns twenty-one," Bellona said, and Adrian thought he saw a shadow cross her face. He would be twenty-one in not much more than thirty days. His legal majority would thereby be attained, and according to Bellona and her sister, then he was gonna die.

Bellona's smile quickly returned, and she said, "She's such a lovely girl."

She and Penny were quite fond of Randi, and suggested to Adrian that he should attempt to woo her away from Gil.

"Don't count on it," he demurred. "I don't want someone else's woman."

"She's likes you very much. *Without a doubt,"* Penny scolded. "We only get so many people in this life that like us the way Randi likes you."

Let's see, Adrian said to himself. *There's Randi. And there was Eileen – Christ, Eileen liked me as much as* five *Randis. And there's Emily, and that cross-eyed chick that Nick mentioned . . . And that's just this year.*

"Arrogance is not becoming in a young man, Adrian," Penny said primly, as if she'd read his mind. "You shouldn't be so cold to Randi."

Bellona's smile flashed brilliantly. "How did those English boys put it?" She sang softly to Adrian. *"Who'd believe you were a beauty indeed, when the days get shorter and the nights get long; lie awake when the rain comes . . . Nobody will know . . ."*

Adrian joined her. *"When you're old, when you're ooold, nobody will know, that you was a beauty, a sweet, sweet beauty, a sweet, sweet beauty, but stone, stone cold!"* He and Bellona dissolved into laughter, but Penny remained stern.

Noticing her lack of a smile, Adrian insisted, "I'm not cold to Randi, Aunt Penny. We're friends. And besides, I could never go for her, even if she was single. Nick would never speak to me again."

"Ah, the towering ego of men," Penny replied. "You speak of yourself and Nick as if the choice would be yours or his. If her circumstances changed . . . The choice would be Randi's."

"And she would choose you. *You may rely on it,"* Bellona said and winked at him.

"Outlook not so good," Adrian returned. "Even in a different world, if Randi was single . . ." Adrian considered it for a minute, then shook his head. "I could never do that to Nick."

"Nothing is so powerful as an idea whose time has come," Penny said and glanced at her sister. Then she said to Adrian, *"Love is the triumph of imagination over intelligence* in Nick's case, Capo. One must accept reality, no matter how unpalatable it might be. There will never be a Randi and Nick."

"But there's definitely possibilities for a Randi and *Adrian. It is decidedly so."* Bellona grinned at him when he shook his head again. She winked at her sister, and let the thought go.

FORTY-SEVEN

At four o'clock on May 25th, Bellona used Adrian's phone to call Mohini's. Bellona told Lily of the plan, then asked her to put Randi on the line.

"I'm so sorry to bother you, dear, but I have an urgent favor to ask." Bellona grinned at her sister, and Penny returned her smile.

They truly are devious, Adrian thought and also smiled. But Nick was still anxious. What if they couldn't get her to come? Then the whole surprise party would be for nothing.

"Your wish is my command," Randi replied with a relieved smile. No one had remembered her birthday, least of all Gil, and if she could go help Miss Bellona in some way, at least she might get to see Adrian.

"Penny has sprained her wrist, and I wonder if you could pick up some Knitbone so I could make a poultice for her."

"Knitbone? A . . . poultice?"

"Comfrey, dear. It's an herb. I'm sure Lily has some in stock. A poultice is a compress. Like a wrapping."

"Do we have any Knitbone, Miss Lily?" Lily nodded, and Randi told Bellona, "I'll be there right away."

"Thanks, Randi. And ask Lily if she would like to close up shop early and come along. She makes a better poultice than I do."

FORTY-EIGHT

Like the considerate girlfriend that she was, Randi called Gil and told him that she wouldn't be right home after work. She explained that she needed to make a quick delivery to her witchy old friends' house first. Gil said okay, told her that he'd see her soon.

Gil knew about the surprise party for his young girlfriend, because the old gals had also invited his other, more mature girlfriend. Nadine told Gil that Penny and Bellona believed that she was sad and lonely since her father's death, and thought that perhaps a party might cheer her up. There was no way for them to know, of course, that Gil had been cheering her up on a regular basis, since long before Sam had passed.

Nadine had called on Wednesday night to let him know about the planned surprise. When Randi answered the phone, Nadine reprised her role as Tim's wife, said she was looking for her husband, and asked to speak to Gil. At first, Gil thought he might just tell Randi about the party: he considered purposely blowing the whole thing. He was resentful that he hadn't thought of it first, and figured that if it was to be held at the old ladies' funky little house in the woods, then Adrian Wilde had to be involved somehow.

But then Gil reconsidered. Thinking up a lie about how he'd found out about it was a logistical snag; besides, he thought he'd enjoy torturing Randi for a few days by pretending to forget her birthday. He knew that she would be thrilled when they all yelled *Surprise!* and she discovered that he'd known about the party all along, that he hadn't forgotten her birthday after all. She'd figure that one of her friends had told him about it. Gil thought that if he could somehow also con Randi into thinking that the whole thing had been his idea, then that would be even better.

FORTY-NINE

Since Will had gone all parental on him at Christmas, Bobby had discovered that he enjoyed a little subterfuge; sometimes he told Mom and Dad that he was going one place when he was really going somewhere else, just because the act made him feel superior: he knew something that they didn't.

Adrian recognized the rebellious streak, as a similar thing had manifested itself in him with his sudden desire to smoke pot and hang out with criminals. "It's just a phase," he told his cousin, from his place of learned wisdom and easily won reform. "Just don't get a mind to start stealing cars."

Bobby's sudden appreciation for deception had led him to want to make sure that there would be no slip-ups before Randi's surprise party: she *would be surprised,* and he would see to it. He'd dug out a set of walkie-talkies he and Adrian had used as children, and he positioned himself behind the living room curtain in his cousin's house. He observed Randi pull up with her boss from Mohini's; they parked in Adrian's driveway. Lily got out and waited by the car while Randi ran up and knocked on his cousin's door. Bobby had known it would go down that way.

Like Nick, Bobby had observed all the ladies that chased his band's singer, as well as the ones that Adrian sometimes allowed to catch him. Bobby didn't envy his cousin for this seemingly endless variety of women; in fact, Bobby knew that Adrian envied *him.* Bobby understood that what Adrian wanted was not a different girl any time the fancy struck him. He wanted just one girl to love and to love him back, for the rest of his life, like Bobby had with Tracy, and Ian had with Daina.

And Randi certainly loved Adrian, so Bobby knew that she would check to see if he was home first before continuing up to drop off her urgent herbal remedy to his aunts. Bobby thought that Adrian could do far worse than Randi. He found her willing to scheme in her pursuit of his cousin – like Gil, Bobby had apprehended her design to kiss Adrian on New Year's Eve – and Bobby admired her stick-to-it-tiveness in going after what she wanted.

Bobby thought that Randi was smart if not learned; willing, capable, easily commanded. He thought she would be a useful and loving partner for his cousin. But Adrian wasn't interested in her because she offered him no mystery, and because she was someone else's girl. Bobby shrugged mentally; Adrian was a big boy. He could make his own decisions.

Now he waited while Randi waited for Adrian to come to the door. When she was sure that he wasn't home, and turned to collect Lily and go up the hill, Bobby said into the walkie-talkie, *"Houston, Tranquility Base here. The Eagle has landed."*

Apollo 11 had touched down on the lunar surface four years before Bobby was born, but Ian had once told him about it. Adrian's dad could tell a good story, and he'd filled this one with thrilling details of cliff-hanging suspense and all-American success. The idea of man's walking on the moon (as related by Ian) had thereby fired Bobby's imagination. He remembered all of Neil Armstrong's immortal words.

"What?" Nick replied.

Bobby sighed. His brother, on the other hand, had *zero* imagination. "Randi's here. She's on her way to your position. Shush everyone up." Bobby waited until Randi and Lily disappeared, then locked up Adrian's house and followed her. He didn't want to miss the big reveal.

When Randi stepped onto the deck, the twenty or so people that Tracy had scared up yelled *Surprise!* and Urban Equinox (sans their bass player) swung into *Happy Birthday.* The crowd sang and Randi grinned from ear to ear. She was completely surprised. She turned around and looked at Lily, who returned her smile. Lily was in on it. Wasn't that nice of her? She saw Bobby behind her. They were all so sweet.

Randi didn't notice Gil standing off to one side with Nadine when she trotted up to Adrian as *Happy Birthday* concluded. *Oh, my God, he* does *like me! This is the sweetest thing anyone's ever done for me . . . Oh, Adrian, you're so awesome!* The only thing that kept her from embracing him was his guitar and the pedals and wires in front of him.

Adrian frowned when he heard her thoughts, but he waited for her to say her piece out loud. "Thank you so much, Adrian!" she cried. "This is just . . . wonderful!"

"Don't thank me, birthday girl," Adrian said into the mike. He turned and looked at Nick, as did the rest of the crowd. They offered a round of applause and Nick bowed humbly and smiled at Randi.

So much for telling her it was my idea, Gil thought.

Randi's smile faltered when she realized it wasn't Adrian who had been so attentive as to devise a surprise birthday party for her.

185

But then her smile returned. No sense hurting Nick's feelings. He was a nice kid. She stepped over the pedals and wires and gave him a chaste kiss on the cheek. "Thanks, Nick," she said softly.

"Cake and ice cream, everybody!" Bellona called from the table across the deck. "Come on, Randi! Make a wish!"

Randi looked around. She found Gil. So he was in on it, too: he hadn't forgotten her birthday! She smiled at him. Gil glowered – she had kissed that kid again – but his jealous expression lasted only a moment.

Gil smiled, came over and put his arm around her. It was her birthday, after all, and Gil had seen her disappointment when she kenned that it hadn't been the eldest Wilde that had remembered her birthday, but the little one that had a crush on her. Gil reveled in her disappointment. Randi had no affection for Nick, and thereby Gil decided that there was no profit in it for him to pretend to be jealous of the little guitar player. He decided that the kid's impossible desire for his woman was just plain hilarious.

The party-goers obediently gathered around and waited for Randi to blow out the candles and make her birthday wish. Gil noted that while Tracy and Bobby, and Nick, of course, had joined the well-wishers beside Randi, Adrian stayed behind and fiddled with his guitar. Gil saw Randi look over everyone's heads for her favorite singer; Gil enjoyed her frown when she saw that Wilde was once again ignoring her.

I know what you're gonna wish for, baby, Gil thought, *but wish all you want. Wilde's afraid of me, and as long as we're together, he's never gonna look at you twice.*

Randi closed her eyes and took a deep breath. Everything was in readiness: evil spirits were known to attack on a person's birthday, and her friends had been gathered around to help protect her from them. The large cake was shaped like a crescent moon, to symbolize Artemis; the candles were there to recreate the moon's glow. The smoke of the extinguished candles would carry her wish to the hidden powers that existed to make it come true.

Randi knew these things because she'd heard tales of them from Lily and Bellona and Penny, and anything the old witches told her, Randi believed as the most absolute of gospel truths. So Randi wished fervently, as fervently as any nine-year-old girl who'd ever wished for a pony on her birthday: *Forces that have always been, forgive my past and future sin. Grant one wish that I do crave, give me what I most would have! Adrian!*

186

Randi opened her eyes and blew out all her candles. As the assemblage clapped and cheered, Gil watched his girlfriend look around for the object of her wish. Unlike his nemesis, Gil was not even vaguely precognitive. He would've laughed at the very idea, because Gil didn't believe in one single thing that he couldn't see or touch. So he hadn't read Randi's mind, although he'd guessed precisely what her wish would be. He was just observant; he knew her.

Gil remembered a time, before Randi had met Adrian Wilde, when that special smile and that glow in her blue eyes had been exclusively for him. It wasn't that she didn't look at him like that anymore, because she still did. But Gil hated Adrian – and he hated Randi a little bit, too – whenever he saw her gaze so lovingly after the uninterested guitar player.

Adrian still ignored her. He'd rather occupy himself with adjusting the strings on his axe than pay attention to this most ancient of birthday traditions. *Well,* Randi told herself, *wishes seldom come true immediately. Perhaps someday . . .*

She turned to smile at her boyfriend, discovered that he was already looking at her with that same jealous glower on his face. But it disappeared immediately, and he smiled at her. "Happy birthday, baby," he said and embraced her. *There's no use acting jealous and ruining her birthday,* Gil thought generously. *Wilde hasn't got the guts to even look at her because he's afraid I'll kill him. So it doesn't matter what she wants . . .*

"I love you, Gil," Randi said from within his encircling arms.

I know you do, Gil thought, then frowned when the idea struck him that Randi only loved him because she couldn't get Adrian Wilde to love *her.* It hadn't always been that way . . .

But for all his jealous and possessive nature, Gil wasn't one to dwell on things that he couldn't change. Wilde was afraid of him, so he would never give Randi what she wanted. He knew Adrian's cowardice was as immutable as Randi's affection, and since he couldn't do anything about that, why worry about it?

"I love you, too, Randi," he told her. "Let's get some cake."

FIFTY

Urban Equinox played their vaudevillian set. When it concluded, the party guests cheered, then resolved themselves into groups of twos and threes and commenced to chatting. Nick set down his guitar and went to look for Randi, to further bask in her appreciation for his mature and thoughtful gesture.

He didn't see her in the crowd, so he looked inside, and when he didn't find her there, he went around to the back of the house. There was only a narrow strip of deck there, between the house and the railing, and Nick didn't really expect to find Randi there. But hey, you never know, maybe she'd looked for a moment of solitude, and if she had, then he would get a chance to talk to her alone.

Nick rounded the corner of the house; Randi wasn't there. In the clearing below, he saw her walking away toward the path. He went over to the railing and called to her. "Where are you going?"

"I'm going to run up to the market and buy one of those disposable cameras. I'll be right back!" Nick watched until she disappeared in the trees. He sighed. *She's so beautiful!*

Nick turned to go back to the party, but when he happened to glance through the window to the spare bedroom, he got the biggest shock of his young life.

The window was large; *it's called a picture window*, some part of Nick's brain gibbered. The picture that it showed him appalled, amazed, *infuriated* him.

Midnight blue curtains decked with golden astrological signs and magical symbols obscured most of the room's interior, but the gap between them allowed Nick to get an eyeful. He marveled at his luck, the serendipity of circumstance. The weather was hot and the window should've been open: if it had been, then the people he saw would've heard him call to Randi. But Adrian's aunts didn't use the extra bedroom, so they hadn't bothered to open its window. Noise from outside was blocked out; the people inside were unaware that Nick had come around to the back of the house. They were entirely oblivious to the fact that he could see them, that he was watching them.

Gil had Nadine pushed up against the door; hungrily, he kissed her neck. She shoved him away playfully. He came back immediately and picked her up. Nadine wrapped her legs around him and they made out passionately for a minute. Then Nadine broke the kiss and Gil set her on her feet again. Her arms were still around his neck; she removed one of her hands to tenderly brush his hair from his eyes. They smiled at each other and Gil kissed her again.

Nick had seen enough. He had seen *more* than enough.

He quickly rounded the corner of the house, then the other corner. Adrian was sitting at the table with his parents and Bobby and Tracy. Nick stopped, caught his cousin's eye, nodded. *I need you to come over here right now!*

Adrian heard Nick's voice in his head, caught the brook-no-excuses insistence. "I'll be right back," he said to his relatives, and arose to join his cousin.

Nick grabbed Adrian by the arm and dragged him around to the back of the house. "You're not going to fucking believe this!" he whispered. "Look in that window. Tell me what you see."

Adrian put his hands around his eyes and did as he was bid. "I see an empty room. It used to be my mom's room, when she was a kid."

Nick shoved him out of the way and looked between the curtains. The door stood open. The bedroom was indeed empty.

"What was I supposed to see?" Adrian asked.

"Oh, my *Christ,* Adrian! It was *disgusting!*"

"What?" Adrian could not imagine what it could've been that had upset Nick so much.

"I was looking for Randi. I came back here, thinking she might've . . . I dunno, I thought she might've wanted a minute alone or something. I saw her going up the path. She said she was gonna go buy a camera. *They knew she'd be gone for a little while, Adrian!"* Nick grabbed his cousin by the forearms.

"Who knew, Nick?"

Nick released him. "I glanced in the window as I went back . . . I saw Gil and Nadine making out, Adrian! He had her backed up against the door, then he picked her up . . ."

Adrian looked in through the window again. He saw Tracy come out of the bathroom and pass by the open door. He looked back at Nick, speechless. What Nick had described *was* disgusting. It was . . . impossible. At last he said, "You couldn't've seen that, Nick."

"Why not?" Nick replied with bitter sarcasm. "Because I'm just a kid and don't know foreplay when I see it?" Adrian winced. "Because Gil is such a fine, upstanding human being that you know he'd never cheat on his girlfriend? Because your aunt is –"

"She's almost old enough to be his mother, Nick!"

189

"So what? Doesn't your mother . . ." Nick thought better of that train of inquiry and let it go. "I'm gonna tell Randi. As soon as she gets back."

"You can't do that." Adrian put his hand on his cousin's shoulder, hoping to comfort him, to calm his righteous anger.

Nick flinched his hand away. "Why not? She should know what a conniving son of a bitch he is! Then maybe she'll see . . ." He looked helplessly at his cousin.

"It's her birthday, for God's sake, Nick. It's none of your business . . ." Nick glared at him: it most assuredly *was* his business. Adrian tried another tack. "You'll hurt her, Nick. She'll hate you for telling her."

This idea gave Nick pause. He couldn't bear it if Randi hated him. "But she has to know!"

Adrian considered. "Maybe there's some way we can make it so she finds out on her own."

"How?"

"I dunno. Let me think about it. Come on. Let's go back. Don't tell anyone else until we can figure this out."

Nick nodded and they returned to the table where their relatives sat. Nick effortlessly blended into the conversation, but Adrian couldn't pay attention to what was being said.

Nick couldn't have really seen what he'd described. That was just nuts. Sure, Gil had repeatedly demonstrated that he was an asshole, with his threats to kill Adrian and his dragging Randi out of the house on New Year's Eve for innocently giving Nick a good luck kiss . . .

Adrian suddenly recalled a term he'd learned in some psychology elective he'd taken in high school: *projection.* Maybe Gil constantly *projected* suspicion and jealousy, because he was secretly a cheating bastard himself. *So, yeah,* Adrian thought, *I wouldn't put it past Gil, but AnTeen . . .*

Christ! She's old enough to be his mother!

Adrian did the math in his head. Gil was twenty-five, and AnTeen was the same age as his mom, so that made her forty-three. Adrian guessed that forty-three wasn't that old, not really. Like Nick had started to say, his mom and dad still . . . But Ian was forty-five, two years older than his wife. *They call that age appropriate,* Adrian thought. *On the other hand, Gil's seventeen years younger than AnTeen!* Nick had to be mistaken.

190

But then Adrian remembered the wickedness he had always sensed in Nadine. He remembered the anticipation, the expectation that he'd read from her when she'd just shown up out of the blue at his eighteenth birthday party, after he hadn't seen her since he was twelve. Adrian remembered sensing a womanliness to her, a dimension that he'd been too young to see before.

He remembered thinking, *AnTeen wants something.* Adrian had first thought that she wanted his dad, but had then decided that it was probably just a boyfriend she was seeking.

But it couldn't be Gil. Gil was such a jerk; but more importantly, he was Randi's boyfriend. They lived together. AnTeen would never stoop so low as to take someone else's man . . .

Adrian thought about it. *One of the biggest mistakes you can make in life,* his Aunt Penny had told him once, *is to believe that everyone thinks just like you do, Capo.* Adrian didn't want someone else's woman, but that was just his own personal philosophy. His AnTeen had come back to town looking for a boyfriend, and maybe she didn't mind messing with someone else's.

Adrian tried to wrap his head around it, but acceptance wasn't coming to him easily. Sure, he had sensed that AnTeen was on the make when she came back to town, but . . . Gil? Then Adrian remembered how she'd laughed and joked with Gil when they'd helped her move, how he'd had to honk the truck's horn to get Gil to come out of the house for one of the final loads. He'd been in there alone with AnTeen . . .

Adrian hadn't thought anything about it at the time, but now that his cousin had put the idea into his mind . . . He looked for Nadine in the crowd, and damned if she wasn't standing across the deck, talking to Gil. Adrian remembered the power, the wickedness that he had always felt within her. Such dark energies could easily lend themselves to adultery, Adrian thought. He tried to read her mind, but since she was neither thinking *at* him nor *about* him, he got nothing.

He and his dad and Gil had helped AnTeen move, going on three years ago; Adrian suddenly wondered if this thing had been going on between them all that time.

FIFTY-ONE

At the same moment that she saw Randi arrive back on the deck, clutching a little blue disposable camera, Nadine also saw Ian sitting at the table, smiling and laughing with his family. Before today, she hadn't seen him since her father's funeral the previous month, and she hadn't had a chance to talk to him since this surprise birthday party extravaganza had commenced.

Nadine waved at Randi, and the dear, ignorant little thing trotted over to them. "Let me see." Nadine held her hand out for the camera. "I used to be a photographer, back in the dim reaches of time." She wound the leader forward on the camera and gestured for Randi to go stand beside her man. "Say, *money!*"

The happy couple said *money,* and Nadine snapped their picture. She smiled faintly at Gil and handed the camera to him, then wandered away. There was no plausible reason for her to hang around with them, so she was free to go talk to Ian without Gil hanging around with her.

There was a lull in the conversation and Daina glanced at the party guests. She saw Nadine take a deep breath, smooth out her clothes, all the while staring at Ian. Daina mused that maybe it was all true, that maybe Nadine might indeed still carry a torch for her husband. She sighed to herself with a touch of conceit. *Wasn't all that just sad? Wasn't it just too bad?*

Nadine walked over, but before she could address her soulmate, her enemy said, "Tell us, Nadine." Daina squeezed her husband's hand. "Do you miss traveling?"

God, how I despise you! Nadine thought. But she smiled and said, "Funny you should mention that. Since Dad's gone, Mom's decided that she wants to go home to San Francisco. She grew up there. My Aunt Ursula is also a widow and has a big empty house, so she's glad Mom's coming back.

"Mom and I are finally gonna get to travel together. We're gonna load up a U-Haul truck and I'm gonna drive her up PCH. We're going to make an adventure of it – visit Carmel and Big Sur; Half Moon Bay. I picked up all kinds of touristy guides and stuff from the Triple A."

"Just the two of you?" Nick asked curiously.

Adrian heard Nick's voice in his head. *Here it comes, Cuz. Just you wait.*

"Actually, Gil has volunteered to ride up there with us." She glanced across the deck to where he was taking pictures of Randi and her friends. "So we'll have someone to take the furniture out of the truck. To help Mom unpack."

What did I fucking tell you?

For Christ's sake, Nick! Her mother's gonna be with them.

Nick blinked at Adrian. *Don't you believe it, Cuz. Don't you believe it for a minute. What's her mom, like ninety? She's not riding in a hot U-Haul truck all the way up the coast. She's gonna fly. It's gonna be just the two of them in that truck. Making an adventure of it.*

"When are you leaving?" Nick asked, thinking that he would go over and visit Randi the very next day.

"Not 'til almost the end of next month. We should be back on the 4th. Just in time for Adrian's birthday." *And his doom,* Nadine thought.

"We'll be gone," Bobby said morosely.

"What?" Nick and Adrian said in unison.

"Dad didn't tell you? He told me." Bobby grasped Tracy's hand, but he didn't smile. "We're leaving for Europe on the second. We won't be back 'til the first week in August."

"But we can't miss Adrian's birthday!" Nick exclaimed. "He's turning twenty-one! He's gonna buy me a beer!"

"Dad's doing it on purpose, Nick. He knows I'm moving in with Adrian when we get home, whether he cuts me off or not, so he scheduled our vacation so we would miss Adrian's birthday. Just to be a dick."

"Flexing a little parental muscle," Nadine said. She reflected that she had never really liked Will, but she applauded his effort to control his son in this case. Anything that spoiled Adrian's good time was okay with Nadine. *Hell, you might never see your cousin again, Red. According to the prophecy, he'll be dead by the time you get back.*

Bobby looked miserably at Adrian. "I said I wouldn't go, but then Mom said she'd bought a ticket for Tracy, too."

"Well, I'm not gonna go," Nick said. "Fuck Dad."

"Yes you are," Adrian said. "You're not gonna give up Europe just for my birthday party." *They won't let you stay behind anyway. You're only fifteen years old. I think that might be illegal.* Adrian put his hands up and mimicked Macaulay Culkin's face from *Home Alone.*

Fuck you, Adrian.

Adrian smiled at Nick, and clapped Bobby on the shoulder. "It's okay, Cuz. We'll just party three times as hard when you get back."

"I'm sorry, Adrian," Bobby said unhappily.

"Not a big deal, my brutha. We've got our whole lives ahead of us.

FIFTY-TWO

As they inevitably do, Randi's surprise twenty-first birthday party drew to a close. The friends that Tracy had invited wished her many happy returns and left in twos and threes. Tracy and Bobby said their goodbyes. Randi, a little tipsy and feeling generous, gave Nick a big hug (Gil frowned), and told him thanks, since he was leaving with his brother. Nick said it was the least he could do. Then Randi and Gil also departed, leaving Adrian alone at his aunts' house with his dad and his womenfolk.

The ladies went inside. "I'm going back to the house," Ian told his son. "I think your mom wants to talk to you. I'll see you later." Ian wouldn't meet Adrian's eyes. Adrian thought that was odd; but his dad had already gone down the steps, so he shrugged and went inside to see what his mother wanted.

A small family of candles was ablaze on the dining room table: three squat, fat ones and two tall, thin ones. Daina and Penny and Bellona and Lily were seated around the table, their attention absorbed by a Tarot lay. When Adrian walked up to the table, the four witches turned as one and looked at him.

Penny began, "The time has come . . ."

"The walrus said." Adrian grinned at his own wit. He'd had a little too much to drink during Randi's interminable party. Just as he'd predicted, her ol' man had spent most of the evening glaring at him, and just as he'd known it was going to be, it had been a drag. And there had been Nick's revelations of seeing Gil and AnTeen making out. *Yuck.* Now Adrian was feeling the four or five beers he'd consumed.

When Penny didn't smile back at him, he smiled at his mom. "Dad said you wanted to talk to me?"

"Sit down, Adrian," Bellona said. "We have to . . . instruct you. The time draws nigh. It's time you learned *The Incantations of Thoth.* So that you may . . . continue."

Adrian flopped down into the proffered chair. He remembered his aunt's mention of the Egyptian deity and his spells the day that he'd gotten out of jail, the day that they'd told him that he was going to die.

Adrian really wasn't in the mood for all that shit at the moment, either. But they were his family and they were concerned for him, and he loved them; he knew he'd have to listen to it. So why not make the most of it? He wiggled his eyebrows at Bellona. "Did you find me a woman?"

"No," Penny said simply. "The woman . . . You'll know . . . when the opportunity presents itself. But first, you have to learn *The Incantations.* So that when the time is right . . . You'll recite them, as you . . ." Penny trailed off. She held Adrian's gaze for another moment, then looked away. Adrian thought she might have blushed.

That surprised him: Adrian didn't think he'd ever seen his stern Aunt Penny blush. He glanced at Daina and Bellona and Lily. Only Lily met his eyes. She smiled.

No one spoke for what seemed like several seconds. Confused by their reticence – his life was supposedly at stake here – Adrian at last said, "Well . . . instruct me, then."

Daina cleared her throat. "Nowadays, sometimes people have babies for a reason, son."

"Babies? How does that . . . What does that have to do with –"

"Yes." Daina cut him off. "Babies."

From his mother's demeanor, Adrian gleaned what was to follow would be a prepared speech. *She's rehearsed this.* The impression was underlined when Daina picked up a folded piece of paper from beside the Tarot lay. Adrian saw it was a Xerox of an article from *The New York Times,* dated June 4th, 1991.

Daina cleared her throat again and read, *"At about eight o'clock this morning, doctors at the City of Hope Medical Center in Duarte, California, plan to transplant bone marrow into a nineteen-year-old girl who is dying of leukemia. The marrow will come from her baby sister. Their parents say they conceived the baby to provide bone marrow to save her sister's life."* Daina looked up at her son; when Adrian only blankly returned her gaze, she continued. *"Ethicists and doctors are asking whether conceiving a child as a source of donated organs violates the principle that individuals should be brought into the world and cherished for their own sake and no other motive. Others argue that the children who are conceived to donate organs are deeply loved and that it is unfair to point fingers at parents who have a child to save another person's life. From the point of view of the child, they say, it is certainly better to have been conceived to donate rather than to have never been conceived at all. It may even be justifiable to abort a fetus of the wrong tissue type, some experts say –"*

"Why are you telling me this, Mom?" Adrian asked in alarm. "I don't have leukemia." He looked at his aunts. "Do I?"

"No," Penny assured him. "You don't have leukemia."

"We just wanted to show you, Capo, that science is catching up with the ancient arts," Bellona said. "After a fashion."

Lily still smiled, still stared at Adrian. "Although it's really not even remotely the same thing."

Again, the room fell silent; again Adrian's mother and his aunts wouldn't look at him. "Who?" he began. "How . . . What exactly are you trying to tell me?"

Then it seemed that they were all speaking at once, except for Lily, who just grinned at him.

"You have to find a girl, son," Daina said. "A healthy, *fertile* girl . . ."

"And then," Bellona continued, "just as you're about to . . ."

"Then, you say the words," Penny said, "and as you . . . Then you will . . . continue."

Silence again. Adrian looked at each of them; his mother looked at the ceiling. Penny looked at the table in front of her; Bellona looked at the floor. What were they trying to tell him? Why were his strong, well-spoken, feminist-minded aunts and mother suddenly behaving like stammering, blushing schoolgirls? Why were they talking about babies, about healthy, *fertile* girls?

Adrian looked at Lily for explanation and her grin widened.

"Ladies, I think you are all too close to this," she said. "I neither birthed him, nor nursed him. I neither bathed him, nor diapered his freshly-powdered bottom. He's nothing other than an attractive young man to me."

Adrian didn't have to read Lily's mind. Her words and her smile, now become slightly feral, spoke volumes. He thought that the temperature in the room might've risen a few degrees. He suddenly felt very uncomfortable.

"So, you all go on, now." Lily nodded at the other witches. "Aunt Lily will tell Adrian about the birds and the bees."

Daina and Bellona and Penny didn't hesitate; they arose and filed quickly out the door. Adrian looked wonderingly after them, then turned back to Lily's wolfish smile. They'd said something about finding him a woman . . . Surely, they couldn't mean . . . Lily, smiling admiringly at him, was neither young nor fertile. Surely they didn't want him to . . . *That's Gil's type of deal,* Adrian thought, a little hysterically.

Adrian glanced over his shoulder in the direction his relatives had fled. They were gazing in at him and Lily through the window.

197

Whatever was going to happen, they were going to *watch*. Surely, they couldn't expect him to . . . Adrian looked back at Lily, perplexed. A trifle fearful.

"Here's how it works, Adrian. There is an ancient, obscure ritual, come down to us from the dawn of history. We know it as *The Incantations of Thoth*. Through recitation of the spell, at the moment of ejaculation –"

"*WHAT?*"

"Hush. You're a big boy. I'm trying to be scientific, here. Clinical. Would you prefer a coarser term? Or perhaps I should go fetch your father, and have him explain it to you?"

"Dad knows about this?"

"Of course he knows. You are your mother's gift to him; his gift to her. You are the incarnation of their love." Lily frowned cynically at this sweet, universal truth.

"Such a thing doesn't happen in all lifetimes. It surely won't happen in mine. But in their case . . . Your mother has no secrets from your father, especially as they might concern you. She has no more devout wish than to save you, Adrian, and by this method, you can be saved. Your father tells himself he doesn't believe . . . But he listens, nonetheless."

Lily sighed. "Your mother and your aunts are embarrassed, even though this is women's work." Lily's vulpine smile increased. *"What the men don't know, the little girls understand.* But your father is no innocent, though he'll play one now. I'm sure he'll stammer through it, effectively enough. Shall I fetch him?"

Adrian, appalled, shook his head vigorously.

"Okay, then. Be silent and heed me. Through recitation of the incantation, at the moment of ejaculation, at the moment of your . . . ending . . . Through the intercession of the ancient forces, the vessel is impregnated. But the child conceived will not be a new soul. The child conceived will be *you."*

Shocked silence gripped Adrian. He believed in the ancient forces, in magic; he knew as fact that the future could be divined. But what Lily was telling him . . . *This is just nuts.* Adrian couldn't suppress a giggle, though he tried mightily. "That's some *petite mort."*

"Literally," Lily agreed, and allowed herself a giggle. Then she sobered. "But I see you have doubts."

Still trying to contain his mirth, Adrian nodded and shook his head at the same time.

"You believe that women will conceive babies late in life to harvest kidneys for their older children, right?" Lily nodded at the copied newspaper clipping. "No one bats an eyelash at that these days. You're just going to create a being, from you, for you – that will *be* you.

"The mysteries are partly revealed to us, Adrian. You believe that, also. *You know it.* Mothers and fathers, lovers, brothers, sisters – in past lives, in future lives, roles are reversed. But basically, a family's souls are all loosely connected – some go off and join other circles, but throughout the ages we remain in the company of the same twenty or so beings, more or less. You are Daina's son; you will be her grandson. The vessel you choose – she will be your woman for a moment – then she will be your mother. But you will continue, Adrian. There will be only your soul."

Adrian remained silent for another heartbeat. He knew a response was expected of him, but he had nothing. It was nuts. "I don't know what to say."

Lily removed a piece of paper from her pocket and handed it to him. Adrian perceived only spidery handwriting, black ink on a white background. "Here is the incantation. Learn the words – the passage is neither lengthy nor complicated. Memorize it, Adrian. Your time is running out."

Lily turned over a card from the Tarot deck and held it up so he could see it. It was The Fool.

"The path of the Tarot is called *The Fool's Journey.* His appearance in a reading is an indication for us to recall our follies, to go back and remember first principles. He is you, Adrian. Change is coming." Lily nodded at the card. "The precipice, the void, they yawn before you. There will be only blackness. Or you can begin *The Fool's Journey* anew."

Again, Adrian knew some response was expected from him. "How will I know . . . who . . . the girl will be?"

Lily gestured for the watchers to come back inside. "You don't have to seek her out." Lily grinned again. "The young ladies always seek you out, do they not?"

"But how will I know . . . when to . . ."

"You're prescient, Adrian. It's the gift you've been granted . . . perhaps as recompense for your short lifeline. All will be revealed when the time comes. In the meantime . . . Enjoy yourself. Don't dwell on it."

Daina stood beside her son, and he hugged her, all the while thinking that she was nuts. They were all *nuts.*

"But learn that incantation," Lily added. "Your majority approaches."

FIFTY-THREE

On Friday, the 28th of June, 1991, Gil feted his girlfriend to a nice, romantic dinner out, followed by a lengthy and loving good-bye. They departed their apartment together on Saturday morning, but left in separate cars, to quite separate destinations. Randi was going to work. Gil was going to pick up Nadine and Irene and start their trip to San Francisco.

Nick called Randi the moment she walked in the door that evening. He asked if he could come over and see her. "I'll make dinner for you again," he promised eagerly. "I'll make chicken enchiladas. With roasted tomatillo salsa. It's one of my specialties." He pronounced it *spesh-she-AL-it-ties.*

But Randi wasn't in the mood for Nick. Not *already.* Gil had said that he'd be gone for almost a week – Nadine planned on a slow, leisurely journey, because her mom wanted to see all the sights – and Randi didn't want Nick to impose on her, didn't want him at her apartment mooning over her every night for all that time. She would let him visit a couple of evenings, maybe, in a few days; she'd even let him cook her dinner. But not *already.*

"Not tonight, Nick. I'm tired. I'm just gonna watch a little TV and then go to bed."

"How about breakfast, then? I'll come over and make you huevos rancheros."

Randi reflected that the kid was a little bit of a one trick pony. It seemed like all he knew how to cook were Mexican dishes. "I dunno, Nick. I'll see how I feel. Call me." *That's what answering machines are for, to allow people to avoid love-sick teenagers.* At least for a few more days.

But Nick was undaunted, and being smarter than the average bear, knowing a little bit more about women than the average fifteen-year-old – even if it was more from observation than from personal experience – Nick was confident that Randi would be more than happy to have breakfast with him in the morning. In fact, he was sure that she'd be willing to spend the entire day with him.

He called at eleven o'clock on Sunday, and as was not unexpected, he got Randi's machine. "Hi, Randi, it's me. Nick. I was just calling to see if you'd like to have brunch with me." He paused, but not long enough for the machine to shut off. Then he delivered the kicker. "I know it's a pain in the ass, but Adrian's all by himself today, so I invited him –"

Nick didn't even get *along* out of his mouth before Randi picked up the phone. "Adrian's wants to have brunch with me? Er . . . With us?"

Nick smiled to himself. "No rehearsal today. Bobby and Tracy are shopping for vacation clothes. She's never been to Europe before. So I felt sorry for Adrian, with no one to hang out with." It had taken the promise of some tiresome guitar tuning, but Adrian had agreed to go. He really didn't have anything else to do that day.

Nick would've rather been alone with Randi, but he knew his cousin's heart and mind. Adrian didn't want Randi, no matter how much Randi wanted him, but Nick knew she'd agree to have brunch with him, if Adrian came along. All he had to do was stand there and look pretty.

"Sure, Nick. That sounds great. When are you guys gonna be here?"

Nick made ensalada de papas y huevos – potato and egg salad. It took a little while to prepare, as he had to boil the potatoes, so the meal turned out to be lunch more than brunch. Randi didn't mind, because while the kid was in the kitchen, she got to look at Adrian; she got to talk to him. She got to imagine what she would do if Adrian would be a little friendlier than *just friends* with her. She thought about that all the time, but it was so much more enjoyable when he was actually present while she imagined it.

Randi asked if there was a blow-out planned for Adrian's twenty-first birthday, and he reminded her that his cousins would be out of the country. "We'll celebrate my birthday when they get home."

"Well, there's still the fireworks. Penny and Bellona invited me for the barbeque, and Gil and Nadine should be back by then. We can still have a little celebration." Randi smiled winningly at him.

"Whatever you say." Adrian frowned at the mention of Gil and Nadine.

He was not as eager as Nick to spill the beans about all that. Adrian had convinced himself that something was indeed going on between Randi's boyfriend and his AnTeen, however unpleasant the thought might be, because this little cozy trip to Frisco had come too hard on the heels of what Nick said he'd witnessed. It was just too pat. Before Nick's revelation, Adrian would've thought that Gil didn't even know Nadine; he'd helped her move, but that had been a long time ago. But after what Nick had told him . . . Adrian couldn't

202

help but notice that they were mighty chummy at Randi's birthday party.

Adrian considered that perhaps Randi would be better off if she didn't find out about it. If Gil had been cheating on her with Nadine for all this time, it only followed that he didn't plan on leaving Randi for the older woman. It was just his thing on the side. In no way did that make it right, but maybe Randi was better off ignorant. Finding out would only hurt her, disrupt her happy little life. It might make her hate Gil, and it would definitely make her hate whoever told her about it. Adrian decided that under no circumstances was it going to be him. Better to let sleeping dogs lie. It wasn't really any of his business.

The three of them caught a late matinee of *The Rocketeer,* and then Nick suggested that they all have dinner. Randi was down; the more time she spent with Adrian, the more she liked it.

When she excused herself to use the ladies' room at the restaurant, Nick said to his cousin, "After we go back to her place, I want you to make yourself scarce."

Adrian grinned evilly. He never ceased to be amazed at his cousin's guts. Nick wasn't even old enough to drive yet, but here he was, talking about – "Gonna make your move, are ya? While the cat's away and all?"

"Fuck you, Adrian. Randi's a nice girl. She's loyal to that bastard, even though he's not loyal to her. I just want to spend a little time with her before we leave the country. I just wanna spend a little time with her when she's not staring at *you.*"

Adrian couldn't escape the truth of that. "Okay, I'll take off after we go back. But how are you gonna get home?"

Nick shrugged. "I'll hitchhike."

"You will most assuredly *not* hitchhike."

"Christ, Cuz, you sound like my mom."

"Just call me from a payphone. I'll come get you."

"It might be late." Nick grinned a little evilly himself. He knew nothing would happen with Randi, but that didn't mean it wasn't nice to think about.

"I doubt it," Adrian replied. "Just call me. I'll give you a ride home."

"I don't care what my dad says about you, Cuz. You're all right."

The trio arrived back at Randi's apartment about seven o'clock. She invited them in, hoping all the while that Nick would hear his mother calling him and have to toddle off to the bus stop and go home. That would leave her and Adrian all alone, with Gil out of town . . . Randi knew in her heart that it wasn't very likely; but newly twenty-one, she'd had a glass of white wine with dinner just because she could. She was feeling a little frisky.

Randi reveled in her fantasy of being alone with Adrian. Nick would do a fade, and she would suggest to Adrian that they watch another movie. Something a little more romantic than *The Rocketeer;* perhaps *When Harry Met Sally* . . . She would dim the lights, and they would curl up together on the couch, and after a few moments of Billy Crystal and Meg Ryan, the movie would be forgotten, because they would start to . . .

But when Randi entered her apartment, reality presented itself in the form of the blinking light on her answering machine. "Hi, baby, we didn't get too far today. We're in Santa Barbara. Here's the number." Randi scrambled to find a pen. She jotted the number down on the same pad where Gil had written Tim's number. "Ask for Room 302. Love you."

Nick frowned, and suggested to his cousin, *He doesn't love her.*

Adrian grinned. *Ah, the pain of passion unfulfilled!*

Fuck you, Adrian.

"Hold on a second," Randi told the Wilde boys. "Let me just call him back really quick." Randi dialed the phone, asked for the room number Gil had given her. The phone rang and rang. Maybe Gil had gone out for something to eat. At last a woman's voice said, "Hello?"

Randi blinked. "Hello? Is . . . Is Gil there?" The phone went dead. Randi blinked again; Adrian and Nick looked expectantly at her. "They must've connected me to the wrong room."

Nick looked at his cousin. "Let me guess. A woman answered."

Adrian glared at him, then told Randi, "You're right. They must've sent you to the wrong room. Call back and ask for him by name."

She's staying in the same room with him, Cuz.

Adrian frowned at Nick. *She's staying in her mom's room.*

Her mom's not there.

You don't know that.

Randi dialed the number again and when the clerk answered, she said, "Could I have Mr. Gilbert Hogan's room, please?" Randi grinned at her companions when her boyfriend answered. "Hi, Gil! How's it going?"

"Ask him if Nadine's there," Nick suggested.

"Shut up, Nick," Adrian advised.

Randi looked at them curiously, and Nick repeated, "Ask him if Nadine's there. Maybe it was Nadine that answered the phone."

"Is Nadine there?"

Gil paused. "She's down the hall. With her mom. Why do you ask?"

Randi laughed nervously. "No reason. I just wanted to say hi." An odd thought began to condense in Randi's mind. Why did Nick want her to ask if Nadine was in Gil's room? Just what was he insinuating?

She listened to Gil talk about the first leg of the trip. He said the U-Haul was clunky and a bitch to drive: Nadine and Irene were fortunate that he was along, because neither of them could've handled the big Ford. He said he hadn't seen any sights that interested him, although Santa Barbara was nice. Randi listened with only half an ear. What was Nick trying to say?

The conversation was brief. Gil stopped talking, and Randi discovered that she didn't have anything to contribute. She laughed nervously again and said, "Well, I'm sure you're tired. Call me when you stop again."

"Okay. Love you."

Randi looked at Nick. He stared steadily back at her. What was he trying to tell her? "I love you, too, Gil. Talk to you tomorrow." She hung up the phone but continued to hold Nick's gaze. It was as if Adrian wasn't even there.

She waited. Nick took a deep breath. "Gil's cheating on you, Randi."

Randi opened her mouth, but no sound emerged.

Adrian warned, *Don't tell her you saw anything. She'll hate you for it.*

At last Randi found her voice. "What are you talking about?"

Don't do it, Nick.

"I bet if you call back and ask for Nadine . . . What's her last name, Adrian?"

"Germaine," Adrian replied evenly.

"I bet if you call back and ask for Nadine Germaine's room, they'll tell you there's nobody registered there by that name. Or her mom's name, either. But I bet if you ask for Mr. and Mrs. Hogan's room . . . He's cheating on you, Randi. Nadine's mom's not there. She probably flew on ahead."

"How do you know that?" Randi asked slowly.

"He doesn't know it," Adrian said. *Don't tell her, Nick. You don't wanna be the one to break her heart.*

"It's just the two of them, Randi."

"How do you know?"

"He doesn't know," Adrian reiterated.

But Randi continued to ignore Adrian, concentrating expectantly upon Nick. He held her gaze for another heartbeat, then looked away, shook his head.

"I don't know anything for sure." He glared at his cousin. "But think about it, Randi. Does he stay out all night a lot?" That was a shot in the dark – Nick knew nothing of Gil's habits – but he knew he'd struck home when Randi's eyes widened. "Nadine isn't married. And doesn't it seem odd that Gil would just out of the blue volunteer to help her and her mother drive all the way to Frisco? Gil doesn't seem to be the helpful type to me. Unless he's getting something out of it."

"Shut up, Nick," Adrian said again. But he knew Nick wasn't going to shut up now.

"Go ahead, Randi. Call that hotel back. Ask for her room." When Randi hesitated, Nick said, "All right. I'll do it." Before either of them could move to stop him, Nick picked up the receiver and hit the redial button. While it was ringing, he asked Adrian, "What's her mom's name?"

"Irene."

"Yes, I wonder if you could connect me with Miss Nadine Germaine's room, please?" Pause. "No? How about Irene Germaine?" Pause. "She's not there either? I'm sorry. I must have the wrong hotel. Thanks for your time."

Nick hung up and looked at Adrian, because he didn't dare look at Randi. He'd just proved that Gil was indeed unfaithful, and he was suddenly afraid that she would hate him for it, just like his cousin had predicted. But she had to know.

"Maybe Gil rented all their rooms under his name," Adrian suggested.

"Maybe. But I think that's ridiculous." Nick at last gathered his courage and looked over at Randi. She was staring blankly at the wall. "I'm sorry, Randi," he told her softly. He let all of his love for her show when he added, "I couldn't just stand around and let him make a fool of you."

When Randi met his gaze, Nick saw the hatred that Adrian had warned him about. But then she blinked and it was gone, replaced by the soft, shy expression that Nick had come to cherish so much. "Maybe . . . Maybe it's not what it seems." Randi looked at Adrian for the first time since this awful . . . *thing* had commenced. "Maybe they're just . . ." Randi looked at Adrian as if seeing him for the first time, and stopped talking. *Oh, Adrian, why would he do this to me?*

Adrian felt her helpless pain and looked angrily at his cousin. "Let's go, Nick. I think Randi might like to be alone."

Randi nodded, sudden embarrassment enfolding her. If it was true . . . Nick was right. Gil had played her for a fool. "Don't tell anyone about this, Adrian."

Randi had a touch of pleading in her eyes, and Adrian's anger bloomed at that worthless son of a bitch for doing this to her, and also at his not-without-ulterior-motives cousin for telling her about it.

"We won't tell anyone," he promised. "Come on, Nick. Let's go."

FIFTY-FOUR

As they walked down the steps from Randi's apartment, Adrian slapped his cousin on the back of the head. "That was cruel, Nick."

"Don't start with me, Adrian. She had to know." They walked the rest of the way to the car in silence. As Adrian backed out of the space, Nick asked, "What do you think she's gonna do?"

Adrian frowned at the hope that tinged his cousin's voice. He remembered Penny's words: *There will never be a Randi and Nick.*

"She's not going to do anything before he comes home. She's just going to sit and stew about it. They've been together for a long time." Adrian pulled out onto the street. "If I was her, I'd want a little more proof."

"We could wait 'til he gets back, then we could follow him. We could –"

"We're not going to do anything like that, Nick, for Christ's sake! This isn't any of our business. Let Randi handle it on her own. She's an adult. You're not her knight in shining armor. You're just–"

"I'm just a kid. Is that what you're gonna say? Fuck you, Adrian. I . . . I love her. I don't want to watch that asshole hurt her anymore."

"What I was going to say was – you're just too close to this. You can't do anything about how she feels, Nick . . . About you or about him. You just gotta let her handle it on her own."

"I can call her. I can let her know I'm here for her."

But when Nick called the next evening, Randi let the machine get it. He figured maybe he deserved that, as the bearer of bad news. It was just like Adrian said. She needed a little time, by herself, to think things out, to decide what she was gonna do.

FIFTY-FIVE

Each evening, when they stopped at another hotel along scenic Pacific Coast Highway, Gil and Nadine did as Prince had suggested in the 80s: *Let's pretend we're married, and go all night.* Nadine was an old hand at traveling, making love in a different room, a different town, each night. But it was all a new adventure for Gil. He decided that he'd like to take a similar road trip with Randi someday.

After Santa Barbara, Gil made it a point to always call and check in with his girlfriend as soon as they stopped. Then it was out of the way. He made sure he actually spoke to Randi. If she didn't pick up, he didn't leave the number on the machine; he just called back until she answered.

Leaving the number had been a mistake. It wasn't like he could forbid Nadine from answering the phone in their room: her mother was also anxious to hear from her each evening, to know how far they'd traveled, how the drive was going. If they were on schedule. As Nick had guessed, Irene had flown ahead to her sister's. She was too old for road trips.

So this is what my daughter's calling a boyfriend these days, Irene had thought. She'd seen Gil leaving Nadine's apartment enough times. She considered him a little young for Nadine, but who was she to judge? Irene was just happy to see that perhaps her daughter was at last settling down. It made it easier for her to leave Southern California and return to her roots when she thought that Nadine wouldn't be left behind all alone. Nadine was happy that her mom thought she was happy, so she allowed Irene to go on believing that Gil was her boyfriend.

It was such a stupid word. *Boyfriend.* Nadine was certainly too old for such a thing. The only *boyfriend* she'd ever wanted had been married to someone else for two decades . . . But Nadine was happy enough with what she had with Gil, even if he wasn't precisely her *boyfriend. He's my lover, my* . . . paramour, Nadine told herself. That had a more sophisticated ring to it. *He's Randi's* boyfriend.

Gil had been seeing Nadine on the side for a long time, and he came to the realization that lately he'd been getting sloppy. Leaving the number for Randi, then going off to jump in the shower, while Nadine was right there in the room – that had just been careless. He knew Randi had never suspected anything, had never even had an inkling that he had been unfaithful to her, in all the time they'd been together. Even before he'd taken up with Nadine. It just wouldn't do for him to start getting stupid and give her reason to suspect him now.

Gil realized with a start that he wouldn't know what he'd do if Randi found out. Nadine was a lot of fun, and he guessed he loved her in a way . . . But Randi *belonged* to him. She was his future. They were going to get married someday, maybe have kids. If Randi found out that he'd been stepping out on her, she'd cry; he'd have to beg for her forgiveness. Gil knew he could talk her down: he'd just tell her how much he loved her. But if Randi found out, she'd just naturally demand that he give up Nadine. And Gil wasn't ready to do that yet. So he had to stop being sloppy, and make sure Randi didn't find out.

FIFTY-SIX

Randi listened to Gil's cheerful patter on the phone each day, all the while wondering if he was cheating on her with that old woman. If he was . . . Then that was truly disgusting, and she didn't want to think about it. But . . . What if he was? Not only was she going to have to think about it, to face it; she was going to have to take action. What was she going to do about it? These thoughts relentlessly tripped over each other in Randi's mind. There had to be some way to find out for sure.

Gil called and actually left a return number on July 1st. They had arrived at Nadine's aunts' house, all safe and sound. Gil would be helping with the unpacking and the furniture placement on the 2nd, and then he and Nadine would be starting back for home on the 3rd.

"We're coming back on the I-5," Gil's message said. "Nadine wants to stop and visit her cousin in Bakersfield, then we'll be home on the 4th."

Randi dutifully returned Gil's call. Nadine answered at her aunt's house and Randi chatted with her for a moment, asked her about the trip, asked her how her mom had fared on the drive. Nadine said that all had gone well. Randi listened keenly to the old witch's voice, trying to figure out if it had been Nadine that had picked up the phone in Santa Barbara. *In Gil's room. Why would she have been in Gil's room if they weren't* . . . There was nothing to a hotel room but a bed and a bathroom. If Nadine and her mom had their own room, there would've been no reason for her to be in Gil's, unless . . . Unless Nick was right.

The woman's voice had just said one word: *Hello?* Randi couldn't be sure if it had been Nadine or not. The whole sordid thing might've just been a mix-up: the clerk might've connected Randi to the wrong room. Buy why hadn't Nadine and her mother been registered?

Maybe Nick made that part up, Randi thought suddenly. *Maybe he faked his conversation with the desk clerk.* Nick had an enormous crush on her, and nothing would make him happier than to see her break up with Gil . . . *Sheesh! I'm getting paranoid. I'm starting to suspect everybody.*

After a moment's conversation, Nadine handed the call over to Gil. He and Randi spoke a few words – he said he was looking forward to coming home to her – then they ended the call.

Nick also called on the 1st of July. Randi didn't want to talk to him. "Pick up, Randi. We're leaving on vacation tomorrow, and we won't be back 'til August. I just wanted to say goodbye."

He sounded so sad at the thought of going overseas without speaking to her, so Randi sighed and answered the phone. She said simply, "You have fun, Nick."

He didn't reply for a moment, then blurted out, "Whatever happens when Gil gets back, Randi . . . I just want you to know that I'll be here for you, just as soon as I get back. Whatever you decide . . . I'll always be your friend."

"I appreciate that, Nick. You have a good time in Europe. I'll see you when you get home."

FIFTY-SEVEN

Gil didn't call home on July 3rd. Randi decided that he was probably having too much fun at Nadine's cousin's in Bakersfield. Or he was having too much fun shacked up in another hotel room with Nadine somewhere en route. Randi decided to just not think about that possibility. There was no proof, not really, so . . . She just wouldn't think about it now.

Randi waited all day on the 4th of July for Gil to return. She started to worry a little bit as the hours passed, but figured that perhaps he'd encountered holiday traffic. She waited until four o'clock. Then she couldn't wait any longer.

Randi went to the grocery store and picked up a case of beer and some potato salad for Penny and Bellona's barbeque. Whether or not Gil was cheating on her, whether or not he was dead on the side of the road due to some horrific car wreck – she would just have to deal with all of that later. She wasn't going to miss Adrian Wilde's twenty-first birthday celebration, no matter how small and not-spectacular it was going to be. Adrian was going to be there: that would make it spectacular enough for Randi.

She returned home from the store to put on her face and get ready to go to Penny and Bellona's; the light was flashing on the answering machine. "Sorry I didn't call you yesterday, baby. George – that's Nadine's cousin's husband – he took me dirt bike riding. It was awesome! I'm gonna have to get me one of 'em when I get home. Anyway, that's also why we haven't left Bakersfield yet. We went out today, too. We're gonna have dinner, then we should be getting on the road. We should get there about the time the fireworks start. Call me. I miss you. Here's the number."

Again, Randi scrambled for a pen. She didn't want to forget it and have to listen to Gil's message again. She didn't want to hear again about how much fun he'd been having with Nadine's cousin's husband. She thought that he used the word *we* a little bit too often, too, a little bit too familiarly. Were he and Nadine a *we?*

Randi jotted the number down on the pad beside the phone. She picked up the receiver and dialed. As the phone started to ring, she glanced down at the pad, wondering if it really, truly could be possible that Gil was cheating on her with Nadine. There was Tim's number, and the number of the hotel in Santa Barbara, where the mysterious woman had answered the phone in Gil's room. Beneath this number, there was the number at Nadine's aunt's house, and now the one at Nadine's cousin's house.

Randi hung up the phone because she remembered Nick's words again: *Doesn't it seem odd that Gil would just out of the blue volunteer to help Nadine and her mother drive all the way to Frisco?*

Randi traced over the phone numbers on the pad with her finger. *All I'd have to do is call Nadine's aunt's house. Ask to speak to her mom. Ask her how their trip was . . .* But that would seem odd. Randi didn't even know Nadine's mom . . .

Does he stay out all night a lot?

On an impulse, Randi dialed Tim's number. She didn't know what she'd say; she didn't know Tim either, had never met him. But she'd spoken to his wife on the phone while Gil was staying there. Or had she? *Does he stay out all night a lot?*

A woman's voice was on the answering machine at Tim's house. "You know the drill. Leave a message at the beep." Was that Nadine's voice?

Randi recalled how eager Gil had been to leave her behind and stay with Tim and his wife, just because she had a sore throat. *He left outta here like a bat outta hell,* Randi said to herself, *or like someone going to get a piece of . . .* She dialed Tim's number again and listed to the brief message. Was that Nadine's voice?

There was only one way to find out. Randi put the receiver in its cradle and dug the *Pacific Bell White Pages* out of the drawer. *Garber, Garcia, Getz, Gonzalez. No, that's too far.* Randi's fingers trembled as she turned the thin pages back. *Germaine, Nadine.*

It was the same phone number.

Randi closed the *White Pages* and staggered to the couch. What Nick had told her was true, every syllable. There was no Tim. There never had been any Tim. All the times that Gil had gone to help Tim fix his car, all the times he'd stayed out all night with Tim, the five days he'd spent at Tim's when she had strep throat – there was no Tim. Gil had been with that old woman. And now, he'd just spent another week with her.

Nick was right. Gil had played her for a fool with some filthy tramp old enough to be his mother. *And she was always so nice to me!*

What am I gonna do? Randi asked herself. *What am I gonna do? That lying son of a bitch!* She took a deep breath, forced herself to calm down, to think. *What was I doing before?* Randi mentally retraced her steps. *I was waiting for him to come home, then I went to the store, because I'm going to Adrian's party . . . Adrian! Oh, my God! Gil's been cheating on me, and . . . Adrian!*

Randi's decision was instantaneous. *Gil wants an old woman? He can have her. I hope they'll be very happy together. I know a man, only a month or so younger than me . . . The most awesome man I've ever met.*

Randi dialed the last number on the pad: Nadine's cousin's house. A man answered the phone. *They must really be where they say they are, this time,* Randi thought. *No need for Nadine to catch the phone and provide an alibi now.* She politely told the man that she was returning Gil Hogan's call.

"Hey, baby!" Gil said enthusiastically. "I was just gonna call you again. We should be leaving here soon, so I'll be home before you know it!"

"I know, Gil," Randi said evenly. She told herself not to get hysterical, not to scream at him. "There's no Tim, is there? You've been seeing that old bitch behind my back all this time!"

Stunned, Gil remained silent for a heartbeat, then stammered, "I don't know what you're talking about."

"Don't lie to me anymore, you son of a bitch. I looked up her number. I hate you. I never want to see you again."

Busted, Gil didn't try to concoct any more lies. He said, "That's gonna be a little difficult, Randi. We live together. If you'd just let me explain –"

"I don't wanna hear it. I'm leaving."

Gil barked laughter before he could stop himself. "Where do you think you're gonna go?"

"It doesn't matter. I won't be here when you get home." Randi hung up on him. As an afterthought, she unplugged the answering machine.

Gil hung up the phone and discovered that Nadine and George were looking curiously at him. "I need to have a word with you," he told his *paramour.* "Can we step outside for a moment?"

The desert sun on the 4th of July was relentless, and George's porch didn't offer much respite. Gil looked at the dirt bikes in the front yard, again thought how much fun they were, then turned to Nadine. "Randi just accused me of cheating on her. With you."

Nadine raised her eyebrows mildly. "Well, you have been, honey."

Gil looked out at the seared yellow Bakersfield landscape. "She says she's leaving me."

Now Nadine laughed, echoed Gil's earlier thought. "Where's she gonna go?"

"I don't know. To her mom's, I guess."

Nadine's lip curled cruelly. Here was relentless fate in action, once again. Gil would either give Randi up and come to stay with her, or . . . Nadine saw her opportunity for revenge, as clear as the cloudless desert sky. The day of reckoning was at hand. All fate needed was a little push. *O, beware, my lord, of jealousy; it is the green-eyed monster which doth mock the meat it feeds on . . . Good heaven, the souls of all my tribe defend from jealousy!*

Nadine giggled, and Gil looked at her in surprise. This was not really a laughing matter. Randi had just found him out, threatened to leave him, and –

"Don't kid yourself, Gilly," Nadine said and giggled further.

He hated it when she called him *Gilly*. *Honey* was bad enough, but whenever Nadine called him *Gilly*, he knew that she was making fun of him, looking down on him, laughing at him. "What do you mean?"

Nadine covered her mouth like a little girl, to disguise her continued giggles. But the malefic mirth shone out from her eyes. "Randi's not going to her mother's. She's been waiting for this moment . . . Hell, for as long as I've known her. You're a cheating bastard and now . . . Now, she's a victim. It's the perfect excuse. The perfect set-up."

"What are you talking about?" Gil demanded.

"Your girlfriend's not going home to Mama, Lover. She's going to Adrian Wilde." Nadine's grin remained. "The question is, what are you gonna do about that?" *And if you wrong us, shall we not revenge? The smallest worm will turn, being trodden on . . .*

Gil was speechless. Then a sense of offended righteousness struck him. Maybe he shouldn't have been cheating on Randi with Nadine all this time. But that wasn't really the issue, was it? Nadine had made a valid point. Randi had just been waiting, biding her time, looking for an excuse to leave him, so she could take up with Adrian Wilde. She'd had a thing for the talentless guitar player since long before Gil had even *met* Nadine.

Randi thought she would take advantage of this little, unfortunate . . . *untruth* on Gil's part to do what she'd wanted to do all along. It was almost as if Randi had been lying *to him* for all this time. All she'd ever wanted was Adrian Wilde, and now she thought she would get him.

216

And Wilde – Gil saw that he'd take Randi. She was cute and she was so obviously willing. She'd say, "I'm free now, Adrian! You don't have to be afraid of Gil anymore!"

And that smart-ass Wilde would smile at her and set his guitar down. He'd say, "Well, it's about time, baby. I've been waiting for you to tell me that since the first night I saw you. Let's go on back to my place, and I'll give you just what the doctor ordered . . ."

Well, now that's just not going to happen. Gil blinked rapidly, furiously. He realized that he was holding his breath. *Wilde's not going to take Randi. He's not going to make a fool of me. I'll kill him first.*

Gil looked blankly at Nadine. When he still didn't speak, she said, "You know, I don't think I want to go home today. It's been a long time since I visited with Allison." She paused, then remembered that she'd heard them talking earlier . . . "She and George are going to see the Bakersfield Blaze tonight. Did you know they're the farm team for the Seattle Mariners?"

Gil blinked again. Why was Nadine talking about a minor league baseball team when Adrian Wilde was about to steal his girlfriend?

"I think I'd like to go to the game with them. There's a fireworks show afterwards. Wouldn't you like to see the fireworks, Gil?" Before he could answer, Nadine continued. "Perhaps not. Perhaps you'd like to make your own fireworks. Back in Riverside."

Nadine glanced at her watch. It was five-fifteen. "The gates open in a half hour or so, but the game doesn't start 'til almost eight. George and Allison are getting ready to go right now. I'll tell them that we've decided to stay one more night.

"We're going to go to the game with them, but you've got to run to the store really quick. You want to gas up the rental car or something. Put some air in the tires before it gets dark. I don't know. Something. You'll meet us there." Nadine paused. "It would be a pity if you couldn't find us in that big stadium. You might search and search. A baseball game's about three hours long . . . But still, you might not be able to find us in all that time. You just might have to meet us back here, after the game's over. Then we'll just go on home tomorrow."

Gil continued to stare at her silently for another minute. Then he said, "You sincerely don't like Adrian Wilde, do you? Any more than I do. I have plenty of reasons not to like him, but what did he ever do to you? You're his *aunt,* for God's sake!"

"He's no blood to me." Nadine sniffed imperiously. "I don't like thieves, honey. I don't like opportunists. Sure, you might be heading into a little rough patch here with Randi. You made a mistake, but you'll tell her how sorry you are, and I'm sure she'll take you back. I'm sure the two of you will get through it. But before you get a chance to talk to her . . . I wouldn't want to see anyone take advantage of Randi at this vulnerable time."

Nadine sighed. "I mean . . . I'm sure you'll forgive Randi. She's a little confused right now, what with all these suspicions she's having. She doesn't have anywhere else to turn. She thinks Adrian's her friend . . ." Nadine lowered her voice. "I'm sure Adrian'll be friendly indeed, now that he thinks you're out of the picture."

Nadine hitched a heavier sigh. "It's not like he'll keep Randi long. When have you ever seen Adrian keep any girl for very long? I'm sure Randi will come crawling back to you, after Adrian's done with her." Nadine patted his shoulder maternally. The only thing he hated more than when she called him *Gilly* was when she patted him maternally. "Everything'll be all right then. I'm sure Randi will come back to you after . . ."

Nadine reached into her pocket and handed him the keys to the rental car. They'd exchanged the U-Haul for it in San Francisco. "I'm gonna go in and tell Allison and George that were gonna stay one more night. I can't wait to see the Blaze! And the fireworks." She took Gil's face in both her hands and kissed him. "The game, the fireworks . . . It probably won't be over before eleven. If you get back before then . . . The game's at Sam Lynn Ballpark. On Chester. Wait for me by the box office."

Gil hesitated for another moment. But Nadine was right. He had to stop Randi before she went crying to Wilde about what a rotten so-an-so he was. He had to stop Wilde from taking advantage of Randi's *vulnerability,* because she would most assuredly allow him to take advantage of it. She'd just been waiting for an excuse. Gil couldn't allow Wilde to make an ass out of him like that. He would stop it from happening, one way or another.

218

FIFTY-EIGHT

Gil put the pedal to the metal, and despite the holiday traffic, he made it back to his apartment in Rubidoux by eight-fifteen. He'd reached a decision about how to proceed – there was no sense going out there to Wilde's house and making a big scene. No sense in getting into a fistfight – Wilde's cousins would be there to back his play, as well as his dad and maybe even the doctor. Gil knew he could take any of them, but maybe not *all* of them. No sense picking a fight when he was outnumbered. They were all such chickenshits – somebody would call the cops. Nothing would be settled, and he might get arrested. Then Nadine would be stranded in Bakersfield. And he'd never hear the end of *that*.

No, Gil decided, this whole situation called for a little bit of stealth. If he was going to take on Wilde *mano a mano*, he'd have to sneak up on him, when his cousins weren't around.

Gil had learned to fight from his father. He'd learned that he *had* to fight from his father.

When Gil was fourteen, there'd been this girl – just like now, it was almost always about some girl. Her name was Rosalinda, and just like that snot-nosed Wilde kid with Randi, Gil had had a fierce crush on her. The age difference wasn't so phenomenally ridiculous between Gil and Rosalinda, however. Where Nick didn't have a prayer with Randi – that five year gulf made them like they were from different planets – Rosalinda had only been just barely two years Gil's senior. She'd been sweet sixteen, and Gil had thought her to be sweet indeed. And he might've had a chance . . . Surely, more of chance than Nick was ever going to get. Or his asshole cousin.

Gil made the mistake of walking Rosalinda home from the market one day, and when they arrived at her gate, her boyfriend James was waiting for her on the porch with two of his buddies. *Big Jimmy,* everyone called him. But not to his face.

Big Jimmy was older than Gil and sweet Rosalinda: he was probably eighteen or nineteen. His friends snickered at the little kid that had followed his girl home, like a lost puppy. Jimmy figured that they were laughing at him.

The pretty girl that Gil wished was his girlfriend told him thanks for walking her home, and went in the gate. When Gil called, "Bye, Rosa!" Jimmy decided that this kid's heartfelt farewell constituted a little bit more familiarity than he was obliged to take. He came down off of the porch to have a few words with Gil about it. His friends followed.

I've put up with a whole lot more than Jimmy did, Gil thought now, as he climbed the stairs to his apartment.

Suffice it to say that Jimmy and his friends pushed Gil around for a while, roughed him up a little bit. "You stay away from Rosa," was the basic lesson. For the next few days, Gil endeavored to do just that: he decided that while she was lovely, she wasn't worth getting his teeth knocked out for.

But Jimmy discovered that the skinny blonde kid with the big green eyes was an easy target; he'd just as soon try to escape as hold his ground, and Jimmy found the kid's lack of fighting skills to be as amusing as hell. So after a while, it wasn't about Rosalinda at all. It was just for kicks. Whenever they caught him out in the neighborhood, Jimmy and his pals would play with Gil, like wolves with a small animal.

Gil went home with a few scrapes on his face the first time; the second time, there was a small mouse over his eye when he sat down at the dinner table. His father looked at him keenly, but didn't say anything. The next time Gil ran into Jimmy and his friends, they sent him home with a split lip and a swollen nose. Gil skipped dinner, but his father came up to his room afterwards.

"It seems to me you've become mighty clumsy lately," Richie Hogan began.

"Clumsy?"

"Yeah. It looks like you've been falling down a lot. And landing on your face." Richie laughed at his own humor. "You want to tell me about it?"

Gil did not. His father was the type of man who acted first and asked questions later, if at all. If he thought Gil was doing something that he didn't like, he'd just as soon smack him or make some cutting remark as inquire as to what his eldest was actually doing. Even if Gil was just standing there.

"Some guys from school have been . . ." Gil almost said *picking on me*. But that wouldn't do. That would sound too much like weakness. Richie had served in Vietnam, had told Gil a million stories about how he'd had to cloud up and rain on anyone that got too lippy with him, while he as over there. Richie didn't have any patience for weakness. He didn't have any patience for much.

"Some guys at school jumped me," Gil told him.

"More than once, by the looks of it." Richie considered his first-born expressionlessly for a moment. "How long are you gonna let this go on?"

"There's more than one of them, Dad, and I'm not –"

"But there's a leader, right?"

"Yeah. They call him Big Jimmy."

"Here's what I want you to do, Gil. The next time you see Big Jimmy, I want you to just walk up and hit him in the mouth. Don't talk. Just walk up and hit him with something. Smack him with one of your schoolbooks. Or a brick." Richie grinned. "Once he's down, I want you to sit on his chest and start bashing his head into the ground. Try to kill him." When Gil blanched at that, his dad said, "Don't be a pussy, son. You're not gonna kill him. Your friends or his friends'll pull you off of him before it gets to that. But he'll think you *wanted* to kill him, so he'll think twice before choosing you again.

"Abraham Lincoln said, *The best way to destroy an enemy is to make him a friend.* I'm here to tell ya, son, that's bullshit. The best way to destroy an enemy is to *destroy him.* Otherwise, he'll just keep coming back to fuck with you."

When Gil didn't immediately agree, his dad smiled viciously. "Here's the deal. If you don't come back from school tomorrow and tell me you beat Jimmy's ass, then I'm gonna beat *your* ass. No son of mine is gonna keep coming home with shiners and split lips because he's a coward."

Gil wasn't a coward. But he was a whole lot more afraid of his dad than he was of Big Jimmy, so he did as he was told. He wound up with a two week suspension from school for it. But his dad was right: Jimmy and his buddies left Gil alone after that.

But even after this schoolyard victory, Gil still got the impression that his dad thought he was a coward. *Dad would definitely think I'm a coward now, the way I've been letting Wilde make time with Randi*, Gil thought. *So I'm just gonna have to handle it, once and for all. Destroy my enemy. Or else he'll just keep coming back, trying to take Randi away from me. If I let that happen . . . Dad's not around to laugh at me anymore, but Nadine is.*

Gil took one of the shotguns out of the closet and laid it on the bed. He'd only gone hunting a few times with his dad. The first couple of times, they hadn't even seen any game, but the last time . . . Richie had spotted a rabbit in the bush, oblivious to the hunters.

Unbidden, unwanted, the memory played in Gil's mind.

"Go ahead, Gil. Shoot him."

Gil didn't want to shoot the rabbit. It was just sitting there, minding its own business. It was so small and stupid, and he and his dad were so much bigger, so much smarter.

"Shoot him, Gil!" his father whispered tersely. "What are you afraid of today?"

Gil didn't want to kill the rabbit, but his father was once again insinuating that he was a coward, and that never failed to infuriate him. He drew a bead on the tiny creature, and thinking that he wished it was his dad, Gil pulled the trigger. The report was deafening. The blast from the shotgun blew the rabbit in half, and the recoil knocked Gil over backwards.

Richie just stood over his son and laughed. He didn't tell him he was a good shot, didn't say he was proud of Gil for killing the very first thing at which he'd ever taken aim.

"You might want to hold on to that pump gun a little tighter next time. Don't be afraid of it, boy." Gil wasn't afraid of the gun, he was afraid of his dad. "All these hippies, always talking about gun control. Gun control means not being intimated by your weapon. A gun is just a tool." Richie grinned at his son. "A tool for killing things."

Gil remembered the night his dad died. Gil had been out late, drinking with some of his friends, and when he staggered up the four steep steps to the front porch, Richie was waiting for him.

"I thought I told you to be home by midnight."

Richie drank Wild Turkey on his nights off, and then the fun would really begin. Gil knew his mother and his brothers were already in bed, either cowering in fear or already asleep. He could smell the whisky on his dad. It was one of the reasons why he hadn't come home before midnight.

Gil was nineteen at the time. He'd never gotten Rosalinda, but he'd had his share of girls by then; he'd been in his share of fights, too. His dad had smacked him around his whole life, but these days, Gil considered himself grown, and the beers he'd consumed gave him an added layer of courage. He decided that he was just about tired of Richie's shit. "Fuck you, Dad," he said.

Richie took a drunken swing at him. Gil sidestepped it, and watched emotionlessly as his dad tumbled down the porch steps. From the way he landed, Gil knew it wasn't good. Or maybe . . . Maybe it *was* good. Maybe the reign of terror that had been Gil's entire existence was finally over. He calmly went into the house and leisurely dialed the phone. "My dad just fell down the front steps," he told the dispatcher. "Yeah, he's been drinking."

Fuck you, Dad, Gil thought again as he found a crumbling box of shells on the shelf and loaded the pump gun. Richie wouldn't be laughing at him if he could see him now. Gil wasn't afraid of the gun, this tool for killing. Not now. Now there was something he *wanted* to kill.

FIFTY-NINE

Adrian Wilde was bummed.

Ian had made a big deal out of taking his son up to Hilltop Market – a place he'd visited almost daily since he'd been old enough to cross the street by himself – so Adrian could officially, legally, buy himself a six-pack of beer. Even though Arnie, the butcher, and Alice, the old clerk, had cheered – and Cindi, the young clerk, had smiled shyly at him – still it had seemed somewhat of a letdown to Adrian. An anti-climax. Sure, he could buy himself a beer now. It was his birthday. He was twenty-one. But no one was waiting for him back at his aunts' house to celebrate the milestone with him.

His cousins, his best friends, *his band,* were half a world away. Since they couldn't be there, Adrian hadn't wanted to throw himself a party. He'd decided that he'd just sit around and eat birthday cake and barbeque with his parents and his aunts. He'd watch the fireworks. And he'd sulk. And since he was twenty-one, since he'd reached his *majority,* Adrian decided he would drink the beers he'd bought. One right after the other.

"No jokes about dying," Ian told him as they returned from his triumphant first alcohol purchase. Adrian had been feeling so sorry for himself because no one was there to party with him, that he'd forgotten all about the prophecy. "All you gotta do is make it through today, son." Ian smiled.

At least he doesn't believe it, Adrian thought. *Any more than I do.*

"When she wakes up tomorrow and you're still with us, maybe your mother will finally see that it's all bullshit. So don't make any smart-ass remarks and remind her about it tonight."

Adrian blew out his birthday candles, and the sentiment they carried to the powers was: *I wish this night was over so my mom will stop worrying.*

Adrian dutifully had a slice of his Aunt Bellona's delicious birthday cake, a la mode. He ate a piece of his dad's Parker, Arizona recipe barbequed chicken – the taste brought back every summer he'd spent waterskiing on the Colorado River – and Adrian was once again confronted with his cousins' absence. *Fuck it,* he thought glumly. *Time to drink.*

Adrian cracked his first beer about five o'clock. No one joined him except for his Aunt Bellona. The six-pack was a birthday memory way before six, so they promptly started in on the twelver that Bellona had stashed away for a rainy day. The bottles were dusty: it didn't rain in Southern California very often.

Randi didn't show up until nearly eight o'clock, because she'd packed her bags. The suitcases were heavy, and it had taken her a long time to lug them down the steps from Gil's apartment, across the parking lot, and out to the car. But Randi didn't want to see Gil ever again; she didn't want to have to go back to his apartment *ever again,* so she had effectively cleared all her stuff out. Randi didn't know where she would be staying tonight or in the future, but she had a hope . . .

Adrian had forgotten that Randi was coming to the barbeque; he was delighted to realize that at least someone his own age was going to be there for his birthday. He leapt up and gave her an exuberant, drunken hug.

Randi was both thrilled and surprised, and looked at Bellona over his shoulder.

"Il capo dei capi è ubriaco," Bellona said and winked at Randi.

Randi, Ian and Daina looked at her in confusion. Adrian didn't care what she'd said; he drained his beer.

Penny translated. "She says, *the boss is drunk."* Penny smiled at Bellona. *"Sei un po 'ubriaco, te, mia sorella."*

"Aqua vitae," Bellona replied, indicating her beer.

Ian smiled. "Not hardly."

"Close enough," Adrian replied and clinked beer bottles with his aunt. He considered Randi, still standing very close to him. "Where's Gil?" he asked, trying to sound emotionless.

Adrian hadn't spoken to Randi since Nick had let the cat out of the bag; he wondered if she'd come to any decision, if she'd taken any action. He wondered if that was why she was here. Adrian thought that might be all right. He was feeling a little lonely, and Randi was –

"Gil's not coming." Randi looked at the old witches that she loved, at Adrian's parents, who had always been kind to her. "Gil and I broke up."

Daina covered her mouth with her hand and shared a glance with her aunts.

"I'm so sorry, dear," Bellona said.

"These things happen," Penny added. "Perhaps the two of you will –"

"No," Randi said firmly. "I'm done. While he's been gone, I've discovered that he's been cheating on me. For quite some time, it turns out."

Oh, shit, here it comes, Adrian thought. *Mom's gonna have puppies when she hears that her childhood friend has been messing around with –*

But Randi didn't name Gil's partner. When it became clear that she would not, Penny observed, "There's a lot of dog in a man."

"Yes. Yes there is." Randi opened one of the beers she'd brought with her, and a little sob escaped her. She looked at Adrian, at his family; she saw that they pitied her. But she didn't want them to do that. Adrian was here, and she'd decided to . . .

Randi realized that she was ruining the party. It was Adrian's birthday – she shouldn't be sitting here crying over Gil. She was done with Gil . . . Here was Adrian . . . She had to stop crying. She suddenly wondered with horror if her make-up was running, like in one of those old black and white pictures from the 60s; like she was someone Nadine's age.

Randi took a swig of her beer, then set it down, laughed shakily. She had to go check her face. She didn't want Adrian to think she was all broken up about this, but she was, really. Even if the thought that she was now free, and Adrian was free, warmed her – the cruelty of Gil's betrayal was still a fresh wound.

"You know what?" Randi said. "I bought another one of those disposable cameras. I left it in the car. I'll just . . . I'll just go get it." She leapt up and ran across the deck, down the steps, then up the path.

"Shit," Adrian said. He started to go after her, but Daina put her hand on his arm. Adrian felt her terror; it broke over him like a thin sheet of ice. It was his twenty-first birthday; his mother didn't want to let him out of her sight. "Let me go see if she's all right, Mom." He looked at his watch: it was getting on to eight-thirty. "I'll be back before the fireworks start."

Daina opened her mouth to forbid him, but closed it again. She hugged him fiercely. "I love you, Adrian."

Adrian looked at Ian over her head. "I love you, too, Mom. Everything's gonna be all right. I can't leave Randi down there, sobbing in her car. I'll be right back."

SIXTY

Randi was pretty much done crying when Adrian caught up to her. She was leaning against her car in his driveway, looking down at the little blue camera. She smiled bravely at him, sniffled back a last tear. "I need to fix my face," she said.

Adrian nodded and unlocked the door to his house. But once inside, Randi's tears began afresh. She turned and hugged Adrian, buried her face in his chest. Adrian hugged her back, stroked her hair. He felt her pain, her sadness, her betrayal.

But there was something else, and when Randi looked up at him, her eyes bright with tears, Adrian knew exactly what it was. She put her arms around his neck. "Kiss me, Adrian."

Adrian hesitated. He admitted to himself that he'd been thinking about it, earlier, when they were at his aunts'. He was feeling a little sad himself; he was more than a little drunk. Randi was cute, and he knew how much she wanted him. But maybe it wasn't the smartest idea. She had experienced quite a shock, and she wasn't in the best frame of mind. The thought crossed Adrian's mind that he might be taking advantage of her at a weak moment. "Randi, I dunno –"

"Gil's gone, Adrian. I need you right now. Kiss me."

Still Adrian hesitated, but Randi wasn't going to take no for an answer. She'd waited for *so long,* had wasted so much time. All the time she could have been with Adrian, if she'd only spoken up before. She'd been loyal to that conniving son of a bitch, and how had she been repaid? He'd been out cheating on her. Adrian was here. The time had come at last. Randi stood up on her toes and pressed her mouth against his.

So maybe I'm not taking advantage of her, Adrian thought and kissed her back. *She's a big girl. She knows what she wants.*

Under the influence of alcohol, and seeking an escape from his uncharacteristic melancholy, Adrian allowed Randi to seduce him. He considered that it was probably not entirely right: he was breaking his own rule, messing around with a girl that had so obviously loved him for so long. He thought of his Uncle Rob's admonition: *Some women are like gum, Adrian. They're sticky. Clingy. They get attached. My advice to you is to avoid them. It's impossible to get them out of your hair.*

Adrian reflected that after this, he might never get rid of Randi. But as she murmured and moaned appreciatively under his mouth and hands, Adrian considered that maybe that would be okay. *Randi's okay.*

He had been without feminine companionship for a while. Adrian liked Randi, even if he didn't love her. He knew that she loved him . . . That would do for the time being.

Adrian picked Randi up and carried her to his bed. The moon was up; it was on the wane but still gibbous, and Adrian noticed that Randi was quite beautiful as she smiled up at him, illuminated by its light shining through the window. She was all right. And tomorrow, when Gil showed up, all apologies and lame explanations . . . Adrian smiled.

This would all serve that cheating bastard right. Adrian would comfort Randi, soothe her hurts. He thought that Randi might eventually go back to Gil – they'd been together a long time. If that happened . . . Adrian decided that that would be all right, too. Either way, his birthday wasn't going to be a total loss.

SIXTY-ONE

Oh, my God, oh, my God, it's finally happening! Randi thought. *Why did I wait so long? He's so beautiful, so awesome . . . All I had to do was ask! Why did I wait so long?*

Adrian smiled at her thought. "It's okay, baby," he said. "You don't have to wait anymore."

Randi cried out in ecstasy: "I love you, Adrian!"

I know you do, Adrian thought. *And right this minute, I love you just as much . . .*

As Randi's fondest fantasy neared its culmination, Adrian heard a strange metallic scrabbling at the front door. Then he saw what would occur next: whoever was working on the door would soon be inside; then he would kick in the bedroom door; there would be a flash of light, a shotgun's deafening roar.

Adrian saw it in a quarter of the time it would've taken to describe it. It was all true. He was going to die. There was no escape. So instinctively, he did as he had been bid by the women that had loved him for every breathing moment of his life. He let go, and recited the words in his mind that were supposed to bind his soul to his seed. The new life that would be created, according to *The Incantations of Thoth,* would not be entirely new. It would be *him.*

Adrian's pleasure was bookended by the concussion of the shotgun. There was no pain; only a flash of light, then darkness.

The nearly point-blank range blew Adrian's body off of Randi, over the side of the bed. Her face and hair were sprayed with his blood. Deafened, she began to scream. The assassin pointed the shotgun at her. She was paralyzed; the twin barrels of the weapon seemed as large as caverns in the moonlight, perfectly round. They mesmerized her.

Then her eyes focused on the killer. He was wearing a ski-mask. He gestured with the gun at the open door to the kitchen; Randi scrambled out of the blood-splattered bed.

She wrenched open the back door, and whimpering, nude, Randi ran through the yard. Not daring to look behind her, she ran across the street, achieved the path. Fireworks bloomed in the sky, and halfway up the path, Randi began to scream again. By the time she reached the clearing, Adrian's family was out on the deck, scurrying down the steps to meet her.

Randi pushed past them and stumbled up the stairs, to the sanctuary at the top, convinced that the murderer was right behind her. She threw herself onto the bed in the extra bedroom, pulled the sheet around herself, then slid off the bed and tried to crawl beneath it.

Penny reached her first. There wasn't space to get under the bed, so Randi was cowering in the corner, sobbing. "They shot him!" she wailed. "Oh, my God, Miss Penny, *they shot him!*"

"*Adrian!*" Daina screamed. "*Oh, my God, Ian! It's happening!*" She turned from the doorway to run to her son, her baby, her darling boy.

Ian caught her, held her to him, as Penny shouted, *"No!* I'll go." Bellona took her place in comforting Randi.

"I have to see him!" Daina cried, but Ian held onto her. "I have to help him!"

"No," Penny repeated. "There is no helping him, child. You don't want to see him. Keep her here, Ian."

Penny hurried down the steps. As she reached the path, another rocket bloomed in the sky. She ran down the hill, crossed the street and fearlessly entered the house through the open front door. She saw the kicked-in bedroom door; the moonlight strode across the bed. Another rocket exploded in the sky outside. Penny smelled the lingering aroma of gunpowder, saw the splash of blood on the wall, black in the half-light. She skirted the bed and beheld Adrian's crumpled body on the floor. A sob wracked her.

What does it matter now if men believe or no? What is to come will come. And soon you too will stand aside, to murmur in pity that my words were true.

Tears blinded Penny as she crouched down and looked closely at her beloved Capo. He was quite dead.

Penny cared nothing about police procedure or disturbing a crime scene: she retrieved a sheet from the hall closet and covered Adrian's body with it, in case somehow Daina broke free from her husband's arms and ran down the hill. Destiny had been fulfilled; there was nothing anyone could do for her son now. *Hell is empty and all the devils are here.* Penny would not allow Daina to see Adrian like this.

She went out to the living room and called the police. She was waiting in the street, Independence Day fireworks filling the sky, when the two cruisers roared up, lights blazing, sirens wailing. Two sheriffs jumped out of one car, guns drawn, and Penny dutifully raised her hands, and pointed at the house. They ran into the yard. Another sheriff got out of the other car.

"Someone has murdered my nephew," she said calmly to the deputy. "His . . . woman . . . She was with him. She got away. She's up the hill at my house."

"Take me to her."

"I don't want his mother to see him," Penny told the sheriff as they trudged up the hill. "Whatever is necessary . . . Whatever . . . *identification* . . .*"* The old lady's eyes blazed at the cop in sorrow and fury. But he saw no fear there. "I don't want his mother to see him."

"I'll do what I can," the deputy promised.

Randi was seated at the kitchen table, still wrapped in the sheet. Adrian's blood flecked her face, clotted in her hair. Ian and Daina, clutching each other beside the table, looked up hopefully when Penny came in, but Randi only stared straight ahead.

"I'm Officer West," the sheriff began.

"Is my son dead?" Daina screamed.

"Yes," Penny said, and shared a look of utter sorrow with her sister. Bellona sobbed and grabbed onto the table to steady herself.

"I don't know," West said. "Other deputies are at the house right now. Could you tell me what happened, Miss –?"

Randi looked up at him and her fear was compounded all over again. Thanks to Gil, she would always be terrified of cops. But she had to tell him. He had to catch who did this. That's what cops were for, wasn't it?

"We were . . . We were . . . in bed. Someone kicked in the door. Oh, my God!" Randi sobbed, put her face in her hands, smearing Adrian's blood. "They shot Adrian!"

The radio on the sheriff's shoulder crackled and he spoke into it. "I'm sorry," he said to them.

Daina screamed and collapsed against Ian.

"I'm so sorry for your loss," Officer West said. "But I'm going to have to get a statement from everybody."

SIXTY-TWO

Clancy Chalmers was enjoying the finale of the 4th of July fireworks show from his front porch when the phone rang. *Ya seen one fireworks show, ya seen 'em all,* he thought, and stepped inside to answer it.

"Someone just shot Adrian Wilde," Deputy West said.

Chalmers looked at his daughter through the screen door, oohing and aahing with her mother outside. *Maybe she doesn't even remember him,* he thought fleetingly.

"Do you wanna take it?" West was saying. "Detective Bixby is on duty, but I thought you might wanna –"

"Yeah. Tell Bixby I'll take it. Hold on." Chalmers set the phone down and retrieved his notepad. He wrote down the details of the crime, then told West he would meet him at the scene.

His wife and daughter saw the look on his face when he came back outside, observed that he had put his gun on. They looked solemnly at him: it wasn't the first time that his job had eclipsed a family celebration.

Chalmers didn't tell AnneMarie what had happened. Not yet. It was the first time she'd been back from college since Christmas, and he didn't want to mar her homecoming with this . . . It wasn't like there was a damn thing she could do about it, anyway. Except mourn.

Chalmers hugged his women and told them that he would return as soon as he could.

As he drove across town to the familiar cul-de-sac, Chalmers thought that he might never tell AnneMarie. He'd tried to protect his little girl from the depredations of the mean ol' world – hadn't he seen enough of them? – and Adrian Wilde had been one of them.

But the smart-mouthed kid hadn't meant anything to AnneMarie. As far as her dad knew, she'd never seen him again. She'd stuck up for him when Chalmers had told her that he'd been caught with a stolen car, though. AnneMarie had been fond of Adrian. What possible purpose could it serve to tell her that he'd been murdered?

Detective Chalmers decided that he wouldn't tell her. Not until he caught the guy.

SIXTY-THREE

Doctor Robert Wilde's answering service caught up with him at the 4th of July barbeque he was attending at a colleague's house. His date, a pretty resident named Michele, watched the color drain from his face as he took the call. *There goes the rest of my evening,* she thought.

Like the detective's wife and daughter, Michele was used to this sort of disruption. Even if Rob wasn't on call, she knew that he was dedicated, and medical emergencies happened. Someone had probably had too much to drink, had taken a tumble, resulting in some kind of traumatic, comminuted fracture. The attention of the area's pre-eminent orthopedist was required.

Michele didn't expect details, and didn't ask for any. This was a doctor's lot; someday it would be *her* lot.

"I've gotta go," Rob said. From the look on his face, Michele thought that the injury must be serious indeed. "Can you –"

"I'll catch a cab," she told him. "Call me later."

Rob nodded absently and left the party.

SIXTY-FOUR

Detective Chalmers was surprised to discover that the scene of the crime wasn't Adrian Wilde's parent's house at all, but the one formerly owned by Allan Coleman.

Chalmers had briefly kept tabs on the car thief: he'd felt more than a little satisfaction when Coleman had packed up his slim jims and his slide hammers and relocated to Moreno Valley. But that was out of Chalmers's jurisdiction, and he'd had other cases to investigate since Coleman and Adrian had skated on that Corvette GTA. The detective had no idea what the fat painter had been up to lately. He wondered if Adrian had known. He wondered if it had gotten him killed.

Chalmers watched the revolving lights on the two cruisers for a moment; he nodded at Harvey from the Coroner's Office, smoking a cigarette and leaning against his vehicle. A shooting was always bad; it was worse when it was someone you knew. Chalmers reflected that maybe he was getting too old for investigating car thefts and murders and anything else that was thrown at him. Not for the first time, he contemplated retirement.

The detective sighed. Maybe next week.

Adrian's house was alive with crime scene techs; they would be there at least until daylight, probably until mid-day tomorrow.

It wasn't necessary for any family members to ID the body. Chalmers saved them the horror and the heartache of that. He lifted the sheet and informed Harvey that the crumpled form upon the floor between the bed and the wall was indeed the earthly remains of Adrian Robert Wilde.

"Aged twenty-one," Deputy West said. "Today."

Harvey made a note of it. Photographs were taken, and the body was soon removed.

Chalmers walked around the house for a while, made a few notes of his own, conferred with the first-responders. Then he crossed the street to interview the witness himself.

When he knocked on the door to Penny and Bellona's house, Ian recognized the detective. "I'm very sorry for your loss, Mr. Wilde," Chalmers said genuinely. "Despite that little trouble he had, I know Adrian was a good kid." Chalmers didn't know how good Adrian really was, but he knew he wasn't Al Capone. He didn't deserve what he'd got. And it was the thing you said to a grieving father. "Do you have any idea who could've done this?"

Ian shook his head.

Penny and Bellona had found some clothes for Randi; they'd gently wiped Adrian's blood from her face, cleansed it from her hair the best they could. She sat at the kitchen table and stared straight ahead. The old women sat on either side of her, ready to get her anything she needed.

Ian introduced them to the detective. Chalmers said to Penny, "I understand you found the body?" She nodded, retold the story of how Randi had come screaming up the steps, how she had gone down to the house, found her nephew, called the police.

"What about you, Miss . . ." Chalmers consulted his notebook. "Miss Green? Did you recognize the guy?"

"Call me Randi," she said automatically. Randi felt like she was in some kind of dream world, half nightmare, half cop show. Adrian was dead and this guy was calling her *Miss Green*. Why wasn't he out catching the guy? "He was wearing a ski mask. I couldn't see his face. Adrian was the nicest guy in the world. Why would someone want to kill him?"

Chalmers expected her to cry then, but she just remained glassy-eyed. He realized that she was on something. He doubted that she had much more to tell him, anyway.

West hadn't mentioned interviewing any other men when he'd arrived on the scene, so Chalmers turned his attention to the guy standing beside Adrian's father. "And you are, sir?"

"This is my cousin," Ian supplied. "Doctor Robert Wilde."

Chalmers glanced at Randi, still staring at the empty air in front of her. "Did you sedate my witness, Doctor?"

"As a matter of fact I did, Detective."

I'm sedated, Randi thought. *It's just like an episode of Law and Order.*

Rob decided he didn't like the cop's tone. "She already gave her statement. I didn't think it mattered subsequent to that." He touched Randi paternally on the shoulder. "But it's not like a couple Valiums gave her amnesia. I'm sure you can —"

"Adrian was your boyfriend, Miss, uh, Randi?" Chalmers asked. He wasn't in the mood for the doctor's self-important offense at the moment.

"No. He wasn't my boyfriend. It was the first time we'd ever . . . been together. My boyfriend . . . That is, my ex-boyfriend . . . We recently broke up. He's out of town."

Chalmers looked at Ian and the doctor. No dawning realization there. They didn't suspect the ex-boyfriend. Chalmers asked for his name, anyway, wrote it down, like the thorough cop he was. But he didn't suspect the ex-boyfriend, either, especially if he was out of town. That was what they called a *red herring.*

Chalmers suspected Allan Coleman. He remembered the way the thief had sold Adrian down the river, just because he believed that it would get the surveillance off of him for a minute. It had been several months ago, but maybe Adrian had recently had a few words with him about it. Chalmers knew Adrian was lippy. Maybe Coleman hadn't liked that.

"Did Adrian say anything to you about Allan Coleman lately, Mr. Wilde?"

Again Ian shook his head. "Adrian gave all that up, Detective. Allan moved away last November. Adrian didn't even help him move. He hasn't . . . *hadn't* . . . seen him since."

"Could I talk to your wife, Mr. Wilde?"

The doctor jumped in, just like Chalmers suspected he would. "She's currently sedated, also. She just lost her only child, Detective. I deemed it a medical imperative."

"I'm sorry if I seem insensitive, Doctor. But I'm trying to conduct an investigation, here, and I would appreciate it –"

"She spoke to the other deputy," Ian said. "Her story's the same as mine. Randi came running up the hill, told us that someone had shot Adrian . . ." Ian sobbed, buried his face in his hands. Rob put his arm around him.

Chalmers looked at Adrian's family. They were grief-stricken. More importantly for his investigation, it was obvious that they knew nothing, suspected nobody. Adrian was the nicest kid ever, didn't have an enemy in the world, as far as they knew. Yet someone had murdered him.

"I'll be in touch," Chalmers said and turned to go.

Don't any of you leave town, Randi thought. She couldn't wait until he left. *Go catch who did this!*

Randi was petrified of cops, yet they'd made her tell the story, more than once. A masked intruder had busted through the door and shot Adrian. What more did they want her to say? She didn't know anything else, and she didn't want to talk to any more cops. Why weren't they out getting the guy?

"Detective?" Chalmers looked back at the old lady, the one who had found the body. "How long before your men are through with my house? How long before we can . . . clean it? I don't want my niece to see . . ."

Chalmers consulted his notebook again. "I thought it was Adrian's house."

"My sister and I purchased it for him. As a Christmas present. Eventually, we intended to transfer title to him . . ."

Real estate transactions, ones that would now never occur, were the farthest thing from Penny's mind. She wanted to know how long the fruitless police red-tape was going to last; she knew they weren't going to catch who did it. Whoever he was, he was an instrument of fate. Such people usually escaped punishment for their crimes, at least in this world. The detective and his investigation could go straight to hell; Penny didn't want Daina to see her son's blood splashed on the wall.

"How long before we can go in?"

"Not more than a couple of days at the most. Maybe as soon as tomorrow afternoon. As soon as they're done. I'll let you know." Chalmers addressed them all. "Again, I'm sorry for your loss."

If you think of anything else, here's my card, Randi thought. But Chalmers didn't have to say it; he'd left one on the table in front of her.

When Chalmers returned to the scene, West told him that Moreno Valley PD had called him on the radio.

His colleague at the neighboring jurisdiction said, "You're in luck, Clancy. We picked up Allan Coleman about twenty minutes ago." Chalmers looked at his watch. Jesus! How did it get to be midnight already?

"Good," Chalmers said. "Charge him with homicide." Sometimes the detective felt like he was in a cop show himself.

SIXTY-FIVE

After Chalmers left, Rob gave Randi another Valium, and the old witches put her to bed in Bellona's room, because Daina was sedated in her old room.

Penny and Bellona hovered in the doorway until Randi drifted off.

"We must tell her everything in the morning," Bellona whispered to her sister. "We must tell her what she has conceived."

SIXTY-SIX

Despite Rob's sedative, or perhaps because of it, Randi dreamed vividly. First she dreamt of Adrian: sweet, beautiful Adrian, making love to her. It seemed so real, so flawless – it was as if everything that happened afterwards was the dream. Adrian wasn't dead; he was here with her. She could smell him, taste him.

But then it happened all over again, the noise of the door hitting the wall, the thunder of the gun. Adrian's blood, hot, splashing her face. Randi didn't scream, but was immediately, completely awake. She still felt Adrian's kiss on her mouth, his blood on her face.

Randi put her face in her hands; Adrian's blood was gone, but she felt the tears, wet on her cheeks. It was all true. Adrian was dead, murdered, shot by some guy wearing a ski mask . . . Who could've wanted to kill Adrian?

Randi wrapped the sheet from the bed around herself and walked out onto the deck. She sat on the bench beside the table and stared out into the black forest. It was there that Penny and Bellona found her at sunrise.

They were practical witches; they knew that Randi was in a delicate state, drowning in grief. Adrian was dead, but Randi was not. She had to eat. So they brought her coffee and fresh-baked rolls, bacon and eggs. She had to keep her strength up, couldn't be permitted to make herself sick with despair.

Randi said thanks; she picked up her fork and took a bite. But Bellona's eggs seemed slimy and flavorless, the coffee tasted like nothing but hot water. After a moment, she gave up trying to eat.

"I'm sorry," she said. "I just can't –"

"You are overwhelmed by the tragedy of Adrian's death."

Penny was stating the obvious, and Randi looked at her in amazement. *No, I'm overwhelmed because I broke up with Gil . . .*

"How would you feel if we told you that Adrian wasn't really gone, Randi?" Bellona asked. "What if we told you that he will continue – because of you?"

Hope, unbounded, bloomed in Randi. Of course! They were witches, magicians, necromancers! They were probably in contact with Adrian's spirit right now! Why hadn't she thought of it herself? The unseen realms! The death of the body was not the end! Adrian's soul lived still; it was eternal. He traveled now among the celestial spheres, across the astral plane!

"Are we going to have a séance? What do I have to do?"

Disconcerted, Bellona exchanged a glance with her sister. "I see that Lily has been allowing Spiritualists back into the shop again."

"Their money's green." Penny looked at Randi again. "But you mustn't listen to their claptrap, dear. They would have you believe that communicating with the dead is as simple and as commonplace as placing a telephone call. Necromancy is far more difficult than they think, and more dangerous –"

"Adrian would never harm me," Randi said. "I loved Adrian, and . . . And he knew it."

"We all knew it, dear," Bellona said. "That's why he chose you."

"What we are going to unfold for you, Randi – you must keep it to yourself." Penny looked steadily at her. "It's permitted for you to wear a pentacle around your neck, nowadays; no one's going to burn you at the stake for calling yourself a witch. But what we're going to tell you . . . If you go around talking about it, someone will say you're crazy. They'll try to have you locked up, say you're delusional, a danger to your child."

"My –?"

"Long before he was born – long before he was even dreamt of – it was prophesied that Daina's son would die young," Penny continued.

"Who –?"

"Through a trivial scry, it was revealed to us," Bellona said. "Daina was hardly more than a child at the time, but her moonflow had commenced, so we asked after the man that would someday walk beside her. Would he be good to her? Or would he bring her heartache?"

Penny still watched Randi keenly. "We were returned that Daina's mate would be for life, that their love would be absolute. We could not see him . . . We didn't see him until right before he entered her life, actually. And even then, it was uncertain. He had a choice to make and he made it.

"But another message was delivered us, when Daina was a little girl – the union of our niece and her true love would produce a child, an exceptional boy . . ."

"But he would die upon reaching his majority," Bellona concluded.

"So, for all of his life –"

"For all of his life, we have prepared for the inevitable." Penny smiled humorlessly. "Adrian was doomed. The future can be glimpsed, but it cannot be controlled, Randi. Adrian Wilde, the face, the body that you knew, is gone. The prophecy is fulfilled. But Adrian Wilde, the person, *the soul* . . . lives on. Within you."

Randi shook her head. "I don't understand."

"Through an ancient rite, Adrian's soul has been transferred to another being. At the moment of his death, at the moment of –"

"You're pregnant, dear." Bellona patted her hand. "Congratulations."

"I'm . . . pregnant? With Adrian's baby?"

Penny shook her head. "The child *is* Adrian. Through *The Incantations of Thoth,* commonplace transmigration of the soul was stymied. A soul waiting to be reborn was diverted, and at the moment of his death, Adrian's soul took its place."

"So it won't do for you to skip breakfast, dear." Bellona smiled and patted Randi's hand again. "You're eating for two now."

Randi sat in silence, stunned. Penny and Bellona expected no other reaction. But they knew acceptance would come, and watched as it dawned across her features.

Randi believed in cosmic forces outside of herself. She knew that there had to be more to life than just the mundane day-to-day grind that she encompassed. She'd seen Lily appear to be decades younger upon a whim: Randi knew her transformations had to be magical, because there was no dye, no cosmetics, that could make a woman of indeterminate age (but definitely past sixty) suddenly appear thirty-five overnight. Yet Randi had witnessed it. The wrinkles, the streaks of gray would reappear, of course. But they would be absent for as long as Lily willed it, usually long enough for her to go out with some young man that had wandered into the shop and struck her fancy.

And Randi had also seen Penny and Bellona's prophecies fulfilled. As Adrian had once said, they were only about missing cats and freak rainstorms – but to Randi, a prophecy was a prophecy. She knew that the old witches could see what was yet to be.

But Randi was unsure now. The sisters knew that she and Adrian had been in bed together when the murder occurred, because they had heard her tell her story to the cops. But they couldn't know that she and Adrian had been in the middle of making love, unless the rest of it was also true, but . . . The whole idea was insane. *Damn right, I won't tell anyone,* Randi thought.

They knew that we were in bed together, so they just naturally assumed what it was that we were doing. And what they'd been doing could've made her pregnant – the thought of protection hadn't

241

entered Randi's mind, because her mind had been filled with Adrian, kissing her, carrying her to his bed, as she'd always dreamed he would . . .

Oh, my God! Could I really be pregnant?

Randi figured that the old fortunetellers were making an educated guess – or maybe, they *had* scryed it. Randi believed in mystical powers – if she was pregnant, perhaps Penny and Bellona could see it – but she wasn't quite ready to believe that Adrian's baby *was Adrian.* She'd never heard of such a thing, and even if it was somehow possible, how would she know? How would that work? Would the baby come into the world and start singing *my, my, my, I'm once bitten, twice shy?*

Randi couldn't quite comprehend all the metaphysical concepts that Penny and Bellona had related to her. She was unfamiliar with the expression *transmigration of the soul;* she wasn't completely sure what *stymied* meant.

But she was sure of one thing. If they were correct, and she was pregnant with Adrian's baby, Randi decided on the spot that she would keep it, and raise it, and love it. She had loved Adrian for so long. Their first, their only, night together had ended in his brutal murder. If a new life had been created out of that, then it had to be some kind of fate – maybe it wasn't exactly what Adrian's aunts were telling her – but it had to be some kind of fate, nonetheless. Randi had loved Adrian, and she would love his baby. It would be like having a little part of him with her. Forever.

A familiar voice said her name, and Randi and Penny and Bellona looked to the deck stairs. Gil was standing there, looking guilty, embarrassed, remorseful.

Randi's heart leapt: five years of thinking you loved someone was not forgotten overnight. But then the memory of his betrayal crashed down on her. She had wished for a future with Adrian, once she'd discovered that Gil was cheating on her. They had begun it, then that future had been senselessly destroyed in an eye blink. But the old witches said she was pregnant with Adrian's child . . . A new future was beginning.

Regardless, Gil was a part of her past. He was a lying, cheating, son of a bitch. Randi subverted the joy her heart felt beneath the memory of that.

"Go away, Gil," she said, and looked out at the trees.

But Gil didn't go away. He crossed the porch. "I made a mistake, baby. I'm so sorry. I never meant to hurt you. It was just a thing . . .

Something that happened. I'll never speak to her again. Please, baby, come on home with me now. You gotta take me back. I love you, Randi."

Gil glanced at the old ladies, wished they would be polite and go into their house, so he could work this out with Randi alone. But they just looked back at him impassively, and made no move to leave.

At last Randi looked at him. "No one told you what happened last night? You didn't see the police at Adrian's house?"

Gil shook his head. "I knew you'd come over here for the 4th of July. Since you said you were leaving me, I figured you'd stay here overnight."

"Someone shot Adrian last night, Gil. He's dead."

"Christ! Oh, my God, Miss Penny! Miss Bellona! I'm so sorry! Who – did they catch – how –?" Gil stammered to a stop. He ran his hand through his hair, his expression the picture of disbelief.

"Someone kicked in the door and shot him. They haven't caught anybody yet."

Gil sat down on the bench beside Randi and hugged her. *"Christ!"* he repeated. "I'm so sorry to hear about this, baby! I know he was your friend . . ."

Gil was disconcerted that Randi didn't hug him back, that she wouldn't even look at him. He was completely surprised that she was dry-eyed. He gently brushed the hair out of her eyes, and at last she met his gaze. "I'm so sorry about what I did, baby," he said with a little sob. "Please come home with me."

Randi opened her mouth, but before she could speak, Penny said, "We've invited Randi to stay here with us for a little while."

Randi smiled gratefully at the unlooked-for out that Penny was offering her. "I don't know if I can forgive you, Gil," she told him. "I need some time to think things out."

"But . . . I love you, Randi. I want you to come home with me."

"I need some time by myself right now, Gil. Please leave me alone."

Gil opened his mouth, then closed it again. Penny and Bellona continued to gaze emotionlessly at him. He'd expected Randi to run into his arms, to forgive him immediately, after the trauma that she'd just experienced. But she was stronger than he'd expected. He'd cheated on her, and even the horror of seeing Adrian Wilde blown away in front of her eyes hadn't erased that from her mind. Randi was pissed about what he'd being doing with Nadine.

But life was long and Gil was confident. Adrian was dead – where else could Randi turn now? She'd have to come back to him. She just needed a little time to cool off.

"All right. I'll go." Gil released her. "But just remember, Randi. Everybody makes mistakes. *Let he who is without sin cast the first stone.*" Her mistake, her *sin,* had cost her lover boy his life. "I'm sorry about what I did with . . ." Gil decided it would be better to not speak her name. "It was a mistake. I'm asking you to forgive me, because I love you. Don't forget that." Gil rose, nodded at Penny and Bellona, and left the deck.

Randi watched over the railing until Gil disappeared at the top of the path. She said to the sisters, "How long before I know if I'm really pregnant? Should I go see a doctor?"

SIXTY-SEVEN

By mid-morning on Saturday, July 6th, the Riverside County Sheriff's Office concluded their investigation of the crime scene. Detective Chalmers was not present; the technician in charge walked up the hill to the little house in the woods and told Penny that it was now okay for her to go back into the house.

It was women's work, cleaning up after the slaughter. In the silence of mourning, after the battle was lost and won, it had always been the women who had bathed and cleaned and prepared their deceased men for burial. Penny and Bellona were spared that; but with soap and sponges and buckets, they took care of the carnage left behind in Adrian's house.

Before they had even begun, Penny had been on the phone, making appointments. After the blood was gone – like the butcher, the baker, and the candlestick maker – the tradesmen showed up, within minutes of each other. The junk man discreetly removed Adrian's blood-soaked bed. While the carpet-layer made measurements and began removing the rug, the painting contractor began his task.

Within twenty-four hours, the place where Adrian Wilde had drawn his last breath was restored to just another bedroom. Penny was satisfied. Daina had worried about the sword hanging over her son's head for his entire life. She would mourn him for the rest of her own. But because of her aunt's diligence, she had not had to bear witness to any aspect of his awful end.

Penny and Bellona drew the curtains and locked the door. Unlike when their sister had died, the disposition of Adrian's belongings was not up to them. Unless his parents' asked them to take care of it, they would leave that task up to Ian and Daina.

SIXTY-EIGHT

On July 7th, Ian sat in his parents' den and shared their grief. The elder Doctor Wilde and his wife – Rob and Will's parents – were also present. Ian appreciated his family's love and sorrow, but there wasn't anything anyone could do for Adrian now. Ian had left Daina at home, asleep, under the caring eye of her Aunt Bellona, and he wanted to get back to her. He knew that his love was the only comfort she had.

But before Ian could return to his heartbroken wife, Rob arrived with his twin brother and his family. They had returned as soon as they could from Europe when Rob told them of the tragedy; he'd just fetched them from the airport.

Will embraced his cousin silently. He had never really cared for Ian, or even Adrian, for that matter. But they were blood, family, and as a father himself, Will tried to comprehend the unspeakable loss that Ian must be feeling, wondered what he could possibly say to ease his cousin's pain. He couldn't think of any condolence even marginally appropriate, so he asked, "Do they have any leads?"

Ian shook his head.

Marta hugged Ian next, the tears streaming down her face. "How's Daina?" she asked.

Again Ian shook his head. "She's sleeping. Rob gave her some sedatives. She's been more or less sleeping since . . . Since it happened."

Ian hugged Bobby and Nick and Tracy; their eyes were red and puffy from crying, from their flight across the globe to return home to this appalling heartbreak. Their expressions were slack and stupefied with grief, with shock and fatigue and disbelief.

No one spoke for a moment, then Nick broke the silence.

"What happened, Uncle Ian?" he said softly. "Dad just told us that somebody . . . killed Adrian. How?" Nick's voice rose. "Who? *Why?* What happened?"

Marta put her arm around her youngest, but Nick refused to be comforted. Everyone present – his parents, his grandparents, his brother, Tracy, Ian's mom and dad – everyone was crying. But not Nick. He had done all his crying on the interminable plane ride. Now he wanted some answers.

All his dad had said was that someone had broken into the house and shot Adrian. That wasn't enough for Nick. He had suffered and grieved with his family for the three days it had taken them to arrange a flight home, nearly twenty hours of which had been spent in airports and aboard planes. Like Rob, his father had given his wife and eldest son and Tracy a sedative; they had slept through the flight, through their initial shock and grief.

But Nick had refused the palliative. He'd remained awake, sharp, alone, as the interrogatives fought with each other for prominence in his mind. His dad had told him all he knew – the *what* and the *when* and the *where,* and even the *how* – someone had shot Adrian at his house.

But Will didn't know anything about the most important details – the *who* and the *why,* and this lack of information tormented Nick.

"Was it an argument? Some kind of burglary?"

Ian shook his head. "No argument. Nothing was stolen. Randi said –"

"Randi?" Nick had not thought of Randi since his father had told him the devastating news. The *who* and the *why* of Adrian's murder had completely taken over his thoughts, had driven out everything else. But now Randi sprung to Nick's mind again. Beautiful, soft-spoken Randi, whom he loved so much, who had loved Adrian so much . . .

Ian nodded. "Randi came running up the hill, screaming. She said someone had kicked in the bedroom door and shot Adrian. She said he was wearing a mask."

Randi said someone kicked in the *bedroom door . . . Randi and Adrian had been in bed together.* Now Nick felt the hot tears stinging in his eyes. His cousin had betrayed him. It was incomprehensible. His best friend in the world besides Bobby, his *only* friend in the world besides Bobby, had stabbed him in the back. Adrian was as big of a bastard as Gil.

Nick's mind teetered. Adrian had shafted him, taken the girl he loved, just because he was older and she liked him. Adrian had stolen Randi from Nick for the same reason that he had stolen that Corvette: because he could.

It's not like he can play guitar better than me, Nick thought insanely. *Oh, my God, Adrian, how could you do this to me? You know how much I love her. But you didn't care, did you? The minute I was out of the picture, you just went ahead and . . .*

Nick glanced at each of his family members. No one felt his betrayal; no one was ashamed of Adrian for being in bed with the woman Nick loved. His family could be excused; they didn't know.

But Bobby and Tracy knew. Tracy wouldn't meet his eyes. Nick saw with a sudden clarity that Tracy had probably heard it from both sides, all along. She had no doubt listened to Randi gush about her desire for Adrian; Randi had never even mentioned Nick. Then Tracy had heard it from Bobby and maybe Adrian himself, about how much Nick loved Randi. And if that wasn't enough, Tracy had witnessed it all with her own eyes. Tracy understood: Adrian had betrayed Nick.

Bobby looked helplessly at his brother; he shook his head, the tears running down his cheeks again. Bobby's expression acknowledged Adrian's betrayal, but –

But nothing that Adrian did matters now. Adrian's never going to do anything, ever again . . .

Adrian's dead, Nick realized, all over again, and he sobbed and put his hands over his eyes, like a little boy. He pushed the meaninglessness of Adrian's transitory betrayal away, and let his sorrow reign.

Oh, Jesus, Adrian! The pain knifed through Nick. He'd loved Adrian, and whatever had happened with him and Randi didn't matter, because Adrian was dead . . . *Adrian was in bed with Randi and someone shot him.*

A picture of the dusty weapons that he'd seen in Randi's closet suddenly manifested itself in Nick's mind; he again heard Randi say, *He's jealous, Nick. He wouldn't like it if he came home and you were here.*

Nick took his hands from his face; his tears stopped abruptly, immediately, like the turning off of a faucet. He blinked in astonishment at his Uncle Ian. Why couldn't he see?

"Gil did this."

His parents and grandparents and Ian's parents all looked at each other in confusion, but Bobby and Tracy's eyes widened. They knew that Gil had threatened Adrian before.

"Who, son?" Will asked.

"Randi's boyfriend. It had to've been him. Gil killed Adrian. He was always jealous, he hated –"

Ian shook his head again. "Randi broke up with Gil, Nick. Besides, he was out of town, helping Nadine and her mother move."

"Gil was out of town fucking Nadine!" Nick yelled. "Her mother wasn't even there."

Nick's grandparents were shocked and embarrassed by his profanity. But then they put it down to the pain of grief, and forgave him. They didn't know who all these people were that he was talking about, anyway.

But Will and Ian and Rob knew, and the three of them flinched as if they'd been slapped.

Will couldn't find his voice, but Rob at last stammered out, "What are you talking about, Nick? Gil and Nadine . . .?"

"That's crazy, Nick," Ian said. He had heard Randi say that Gil was cheating on her, but it couldn't have been with Nadine. "She's old enough to be Gil's –"

"I saw them," Nick explained. "They were making out at Randi's birthday party. That's why he wanted to go out of town with her. Her mother wasn't really with them. I called the hotel . . . It was just the two of them. I . . . I showed Randi what he was doing to her . . ."

That was why she was in bed with Adrian. I did this to myself. Adrian told me she'd hate me for telling her that Gil was cheating on her. When she finally made up her mind about it . . . Did I really expect her to run to me?

Hatred, bitterness, remorse, grief warred within Nick. These powerful emotions, swirling and sloshing around in his mind, nearly undid him. He reached out and held onto the back of a chair for support.

No, Nick said viciously to himself. *I'm just a fucking kid. She never so much as glanced at me, but Adrian . . . The way she looked at Adrian. Randi loved Adrian. She'd always wanted him. She didn't even care that I was alive.*

I told her Gil was cheating on her, so immediately, she ran and jumped in bed with Adrian.

He could've told her no . . . But . . . I'm just a kid to him, too. He didn't care about what I felt . . .

Again, the rational part of Nick's mind told him that none of that mattered anymore. *Oh, Christ, Adrian!*

"Gil did it," Nick said again. "Why can't you people see that? Randi dumped him because he was cheating on her and then she ran to Adrian. Gil was jealous, so he shot –"

"Gil was out of town, Nick." Ian said again. "He couldn't have done it."

Ian obviously didn't believe that the blinding force of jealousy could drive a man to murder. But Nick believed it. He had just felt it in himself. His best friend in the world, his cousin, his blood, was dead, shot in cold blood, ambushed, murdered . . .

But for a moment, Nick's overwhelming grief had vanished.

For a moment, all Nick could do was hate Adrian, utterly, for betraying him, for taking Randi away from him. And Randi hadn't ever been Nick's. She would never be Nick's. Hatred for his cousin had seized Nick; he had felt a capacity for revenge within himself.

Nick had never possessed Randi, and he loved Adrian. Gil thought he owned Randi, and he hated Adrian. Why couldn't they see? It couldn't have been anyone else *but* Gil.

Nick looked at the sad faces of his relatives. They all thought he was just a kid; hysterical, grief-stricken, grasping at straws. Gil was out of town, so he couldn't have murdered the guy he'd threatened to murder, if he did just what he had been doing. Right.

Nick looked at his brother, but Bobby didn't believe him either. Just like Ian, Bobby had never suffered through the agony and bitterness of love unrequited. Neither Ian nor Bobby had ever felt the anger and hatred when the object of their affections looked with affection at someone else. They had never felt jealousy.

But Nick understood jealousy and hatred and a sudden thirst for revenge. And he knew beyond a shadow of a doubt that Gil understood them, too. Nick knew that Gil had acted on these emotions.

Gil shot Adrian.

But Nick's family didn't believe him. So Nick shut up and sat down.

Another silent moment passed, then Ian said, "I've gotta be getting home to Daina." The large Wilde clan enfolded him in their arms, their love, their sorrow. "I'll let you know about the service," he said and departed.

SIXTY-NINE

Rob drove Will and his family home in silence. When they arrived, Bobby mumbled something about having to take Tracy home, and he and his brother transferred her suitcases to his car. Then Rob hugged his twin and his wife, his nephews and Tracy, and went on his way. Marta and Will went inside.

"Can I go with you guys?" Nick asked Bobby.

"Sure, Nick," Bobby said and ruffled his hair.

When they got to her parents' house, Tracy said to her fiancé, "Just put my suitcases on the curb, Bobby. If you go into the house . . . They'll want you to go through the whole story. I'll tell them that you just . . . had to go."

"Thanks," Bobby said simply and hugged her. "I'll call you later."

As they drove away from Tracy's house, Nick said, "Take me downtown, Bobby. To the police station. I'm gonna tell 'em Gil did it."

"Gil was out of town, Nick." Bobby looked over at his brother. "Why didn't you tell me about him and Adrian's aunt?"

"Randi made me and Adrian promise not to tell anybody."

"But I'm your brother, for Christ's sake . . ." Bobby sighed.

"Gil did it, Bobby. I saw guns at their apartment. You know how jealous he is."

"He was out of town, Nick!"

"Take me to the police station, Bobby. If you don't, I'm gonna get out right now and walk. I wanna make a statement. You're obstructing justice."

"This isn't *Law and Order,* Nick. They're not going to listen to you."

But Clancy Chalmers did listen to him.

Allan Coleman had an alibi for the time of Adrian's murder, air-tight, ironclad. At eight-forty-five on the 4th of July, he and two of his buddies had been talking to one of Moreno Valley's finest. It seemed that someone had lit off a bottle rocket from the vacant lot beside his shop, and it had landed on one of the cars Allan was supposed to be painting, and had done some minor damage. As a tax-paying citizen, outraged Coleman had felt it his duty to report it. In case he had to take actions against the little bastards himself.

The report said that the complainant mentioned that his wife had left him, and he was currently forced to live at the shop, so he couldn't be having juvenile delinquents burning the place to the ground, just because it was Independence Day. The Moreno Valley cop had walked around the lot, but had turned up nothing. He concluded the call at 9:15, just about the time Adrian's aunt had discovered the body.

Coleman had been in the company of the law when Adrian was murdered. He couldn't have done it. Chalmers had to release him.

The idea that it could all be part of a plan hadn't escaped Chalmers, however. It all seemed a little convenient – Coleman was talking to the cops when Adrian died – maybe he'd sent someone else to do it, and then called the police to give himself an alibi.

But Chalmers thought that it wasn't very likely: Coleman had neither the resources nor the smarts to pull off something like that. Neither did he really have a motive for murder – if his wife had left him, Chalmers imagined that Coleman had other troubles in his mind past a months' old beef with some kid he hadn't even seen in all that time.

And Coleman had seemed genuinely saddened when Chalmers told him that Adrian was dead. He was stunned that Chalmers could even suggest that he'd done it. "I thought Adrian was a great kid. What reason would I have to kill him?"

Detective Chalmers was back to nothing. So he listened to Nick's story.

Chalmers was surprised to hear that Wilde's girl's ex-boyfriend had been nailing the old gal that he was helping to move. But on the other hand, Chalmers wasn't that surprised. That kind of thing happened every day. What also happened every day, what had also occurred in this case, was that the cheated-upon party had found out about it, and had broken up with the cheater. And the cheater hadn't cared too much about all that. He hadn't rushed back to town and murdered his girl's new boyfriend, as this kid was trying to tell him. That kind of shit only happened in the movies. He'd gone to a baseball game instead.

"He's got an alibi, kid," Detective Chalmers told Nick. "He went to the gas station to fill up the rental car, then met his new girlfriend at a baseball game. I already talked to them."

"Maybe she's lying for him," Nick said. Bobby rolled his eyes.

Chalmers took in the kid's grief, his sincerity. "Maybe she is. Maybe he did it. But there's no way for me to prove –"

"Did you see Gil's guns?"

"Yes, I did, Mr. Wilde. It's all part of the investigation."

"Were they clean? Because when I saw them, they were dusty –"

"Just because a man cleans his guns doesn't make him a murderer, son. It's part of the upkeep."

"Randi said he never used them!"

"Then why do you think he used them now?"

"He's jealous! He hated Adrian!"

Chalmers appreciated the kid's desperation, his relentless need to find out who killed his cousin. But there just wasn't any evidence. "He wasn't here. He couldn't have done it."

"So you're not going to do anything else?"

"I'll go out and talk to him again. But don't get your hopes up. He's got an alibi, witnesses that put him in Bakersfield at the time of the murder. And none that put him here."

Nick looked at his brother. Bobby nodded at the door.

"Okay," Nick said. "Thank you, Detective. I guess I can't ask for more than that."

SEVENTY

Bellona saw to the arrangements. Adrian was to be cremated; Bellona picked out a beautiful onyx urn. A memorial service for Adrian's family would be held on the morning of Wednesday, July 10th.

Rob stayed at Daina and Ian's the night before, sleeping fitfully on their couch. He didn't notice the discomfort. Adrian was dead, murdered . . . Rob felt Adrian's loss, the incomprehensible suddenness of it; the utter lack of reason – why would anyone want to kill Adrian? But Rob knew his own numbness and disbelief was infinitesimal compared to Ian and Daina's.

Ian wanted to remain by his wife, sought to relieve her of her stupefying grief, like a Kaparot chicken absorbing sin. Rob wanted to stay by his cousin and perform the same function.

Daina welcomed the sedatives that Rob provided, but Ian didn't want to sleep. He wanted to be awake and alert if she should request anything of him. He was up at six am on the day of his son's service, even though it wouldn't commence until hours later. The morning had dawned foggy; Rob sat with him on the porch in the unseasonable gloom.

Ian said, *"By the clock, 'tis day, and yet dark night strangles the travelling lamp: Is't night's predominance, or the day's shame, that darkness does the face of earth entomb, when living light should kiss it?"*

"'Tis unnatural, even like the deed that's done," Rob replied.

Even in grief were the Wilde cousins simpatico. The ancient, immortal words were a comfort. Duncan's murder was no more unnatural than Adrian's.

"Who could've done this, Ian?" Rob whispered helplessly.

Ian shook his head. "The cops say it was a botched robbery."

Tears welled and fell unnoticed. His son was dead . . . Ian tried to escape the fact that Penny and Bellona had predicted it, before Adrian was born, when his mother was just a girl. They had predicted it, to the day. Adrian had died upon reaching his majority, murdered in his bed by person or persons unknown . . .

Not only had Daina's aunts foretold Adrian's death, they had also planned ahead for the inevitable. Ian had never believed . . . It was just too horrible a thing to contemplate, that his son would cease to exist, and right on schedule, just because they said he would. That Adrian would die was ridiculous; Penny and Bellona and Daina's way for him to circumvent his inexorable fate was downright hilarious.

Ian had laughed out loud after Daina explained how it was supposed to work. She had not appreciated his laughter, so Ian had tried to choke it back. She was so solemn, so serious . . . Tears had squeezed from Ian's eyes then, too, but they had been tears of mirth . . . Adrian was gonna die, but only for a moment; then he would be reborn as his own son . . .

Ian feared for Daina's sanity for a moment, but then realized that she had been raised on this kind of fanciful, magical mumbo-jumbo, curses and predestination. She believed that her aunts were *never wrong*. This fantasy of Adrian's *continuing* after his untimely demise was not a new delusion on Daina's part: it was just part and parcel of the overarching delusion of unseen realms that she had been taught.

But Ian couldn't deny that Penny and Bellona had accurately predicted that he and Daina would fall in love. And the child produced by that love had died on his twenty-first birthday, just as they had foretold that he would.

Ian had read an article in *Psychology Today* that suggested that future events had been predicted with a startling statistical accuracy. The authors concluded that more studies would have to be conducted before definitive answers could be stated, but . . . Ian had seen the future predicted to his eternal joy and his eternal sadness. It was impossible for him to deny that precognition could exist.

From the moment he'd stepped foot into this strange little neighborhood on All Hallow's Eve, Ian had accepted that he was in the Twilight Zone: air that should be empty and incorporate sometimes shimmered and moved, if only for a second; statements that should've been just words and breath and wishes became boons and curses . . . He had discovered to his joy and agony that such things were as inevitable as that sunrise, which, if it was sometimes inexplicably delayed, like today . . . always arrived in the end.

But this other thing, this *continuing* that Penny and Bellona and Daina awaited . . . It was madness. Adrian was dead. Ian would not allow himself even at atom of hope . . . It was crazy, impossible. He would *not* believe it.

SEVENTY-ONE

The Wildes didn't follow any established religion, so no man of the cloth was present at Adrian's service. The funeral director observed a moment of silence, then invited Adrian's family and friends to come up and say a few words. For a heartbeat, no one moved.

Adrian had been beloved by his family; their grief at his sudden, senseless loss was so profound that they didn't feel it necessary to speak to each other of their love. An additional ceremony was planned for Adrian's legion of friends and fans, after his family had gone. Randi had arranged it. Let them offer funny anecdotes and offer tribute. Adrian's family remained speechless.

The funeral director paused for another moment. This had never happened to him before, even when the deceased had been murdered, like in this case. Family always wanted to talk, to help ease their grief. He was not sure how to proceed if no one was going to speak . . .

To the funeral director's relief, Nadine arose and walked up to the podium.

"I knew Adrian all his life," she began, and met Ian's eyes. She couldn't see her aunts', or Daina's, or Lily's eyes, because they were veiled, as good witches always were at funerals. "I wasn't around a lot, but he was always in my thoughts. I offer this simple verse." Nadine read from an index card. "A heartfelt prayer: Musician sheer, always in memory. Now dreamers wince, but will endure. Parting for a while; saddened never." Nadine turned, grinned to herself, although nothing but sorrow showed on her face. She set the card down next the urn, touched the top of it. "Goodbye, Adrian," she whispered, then returned to her seat. No one else spoke, and after a short time, Adrian's family went home to suffer their grief in private.

There were tributes aplenty at the more public service that followed. Young men that had enjoyed Adrian's music spoke of his talent. Emily was there, and AnneMarie, and a host of other girls that had loved the black-haired singer, if only for a night or a few days. Several of them also tearfully said a couple of words. One girl, like Nadine, read a poem.

Randi felt no jealousy at these girls' outpouring of love for Adrian: if Penny and Bellona were correct, she would have more than anything that these girls had ever received from him. Randi would have more than just fond memories, now turned to sadness. She would have Adrian's child.

Being young and divorced from the traditions of death, Adrian's friends left flowers and cards on the table around his urn, like at some roadside memorial. When the last mourner left, the funeral director offered Randi a manila envelope for the cards. He suggested that perhaps Adrian's mother would like to have them. He said he would take care of the flowers.

Randi had not spoken more than a few words to Adrian's mother since the night of the murder. Daina had been in seclusion. *Sedated,* Randi thought.

Now Randi sat with Adrian's grieving parents in the living room of the house where Daina had raised her son.

"Could we have a moment, Mr. Wilde?" Randi asked.

Ian hesitated; he had become Daina's shadow, seeking every waking moment for any means to relieve her relentless sorrow, even if it was just temporarily, for a brief moment. And he didn't want to leave her yet. Their lives had been shattered, irrevocably.

But then Ian realized that even in the aftermath of this devastation, some normalcy would eventually return. He knew that he couldn't hover over Daina forever. Ian nodded at Randi and went outside.

Daina sat on the couch with her hands folded in her lap. She stared fixedly at the urn that held Adrian's ashes. She ignored the envelope full of cards.

In the short span of time since Adrian's murder, Randi had done a lot of thinking. It was still too early to tell if she was indeed pregnant: the nurse at her doctor's office had laughed – "Come in after you've missed your period, honey," she said. "We'll be able to tell you for sure, then."

That wouldn't be for a few more weeks. But Randi hoped it was true; she believed in the old witches' predictions, and she wanted to have Adrian's baby. Penny and Bellona had taken her aside at the service and told her that the time had come for her to tell Daina.

Randi opened her mouth to speak, but no words came out. She cleared her throat and tried again. "Mrs. Wilde?" When Daina slowly dragged her sad eyes from Adrian's urn to Randi's face, Randi continued quickly, "Miss Penny and Miss Bellona have told me that I'm pregnant."

Daina blinked, also slowly. Randi realized that Adrian's mom wasn't only sedated, she was *heavily sedated.* Penny and Bellona had said that Daina had anticipated, had dreaded Adrian's death since long before he was even born. And the prophecy had come true, right on schedule.

That's a lot to take, Randi thought. *I'd wanna be sedated, too.*

"Are you sure?" Daina said at last.

Randi shook her head. "The doctor's office said not to bother to come in until next month. So I made an appointment for the 2nd of August." Randi paused. "But I hope . . . I hope it's true, Mrs. Wilde. I loved Adrian."

"I know you did, Randi."

Daina continued to stare blankly at her, so Randi added, "Penny and Bellona . . . They told me that . . . They told me about . . . Adrian's soul."

Randi saw a flare of hope in Daina's light blue eyes. It blazed there for a moment, combating the tranquillizers. "Do you believe what they told you?"

Randi hesitated. She couldn't quite accept that the baby would *be* Adrian; such impossible, magical wonders were too much to think about right now. Contemplation of such concepts was just a bridge that she would have to cross later. Randi wasn't quite sure that she wanted to believe it.

But she knew that Penny and Bellona believed it, and Miss Lily. And perhaps most poignantly of all, Randi knew that Adrian's mom believed it, because the old witches had told Randi that she did. Daina would not lose her beloved son at all; she would get to see him grow and thrive and live again.

So what could it hurt? Randi had loved Adrian from the moment she saw him, but his mom had loved him for his entire life. Randi had been devastated by his murder, but the hope of bearing Adrian's child had helped her cope. If the belief that the baby she carried (if that was even so) was Adrian would also give Daina hope, if it would help her start to make the climb out of grief – what harm could it possibly cause?

"Of course I believe them," Randi told Adrian's grieving mother. *"They know things."*

"They're never wrong," Daina agreed. Then she said, "They warned you . . . not to . . . tell anyone?"

Randi nodded. Penny had been one hundred percent right. It was all just crazy. Randi completely believed that telling people that her baby was not really her baby but was in fact his father reborn would get her 5150'd quicker than telling them that she believed she was Napoleon. There would be cops. Handcuffs, maybe. A padded cell.

"I think it's for the best, to keep it between ourselves."

"It's not like it's something that happens every day." Daina laughed shakily, and Randi's heart soared. It wasn't much of a laugh, but it was still a laugh, and that was progress.

"Who all knows?" Randi knew that Penny and Bellona knew, of course, and Miss Lily. But Randi didn't know how much the mysteries of the universe were shared with the rest of Adrian's large family, so she wanted to be sure. She didn't want to make a seemingly delusional comment in front of unbelievers.

Daina recited the three names Randi already knew, then added, "And Ian. But he doesn't believe. We'll wait to tell him, until the doctor tells us that you're definitely pregnant. Maybe he'll believe then."

SEVENTY-TWO

Randi went back to work on July 15th. At quitting time, she walked out to the parking lot behind Mohini's, to find Gil leaning against her car, waiting for her.

Again, Randi's heart jumped into her throat: her heart still loved Gil, even if her mind had resolved to be done with him. She took a deep breath and walked over to confront him.

"What do you want?" she said, as cruelly as she could.

He looked sad and tired. "You haven't answered any of my letters."

Randi had been spared the harassment of pleading phone calls from Gil, because Penny and Bellona didn't have a phone. But still Gil wouldn't leave her alone. Like some throwback to a different age, she had received a letter from him every day. Randi had discarded them, unopened.

But it was more difficult to ignore him when he was standing right there in front of her. Randi didn't tell him that she hadn't read his letters – why hurt him unnecessarily? She said, "I'm going through a lot of changes right now, Gil. I'm not ready –"

"When do you think you might be ready?" he demanded angrily. "I did a stupid thing. I told you I was sorry. I think you should at least give me a chance to make it up to you, to show you how sorry I am. To show you how much I love you. I think I deserve a second chance." Gil's tone softened. "At least come and have a drink with me. I miss you, baby."

At the mention of a drink, Randi thought of the child she may or may not be carrying. Her doctor's appointment was still two weeks away, and even though she looked at herself minutely in the mirror every morning, she could perceive no changes. Penny and Bellona were convinced: they said that they could already see the legendary maternal glow about her. But Randi was unsure.

Despite herself, Randi had to admit that it was great to see Gil. She was lonely. Adrian was gone, and there wasn't a lot to occupy her time at Penny and Bellona's house. She studied the old arts with them most nights. Currently, she was learning how to scry, to induce a kind of trance within herself. She would stare into the glow of a candle behind the glass, then unfocus her eyes . . .

What she perceived next was supposed to hint at the future. But all she ever saw were images of the past. All she ever saw was Adrian.

Penny said it wasn't necessary for Randi to pursue the other realms every day. The visions would come when they would come, if at all; they could not be forced to appear. So Randi also read a lot. But mostly she was bored. Penny and Bellona didn't even have a television.

She looked at Gil, and the memories of the fun years they'd spent together flashed through her mind. She'd loved Gil, right up until the moment when she knew for sure that he had betrayed her.

But she didn't want Gil anymore. She had found a new family, people that loved her. She was going to raise Adrian's baby with them. They would all tell the child what a great guy his father had been; Adrian's memory would live on.

So now, Randi pushed the memories of better times with Gil away. Gil was her past. She told herself that she didn't want anything to do with him anymore. It was difficult . . . But then Randi imagined the scene of Gil and Nadine, in bed, locked in embrace . . .

An idea struck her.

"I need a little more time, Gil. I have a doctor's appointment on the 2nd, so Lily gave me the day off. Why don't you –"

"Are you sick?" Gil took a step back.

"No. It's just time for my annual check-up. Why don't we have lunch together after I'm done?"

Here was the perfect solution. If Randi was indeed pregnant with Adrian's baby, Gil would be outraged, disgusted. He wouldn't want her anymore. He would finally leave her alone to get on with her new life.

"The 2nd is a long time from now, Randi," Gil said. "I don't want to wait that long. I miss you."

I don't care what you want, you cheating son of a bitch! Randi thought. "I'm not ready to see you right now, Gil," she said firmly. "Take it or leave it." She unlocked the door to her car and got inside.

Gil frowned in through the window at her. "I guess I don't have any choice. But I want you to know that I'm not going to give up, Randi." *You belong to me. I killed a man because of you.* "I'm going to make you see how much I love you."

Randi regarded him impassively, a trait that she'd picked up from Penny. "I'll see you on the 2nd, Gil." She started the car, and when he didn't step away from the window immediately, she put it in gear. He stepped back then, and Randi drove away.

"She's making me wait another two weeks," Gil told Nadine from a payphone.

"I'm sorry, honey," she replied. "I'm sure she'll come around. I know that infidelity is a difficult thing for a young girl to get over . . ." *Who knows better than me?* Nadine thought. *I'll never get over it, even though the powers have at last seen to my revenge . . .*

"But you're so sincere," Nadine told Gil. "She'll come back eventually. Just be patient. Come on over. I'll make you dinner."

SEVENTY-THREE

Randi's pregnancy test came out positive. Based on the dates she provided to the doctor, the augury of modern medicine led him to predict that her baby would arrive sometime around the second week of April.

Randi called her old apartment, and Gil picked up on the first ring. He'd also taken the day off, just so he could have lunch with her. She told him to meet her at Mickey's, a little bar down the street from where she worked.

Gil walked up to the bar and ordered himself a beer, then proceeded with it to the booth where Randi was waiting for him. She got directly to the point. "I'm pregnant, Gil."

Gil blinked, stunned; after a moment to comprehend her words and their ramifications, he smiled. He was gonna be a daddy! "That's great, baby! We'll have to get married right away!"

But Randi didn't smile. "It's not yours, Gil. Adrian and I . . . The night he was killed . . ."

Gil stared at her silently. "That son of a bitch just moved right on along, didn't he? He'd just been waiting for his chance to –"

"It doesn't matter now, does it? I don't want to talk about it."

"You can't be sure. Right before I left town, we . . ." But Gil didn't want Randi to think about when he'd been out of town. He didn't want her to dwell on what she'd discovered about him and Nadine whilst they were gone. "You can't be sure it's not mine."

Gil didn't know all that much about the inner workings of the female anatomy, but he knew that much. Randi had been with him just days before her interrupted roll in the hay with Wilde . . . It could be his baby.

"I'm sure, Gil," Randi said, steeped in feminine mystery. "The baby's not yours."

"You can just get rid of it, then," he growled.

"I knew you'd say that." Randi smiled. A kind of sadness, mixed with relief, washed over her. "I'm not getting rid of Adrian's baby."

I loved Adrian, she thought, *and for a few minutes, he loved me. Now I'll have a piece of that love forever.* But she didn't say these things to Gil.

"Adrian was kind to me, after I found out that you –"

"Is that what you call it? *Kindness?* Where I come from, we call that a mercy –"

"Shut up, Gil!" Randi shouted shrilly. A few of the bar's other patrons turned around and looked at her. She lowered her voice. "I'm not getting rid of Adrian's baby. So I guess this is goodbye." Randi stood up.

Gil grabbed her wrist. "Wait, Randi. Don't go."

Gil held onto her; the curious bar patrons continued to look at them. The thought that someone might call the cops if she continued to argue with Gil crossed Randi's mind. She surely didn't want that; she hated cops. So she sat back down. She would just have to be calm and resolve this quietly.

"I guess we're even now," Gil said. "Me and Nadine, you and Wilde . . ."

Randi barked laughter. "You've got to be kidding, Gil. It wasn't hardly the same thing. You were carrying on behind my back with that bitch for *months."*

Years, Gil thought. "At least she wasn't dumb enough to let herself get pregnant."

Randi narrowed her eyes. "I think she's too old to get pregnant, Gil, even though she's obviously not too old to –"

"Look, Randi, I don't want to argue with you."

There was a note of pleading in his voice, in his green eyes. It was something that Randi had never seen in him before. He still held tightly to her wrist.

"I love you. I want us to be together. I don't care that the baby's not mine. It's yours. That's good enough for me. We can get married. Raise it together. It's gonna need a father . . ."

Randi snatched her hand away from his grasp. "That's the most ridiculous thing I've ever heard, Gil. I don't want to marry you." Yet Randi's heart was touched by the sadness in his eyes, by the honor of what he was suggesting. Maybe he really did love her. Her righteousness slipped a few notches. "But there's no reason we can't be friends."

Gil's smile blossomed. *Goddamn, I'm good!* he told himself. "I'll take friends, for now. Let's get out of this bar. Go someplace nice for lunch."

Adrian was gone. Randi would always have his baby to remember him by, but . . . It would be okay to be friends with Gil.

They left Mickey's. Gil didn't bother to call Nadine and tell her that he wouldn't be there for dinner, because Randi would wonder who he had to talk to all of a sudden; she'd be immediately suspicious again. Randi had just taken the first step on the road to coming back to him. Nadine would get over it. Gil would just call her with the good news later.

SEVENTY-FOUR

Urban Equinox died with its singer.

Bobby and Tracy and Nick fled the funeral home before the memorial service attended by Adrian's friends and fans, because, like the rest of the Wilde family, their grief was suffocating. It was too painful to listen to strangers talk about Adrian, even if their words were in loving tribute.

Bobby had a key to Adrian's garage door. He lifted it, and the three of them looked in at their equipment in silence. Bobby put one arm around Tracy and one around his brother. They stood there for a long time.

"We should put it all in storage," Tracy said at last. "Maybe his aunts will want to sell the house . . . It'll just be in the way . . ."

"Bury it all," Nick said. "Try to forget." He was dry-eyed, furious. "I can't do that, Trace. It would be like killing him all over again."

"I'm done, Nick," Bobby said. "The band . . . I can't . . ."

"I know, Bobby. The band's over. There is no band without Adrian. But I'm not putting his guitar in storage. Or mine, either. I can't just forget about Adrian . . ."

"Nobody's saying you're supposed to forget about him, Nick," Tracy said gently. She looked at Bobby. "It's just . . . The band . . . We . . . We can't . . ."

"I'm gonna live for another *seventy years,* Tracy. There'll be another band someday. I can't give up music, just because it hurts so much right now." Tears threatened, but Nick blinked them back. He looked at his brother. "It's what we did with him, Bobby. It's what we *were.* Adrian wouldn't want us to –"

"I can't, Nick . . . Like you say, maybe someday. But not now. You take Adrian's guitar, and your own. But the rest of it . . . I'm going to have it put up. I can't stand to look at it right now." Bobby's tears fell again; Tracy held him.

SEVENTY-FIVE

Marta lent her vacation house in Lake Elsinore to Ian and Rob and Bobby and Tracy for Labor Day weekend. Neither Daina nor Nick could be persuaded to accompany them, but Daina insisted that Ian go.

There were a million boats on the lake for the last big weekend of the summer; a festive atmosphere reigned for everyone but the Wilde cousins. They pulled Tracy skiing a couple of times, but Bobby couldn't bring himself to get in the water. Rob's heart wasn't in it either. Ian skied a couple of times, but it had suddenly become like work to him.

The family went through the motions of a barbeque on Saturday night, but it was a silent affair. They locked up the house early Sunday morning and went back to Riverside. Ian said he wanted to get back to Daina, but the truth was, he didn't want to ski anymore. Like with Bobby and the band, his once favorite activity now just held too much of Adrian. He backed *One Wilde Ride* into the garage and parked his ancient truck in the space between the side of the garage and the fence. Ian didn't want to look at it anymore.

SEVENTY-SIX

Daina spent a lot of time sitting on her aunts' deck, staring out into the forest. She tried to bond with Randi, to absorb some of the younger woman's cheerfulness. Randi wasn't sad. She was young, and she was pregnant with Adrian's child; she looked to the future.

Daina performed the ancient rituals with Randi and Penny and Bellona, and occasionally Lily; something she hadn't done since childhood. Daina discovered that she believed again, that she had never really ceased to believe. The forces existed; they had taken her son from her, just as she had been forewarned they would. There was no profit in attempting to ignore them now.

On the Sabbat of Hallowe'en, Penny and Bellona called for a celebration. They would not term it a remembrance of their beloved Capo, but they insisted on a little family get together, anyway.

"Life *must* go on," Penny told her niece. "Your husband is here. He's always been here, but you've neglected him in your grief. That must cease, Daina. Your love for each other created Adrian. Such a love was something Adrian sought for himself; he admired what his parents share. He wouldn't want you to allow it to wither in his absence."

The old witches had recreated their famous hot cider for the holiday, and Daina imbibed gratefully, attempting to do as Penny suggested, to remember the first night she had met Ian, long before the tragic blot of their son's murder had stained their lives.

The cider worked its subtle magic. Ian and Daina's spirits were lifted. They were successful in remembering that long ago night. It was a simple enough truth, but even though Adrian was gone, Ian and Daina would always have each other. That had been part of the prophecy, too.

Four months along, Randi's flat belly had just begun to swell; Adrian's child was in there. Daina wanted to believe that it was Adrian, but she realized that it would be years, perhaps decades, before she found out if *The Incantations of Thoth* had been successful.

"How will we know?" Daina asked her aunts, nodding at the mother-to-be. Randi gazed solemnly at the seeing sisters; she wanted to know, too.

Ian shook his head. He was overjoyed that he was going to be a grandfather in five months or so; he was grateful that a part of himself, a part of Adrian, would live on. But he didn't believe, not for a second, that the baby *would be Adrian.* He couldn't believe, not even partially like Randi, nor hopefully like Daina, nor completely like Penny and Bellona. It was the stuff of fantasy. It was impossible.

Penny ignored Ian. "It's not so much how, Daina. It's when. He will have to grow and learn, just like any other child. But one day, he will see . . . He will know! He will recognize us for what we were to him before."

"What if it's a girl?" Ian asked irritably.

"It's a boy," Bellona replied, as surely as if Ian had asked her the date. *"The Incantations* made it so."

Ian shook his head again. He said to Randi, "Have you thought about a name?"

"I've always liked the name *Leo,"* she replied in a small voice.

Randi reckoned that her baby's grandmother and her aunts would want her to christen the child with his father's name. But Randi couldn't do that. She looked to the future – calling the baby *Adrian* would keep her in the past eternally, would never allow her to forget his father's bitter end. She couldn't call him by his father's name.

And Randi had Gil to think about. He had been so good to her since Adrian died. He visited her almost daily, remorseful, contrite, sweet. He told Randi that he knew that she hadn't forgiven him yet, but talked about a future where they would be together again, because he loved her. Gil told her over and over again how sorry he was; he told her over and over again that he couldn't live without her.

Gil patiently took Randi to all her doctor's appointments. He tenderly patted her belly, as if the new life in there was his own. Adrian was dead, cut down by some anonymous lunatic. But Gil was here, and he was good to Randi.

Naming the baby after his deceased father would be a slap in the mouth to Gil. It would make him believe that Randi would rather live in the past with memories of the dead, instead of looking to the future. Randi would have Adrian's son for the rest of her days; and she knew that Gil would be beside her. Not yet, of course, but Randi knew she would take him back eventually. He loved her, and she couldn't imagine life with anyone else. Adrian's son would have his own name.

"Leo is a nice name," Daina said, relieved. She had feared that Randi would want to name the child after his father; Daina didn't think she could've borne it if she did. *Life must go on,* just like

Penny had said. Hearing her son's name every day would only keep the wound open.

"It's a fine name," Ian agreed. Once Leo was here and the women realized that he was not Adrian . . . It would be good that they had given him his own name.

Penny shared a glance with her sister that said, *It doesn't matter what he's called. He will be Adrian.* Bellona opened her mouth to give breath to this thought, but Penny shook her head.

Instead, Bellona said, "A regal name. Strong. Masculine. *Leo.* The lion. Popes, emperors and kings have been called *Leo.*" She smiled at Randi, who still looked nervous. "An excellent choice, dear!"

Realizing that none of this wonderful family that she had . . . *mated* into had any objections, Randi smiled back at them. She would call Adrian's son *Leo.*

SEVENTY-SEVEN

The elder generation of the Wilde clan saw Randi's pregnancy as a blessing. They would've preferred it if Randi and Adrian had been married, of course, but these things happened nowadays. They had always happened. Adrian himself had arrived suspiciously, impossibly early. Despite a lack of social etiquette, nature had taken its course and the Wilde dynasty would continue. That was really all that mattered.

The youngest Wilde (so far) had mixed emotions about the imminent existence of Adrian's heir. Every time he looked at Randi's growing belly, Nick was perennially, inescapably, reminded of his cousin's betrayal. Adrian had disregarded Nick's love for Randi. He had just gone ahead, *and if he was still alive, Randi would be his now, regardless of what he knew I wanted . . .*

But Adrian was dead, and Nick missed him every day. He couldn't hate Adrian. Nick knew that had Randi had the choice between himself and Adrian at the time, if Nick had been in Riverside on that fateful 4th of July, instead of seeing the lights of Paris – Randi would've chosen Adrian. Even if his cousin had done the honorable thing and turned her down, Nick knew that she never would have chosen him. He would always be just a kid to her.

So as the days passed, Nick forgave Adrian his trespass. He was gone, and his final act had produced a new life. Nick knew that Adrian's witchy aunts had predicted that the child would be a boy, and he hoped that it would look like Adrian.

Nick vowed that he would be the best cousin ever to Adrian's son. He would teach him how to play the guitar; he would tell the boy about all the fun that Nick and Bobby and his father had had growing up. He would tell him what a great guy Adrian had been. Nick would keep his cousin's memory alive for Adrian's son.

SEVENTY-EIGHT

As Randi's pregnancy progressed, so did her reconciliation with Gil. They held hands, and he would hug her and he would give her warm kisses hello and goodbye. But he never made any kind of suggestion that they should take their renewed relationship to a more physical level. Randi supposed it was out of respect for the fact that she was pregnant with someone else's child, even though everyone at her obstetrician's office, everyone she knew, in fact, thought that the baby was Gil's. Everyone, of course, except for the Wilde family.

None of them had even raised an eyebrow when Gil started coming back around, paying court to Randi again. Adrian was gone, and it was not as if he and Randi had shared a relationship before . . . They had shared only one fortuitous moment, and none of his family expected Randi to pretend otherwise. They knew she had to go on with her life, and they all found her former boyfriend to be pleasant and charming. He would make a good father.

Everyone accepted Gil's return to Randi's life. Adrian's family welcomed him with open arms, except, of course, for Nick. Gil's presence was a solid brick barrier to Nick's eternal hope that one day he and Randi might get together, but more importantly, Nick believed, beyond a shadow of a doubt, that Gil had murdered Adrian.

Nick pestered Detective Chalmers for the first few months. He called, showed up at the station, asked constantly if the cop had figured out how Gil had managed to return to Riverside, shoot Adrian, then flee back to Bakersfield. Chalmers listened patiently to Nick's theories. He humored the kid, because he admired Nick's single-minded determination to solve his cousin's murder.

It was a sad and painful fact of life, Chalmers knew, but people forgot about murders. Even for family members, the wounds eventually healed. Adrian was gone, and life went on. Nick would soon be sixteen; he would be driving, he would become enmeshed in the new and exciting world of high school and girls. Chalmers knew that the young man would slowly but inevitably forget about Adrian's brutal ending. Time heals all wounds.

But for the moment, Nick was like a puppy worrying a bone. He believed that Gil Hogan, in some kind of premeditated fit of jealous rage, had planned and carried out Adrian's murder. Chalmers considered that it might be possible, especially if life was like a Hollywood thriller. Plots were always complicated and twisty in the movies; timing was always flawless. Some fortuitous witness always saw the perp when he was where he wasn't supposed to be, and then the gig was up, then the crime was solved . . .

But that wasn't the case, here. No one had seen Hogan anywhere else but in Bakersfield.

Chalmers had heard the story over and over again from young Mr. Wilde: he'd told the Green girl that Hogan was cheating on her, while he was out of town with the other woman.

At approximately four-thirty on July 4th, 1991, Miss Green had told Hogan that she was leaving him; she said that Adrian Wilde had not been mentioned, however.

Nick believed that Hogan had then driven back to Riverside, making phenomenal time through killer 4th of July traffic, shot Adrian when he found him in the kip with his girlfriend, then drove all the way back to Bakersfield.

But no one had seen him do any of it.

There were just too many holes in the kid's theory. There was no possible way for Hogan to make the trip without being seen, *somewhere* along the route, and witnesses placed him at Sam Lynn Ballpark. It was true that no one put him there at the exact time of the crime, but he was there nonetheless. He'd walked out of the place with the Germaine woman and her relatives at eleven-forty-five. They hadn't sat together during the game, because she had gone back to the gate to fetch him. Seats with her relatives had filled in, and they'd sat somewhere else. It was a little bit incriminating, but . . . Chalmers shook his head. There wasn't enough time. This wasn't Hollywood.

Besides, why would the Germaine woman provide an alibi for Hogan if it wasn't true, when it had been her nephew that had been murdered? It had come through in the interview Chalmers had conducted with her – not only was she devastated, beside herself with grief over Adrian's death – it was also obvious to Chalmers that Hogan meant nothing to her. Sure, they had had a little thing on the side, but she made it clear that theirs had been no monumental love affair. Chalmers got that she was glad that it was over, that she was embarrassed at the age difference. If Hogan hadn't been there at the game with her, if there was one single possibility that he could've done it, then Chalmers was sure that the old gal would've fingered him.

Hogan had the right kind of weapons, but so did a million other registered gun owners in Riverside County, hunters and home-protectors. Not to mention a million other unregistered ones. No shell was recovered at the scene, so that could mean that the gun that killed Adrian had been pump action, like one of Hogan's. Or it could mean that the assassin had just been careful enough to retrieve the spent shell after it had been ejected from another type of shotgun. Unfortunately, ballistics was non-existent for scatter guns.

Chalmers had another open case – a store clerk had been blown away by a shotgun a few days after Adrian's murder, at a convenience store not six miles from his house. No witnesses to that one either. It was Chalmers' theory that the same guy had committed both crimes. He'd broken in to rob Adrian's house, because the house was dark. He'd been surprised to find that someone was home. He'd panicked, killed Adrian, then fled without stealing anything. Then a few days later, he'd hit the convenience store. Emboldened that he'd got away with one murder, he'd committed another one. It happened every day.

The memory of his cousin's murder might still be fresh in Nick's memory, and Detective Chalmers was sorry that Adrian was dead, but there just wasn't enough evidence to keep harassing Gilbert Hogan about it.

Other cases came across Chalmers' desk. By the time 1992 arrived, the Wilde murder had been relegated to the cold case files, and Chalmers accepted that it was one that wasn't going to get solved. That happened every day, too. It was only on television that the cops always got their man.

SEVENTY-NINE

Nick asked Randi out to dinner for Valentine's Day, but she turned him down.

He didn't press it; he knew who'd be having dinner with her. Nick's hatred for Gil bubbled in his mind like hot acid, and a little of it spilled over: he found that, at times like this, he hated Randi a little bit, too, for letting the cheating, murdering son of a bitch back into her life.

Nick had tried to tell Randi of his suspicions, but she had shut him down completely. "You're just being jealous, Nick," she'd told him. "You're being ridiculous. Gil couldn't kill anybody, not to mention that he was out of town at the time." Randi crossed her hands across her tummy, grown ample. "I don't want to hear about all that nonsense. If you bring it up again, I won't talk to you anymore."

Nick was resigned. His family didn't believe him; the cops didn't believe him; Randi didn't believe him. Or, he thought keenly, Randi *didn't want to believe him.* She knew what a jealous bastard Gil was – hadn't she showed Nick his guns? Nick believed that Randi knew, just like he did, that it couldn't have been anyone else. Gil murdered Adrian.

Randi was deceiving herself about Gil's guilt. Why else would she forbid Nick from mentioning it? Why else would she threaten to end their friendship if he brought it up again? Adrian was dead, and Gil was back, and Nick knew that Randi depended on him, that she *loved* him . . . There was no way Randi was going to allow herself to see the truth.

Nick didn't bring it up again, but his abject love for Randi curdled a little bit. He was convinced that she knew the truth, yet she had allowed Gil to come around again. She was going out to Valentine's Day dinner with him.

But a portion of Nick's love for Randi was inextinguishable, and there was also the fact that Nick wanted to be a part of Adrian's child's life. He didn't want Randi to end their friendship over something he couldn't prove. *I can't prove that the earth revolves around the sun either,* Nick thought, *yet I know it's true. And so does she.*

But Nick didn't want Randi to cut him out of her life, so he knew that he couldn't continue to tell her that Gil had done it, couldn't continue to try to *make her see it,* make her admit it . . .

Nick knew that Gil had killed his cousin. He knew it like he knew that that same sun, the one around which the world revolved, would come up in the morning. But for now he kept it to himself. And he waited.

Nick was unfamiliar with witchcraft, but the idea of karma was not unknown to him: *what goes around comes around.* He believed that Gil would get his, sooner or later. He would not get away with killing Adrian. Nick wasn't sure how Gil's comeuppance would occur, but he believed it would happen someday.

Nick had to believe it, or else all the concepts of right and wrong upon which he'd been raised were lies. The good were rewarded, the bad punished. Life was long. Nick wasn't patient by nature, but he assumed the virtue, at least around Randi. He didn't mention Gil's guilt again. He waited.

EIGHTY

Gil thought that Randi was looking exceptionally lovely as she sat across from him at dinner on Valentine's Day. He'd made reservations far in advance at Paul's, the most expensive restaurant in town. It was a no-brainer: if Randi had refused to accompany him, he would've taken Nadine. Gil saw himself in the catbird seat, *living the life of Riley,* as Richie used to say. Everybody should have two women.

Taking Nadine would've been risky. Someone might've seen them together. But if Randi had turned him down . . . What the hell, why not?

Gil had assumed a whole new layer of secrecy in his relationship with Nadine. When he spent the night at her house, he made sure he left his car at home, and took a cab over there. It was a drag – he wouldn't even let her come to his neighborhood to pick him up – but he was done with being sloppy. He was on the road to getting Randi back, yet he'd discovered to his delight that it was still possible for him to keep Nadine on the side, too. He just had to be careful.

Tonight, Randi's eyes sparkled; her skin and hair seemed to glow. She was beautiful, and Gil was even able to forget that she was pregnant, because he couldn't see her bulky belly when she was sitting at the table.

Gil thought about how Randi had been before, thin and sexy; he remembered how eager and accommodating she'd always been. She'd be thin again, willing again . . . Gil thought about how great it was going to be . . .

Then Randi excused herself to go to the ladies' room; as she waddled away, Gil's fantasies evaporated. The thought of being with her now . . . That was just disgusting. *She was disgusting.* The whole situation was *just disgusting.* The very idea . . . There was no way. But she wouldn't be pregnant forever, and then . . . Gil thought that he would take out his lust for the Randi that used to be, the Randi that would be again, on Nadine tonight, just as soon as he dropped his Valentine's Day date back at the old ladies' house.

Randi touched up her make-up in the mirror, side by each with all the other women out on Valentine's Day dates with their husbands and boyfriends. There was even another girl that was pregnant, and she and Randi smiled at each other.

Randi sighed. She thought about all these other lucky girls, how they'd be cuddled up with their men later, showing their gratitude for the Lover's Day dinner. But not Randi. She would go home to her room at Penny and Bellona's house; she would sleep all alone.

Randi had discovered that being pregnant had not dimmed her desire for a man. Sometimes it seemed that being pregnant had increased it. Sometimes, she would lie awake at night, unable to get to sleep . . .

Randi would try to think of Adrian, then, try to remember him . . . But her recollections were dim, unclear, unsatisfying. She found that she had a little trouble remembering Adrian's face, nonetheless anything else. They had only had a brief moment together.

Thinking about Gil was easier. Randi wondered if he was having the same desires as she was . . . If he was, Randi just wouldn't think about how he might be taking care of them. He had promised, repeatedly, that he would never speak to Nadine again, and Randi had made up her mind to believe him. Gil said he loved her. Randi was sure that he went home to his bed alone every night, just like she did.

Randi missed Gil. Unlike her baby's father, Gil was here, alive. He smiled at her, told her he loved her. He'd taken her out to dinner at Paul's for Valentine's Day.

But Gil hadn't made a pass at her, not tonight, not ever; not even a hint of one, no doubt because she was fat and ugly right now. But she wouldn't be this way forever. Just another couple of months. And then . . .

Randi thought that Gil looked exceptionally fine tonight; she knew that she would be thinking about him later. Randi longed for the baby to be born, so she could be released from this fat, uncomfortable, celibate prison. After Leo was born, she would ask the doctor how soon . . .

Randi resolved to surprise Gil at the first opportunity. She looked forward to it. It would be *awesome.*

EIGHTY-ONE

Leo Adrian Wilde was born on Wednesday, April 8th, 1992. Gil had been Randi's Lamaze coach, so he was in the delivery room throughout the whole ordeal with her, enthusiastically encouraging her to pant and push. They worked well as a team; the delivery went smoothly.

Afterwards, the new father laughed and joked with the nurses for a moment before he left. Mom and baby were resting comfortably. "My work here is done," Gil told them with a smile.

Most new daddies were silent, dazed and a little awed by the wonder of childbirth, but the nurses found Gil to be talky, friendly and charming; they remembered his name. So there was surprise, and more than a few sidelong glances between the staff on the floor the next day, when Randi put someone else's name down under *Father* on her baby's birth certificate.

Standing in the hall outside the nursery, Daina and Bellona, Penny and Lily smiled smugly at each other. Leo had come into the world with a wild thatch of black hair, as had his father. He had dark blue eyes. The witches thought that he looked just like Adrian; their belief that *he was* Adrian was reinforced.

Ian thought they were ridiculous. Of course Leo would look like Adrian; he was Adrian's son. Ian also thought he looked a lot like his mother; Randi was also black-haired and blue-eyed. On more than one occasion, Ian had remarked to his wife that he thought Randi looked a little bit like she had at the same age; he'd observed that Randi and Adrian looked almost like brother and sister.

After the Wildes had effusively congratulated her and gone home, Randi had Gil call her mother to let her know that Leo had arrived. Since she'd left home at sixteen to live with Gil, Randi had ceased to be close with her family. Her mother still reproached her for not finishing high school, and Randi hadn't wanted her there for the delivery.

Mrs. Green and her other children had never heard of Adrian Wilde. They thought that Leo was Gil's baby. Sure, he didn't look like Gil; but he looked like Randi, so they thought nothing of it.

Gil saw only Randi in Leo, and knew that other people would, too. They would think that he was Leo's father. So what if the kid didn't look like him? He looked like his mother. That was good enough.

Randi saw Adrian in her baby, but like Gil, and her family, and Ian, she also saw herself. She could not believe that *The Incantations of Thoth* had taken hold. She couldn't make herself believe that the little squalling bundle in her arms *was Adrian*. She loved Leo; he was her son, and it didn't matter that he wasn't Adrian. She had never quite believed all of that, anyway.

Randi spent the night of Leo's birth in the hospital. In the morning, she was given a clean bill of health and the doctor released her. While Gil was still out of the room, Randi casually asked the doctor how soon she could resume marital relations.

The doctor blinked expressionlessly, and handed Randi a pamphlet. He took care of babies before they were born, and he delivered them; but it occurred to Randi that apparently a discussion concerning how babies were created and how soon such a thing could again be attempted was not his cup of tea.

The literature said Randi should wait four to six weeks – that was an eternity! – but it also said that she should listen to her own body and go at her own pace. It advised her to take the whole thing slowly, and reminded her to use birth control if she didn't want to go through this whole ordeal again immediately.

Randi didn't. She bought a box of condoms at the pharmacy after Leo's one month check-up; the lady behind the counter didn't bat an eyelash. Randi was a mom now, an adult. Birth control wasn't a dirty secret to the lady at the pharmacy. She understood.

EIGHTY-TWO

At his one-month check-up, the pediatrician told Randi that Leo was healthy, that everything was progressing as it should. When she returned home, she related the news to Daina and Penny and Bellona.

Then Randi told them a little fib.

"My mother is down with strep throat. I told her that I'd go sit with her for a while, but . . . I don't want to take Leo. Because of the germs. Could you guys watch him for me for a few hours?"

"Of course, dear," Bellona said. "Let me whip up a little herbal remedy for your mother. It'll help with her sore throat."

Randi waited patiently. Then, potion in hand, she kissed her newborn goodbye and flounced happily down the hill.

Randi had called Gil from the doctor's office after Leo's visit. She told him that she had forgiven him. Gil was waiting for her at his apartment.

Wordlessly, Randi put her arms around his neck and kissed him, the moment he opened the door. Gil was tender, gentle with her. He found Randi to be different than he remembered: rounder, softer. She'd just had a baby, he reasoned . . . But she was still his Randi, as eager and passionate as she'd always been.

Gil congratulated himself. He'd known all along that she would come back to him. Adrian Wilde was dead. Where else could she turn?

Gil was a little disconcerted, therefore, when Randi arose from their bed and began to put her clothes back on. "Where are you going? I thought that you'd stay the night. I'm sure the baby will be all right with –"

"I have to nurse him, Gil."

Gil had forgotten about that. "Go home and get him then. Bring him back here." He grasped her hand. "I want us to be together again, Randi."

Randi was unsure. It had been great tonight with Gil, but she also liked her freedom. She liked Penny and Bellona's weird little house in the forest. It was quiet there; it was noisy, comparatively, at Gil's. Randi thought she could hear ever car that passed by on Rubidoux Boulevard.

"This place is too small, Gil," she said. "Leo wouldn't have his own room . . ."

"He doesn't have his own room where you are now," Gil countered.

Randi allowed him to embrace her. "True. But no one is there with him but me. We couldn't have him in here with us . . ."

"We'll get a bigger place, then. I love you, Randi. I want you here with me."

"Let me think about it."

Gil walked Randi out to the car, kissed her goodbye. As she pulled out onto the street, he looked at his watch, then bounded back up the steps to his apartment. It wasn't that late; there was plenty of time for him to hop into the shower, then cruise over and see Nadine. *Fuck taking a cab,* Gil thought. *I'll just risk it.*

Life's good, Gil said to himself as he turned the hot water on.

EIGHTY-THREE

Upon her return to Penny and Bellona's, Randi fed her hungry baby, then fell into a deep and satisfied sleep.

She saw Gil in her dreams. He was wearing the same green tank-top, the same jeans that he'd had on the first time that she'd ever seen him. Gil looked fine: blonde, green-eyed; muscular, a little bad-ass. Sexy. He was smiling slyly at her, just as he had tonight when she'd kissed him for the first time after so many months.

In her sleep, Randi sighed and smiled back at her boyfriend. But he didn't acknowledge her smile; Randi realized that Gil wasn't smiling at her at all, but at someone else. She looked over her shoulder to see who it was – her action was in slow motion, because it was a dream.

Nadine was standing behind her, smiling at Gil. Like Lily sometimes did, Nadine seemed younger than the last time Randi had seen her – how long ago had that been? It was at her twenty-first birthday party, before she had gone out of town with Gil, before Randi had found out about them, before Adrian, before . . .

Randi knew that Nadine had been by the hospital to see Leo. She knew that she visited Daina and Ian, and Penny and Bellona – they were the only family she had in town. So Randi knew that Nadine was aware of her pregnancy.

Gil had calmly told her that he had seen Nadine standing outside the nursery. He reminded Randi that Adrian had been like a nephew to her, so she had just naturally wanted to see his son. Gil swore that he hadn't spoken to her, though; he told Randi that when he saw her there, he had scooted back into her room until his former . . . Until Adrian's aunt had left.

But what if he was lying? What if Gil was lonely? Randi had just tonight resumed their relationship . . . She had been cold to Gil for so long. What if he still thought about Nadine?

In Randi's dream, Gil ignored her, as if she wasn't even there. She *hadn't been there,* for a long time. He embraced Nadine, kissed her neck. She murmured in enjoyment, said, "It's okay, honey. I still want you, even if Randi doesn't . . ."

Randi snapped awake. She did still want Gil. She just hadn't been able to prove it to him until tonight.

Randi remembered the hurt look on his face when she'd told him that she'd need to think about moving back in with him. Randi arose and picked Leo up out of his crib. She gently hugged the newborn, and took him back to bed with her.

What do I need to think about? Randi asked herself. *Gil loves me.* He'd showed himself ready and willing to take on the responsibility of a baby that wasn't even his . . . *He loves Leo, too.*

There was nothing to think about. Randi would wipe all thoughts of Nadine from Gil's mind. She would be the only girl for him, like she'd once been, before he'd meet that old bitch, before she'd met Adrian . . .

The thought struck Randi so suddenly that she blinked. Maybe it had all been partially her fault. Maybe she'd drove Gil into Nadine's arms, by the way she'd always mooned and sighed and stared at Adrian . . .

But all that was in the past. Adrian's son was her future, but so was Gil. Randi made up her mind. She would thank Penny and Bellona for their enormous kindness in letting her stay with them, but first thing in the morning, she would tell them: she had to get on with her life. She was taking Leo and moving back with Gil.

EIGHTY-FOUR

Penny and Bellona met the news with stony silence for a moment.

The moment lengthened, then at last Penny said, "We had hoped that you would stay with us a little longer, child. At least until you were prepared to go back to Mohini's."

"We'd hoped to look after Leo while you worked. If you move away . . . Who will you get to watch him?" Bellona asked.

Randi hadn't thought that far ahead. Lily had given her the last two months of her pregnancy off; she'd said that Randi could return at her leisure. Penny and Bellona had been footing the bills for all that time, feeding her and housing her . . . Daina and Ian had purchased Leo's car seat and his crib, and all the little t-shirts and onesies that he wore. If Randi wanted her life back, she would have to return to work soon.

The old sisters had a valid point. Who would watch Leo whilst she was at work?

Her own sister? No. Beth had kids of her own, and a string of boyfriends . . . *Mom? Oh, hell, no.* Randi had not thought her mother had done a very good job raising her brothers, and she didn't speak to her mom too much anymore. Randi wasn't going to just show up on her doorstep and ask her to watch Leo.

"If you guys want to watch him . . . I could just drop him off in the mornings. Before I went to work."

Another heartbeat of stony silence. "That seems like a lot of extra work, dear," Bellona said, stating the obvious. "And Daina will be so disappointed if she can't visit with Leo in the evenings anymore."

He's not Daina's baby! He's my baby! Randi's mind protested. But then she felt guilty. Daina's son was dead and gone. Murdered. Randi believed that Daina's only joy in life these days was her grandson.

"Rubidoux's so . . ." Penny frowned. Rubidoux wasn't the best part of town to be raising a baby. But Penny didn't mention that. "Rubidoux's so far away. We'll hardly get to see you."

Rubidoux wasn't that far away, probably only eight miles or so. It was even in the same zip code. But Randi knew the sisters were right. She could picture herself, tired after working all day, anxious to get back home and start dinner for Gil and Leo. She wouldn't want to be hanging around every night, visiting with Daina and

Penny and Bellona. They would be relegated to the role of babysitters, employees.

But Randi wanted her old life back. She wanted to create a new life with Leo and with Gil. She wanted her own place, wanted to run her own household, be a mother, be a . . . *wife*. She and Gil and Leo didn't have to remain in Rubidoux. They could find a bigger place, in a safer neighborhood. Randi thought of decorating a little room for Leo; she pictured cooking Thanksgiving dinner for her family, she thought of Christmas trees, and telling Leo about Santa . . .

"I think I have a solution, Randi," Penny said with a rare smile. She clapped her hands together. "It will serve us all! Bellona and I, Ian and Daina – we'll all get to see Leo as often as we want! You won't need to find a new babysitter." Penny looked at her sister, and Bellona smiled.

"You can live in . . ." Bellona almost said *Adrian's house*. "You can live in the house across the street."

Bellona didn't have to say *Adrian's house* for Randi to have just that thought. That 4th of July night came back to her all at once – the noise, the blood . . . "I could never go back . . ."

"Don't be ridiculous, dear," Penny said emotionlessly, her smile draining away. "Of course you can."

"Leo can have his own room," Bellona continued. "And there's a yard for him to play in when he gets older. And we can still see him every day. Look after him while you're at work, without a tiresome drive."

Randi was overwhelmed by the old witches' generosity, even though she saw that the arrangement would be of benefit to them, also. Leo would still be in their lives as completely as he had been since the day he was born; he'd be just across the street. And his grandmother would also get to see him every day . . .

"What about . . . ?"

"Of course, Gil can stay there with you," Penny said and gave Randi's arm a little pat. "He's your man." She touched Leo's cheek. "He'll be like a father to your son."

Randi brightened. It really was the perfect solution. She loved Gil . . . But she also loved Adrian's family. They were Leo's family, and he should be around them as much as possible.

Randi had never liked Rubidoux, anyway. She'd grown up there, and she'd much rather see her boy grow up out here, a little farther from the noise and traffic of the city, where the air was a little fresher . . . Where his father had grown up.

"I'll ask Gil," Randi promised them.

EIGHTY-FIVE

When Randi told Gil about the sisters' magnanimous offer, he gave her the same silent stare that Penny and Bellona had given her when she'd told them that she wanted to move back in with him.

Gil considered. It was a nice house. "What about rent?"

"They didn't say anything about rent," Randi answered immediately. She'd already considered that: it would be taking advantage of the old ladies' kindness, of their desire to be close to Leo, if she and Gil just lived there for free. "I'm sure we could offer them something reasonable."

"Reasonable," Gil repeated. He discovered that he was warming up to the idea. There was something fitting to it. Wilde had tried to take Randi away from him, but Gil had nipped all that bullshit right in the bud, with one shell from Richie's dusty ol' pump gun. And now, not only would he be living in Wilde's house at a *reasonable* rent, he would be raising his son. He would get to do Randi every night in the very room in which he'd killed Wilde. Gil smiled. He'd get to do Randi . . . He would laugh at Adrian's ghost.

"It sounds great, baby." Gil acquiesced. It was a perfect set-up. The old ladies were always nice to him, and he would get to check out Wilde's mom whenever she popped in for a visit. Sure, she was no spring chicken, any more than Nadine, but she was still nice to look at.

Gil smiled again. And wouldn't Nadine think it was funny? Her parents were gone, Wilde was gone . . . And he wound up living in her old house. *Maybe sometime, if Randi's ever out of town . . . Maybe I could just sneak her in a side door and help her reminisce . . .*

"When can we move in?"

"I'm sure we can move in as soon as possible. Today, if you want. Only . . . Gil? If we're going to be living in . . . If we're going to be living *there* . . . I don't want you to . . ." Randi stammered to a stop.

"What, baby? You don't want me to . . . what?"

"After what happened to Adrian . . ." Randi saw Gil wince at the name. She had never said it to him, not once, all the time she'd been pregnant. Not once since Leo had arrived. "I don't want you to bring those guns." She nodded toward the bedroom. "Just like your mom, your little brothers . . . I don't want them in the house with Leo."

Gil laughed before he could stop himself, then quickly grew somber. "I thought that you might never come back to me, Randi. I thought about that a lot, all alone here. A couple nights, I looked at the old man's guns, and thought – if Randi won't come back to me, what do I have to live for?"

Gil had a hard time keeping his solemn expression, because Randi was buying it, hook, line, and sinker. "So, I got rid of them. In case I got drunk some night, in case I was feeling sad . . . I didn't want to have that option just staring me in the face. You don't have to worry about Leo being around any guns. I sold them to one of the old guys at work. He hunts."

EIGHTY-SIX

It had been extremely boring to Nick to visit his baby cousin at first. He'd discovered that babies didn't do a lot, not much past gurgle and drool, cry and eat (messily) and need their diapers changed. But there were smiles, too, so Nick had persevered – he was an old soul, and he realized that Leo wouldn't be a tiny, mindless *thing* forever. Nick wanted Adrian's son to know him from the beginning. So he took the bus out to see Leo almost every day after school.

Nick played with his cousin, brought him toys; he'd put the baby in the stroller and take him up to Hilltop Market, or walk him around the block. Nick made sure that he was always back at Penny and Bellona's with the baby by the time Randi got home from work. Then he'd go back to Adrian's house with her and help her to feed him and change him and bathe him. Randi would start dinner, and Nick would take his leave.

The only time that Nick saw Gil was at 1992's sad and solemn 4th of July barbeque. The fireworks went off as usual. It was Independence Day – the world went on – even though Adrian Wilde was gone, murdered on his birthday the year before.

Nick sat in seething silence and watched while his Uncle Rob and his Uncle Ian, his Aunt Daina and the old ladies went through the motions of cooking and eating; the fireworks exploded, but no one oohed or aahed. Nick watched his cousin's murderer and the woman he had once loved and Adrian's three-month-old son. Randi saw his angry mood and ignored him. Gil always ignored him.

Nick had been speechless, appalled, *outraged* that Penny and Bellona had given Adrian's house to them. But he swallowed his anger, as he'd recently learned to do. Nick kept his mouth shut. He recognized that Penny and Bellona had had no other choice. It was the only way to keep Leo nearby. Randi would've taken off back to Rubidoux with that son of a bitch, otherwise.

Now it was almost Hallowe'en again; Leo was going on seven months old. Nick had missed his usual bus – he'd been talking to Maria Sanchez for a moment after last bell, and the time had gotten away from him. He knew that Randi was already home from work, so he rang the doorbell at Adrian's house. He'd just say hi to Randi, hold Leo for a few minutes, then go on back, before Gil got home.

Nick was thinking that he might call Maria later, see what she was up to . . . When Gil opened the door, carrying Leo.

Since the 4th of July, Nick had purposely avoided seeing Gil and Randi together. Nick loved Leo, but he didn't love Randi so much anymore. The horrendous events of the past year had matured Nick. Gone were his fantasies of *maybe someday* with Randi. She had made her choice, and the choice she had made, made Nick hate her a little bit.

Nick was sure that Gil had murdered Adrian, and so far, he was getting away with his crime. Nick had felt the rage and violence stir within him on the 4th of July; he'd barely been able keep it contained. Nick wanted to hurt Gil then, to beat him to a bloody pulp . . . Nick found that he also wanted to smack Randi for refusing to see the truth.

But Nick wanted to remain in Leo's life, to watch him grow, to tell him all about his dad . . . So he had avoided running into Gil, because he thought that he might find it impossible to stop himself from picking a fight. Nick knew that he would feel his hatred keenly if he was forced to watch Gil and Randi interact – and he didn't want to give Randi a reason to forbid him from seeing his cousin.

Concerned with his own ability to keep his anger in check, Nick had always made sure he was gone before Gil got home from work. Until now.

Gil's mouth dropped open in surprise. "What the fuck do you want?"

Nick thought that maybe he should just go. *But if I just turn tail and leave, he'll think I'm afraid of him. Then it'll just be more of a pain in the ass the next time.* Nick reasoned that he couldn't avoid this asshole forever.

"I'm here to see my cousin." Nick held out his arms for the baby and Gil hesitated just long enough to let Nick see that he didn't want to hand Leo to him.

Gil watched Nick bounce Leo in his arms a couple of times. He smirked at both of the youngest Wildes. "Your cousin. You mean my son."

Nick had been smiling at the baby. Leo smiled back. Nick was glad that he had toughed it out through the boring newborn months, because it gave him joy to see that Leo always recognized him now. Leo was always glad to see him.

Nick's smile evaporated. He felt a tremor of anger well up in him. He didn't want to be holding Leo while he experienced this fury, so he pushed past Gil into the house, and sat Leo down in his playpen.

Nick smiled at the baby again, then turned. He discovered that Gil was leaning cavalierly against the doorframe to the open front door, watching him, still smirking.

"Is that what you tell people? That Leo's yours?" Nick reached over the side of the playpen and tickled the baby. He kicked and gurgled gleefully. Nick straightened up, looked at Gil again. "Too bad nobody's gonna buy it. He doesn't look anything like you."

Gil wouldn't be baited. He shrugged, grinned. "But I'm gonna raise him. He's gonna think like me, talk like me. The first word out of his mouth's liable to be *Daddy*. And he's gonna say it to me."

Nick would talk to Leo while he fed and bathed and played with him, as if the kid could already understand. *Your daddy did this,* Nick would say, and, *Your daddy did that.*

"You look just like your daddy," Nick would tell his cousin's son.

Now Nick realized that if Gil had his way, Leo would grow up believing that Gil was his father. Nick imagined the murdering son of a bitch conning Randi into it, telling her that it would just be bewildering to Leo; he wouldn't understand why his real father wasn't around, he would be confused; telling him that Adrian was dead would traumatize him, blah, blah, blah . . .

We'll tell him the truth about Adrian someday, baby, but for now . . . We'll just let him think that I'm his dad . . .

Nick speculated that maybe Adrian's parents and aunts wouldn't put up with such a trampling of his cousin's memory, but on the other hand, they'd allowed this bastard to just move on in *and pretend that he was Leo's father,* so far. Who knew what else they might let happen?

It didn't matter what the rest of them thought. Nick wouldn't let Leo forget Adrian; he wouldn't allow this murdering bastard to masquerade as Leo's father.

"But you're not his daddy, bitch-boy," Nick said. He smiled when Gil's own smile vanished.

Nick was almost sixteen now. He'd come into the height he'd inherited from Will; Nick was no longer an old soul trapped in a little boy's body.

And Nick had been in his share of fights. Being observant, he'd sometimes made comments to his peers that they didn't appreciate. Nick knew that fighting while he was angry was a sure way to lose; but if he could incite his opponent to anger . . .

Nick had never been afraid of Gil, and he was sure that he could take him now. Nick didn't care if Randi would be pissed; he realized that he would completely relish whipping Gil's ass right this minute. He didn't care if Randi would try to cut him off from seeing Leo. Adrian's parents and Penny and Bellona would make sure that he got to see Leo.

Come on, swing on me, you worthless bastard!

But calling him *bitch-boy* hadn't made Gil angry enough to want to fight. He still just stood there, leaning against the door frame. Nick decided to try a little harder.

"He's never gonna call you *Daddy.*"

Gil laughed. "And why is that?"

Nick grinned. "Because I'm gonna see to it."

Gil laughed again, shook his head. "Right. Well, see to it some other time, kid. You've visited Leo. Tell him goodbye. It's time for you to get the fuck out of my house."

Nick smiled down at the baby. "Bitch-boy's sure gotten uppity in his old age, huh, Leo?" Nick looked at Gil. "This isn't your house. You're only here 'cause Adrian's not, and Randi decided to give you sloppy seconds. She decided to *settle for you,* since the better man's gone. Is she different, since she's been with my cousin, Stud? Since she's had his baby? I bet she still gets that faraway look in her eyes when she thinks about him –"

Gil took a step forward and swung on him then, but Nick was ready. He ducked Gil's fist and went in low, driving him up against the wall behind the door. One of Gil's arms was stuck behind him; Nick pinned Gil's neck to the wall with his forearm. With his other hand, he pinned Gil's wrist, immobilizing him. Nick slammed the door with his foot.

"Hold still, or I'll break your nose," Nick warned. An idea had come to his mind. Gil stopped struggling. "Here's what you're going to do, Gil, you worthless sack of shit. I'm not going to have to see to it that Leo doesn't call you *Daddy,* because you're going to see to it."

"Let me go, or I'll –"

"Let me go or I'll is not much of a threat." Nick pressed his arm harder against Gil's throat. "Shut the fuck up or I'll crush your windpipe. Now that's a threat. I've never liked you, and I've got absolutely nothing to lose."

Nick saw a spark of fear in Gil's eyes. He grinned, and before Gil try to break his hold again, Nick managed to swing him around and slam him onto the carpeted floor. Nick pinned one of Gil's arms behind him; he scrabbled uselessly with his other hand. Nick put his knee into the small of Gil's back.

Now Nick had him; Gil wasn't going anywhere. No one was more surprised about it than Nick himself.

"You're not Leo's father, and there is no way that you're going to let him think you are. Not for one fucking minute. So here's what you're gonna do. You're gonna tell Randi that you want Leo to call you by your name. You're not his father, so –"

"Why would I want to do that?" Gil gasped out.

"Because I said so, that's why." Another idea struck Nick and he grinned again. "Because if you don't, then I'm going to become your shadow, son. I'm going to follow you to work. I'm going to follow you home from work. I'm going to follow you to the market and to the bar . . . And wherever else you have a mind to go. I'm gonna be on you like white on rice, like ugly on a bulldog, you cheating son of a bitch."

"I don't know what you're talking about. I'm not –"

Gil's denial proved his guess to Nick. He didn't care that he had guessed correctly: Nick thought in a flash that Randi deserved it, for taking the conniving, murdering son of a bitch back. "If I hear Leo *ever* call you *Daddy,* I'm gonna take pictures, Gil. And I'll send 'em to Randi. So, unless you've become a choir boy, which I sincerely doubt . . . You're gonna do this favor for me."

"You wouldn't tell Randi. . . She hates you for telling her the first time." His face in the rug, Gil still managed a grin.

"Then why would I care if she hates me some more? She doesn't have to know it's me. I'll send the pictures to her job. Anonymously."

Gil considered. What did he care what Wilde's kid called him? He would still be Leo's daddy, regardless. Gil would be the one raising him; Gil would be the one disciplining him. Gil would be Leo's father in everything but name. Not Adrian, gone to his reward, and not his surprising, quick young cousin.

How did I let this lippy bastard get the jump on me? Gil asked himself. *I must be getting old. Slow. All this good livin' . . .*

Nick ground his knee into Gil's back. "So what's it gonna be, asshole?"

"All right. I'll tell Randi I want Leo to call me by my first name." Gil didn't want this little shit shadowing him. Everything was great, just the way it was. He had his happy little domestic life with Randi, and he had a couple of wild, intense afternoons every

294

now and then with Nadine. He didn't want to give that up. What difference did it make what Leo called him?

"I thought you'd see it my way. I'm going to let you up now, and I trust you to act like a gentleman." Nick didn't trust Gil at all. He was a murderer. He didn't even know the meaning of the word *gentleman.* "My cousin's seen enough violence for one day. But if you try to swing on me again, I'll make sure he sees your blood."

"Fuck you, kid. First chance I get –"

"But that's not gonna be today," Nick said. In one fluid movement, he stood up, turned, and opened the front door. *He who fights and runs away,* Nick thought, vaulting over the fence, just as Gil appeared in the doorway, *lives to fight another day.*

Nick sprinted across the street. He turned and flipped Gil off, then ran on up the path to Penny and Bellona's.

He couldn't believe that he'd just slammed Gil against the wall, pinned him to the floor. It couldn't be said that he'd kicked Gil's ass – *I should've hit him at least once,* Nick thought, *broken his nose –* but it still felt good. It felt great, in fact. Nick had surprised Gil, made him look like an ass.

He won't tell Randi, Nick realized. *What's he gonna say? You're teenaged boyfriend jumped me and slammed my face into the rug?*

Nick trotted gleefully up the path. He'd just pop in and say hi to the old ladies for a minute, then sneak down the path that ran behind Ian and Daina's garage and sally on up the hill to the bus stop. Despite his *flawless victory,* no one could say that Nick Wilde didn't understand the better part of valor.

Nick reminded himself to call before he just showed up at Randi's house in the future. Subduing Gil had been a lucky shot. Nick thought of Adrian, and reckoned that he might not be so lucky if he tangled with Gil again.

Also by LM Foster

A Passing Resemblance
Contrariwise – A Tale of Twins
Corvino
Crypsis
Duck Feet
Peter's Sisters

Two Green Keys:
Two Green Keys
Adapted for the Screen

One Wilde Ride Trilogy:
Part One: It Might Have Been
Part Two: An Exceptional Boy
Part Three: What Should Never Be

Stars and Guitars:
Talk To a Movie Star
Where The Guitars Play

Tom and Wiley:
This Carnival of Strange
Wiley Royce
Generally Recognized as Safe
Wiley Royce Versus The Martians